To
Kufstein

Knight's Cross
■ drop zone

Brooks's
command
■ post

ad
all

● W

Tulfes ●

S T R I A

■ Schafer's team
Steinach ●

■ Bridge at Stafflach

Brenner
Pass

ITALY

Miles   10

Km.   10

Knight's Cross

Knight's Cross

A NOVEL

by E. M. Nathanson
and Aaron Bank

A BIRCH LANE PRESS BOOK
Published by Carol Publishing Group

A Birch Lane Press Book
Published by Carol Publishing Group
Birch Lane Press is a registered trademark of Carol Communications, Inc.
Editorial Offices: 600 Madison Avenue, New York, N.Y. 10022
Sales & Distribution Offices: 120 Enterprise Avenue, Secaucus, N.J. 07094
In Canada: Canadian Manda Group, P.O. Box 920 Station U, Toronto,
    Ontario M8Z 5P9
Queries regarding rights and permissions should be addressed to
Carol Publishing Group, 600 Madison Avenue, New York, N.Y. 10022

Carol Publishing Group books are available at special discounts for bulk purchases,
for sales promotions, fund-raising, or educational purposes. Special editions can be
created to specifications. For details contact: Special Sales Department, Carol Publishing
Group, 120 Enterprise Avenue, Secaucus, N.J. 07094

Manufactured in the United States of America
10 9 8 7 6 5 4 3 2 1

Library of Congress Cataloging-in-Publication Data

Nathanson, E. M., 1928–
    Knight's Cross : a novel / by E.M. Nathanson and Aaron Bank.
    p.   cm.
    "A Birch Lane Press book."
    ISBN 1-55972-168-5
    1. World War II, 1939-1945—Fiction.   2. Hitler, Adolf, 1889–1945—Fiction.
  I. Bank, Aaron, 1902–   .   II. Title.
    PS3564.A85K58   1993
    813'.54—dc20   92-35891
                                                                              CIP

To my wife Catherine
and my daughters Linda and Alexandra
who favored me with loving support and encouragement
—AARON BANK

"Hitler will probably die under the hand
of an assassin. . . . The world will probably never
know the precise details of his death. . . ."
　　　　　—Wilhelm Wulff
　　　　　　Astrologer employed by
　　　　　　the Nazi *Schutzstaffel* [SS].
　　　　　　(As reported by John Toland
　　　　　　in his biography *Adolf Hitler*)

Preface

✠   In the winter of 1944–45 I was given the most extraordinary assignment of my career as a Special Operations officer with the Office of Strategic Services (OSS). My mission was to kidnap Adolf Hitler.

Much of this novel is based on the planning and training for that mission and my attempt to carry it out.

During the time that my unit was operational, it was announced in broadcasts by the Nazis that Adolf Hitler and Eva Braun, his mistress, had committed suicide in his command bunker in the Chancellery building in Berlin. The details divulged then and during the early years after the war became the popularly accepted version of their deaths. Since then I have read of new and differing assessments of the same testimony and evidence and of other theories about what might have happened to Hitler. Those suppositions dispute the early *Götterdäm-merung* version of his death that was told by Hitler's loyal Nazi associates—the same story, with certain important variations, that was later put out by the Russians, who claimed to have dug up the burned corpse of Hitler.

Since no irrefutable, identifiable evidence of Hitler's remains was ever proven beyond a doubt, a gray area of speculation was created concerning what had really happened to him. As recently as 1987, a Canadian dentist reported to the American Academy of Forensic Sciences that photographs of the teeth of the burned corpse said to be that of Hitler do not match pictures of his teeth taken while he was alive.

That—and more—is certainly within the realm of possibility.

There are episodes in *Knight's Cross* where the fictional Dan Brooks and other fictitious characters take over my story, but I think it would be imprudent of me at this late date to tell you exactly when. And, besides, I really don't want to spoil the book for you.

Aaron Bank
Colonel, U.S.A. (Ret.)

One

Berlin—April 30, 1945

✠ *Obersturmbannführer* Dietrich Reiter knew now that Dante's *Inferno* existed. Berlin was exploding all around them as he helped his dazed passenger out of the army sedan he had finally been able to drive through the fire and rubble to what was left of Unter den Linden and the east-west axis of the Tiergarten.

The sights, sounds and smells of hell were right here this night. The SS lieutenant colonel's eardrums ached with each new explosion of Russian artillery and bombs. Wherever his eyes darted they saw erupting flames, burning buildings, grotesque corpses and staggering figures. Wehrmacht, SS, Volkssturm, Hitler Youth, armed and unarmed, alone or in shattered units, moved through the streets among the terrified populace. Those with weapons fired at perceived enemies, deserters and each other.

More macabre than any of the other images was the sight of his companion completely wrapped like an Egyptian mummy in layers of white gauze, except for eye slits and nose and mouth holes. *Herr* Siegfried Schmidt—the new identity his charge had prepared weeks in advance but had taken on only this night—had become weak and compliant in his unaccustomed condition. Only hours before, he had gloated over his choice of his new name. None was more popular and numerous in the world, he had said; none brought him closer to the *Volk* or made him more Everyman among the German people. Yet, also, no name soared higher above them than Siegfried. It reverberated out of noble Teutonic myth and resonated from the music of Wagner, his favorite composer.

Schmidt...Schmidt...Schmidt..., Reiter had been thinking and saying to himself over and over again so that he would never make a mistake.

1

Herr Schmidt, of course. The respect due him must still be given. Though prudently, not fawningly.

Now—his injuries barely a few hours old, his senses dulled by painkiller—Siegfried Schmidt seemed in another world already and moved stiffly, as Reiter had seen zombies newly risen from the grave portrayed in cheap American movies. Reiter wondered how much pain he felt—or if he felt any. The more bizarre and ironic aspect of what had happened to him was that Schmidt already had been wearing bandages wrapped around his head even before he had been wounded. It had been a vital part of the escape plan.

The car that had carried them this far through the inferno to Unter den Linden was the second they had used this night. The first had been tossed on its side by the shock wave of a Russian artillery barrage before they had moved a hundred meters from the *Reichskanzlei*. The closest round might have killed them.

It had exploded five to ten meters beyond the passenger's side of the car, blowing the vehicle over onto the driver's side. Reiter had had to squirm out from under his companion. Schmidt's head and hands had been burned by phosphorous, and he had tried to smack out the flaming stuff that stuck to him. The fire had burned his clothes and brown fedora. The gauze wrappings underneath had caught fire, then burned his hair and flesh. Skin had bubbled up into blisters, charred blotches and cauterized vesicles. Reiter had used a blanket to smother the flames. After an initial cry of outrage, Schmidt had gone into shock. He was no longer recognizable as the man he had been a few minutes earlier.

Reiter had rushed back to the emergency hospital under the *Reichs-kanzlei* and obtained ointments, drugs, bandages and detailed instructions how to use them. To have brought a doctor back with him to treat *Herr* Schmidt would have been impossible because of the secrecy of what they were doing. To have stopped for extensive medical treatment would have destroyed weeks of careful planning. His assignment—perhaps the last he would ever perform for the Third Reich—was to get Schmidt out of Berlin this night, out of Germany.

Remarkably, when he had returned to where he had left Schmidt lying on the ground against the overturned car, he had found his charge able to stand and walk. He had spoken softly in a strange voice that did not sound like him. He had done exactly what Reiter asked him to do, and helped to peel off his burned clothes.

Under the continuing fury of the Russian barrage, the *Obersturmbannführer* had made his charge swallow tablets to prevent further shock, alleviate pain and fight infection; and he had applied an anti-bacterial compound and soothing ointment to his burns and wrapped bandages around his neck, face, head and hands. Then he had helped him change into fresh clothes and another hat taken from one of the suitcases.

2

Afterward, the SS lieutenant colonel had commandeered another car, transferred all their luggage, made *Herr* Schmidt as comfortable as possible and continued to drive through the inferno.

They had a rendezvous to keep with an airplane that was to land on the east-west axis through the Tiergarten, between the Brandenburg Gate and the Victory Column. An emergency landing strip had been created there during the last weeks in the midst of battle by removing *Herr* Speer's ornamental bronze lamp posts and *Herr* Hitler's prized linden trees. The pilot Reiter had selected through devious SS channels was supposed to be daring and skillful enough to accomplish the mission. He would never know who his passengers were.

Now, having reached the rendezvous site, Reiter realized the impossibility of what he had planned. It would be a miracle for a pilot to get through enemy-controlled skies and land in this hell without crashing or being blown up. They had been late arriving, but he was sure the pilot would not have dared take off without them. His great concern had been that they would never make it this far. Now he worried that they would be stranded at this exposed place on their escape route because the plane would never arrive; or, arriving, that it would never be able to take off.

He doubted that it would be long before Russian tanks and shock troops loomed into view. Like a new major chord rising through the pandemonium of the night, he thought he heard heavy engines and clanking treads moving on the Tiergarten from the east, north and south, tightening the ring of steel around the city's center. Or did he imagine it?

And did he imagine what he thought he saw now? No, it was quite real! Silhouetted against the flames and smoke above the Tiergarten—as if sent from Valhalla by Wotan himself—a Fieseler Storch light plane descended from the sky. It landed on the broad highway of the east-west axis and taxied toward where they waited near the shell-damaged columns of the Brandenburg Gate.

"*Herr* Schmidt, the plane is here!" Reiter cried out.

If there was a reaction from his companion he neither heard it nor saw it. The man just stood there slumped against the car where Reiter had placed him. The lieutenant colonel grasped him firmly under the arm and rushed him toward the aircraft as it spun around, ready for takeoff.

The pilot set the brakes, opened the door and leaped out. He stared wide-eyed for a moment at the macabre, bandaged civilian standing limply beside the SS officer. Then he averted his gaze and raised his arm stiffly to salute the *Obersturmbannführer*.

Reiter started to respond and then shouted, "The hell with that! Help your passenger into the plane and belt him in. Be careful. He is badly hurt. Then help me transfer the luggage from the car."

Minutes later, miraculously, the Fieseler Storch rose out of the maelstrom of fury and flames and flew toward the west at rooftop level, buffeted about by the explosions of Russian anti-aircraft shells. The beams of searchlights and the bright flames of the burning city flickered over the fuselage and single high wing and illuminated the cabin through the wide expanse of windshield and forward windows. Then the pilot suddenly zoomed upward steeply at maximum power to escape the illumination and flak, and he turned and twisted the Fieseler Storch onto a new course to the south.

Obersturmbannführer Dietrich Reiter gazed in horrible fascination at the full spectacle of doomed, burning Berlin beneath them. Never had he imagined that the thousand year Third Reich could come to this!

Two

London—November 15, 1944

✠   London was even bleaker than when Captain Dan Brooks had left it five weeks earlier.

On the drive to Grosvenor Street in the early dawn, sitting in the passenger seat of a jeep, he saw fresh craters in the roadways and new cavities among the rows of brownstone buildings in residential districts, caused by the German V-2s. Smoke hung in the air near Mayfair and the acrid smells of burning stung his nose. Sergeant Fred Blumberg, sitting in the back of the jeep with their rucksacks and weapons, was cursing: "Fucking lousy Nazis!"

It would be ironic, thought Brooks, if a V-2 got him and Freddy while they were here in London, theoretically out of danger, when four nights earlier he and a partisan band had been in a fierce fire fight against German troops on a mountain road in Italy while ambushing a supply convoy south of the Brenner Pass.

His extraction from the *Süd Tirol* with his radioman had been uneventful. The small Lysander that had snuck into Italy to bring them out had flown them to an Allied airfield in France, where they had boarded an empty bomber and flown through the night to its base near London. The jeep and driver had been waiting when they landed.

It was still quite early when the driver pulled up before the red brick Georgian mansion that was the European headquarters of the Office of Strategic Services. There was no outward indication that inside the former private residence clandestine operations were concocted.

The security detail showed no surprise at the arrival of two men in strange costume, carrying rucksacks and weapons. They were directed to the duty officer, where they turned in their mission gear, weapons and Dan's remaining operational funds.

5

He always treated the large sums entrusted to him on his missions with disinterest, though he sometimes wondered how he might use the money if it was his. He had once had a modest inheritance and had used some of it on travel and good living and had liked that a lot; but the stock market crash and Depression had wiped out the rest. After that, he'd made his career in the army.

Two hours later, Brooks reported to Special Operations branch on the third floor. He was all tidied up in his winter Class A's. Walking through the big Plans and Operations room toward Major Alan Blakely's office, he noted the much reduced staff. Special Operations was withering away, in danger of being made superfluous by the swift advance of Allied armies. There was only one small area of activity where a typewriter clattered. A blonde with fashionably coiffured hair caught his eye. Not until he came abreast of her did he take in the full profile of a very pretty woman in her early thirties, striking the keys with rapt attention and great energy. An exquisite pair of legs were positioned sidesaddle over the edge of the chair, extending out from under a skirt that had been hiked up as she tried to make herself comfortable.

When she became aware that someone had stopped beside her and was gaping, she ceased typing, turned her head and sized him up coolly with her large blue eyes. Then her challenging demeanor and icy expression changed in an instant, as if something more salutary or calculating had crossed her mind. She stood up, smiling and animated, and extended her hand.

"You're evidently Captain Brooks," she said.

Her voice had a warm, sensual timbre. She wore a long-sleeved, crisp white blouse over a blue tweed skirt. A jacket had been draped casually over her shoulders, as if she couldn't make up her mind whether she was hot or cold. With a few simple pieces of jewelry, one of them a string of pearls framing a discreet dècolletage, she looked very elegant.

"Sure thing," Dan responded, grasping her hand. Her grip was firm and she let it linger. "How did you know?"

"I'm among the few left and I do all the major's typing. I'm Ann Jordan."

"Glad to see you, Ann. Without your shining presence, the place would look like a morgue."

She tilted her head, her eyes assessing him, her expression accepting the flirtatious banter but not quite encouraging more of it. "Go right in, Captain," she said, withdrawing her hand. "Major Blakely is expecting you."

Dan continued to stare at her appreciatively as she sat down again and demurely adjusted her skirt. Then he turned away and walked toward Blakely's cubbyhole.

6

"Jesus, it's you again," Blakely said with feigned irritation when Dan extended his arm through the open doorway and rapped on his desk.

It was a small room with hardly enough space for another person to sit in the extra chair. Blakely had been studying a file of papers in a green folder and Dan had just enough time to catch the large, boldly printed *TOP SECRET* designation before the file was folded closed. Blakely was the plans officer for SO and most of the stuff that came across his desk was marked *TOP SECRET*.

"I thought we sent you to Italy on vacation," he continued dryly.

"Apparently somebody wanted me back. Wasn't it you, Alan?"

"Me? Not particularly. You were a pain in the ass last time you were here. That's why we dropped you on the Italians." Then he stood up, smiled warmly and shook hands. "Welcome back, Dan. It's good to see you. How did you find the dark-haired, brown-eyed signoras?"

"I didn't," Brooks complained. "Only a bunch of mountain men, Kraut-speaking Italians who used to be Austrians when there was still an emperor in Vienna and a Kaiser in Berlin."

"How proficient is your German these days?"

Brooks sat down on the chair adjacent to the desk and scrutinized Blakely's expression for clues. It had been a mission into Germany that he'd really wanted before they sent him to Italy.

"Pretty good," he answered offhandedly. "Couldn't say I was a stickler for their grammar, but the same might be said for my French and sometimes my English. My eyesight's pretty good too. Where'd you get that chick who does your typing?"

"You mean Ann, the one and only," Blakely responded in a possessive tone. "Had her bunked away in another office doing translations when you were here last." His eyes rose in an allusive gesture. "You wouldn't believe it, but she's a recent widow. Her husband was a pilot. Caught it on one of the Schweinfurt raids a few months back. I guess I've helped her," he added, trying for a humility that didn't go with the look on his face.

"She gives me the impression she's overqualified."

"Yeah, she sure is," Blakely agreed. "She's trilingual, but we've been winding down and there isn't any need for her as a translator, so we had to settle for the slot she's got now."

"You sure latched onto a beauty," said Dan with genuine appreciation in his voice.

"Yeah, and I'm going to hang onto her," Blakely snapped back. He smiled to soften the tone. "Enough of that. We've got a briefing laid on for you in the conference room."

They walked down one floor, and as Brooks moved through the corridor he carelessly brushed against someone just entering the hallway from another office. He immediately said, "Sorry," caught sight of a dark blue naval officer's uniform and heard a gruff voice begin to berate him,

"Why the hell don't you watch where—!" then stop, shift gears and say, "Just the man I'm looking for."

Lieutenant Commander Francis Cassidy, Chief, Secret Intelligence, OSS, London, was smiling at him instead of glaring, and had his hand extended in greeting. Behind him were two men in army o.d.'s without any insignia of unit or rank. One man was of medium height and stocky, with brown, straight-combed hair and broad cheekbones that made his brown eyes appear deeply recessed. Brooks guessed his age to be about thirty-four. The second man was seven or eight years younger, tall and thin, with sad, pale eyes and thick black hair combed in a way still fashionable among European civilians.

Agents was the first thought that leaped into Brooks's mind. Two agents working for Cassidy's Secret Intelligence branch, either on the way out or on the way back from a mission. Dan reluctantly shook the lieutenant commander's hand, then decided to force an I.D. out of the other two men. He stuck his hand out in a quick gesture toward the stocky one.

"Dan Brooks," he said with a big grin.

The man hesitated, looked at Cassidy for approval and, getting the nod, took Dan's hand and said, with a little bow and almost a click of the heels, "Bergen. Karl Bergen. A pleasure to meet you, sir."

The English was good. The accent was German. Dan leaned toward the taller man, extended his hand again, fixed his gaze on the fellow's sad eyes and repeated his name once more in the same tone of joviality.

"Pleased to meet you, sir," the man responded in a soft voice. "I'm Willy Hupnagel."

The accent was American Midwest with just a touch of German, like Freddy Blumberg's accent. Blumberg had been born in Germany and had come to the States with his parents as a fourteen-year-old refugee from the Nazis in 1937.

"You really ought to join my team, Danny boy," Cassidy's gravelly voice prodded. "There's no room for you operational hotshots anymore."

Dan felt his anger rise. "There's still a war out there, Francis. You ought to visit it now and then so you know what you're talking about."

"I've got carte blanche to pull in anybody I want, Captain," the SI chief bristled. "That goes for you, too. Isn't that right, Blakely?"

"So I hear, Frank," Major Blakely said.

"You can take your carte blanche and shove it, Francis," Dan said with a big, put-on smile. He knew Cassidy wanted to be called "Frank" or "Commander," and that he hated to be called Francis.

"Your boy's going to have to deal with me one way or another," declared the naval officer.

Dan was about to retort, but the major took his arm and swept him along the corridor. "What did he mean by that?" Dan demanded.

"You'll find out eventually," Blakely told him. "But he's not co-opting you, much as he'd like to."

8

"Who are the two Kraut agents?"

Blakely stared at him and shook his head. "You don't need to know that yet."

He knocked on the door of what once had been the formal dining room of the mansion. The room was elegantly carpeted and paneled in dark wood, and there were war maps on the wall. Three men sat in leather chairs at a refectory table. Dan greeted them respectfully and each welcomed him with more than his usual formal courtesy. They seemed genuinely glad to see him, as if they'd been waiting anxiously, uncertain of his safe arrival back from behind German lines.

The three men were Colonel Robert Hoose, Chief of the London headquarters, in command of all the agency's European operations; Lawrence Dillard, the civilian Chief of Special Operations; and Lieutenant Colonel Ted Pearson, head of the Paris branch.

Colonel Hoose began the briefing. "Have you ever heard the phrase, 'the Last Redoubt,' Captain?"

"Yes, sir. But I've never put much stock in it," Brooks challenged.

"General Eisenhower does," Hoose responded crisply. "SHAEF is making plans to deal with it. Allen Dulles, our man in Switzerland, believes it exists and his intelligence has high credibility. The Germans refer to it also as the National Redoubt. The reports we've received say they're building an *Alpenfestung*, a vast, impregnable fortress in the Alps where the government and high-ranking Nazis and their families will take refuge, to be defended by as many as twenty-five divisions. They're supposed to be storing huge caches of ammunition, fuel, food and weapons in caves and building underground factories dug deeply into the mountainsides."

"It can extend the war by a year and cost more dead and wounded than we've already suffered since D-Day," Larry Dillard interjected.

Brooks wondered what they were driving at. It certainly didn't sound like a target that could be eliminated by a Special Operations mission—or a thousand of them.

Colonel Hoose narrowed the perspective. "The Redoubt will make your assignment more difficult, Captain Brooks," he said, "But attacking it is not the primary objective of the mission we have in mind for you."

"We do want you to continue the sort of operations you're accustomed to, Dan," Major Blakely added ingenuously, as if he were sending him around the corner with a grocery list. "Ambushes, raids, sabotage, harassing lines of communications, subversion and generating guerrilla groups. We want you to do as much damage as possible to the enemy war machine in your zone of operations, but not when it compromises your main mission."

"What *is* the primary objective?" Dan asked, glancing at each of them in turn.

The colonel rose from his place at the head of the table and strode to

one of the war maps on the wall. "First, your zone of operations, Brooks."
He was a tall, slender man, elegant in tailoring and manner. A wealthy
socialite, he had been a successful lawyer and diplomat before the war.
He used a long pointer and began to identify places in the mountainous
south of the shrinking Third Reich. Dan felt a surge of excitement when
the pointer momentarily tapped Berchtesgaden in the southeast corner of
Bavaria where Adolf Hitler's personal mountain retreat was located. But
then Hoose said, "That's only for reference, Captain. We won't expect you
to cover that much territory." He moved the stick down across the border
into the Inn Valley of Austria.

"Here's the territory we have in mind," he said, pointing to the
mountainous area that rose steeply on all sides of the city of Innsbruck.
"You will select the landing zone yourself, of course, but this is the
general locale of your mission. SI men working for Commander Cassidy
have already begun transmitting intelligence to us about German deployment there and in other parts of the Tyrol."

"Would two of those agents be named Karl Bergen and Willy Hupnagel?" Brooks asked.

Colonel Hoose looked at him sharply. "You do get around, don't you,
Captain, where you're not supposed to. But I guess that's what we pay you
for, isn't it?" he said, adding a smile. "In this instance, however, the
intelligence comes from other teams. Bergen and Hupnagel haven't been
out yet. It might even be good to overlook compartmentalization this
time and have you talk to them. They'll be going in a lot sooner than you
will."

Brooks agreed. "If their intelligence will be important to my mission
I'd like very much to meet with them before they leave."

"You won't have to depend only on SI's people," Lieutenant Colonel
Pearson spoke up. "You'll have your own agents too, We'll provide
whatever personnel you need for the job. There is also an Austrian
resistance movement developing, so by the time you're on the ground you
might have help from some of the civilian populace, as you did in
France."

But none of them had told him the point of it all yet, as if the purpose of
the mission was so secret that it could not even be mentioned. "What *is*
the mission, sir?" he tried again softly. "The main objective."

"To capture all the high-ranking Nazis you can bag," Hoose said. "Not
kill them, Brooks, but kidnap them right out from under the noses of the
SS. The job of your agents will be to pinpoint the exact places where the
top Nazis hole up."

"They're either going to make a run for it, Dan, or fight to the death in
the National Redoubt," Larry Dillard spoke up. "If you capture the
leaders, not the military commanders but the political leaders, and the
higher up the better—Göring, Goebbels, Himmler, any one of those

bastards—we can use them to effect a surrender. The fanatics won't quit unless the top Nazis order them to. That's why they have to be taken alive."

Dan felt the adrenaline hit his blood stream. He realized there was one name that hadn't been spoken yet—Adolf Hitler! By its absence, he understood what they had in mind but wouldn't reveal to him yet.

"One matter of vital importance, Brooks," declared Colonel Hoose. "No matter who you capture, you must keep their identities secret until we tell you otherwise. By secret I mean it would be best if only you knew their identities, though I realize that might be impossible under certain circumstances. Nevertheless, take with you the means to disguise your captives. If you have to let a few of your men know the sort of quarry you're after, they are never to talk about it with each other or anybody else. You are not even to tell *us* until we order you to. Even if it is Hitler himself."

What the colonel was really saying was, *It is Hitler you are going in to get! But the situation is so fraught with international complications and peril that even we who give you this mission can't call it by its rightful name. It must be kept from strangers and from your men. From us, partly. And, if it were possible, even from yourself.*

Dan asked, "What about personnel?"

"What we have to start with," Lieutenant Colonel Pearson began, "are forty-five anti-Nazi Germans in a holding compound at St. Germain, outside Paris...."

In the next minutes, Dan felt himself gripped by the audacity of what Pearson told him. Some of the lieutenant colonel's Paris staff would assist him in selecting cadre and personnel from a unique, predetermined complement of candidates. Housing and training facilities for a company-size unit were already waiting for him in St. Germain.

"All we've got now is the outline of a plan," continued Colonel Hoose. "Pearson and Blakely worked it up as far as they could go. It will be up to you now to write a complete plan. If you don't think the mission can work, you're to speak up strongly, giving the reasons why. Do you understand?"

"Yes, sir. How quickly do you want it?"

"Three days. If our advance into Germany continues as quickly as it's going now, we'll need your unit operational by February or March. Mr. Dillard has suggested that eight weeks of training would be adequate. What do you think?"

"That should be sufficient," Dan agreed. "Is there a code name for the mission?"

"Knight's Cross."

Three

✠   Ann Jordan smiled sweetly over the rim of her glass of gin and bitters at the man sitting across the table from her. He had just used one of his charming little Russian phrases, which he would translate when she asked him to, always in a way to please her, but Lord only knew what they really meant. He might be murmuring the most sexual of things. Her eyes traveled over the well-tailored gray suit he wore. It was obviously made by a good firm in London. Clothing made in the Soviet Union was generally quite dowdy, especially now.

Ann was glad that Major Schepilov preferred small Bohemian restaurants like this one in Soho, rather than the officers' clubs where the variety of liquor seemed unlimited and the food better than the public spots could offer with the strict rationing. She would have hated running into Alan Blakely after the snit he'd been in that morning, nor would she have liked being seen by any of the other OSS personnel who presumed that she and Blakely were an item.

They had had an awful row in the office when she told him she wouldn't be able to see him tonight. Fortunately, no one else had been close enough to hear them. She had begged off for the night and Alan had accused her of flirting with Dan Brooks and making a date with him. She had denied it, of course. But Alan had kept after her and she had finally stalked out of the office in a tearful rage, telling him it was none of his damned business what she did on her own time. Blakely thought he owned her, but she didn't want to be owned by anyone and she'd already given him more than she should have.

Drew Jordan had owned her for a brief time and she had loved the glamour and excitement of being married to a bomber pilot and being there in London for him when he returned from his missions over the continent. They had known each other as friends at home. The men of their social set on Long Island either went into the air corps or intelligence, maybe the navy. Even some of the women were in uniform, but she hadn't wanted that. When some of her friends had joined what their detractors called "Oh, So Social" and "Oh, So Secret," she too had applied, for a lark, and found that her background, travel experience in Europe and trilingual education in Switzerland made her an ideal civilian employee of the agency.

When she had run into Drew in London they had begun to date right away, had fallen in love and into bed quickly, though she was never sure which had come first, and then had been married by the rector of St. Paul's, all within the space of a few whirlwind months. Then Drew had had the damn fool luck to get himself killed. It had been a terrible blow to her and she had hardly known how to behave, except that Drew, with his have-a-good-time-while-you-can philosophy, had prepared her for it. His death had not devastated her the way she had seen it happen to other war widows. She and Drew had had their glorious loving months together and that had been that. She was luckier, Ann supposed, than women at home who sent their men off to war and never saw them again.

But death could happen to her over here too, just as it had happened to Drew. If Jerry sent one of his V-2s at her in Soho this night, they would ship her home in a box if they could find anything left. Which was why she had not let herself sink into despondency and mourning too long. Alan Blakely had been there at the office, only too ready, willing and able; though she'd had no intention of getting into a permanent thing with him. He would be livid if he knew that at one of the diplomatic cocktail parties he had taken her to she had slipped her phone number to an officer who had been discreetly flirting with her that night, the man who sat across the table from her now. Major Mikhail Schepilov of the Soviet Mission in London.

When he had ordered dinner for both of them and the waiter left, he asked, "How does your work go, Ann?"

"Work? What work, Mikhail?" she teased. "I told you last time that I'm the daughter of a wealthy capitalist whom you people, no doubt, would disapprove of... or shoot. I don't have to work."

Mikhail smiled. "I do not believe you, Ann," he said. His English was quite fluent, his speech courteous and respectful and he tried to keep any note of reproach out of his voice. "Surely you are not here as an American tourist. Even I know that this is banned now in wartime."

He had not asked her about her work on their first date a week earlier. They had merely talked about their countries, their personal backgrounds, interests and general outlook on life. Ann had let him know right away that she had no qualms about communism, having absorbed the influence of sympathetic or politically radical students and professors at college. Mikhail had been tender and compassionate when she told him her husband had been killed over Schweinfurt a few months earlier. They had walked through the blacked-out London streets after dinner as he escorted her to her apartment. She hadn't invited him in, although she had been tempted to do so even on that first date, and she had been almost disappointed when he hadn't even tried to embrace her.

He was indeed a charmer, though. Tall, broad-shouldered and slim-waisted, and when he smiled his brown eyes twinkled invitingly. His complexion was somewhat swarthy, being part Tatar, which accentuated the whiteness of his teeth. She had felt very drawn to him and was glad that he had called her again.

"I just do some simple secretarial work," she finally said. "Nothing of importance . . . or even of interest."

Mikhail scoffed at that. "I cannot imagine you doing anything of no interest," he said. "You are too bright, too well educated, For instance, how many languages do you speak?"

"Three. French, German and English. And now with you, a fourth," she replied, reaching out across the table and touching his hand.

"And what is that?"

"Russian, of course."

His eyes looked at her harshly for a moment, as if she had deceived him. "I did not know that you understand Russian."

"Only the phrases you've taught me," Ann replied, laughing. "I wish I did speak it fluently. It might be amusing to make love in Russian."

The major colored slightly, looking away in embarrassment. She was going too fast, thought Ann. Men were really so innocent, despite their highly vaunted libidos. Basically such little boys. Even a man as sophisticated as she imagined Major Schepilov to be.

He recovered and waved a finger at her roguishly. "Like Mata Hari, perhaps? But she, of course, spied for the Germans against the French . . . and the French shot her. Very unlike them to do a thing like that, isn't it?" He stared into his gin and bitters for a moment, his face dark. Ann wondered if he would have preferred vodka, which all Russians were supposed to like. Then he went on, looking at her directly. "But that was another time. Are you a spy, Ann?" he asked smiling.

She laughed. "No, my dear Mikhail. I have aspirations to be a *femme fatale*, but nothing beyond that." She wondered if the Russians *would* consider someone in her line of work a spy. She was, of course, only a secretary, as she had told him, and sometimes a translator, but the people she worked for did more interesting things than that. She loved being in the know on Special Operations' cloak-and-dagger activities, and was thrilled by her brief contacts with daring field operatives like Dan Brooks. But no, she wasn't a spy. Though OSS was in the spy business.

"I do not believe that someone with your abilities is used by your government only to do simple secretarial work," the major insisted. "If you were employed by the Soviet Mission you would have a more important job, I assure you."

Ann tilted her head and looked at him searchingly. She thought she had better smile, and she did. "Are you offering me a job, Mikhail?"

"I do not think it would be proper," he replied. "Besides, I do not even know what you do now. This simple secretarial work that you do. Is it for your embassy? Or one of your government's agencies? Or the military?"

Ann did not think there would be anything wrong in replying to that in vague terms. "One of the agencies," she said.

Major Schepilov did not pursue his questioning to the next logical step, and Ann was relieved. He said, offhandedly, "I will ask my superiors at the Mission and see if there is something available."

Ann realized that he was not merely being polite, he was quite serious, and she wondered if she ought to take him up on it. There was no telling how long her job with SO would last. The only reason she was still there was Alan Blakely. She would hate to be let go and sent home. She would miss the excitement of life in London, and she did feel she was making at least a small contribution to the war effort. But of what use could she possibly be to the Russian Mission?

"That's awfully sweet of you, Mikhail," she said. "Thank you." Then she turned her mind to contemplating what she would say or do with him when he took her back to her apartment. She felt magnetically drawn to him. She thought she understood the male's feelings of desire as well as she did her own. But Mikhail was different. There was something exotic about him, not only physically but also the way he spoke to her.

Karl Bergen swaggered down the corridor toward Lieutenant Commander Cassidy's office, with Willy Hupnagel a step behind. It seemed to Willy that this was the way they had moved in tandem ever since they met, always letting Karl take the lead. Cassidy had even appointed Karl the team leader, though Willy had outranked him from before the time they started training together six months earlier. Radio men were never appointed team leaders. They were always an adjunct.

He had come into OSS as a T4 radio operator from the air corps and Karl had signed up as a corporal from an armored division. Now Willy was a tech sergeant entitled to wear three stripes over two rockers and he still outranked Karl's three buck sergeant's stripes. But their ranks weren't important except on paydays because Cassidy had told them not to wear any grade insignia or unit designation and to practice thinking and talking like civilians—in German.

It seemed to come more naturally to Karl, Willy thought, maybe because he had been born in Munich and had lived in Germany until he was twenty-four. Karl liked to point out repeatedly that Willy was "only an Austrian like that son-of-a-bitch Hitler who came across the border, stuck his nose in other people's business and fucked up Germany." He didn't like Karl, but Willy figured he would be a good man to keep them out of trouble once they parachuted into Austria. He hoped Bergen was still one step ahead of him and took the first bullet if they ever walked through the wrong door and the shooting started.

Lieutenant Commander Cassidy smiled, stood up and extended his hand when the two agents were passed through by his secretary. He still tended to follow the courtesies he had used as a civilian lawyer ingratiating himself with clients shown into his office.

"Well, how's the 'Bluenose' team today?" he asked jovially.

Cassidy, who had been a naval officer only a very short time before transferring into OSS, wasn't a stickler for the military formalities of saluting and reporting, despite his conservative nature. He was more concerned about the individual qualifications of personnel selected for a specific job, about motivating them to do that job superbly and inspiring them to strong personal loyalty to him. In these two agents he felt he had a pair of winners, though they had no experience in the field yet.

"Pretty good, sir," replied Bergen. He opened his mouth to add something, then hesitated, gathered his thoughts and finally decided to get what bothered him off his chest. "I do have one question to ask you, Commander."

Bergen would pass easily in the Reich, Cassidy thought, provided that every item of clothing and personal possessions the supply people issued to him and Hupnagel, and every I.D., passbook and piece of paper they took with them, did not vary from what was in use there now.

"Sure. Pull up a couple of chairs and tell me what's on your mind," invited the SI chief.

Karl Bergen was not a type Cassidy would have dealt with on Wall Street. Maybe over near Foley Square if he'd been in the criminal law business, but certainly not among the genteel, monied clientele he'd been accustomed to. Cassidy always covered his feelings nicely with his toothy smile and firm, rank-dispensing handshake, but there was something intimidating about Karl's stocky presence. The man looked like a brawler. His hands were big, hard and rough to the touch and his knuckles were puffed. His left ear was cauliflowered, a sign of having taken a lot of punches there, and his cheekbone on that side was enlarged, making his left eye appear deeply recessed and slightly higher than the other.

According to his service records, which Cassidy had studied carefully, Karl actually had been in the ring for a while and later had worked as a beer hall bouncer in Yorkville, the old German section of New York City. He had told that to the army recruiters who accepted his enlistment in 1942 and he also had admitted to them that he had jumped ship in New York harbor from a German freighter in 1934 and had been in the U.S. illegally for eight years. Enlistment in the army had allowed him to apply for legal citizenship and expedite the process.

A year later, an OSS recruiter scouting for agents had made contact with Karl while he had been on leave in Yorkville. The OSS man had spotted Bergen in a restaurant, drinking beer and eating wurst with a bunch of his civilian friends. They had been loudly and heatedly discussing the war news in their native tongue, and Karl had been roundly cursing the Nazis, wondering if the American army would ever give him a crack at them. The recruiter had arranged to talk to him alone and found him very interested in his proposal. Some weeks later Bergen, having undergone and passed an investigation, was transferred out of his former unit into OSS and became a very enthusiastic candidate for an agent's assignment in the Reich.

He and Hupnagel moved two chairs closer to Cassidy's desk and everybody sat down. Karl squirmed a bit. "This 'Bluenose' word," he muttered. "It is a joke? It is something bad?"

"Of course not, Karl. It's just a code name I pulled out of the air. As far as I know it has no other meaning. Whatever gave you that idea?"

Karl was embarrassed. "First I assure you, sir, that I have told to nobody anything about our 'Bluenose.' Total secrecy, as you instructed. But I have thought about it and it seems to me like a bad word . . . and I do not know if you are making a joke. Is it proper and dignified for such an important mission?"

Lieutenant Commander Francis Cassidy was totally bewildered. "I don't get you, Karl. What do you mean?"

"You have heard the American slang word 'brown nose'?"

"Yes, of course." Sudden perception hit Cassidy. He almost laughed but thought better of it.

"My English perhaps is not so good," continued Karl gravely, "But I think 'brown nose' means kissing somebody's ass. What does it mean, 'Bluenose'?"

"Your English is just fine, Karl," Cassidy spoke up quickly. "But two nights from now you'd better forget you speak it."

"We are going!" Karl said happily.

"Yes . . . and rest assured," the SI chief said, "there is no derogatory meaning to 'Bluenose.'"

Cassidy dropped the subject, but noted for future reference that Karl, despite his toughness, was very sensitive to imagined slights and insults. He remembered too that some of the staff who worked with the agent teams had told him that Karl Bergen was an ass-kisser regarding rank and authority, but otherwise tended to be overbearing and supercilious. Neither character trait would impair him for the mission, Cassidy thought.

Willy Hupnagel, on the other hand, had a more reserved and gentle personality, though the tough agent's training courses, including parachute jumps, hadn't scared him off. According to his service records and the OSS probe of his background he had been brought to the States from Austria by his parents when he was seventeen in 1938, just after the *Anschluss* between Austria and Germany. They had seen what was coming and, good Catholic country people that they were, they wanted no part of it. They remembered the 1914–18 war too vividly and didn't want to be on the wrong side again, so they had followed the example of relatives who had emigrated many years earlier and joined them in St. Louis, where young Willy learned English, finished high school and was working in his parents' bakery until the time he volunteered for the air corps. He had already tinkered with crystal sets and radio kits and he knew Morse code, so when he took the radioman's aptitude test given to all recruits he passed easily and had gone through basic and radio training in the air corps before being recruited into OSS.

Hupnagel was a good balance to Bergen's aggressiveness, Cassidy thought. More important, he also had an aunt who owned a *Gasthaus* on the southern outskirts of Innsbruck. The head of Secret Intelligence now began to tell them in greater detail than they had been told before about those things that "Bluenose" was expected to do in the area of the Last Redoubt.

Four

✠   Upstairs on the third floor of the OSS headquarters building, Captain Brooks was at work again Saturday morning, sitting in the big Plans and Operations room. Major Blakely's outline had been an adequate beginning, but to flesh it out and give it substance Brooks had worked diligently for three days and was going over it again now before submitting it to his superior.

He had noticed Ann Jordan pounding her typewriter far across the room, had greeted her just once out of courtesy and then had forgotten about her. For him, nothing existed now but the mission.

The Inn Valley was not an unknown place to him. Before enlisting in the army in the mid-1930s, he had worked a number of summers in Biarritz, France, as a lifeguard and swimming instructor, and had traveled extensively in France, Germany and Austria. He had learned French and German earlier from some of his family in New York, had studied the languages further in school and ultimately had acquired greater proficiency working and traveling in Europe. With that sort of background, he had been a natural for recruitment by OSS. They had, in fact, saved him from the dullest of duties as a training officer. Two years earlier, his basic branch, the infantry, had considered him too old at thirty-seven for a combat troop assignment.

Appraising what he remembered now of the terrain of the Tyrol, Brooks felt that the high mountains and glaciers, the deep valleys, woods, farms, isolated hamlets and villages would work in favor of success. If the Nazi leaders expected to find refuge there, so could a highly motivated, superbly trained force of well-equipped, clandestine hunters bent on rooting them out and kidnapping them. No matter what places the Nazi fugitives went to ground, he thought it highly unlikely that there would be twenty-five SS divisions around to defend them.

He wrote his plan in longhand on a yellow pad, then added his personnel requirements, an equipment annex and requirements for support from OSS's Special Operations Wing for infiltration, resupply and recovery. He completed his detailed plan with a memo to the documentation branch of OSS requesting cover stories and I.D.'s for himself and the personnel who would go in with him.

Sergeant Blumberg entered the Plans and Operations office just as Dan was finishing up. He had asked his radioman to meet him there at 1100.

"How'd you like to join me on another little trip?" he asked.

"Where to?" asked Freddy.

"Can't tell you."

"Sounds familiar. I've been there before, Captain. I liked it a lot. I'll go."

Dan smiled at him. He would have let him refuse, but he would have hated to lose him. They had always made a good team and he trusted him in all matters. "I can tell you this much, Freddy," he said. "We'll be in France for a couple of months. That isn't much of a secret. Everybody goes to France these days."

"Yeah, I know. I've been there too," Blumberg joked. "Fine food, Good wine. A really swell country for a vacation." Last time they had been there, in the south of France, they had been operating in the middle of German General Blaskowitz's XIXth army.

"First assignment, Freddy, is get me another radio operator just as good as you," Dan told him. "He also has to speak German well enough to pass for a Kraut."

Blumberg looked at him and smiled. The captain had told him nothing and yet had told him everything. "No problem, sir," he said. "I know a lot of those guys."

"Wait here for me, will you," Dan told him, gathering up his yellow pages. "I've got to go in to see the major. Shouldn't be too long."

"Sure, Captain," Blumberg said, settling down at an adjacent desk. "I bought *Stars and Stripes* and *The Times* on the way over. I want to find out who's winning the war. Maybe I should have picked up the *Völkischer Beobachter* or *Frankfurter Zeitung*, huh? Just to get in some practice," he added with a knowing grin.

Dan raised his eyes, shrugged and walked toward Alan Blakely's little cubicle, nodding to Ann Jordan as he passed. She was flipping through the pages of a magazine, apparently with nothing else to do at the moment, and she smiled at him.

Half an hour later, Sergeant Blumberg was laughing at Bill Mauldin's latest "Willy and Joe" cartoon in *Stars and Stripes* when he became aware of somebody staring at him from inside the doorway of the Plans and Operations room. Blumberg thought the man in the unmarked o.d. uniform looked a bit like Max Schmeling might have appeared a few weeks after his second fight with Joe Louis: healed, but too late to undo the damage.

"Hello. Looking for somebody?" Blumberg called out, adding a belated, "sir."

In the halls of this building you never knew when rank was traveling incognito, so he always thought it best to render the military courtesies, whether they were necessary or not.

"Yes, please. Captain Brooks," Karl Bergen said.

Blumberg tuned right in on the German accent. He had heard more tones and inflections like that since joining OSS than he had ever expected.

"Pull up a chair. He ought to be out in a few minutes. I'm Fred Blumberg."

The man looked Blumberg over in a way that said he wasn't yet sure of the amount of deference or courtesy due him. His stare was presumptuous. "Blumberg? Blumberg?" he repeated, chewing the name over and tilting his head to the side as if to give greater scrutiny to the unexpected person before him. His deep set eyes darted from shoulder to sleeves and settled on the buck sergeant's stripes. They were of equal military rank, he noted with satisfaction; and the slight German accent he also had detected induced him into assuming an attitude of familiarity. "*Ich heisse Bergen...Karl...Unteroffizier.* My name is Bergen...Karl ... Sergeant," he said, dropping into a chair at the next desk.

"In which army, Sergeant?" Blumberg joked.

But Bergen didn't know how to joke. He took immediate umbrage at Blumberg's cheerful remark, and switched to English. "In the American army, of course," he said. "Just like you." Then, in German again, "*Blumberg...Blumberg...Sind Sie ein Jude?* Are you a Jew?"

"*Ja,*" the radioman replied crisply. He watched the man weigh the answer, look at him slyly and file it away. "And you, Bergen? Also Jewish?" he added.

"*Bergen? Bergen? Ein Jude?*" He switched to English. "Don't be ridiculous."

Blumberg clenched his fists, leaned toward the other man and tensed himself to spring. "Look, fella, I don't know who the hell you are, but your German is crude and your English is either ignorant or insulting. I'll give you the benefit of the doubt and say it's ignorant."

Bergen was taken aback by Blumberg's unexpected and instant shift in manner from open and friendly to antagonistic. He stared uncertainly at the stocky man with the outthrust chin and recognized the type, for he was one himself—a brawler with a hair-trigger temper ready to explode. In the States, Karl's friends knew him—as the army and OSS did—as a one-time preliminary fighter in the ring and a beer hall bouncer. But none of them knew about his years of political brawling in the streets of Germany from Munich to Berlin, some of it organized, some spontaneous, all of it done with relish, until Hitler had shown his true and treacherous colors.

21

"No, no. I did not mean to insult," Bergen said. "Maybe it is my bad English." He heard footsteps coming toward them from the other end of the room, looked up, then leapt to his feet and stood at attention as Captain Brooks stopped beside them.

"Man's looking for you, Captain," Blumberg said, eyeing Karl with amusement now rather than anger.

"Hello, Bergen. Your boss ready for me?"

"Yes, sir."

Brooks looked from one to the other and sensed that he had interrupted something. Whatever it was, he knew that Blumberg would never bring it up on his own, so he would have to ask him about it later. Anything at all he could learn about Bergen might be important. He glanced at his wrist watch. "Better start on that first assignment we talked about, Freddy. I'll see you back here at 1500."

In the first minutes of their meeting, it became apparent to Brooks that Lieutenant Commander Cassidy was jealous and angry that the Special Operations branch, rather than Secret Intelligence, had been designated to carry out Knight's Cross in the Reich. They were alone together in Cassidy's private office on the second floor. Bergen and Hupnagel were waiting to be summoned from the outer room if Cassidy ever deigned to grant Dan's request to interview them.

The head of SI had insisted, "Information on a need-to-know basis, Captain. There is no reason I can think of for you to talk to Bergen and Hupnagel or know anything about them. That sort of information could compromise their mission and endanger their lives."

"What's the code name for their mission?" Dan persisted.

Cassidy gave him his toothy grin and waggled a finger at him as if he were being a naughty boy.

"They're going to be gathering intelligence for Knight's Cross, aren't they," Dan reminded him.

"But they're not working for *you*, they're working for *me*," Cassidy said. "They'll have other things to think about besides Knight's Cross. Anything of interest to you will be passed along through channels."

The naval officer seemed to consider all of Germany and Austria as SI's private preserve and his agents as part of his own personal fiefdom. Dan began to steam, but he knew that anger wasn't the way to get what he needed. Nor did he want to invoke the authority of Colonel Hoose to get the naval officer to cooperate. He wanted him to do it on his own.

Then Cassidy started to denounce Knight's Cross itself.

"It's a redundant operation, Captain," the SI chief insisted.

"The boss doesn't think so, Francis, " Brooks responded.

"I wish you'd stop calling me that. I prefer Frank."

"Sorry, Commander...Frank," Brooks acknowledged. He stopped

baiting Cassidy, but would not tolerate any interference in Knight's Cross, whether by intervention or omission.

"We've already got agents in the Tyrol, Brooks. More going in and resistance groups becoming active under SI's auspices," Cassidy blurted.

In the instant of saying it, he realized that he had divulged information he had had no intention of revealing to Brooks or anyone else in Special Operations, but it was too late.

Dan scrutinized him closely to see if he was speaking the truth. "Where, Frank?" he asked warily. "If freelancers are in there now they can fuck up everything."

Cassidy glanced away in embarrassment, knowing he'd been caught out. There was no point in trying to dissemble any further. Better to boast of his coup. "Kufstein," he said. "We have a two-man agent team in the area. A local resistance group requested arms. We complied and sent in weapons for a band of thirty partisans."

"That is *not* an SI function, Commander, and you know it!" Dan declared heatedly. The man wouldn't last two seconds under Gestapo interrogation, he thought. "Secret intelligence quietly gathered... *that's* what your agents are supposed to be doing. They're not supposed to engage in covert actions against the enemy. That's the function of Special Operations. That's *my* job."

"What do you expect me to do, Brooks, ask the partisans to return the guns we've dropped to them?"

Dan realized that what Cassidy regretted more than his inadvertent confession was not having control over what SO teams did in Germany and Austria. If he couldn't control SO's unconventional warfare operations, he wanted to isolate SI's role from them completely. Dan had also suspected, early on, that the SI chief was the sort who might attempt to go beyond his branch's functions and set up his own independent covert actions against the enemy. Now he had Cassidy's admission of doing the very thing that his standing orders forbade him to do.

"Does Larry Dillard know about this? Or Colonel Hoose?" Dan pressed.

"No, And I would like you to keep it that way."

"Very well, But I want something from you in return."

"What?"

"To have a friendly little chat with Bergen and Hupnagel, and then for you to give me, before I leave for Paris, complete copies of their service records, their civilian files and the OSS intelligence reports on them."

Cassidy thought about Dan's request. "Very well," he finally said. "Since they will be gathering intelligence pertinent to your mission, perhaps you're right. But you are to treat their records with the strictest confidence. No one else is to see them."

"Of course, Frank. Information on a need-to-know basis."

"And I want a copy of your Knight's Cross plan."

Dan put as much deference into his voice as he could muster. "I'm sure, Commander, that you'll understand why I can't do that. There's a TOP SECRET classification on it. They'd have my ass if I violated it."

"Yes, of course. Thank you, Brooks. I'll call the men in."

Five

✠ The combat zone had moved east to the German frontier and beyond, but there was still need for subterfuge as they left OSS's Paris headquarters just off the Champs Élysées.

Brooks's shabby, dark suit was on the full side, as if he'd lost weight and was still hungry after four years of Nazi occupation. He carried a light coat and fedora appropriate to the vagaries of late November weather. Captain Robert LeGrange, his liaison officer, a slim man with sharp features, also dressed in civvies.

They drove in a small black Citröen to an apartment on Rue Maillot near the Bois de Boulogne, where three civilians joined them soon after their arrival. Each wore workmen's clothes and caps which they removed and held politely in their hands.

The leader was introduced as Dietrich. He was a slender man about sixty years old with gray hair and wire rim glasses. Speaking French with a German accent, and staring warily at Brooks, he introduced his companions as Hans and Walter. Dan thought one looked like an assassin, the other a con man. He greeted them in German and they fell more comfortably into an exchange of pleasantries in their native language. All three smiled with pleasure when LeGrange waved them to the dining table for brioches and coffee.

"Do you have the lists?" LeGrange asked.

Dietrich lifted his coffee cup, inhaling the aroma with gusto. "Of course," he replied.

"Dietrich is the contact man," LeGrange explained.

"I'd prefer him to be the cut-out man after he turns over his list of names." Dan stated bluntly. "Neither he nor any of his people, including Hans and Walter here, if we decide to use them, are to be exposed to anything except what concerns them directly."

"Agreed," said LeGrange, "but Dietrich must help us establish the bona fides of the men we'll be seeing. He'll also be able to vouch for us with them, since he has a certain amount of credibility among them."

25

Dan saw the practicality of that argument and did not question it further. Though there would be more chances for Knight's Cross to spring a leak, he also thought the recruitment team might need additional interviewers to accomplish the job quickly. Besides LeGrange, himself and Sergeant Blumberg, a couple of German-speaking OSS linguists would join them, and now he would have Dietrich too.

Freddy would be good at sniffing out unreliable candidates. He had already allowed, with some prodding from Brooks, that there was something fishy about Karl Bergen. That opinion reinforced Brooks's assessment after his talk with the Bluenose team in Lieutenant Commander Cassidy's office. Later, he had let Blumberg read the Bergen and Hupnagel records and Freddy had spotted the same holes he had—a very inadequate account of Bergen's years in Germany prior to 1934 when he claimed to have sailed from Hamburg and jumped ship in New York.

Brooks chatted casually with the three civilians while LeGrange plied them with more coffee and brioches. He learned enough about them to assuage his innate wariness. Though Dietrich was German, Hans and Walter were Austrian. Of special interest to him was Hans's claim that he knew the Inn Valley well.

The man was built like a weightlifter. He was just under six feet tall, had a solid, square jaw and a bull neck. He was somewhat ponderous in his movements, but this lack of agility was more than compensated for by his strength. Walter was of medium stature, spoke persuasively and had a lot of *savoir faire*. He was definitely an operator, Dan thought. They certainly complemented one another.

All three men said they had fought in Spain seven years earlier on the side of the Republican government. More recently they had fought with the French Resistance. That made Brooks feel more comfortable with them, for there were ways to verify that part of their stories.

"Are you able to leave with us tomorrow?" he asked Dietrich.

"Of course."

Dan looked toward Walter and Hans, still waiting for him to say whether they would be agents or not. "All right, I can use you," he granted, and they beamed as if he'd bestowed a coveted award upon them. To LeGrange he said, "Cut travel orders for them to leave tomorrow for our training facilities in England."

To the two Austrians, he warned, "You must maintain absolute secrecy about your association with us. You must not breathe a word of it to anybody. Not to your friends or your relatives. Your lives depend on that. Do you understand and agree?"

"Absolutely, *Herr Hauptmann!*"

With handshakes, *danke sehrs* and *auf Wiedersehens*, the three civilians left the apartment. Brooks and LeGrange returned to OSS headquarters, changed back into their uniforms and traded the Citröen for a jeep.

On a quiet residential street in the village of St. Germain, west of Paris, LeGrange parked beside a large private house similar to others adjacent to it. The door was opened by an OSS sergeant wearing a holstered .45. He saluted, checked their identities, then escorted them through the interior and out into the extensive rear grounds where they found Lieutenant Frank Chadwick refereeing a soccer game.

Chadwick was a tall, broad-shouldered man with a genial gaze that looked out at the world through steel-rimmed glasses. He had been put in charge of the German civilians staying there while waiting for assignments, and also in command of the OSS housekeeping detail at the training base a short distance away.

"Hope you've got something in mind for these guys," he said. "I'm running out of ideas how to be a good den mother. We're down to a soccer tournament and the local whorehouse."

"Interrupt the game for a few minutes," Dan said.

Chadwick blew his whistle and called the group to gather around him, speaking German just adequate for the job. When Brooks was introduced as the officer who would screen them for assignments, they moved in closer. They wore a motley assortment of drab wool trousers, sweaters and jackets. Their footgear ran from canvas tops to old brogues, brogans and boots. In age they appeared to be between twenty-five and fifty. In physique they ranged from skinny to brawny, from average to tall.

Brooks spent fifteen minutes with them, speaking in German they seemed comfortable with. Most of them, he learned, had been with the French Resistance. All of them had volunteered to serve with the U.S. in a covert capacity.

"We'll start training in about two weeks," Dan told them. "Meanwhile I want you to do more than just hang around, play soccer and visit the local *maison de joie.*"

He paused to allow for the laughter, and when it had quieted down, he continued, "I want you to assume you're in the army and begin physical conditioning, running and close order drill. Soccer and other games will be fine for your off hours, but you're going to need a lot more than that to toughen you up for my program. The lieutenant will post your new schedule this evening and it will commence tomorrow at 0600."

There were a few groans, but Brooks ignored them. The slackers would make themselves apparent soon enough. and getting rid of them before the real training began would make his job easier later on. He thanked the group for volunteering their services and dismissed them back to their interrupted soccer match. Brooks returned to the house with Chadwick and LeGrange and was given a tour of the building. It was set up like a barracks, with every room except the main salon crammed with cots.

"I hope to hell we've got more room at the other place," Dan remarked to LeGrange.

LeGrange frowned, but then quickly changed to a rather smug expression. "What did you have in mind, Captain?"

"Milton Hall."

Milton Hall was the magnificent estate just outside Peterborough in England that OSS used as a training facility. It was more like a resort. No man who had stayed there could ever forget its elegance—and its rigors.

LeGrange and Chadwick looked at each other and smiled. Dan thought it was with fond memories of Milton Hall. "I want to see the training setup now," he said.

He hopped into the passenger seat of the jeep, gestured for LeGrange to get in the rear and Chadwick to take the wheel. "How much do you know about our assignment, Lieutenant?" he asked Chadwick as they drove along the quiet residential streets of St. Germain.

"Not a damn thing, sir, and if I did I wouldn't tell you."

"You'll do just fine, Lieutenant," Dan said, grinning at him. "I'll tell you what you need to know when you need to know it."

"If it's agreeable, Dan, I can order in the rest of the cadre," LeGrange shouted from the back seat. "They can help whip the civilians into shape while we're out rounding up the troops. There's only the housekeeping staff at the training base now."

"Sure, get them here as quick as you can. Frank, you assign them billets and let them start drilling the fundamentals into the civilians. The cadre can stay at the training base, but we won't move the candidates over till I get back."

The lieutenant acknowledged the instructions, then turned into another street and drove slowly alongside a high masonry wall. He stopped at a vehicle entrance barred by two large iron gates. Brooks caught a glimpse of extensive grounds. LeGrange opened the gates to allow the jeep to be driven through. Back in the jeep, he leaned forward to catch the expression of wonder on Dan's face as they drove up the long driveway to the main house.

"Ver-r-ry impressive." Brooks said enthusiastically. "Now I know why you guys looked so damned smug when I started bitching about the accommodations at the compound."

It was a breathtaking estate. As they stood at the front entry of the Normandy style manor house, LeGrange rambled on as if delivering a travelogue. "*Regardez la Fôret de Saint Germain!*" he proclaimed, waving his arm beyond the beautifully groomed grounds toward the woods in the near distance. "Not only do you have these vast grounds, *Monsieur*, but you have ready access to the forest and surrounding countryside for field training."

Only one thing spoiled the grace and serenity of the vista. Squad tents were pitched close to the main house. "For your trainees," Chadwick said. He and LeGrange, quite pleased with themselves, led Brooks on an inspection. Inside the tents were cots and steel lockers awaiting the men. Close by, in other tents pitched in tandem, were the day room and mess. Elsewhere, enclosed latrines and portable showers had been constructed. Finally, there were the storerooms for weapons and supplies, the ammunition and demolitions bunkers and a motor pool with jeeps and two-and-a-half-ton trucks.

Brooks took it all in with satisfaction. He had not been aware of the enormous amount of quiet, behind-the-scenes preparations that had gone into Knight's Cross before he had been given command.

"You've done a fine job." he said with more effusiveness than usual.

Chadwick responded with the élan of a proud maître d'hôtel. "Accommodations for you and your staff are in the manor house itself, of course. Would the captain care to inspect his quarters now?"

"*Mais oui, s'il vous plaît!*"

The lieutenant led them into the grand entry hall of the mansion and they climbed the wide stairway to the second floor. The suite they entered was the master bedroom, with adjacent bath. It was large and airy, with glass doors opening onto a balcony that faced the huge, well-manicured grounds and forest. All of the fine original furnishings were still there, including a large, functional desk with beautifully carved legs.

Dan felt almost guilty. "Unless there's an office for me downstairs," he said, trying to sound practical and untouched by the unexpected luxury, "this will serve very nicely."

Chadwick took them all through the numerous rooms. The dining room would serve as the mess for all OSS personnel. The kitchen was large enough and sufficiently well equipped to prepare food for the entire training unit and station complement. Sleeping quarters for housekeeping staff and cadre were luxurious. The salons which would be used as classrooms were large and well lighted.

"I've stayed in a lot of swanky places," Dan commented finally when he had completed the tour, "but this beats them. Nobody in the world would envision this place as a training base. It even puts the Congressional Country Club to shame."

That large playground near Washington, taken over by OSS a few years earlier, had been his first duty station after the swampy maneuver area in Louisiana from which the agency had co-opted him.

"Don't let it soften you up," LeGrange joked. "We don't want you to think you're on leave."

"No danger of that," Brooks replied coolly.

He thought of the many quid pro quos he'd given—though not without a certain perverse pleasure in his work these past two years. Yet he also wondered if that was a smile or sardonic grin on LeGrange's face. Why was OSS being so good to him? Was he a calf being fatted for slaughter? It was the nature of his trade to be suspicious, to accept nothing at face value—even from friends and allies. It was how he had managed to survive so long in an exceedingly treacherous business.

Six

✠ *Oberfeldwebel* Helmut Jung, prisoner of war, had looked forward for many weeks to this day in late November of 1944.

As long as the war continued, he knew he would rot in this stinking stockade, surrounded by Nazis he had tried to ignore at home, in the army, in combat and now as a captive of the French. But a possible outlet for his frustration and anger had been broached to him some weeks earlier and now the moment was at hand. He was going to be offered a chance to help end the war and, if he survived, to be among the first prisoners to be allowed to go home to Germany.

A message had been smuggled into camp from an anti-Nazi group of Germans based in Paris. He didn't give a shit about politics, except that he hated the deceitful government and corrupt bureaucrats who had brought the Wehrmacht and old soldiers like himself to their present low estate.

Now the American recruiting team—at least that's who he suspected they were when he caught sight of the six strangers dressed in the shabby clothes of low-level French civil servants—had actually arrived in his camp at Lyon. Helmut Jung waited eagerly, though not without some anxiety, for his turn to see them. He stood in a line with about thirty other prisoners outside one of the big mess halls. They had been culled from the ranks of many thousands in the camp and he supposed each had been approached secretly in the same way.

A secondary assessment of Jung had already been made by unknown persons within the camp. Then a not-so-subtle approach was made by another prisoner. In his case it had been *Stabsfeldwebel* Gunther Ferber, a man he had not known before, but an old soldier like himself, one whose demeanor rather than his slightly higher rank had commanded Jung's respect. The purpose of their talk had been to determine how much of a Nazi or anti-Nazi he was—and, if the latter, how much he would be willing to do to end the war quickly and free Germany. There had been a

31

few more conversations with others, always with the fear that any of them could be a spy or provocateur for the die-hard Nazis. He had then been told privately to await a call to a very important interview.

The area around the mess hall had been cleared of all other prisoners and was guarded by French soldiers. Three POW's had gone into the building to start with, and now, after about fifteen minutes, the rest were being admitted one by one. Whatever was going on in there, Jung realized it didn't take long. Those inside were apparently leaving by another exit to prevent them from letting the waiting men know what to expect, and to shield them from the attention of the rest of the prisoners in the camp.

Finally it was Helmut Jung's turn.

Captain Brooks took special note of *Oberfeldwebel* Jung the moment he entered the room. Sergeant Blumberg, also dressed in mufti, sat close enough to his CO's table to be an observer but not take part in the questioning. At separate tables elsewhere in the room, two OSS linguists were also interviewing. LeGrange sat with one of them, though he could hardly follow the German being spoken. Dietrich sat with the other linguist and had been moving about as needed to reassure the POW's that they would be treated well in the unit for which they were volunteering and would have a chance for early release at the end of their service.

Brooks had instructed his team and the guards at the door that he would personally interview any candidates above the rank of corporal. Therefore, Master Sergeant Jung was sent directly to his table. Brooks noted his soldierly bearing, his smooth, rapid approach and the click of his heels as he halted at attention, looking straight ahead until Brooks spoke to him pleasantly and invited him to stand at ease.

"Rühr dich, Oberfeldwebel."

It was the way his interviewer used the correct military expression in German that made Jung decide this was a soldier he faced. At first sight he hadn't known what to make of the civilian in the ill-fitting dark suit. He glanced at the second man sitting near the table, noted similar setups at the other tables and decided his attention was to be given to the primary interrogator, not the observer.

Dan noticed Jung didn't slouch as others had, but assumed a proper at-ease position with his feet slightly apart, his hands clasped behind his back and his eyes focused attentively upon his interviewer. His gray wool field uniform was clean and unrumpled and bore the various embroidered collar patches, shoulder straps and sleeve insignias stitched upon a dark green fabric background which signified he was an *Oberfeldwebel*, a master sergeant, in the armored infantry.

The man was taller than average, big in the chest and shoulders, and had a wide jaw. His appearance, demeanor and voice, though respectful, fit the popular sterotype of the brutal, barking Wehrmacht noncom. He

32

gazed intently at his questioner with dark brown eyes, trying to read deeper into what Brooks's expression might reveal.

"How am I to address you, sir?" Jung asked directly.

"I'm an American captain," Brooks replied, and his answer appeared to please the German.

"*Danke, Herr Hauptmann.*"

There were four standard, simple queries put to each candidate: name and rank, civilian occupation, years of service and duties, reason for volunteering. There was not enough time to ask for more or to probe deeper. After each interview was concluded and the POW had left, assessments were made on the spot by the interviewer and the observer regarding the volunteer's physical fitness, his attitude toward the questions and his examiners, and any signs of deviousness in responses.

Though Brooks already had the name and rank of Jung on his list, he asked him to state it again. Then he asked what the *Oberfeldwebel* had done in civilian life. Jung smiled, but with an expression more bitter than cheerful.

"I do not think that I have ever been a civilian, *Herr Hauptmann*, except when I was a child."

"Where was that, Jung?"

"Hamburg."

"East or west of the Alster River?"

"You have been there?" Jung asked with some elation.

"*Ja.*"

Jung's smile became warmer. "In the *Altstadt*, east of the river, *Herr Hauptmann*. My father was a foreman on the docks. I too worked as a stevedore for a little while, but then I joined the Wehrmacht in 1923 and it has been my home and career ever since."

Brooks looked at him closely. They were about the same age, though Jung appeared older than Brooks's thirty-nine years and he had been in the army twice as long.

"I remember Hamburg very well," Dan related in a friendly voice meant to put the master sergeant at ease. "The canals in the *Altstadt* were sometimes full and sometimes practically dry, depending on the tides of the Elbe River. In warm weather they stank!"

"*Ja*, they sure did," Jung acknowledged, grinning and shaking his head. "But when the basins were full, it was our Venice," he added with a nostalgic memory of home.

"Are you a member of the Nazi party, Jung?" Brooks asked quickly, hoping to catch him off guard.

The *Oberfeldwebel* bristled. "No, *Herr Hauptmann*. I am a soldier, not a politician."

"What's your reason for volunteering for my group, Jung? You've been told, haven't you, you may have to attack and kill German soldiers?"

Jung was pensive for a few moments. "I will tell you the truth, *Herr*

33

Hauptmann. I would not want to hurt the ordinary *Landser* of the Wehrmacht, what you call GIs in your army. Maybe some of them are bad, but most are decent men. They are not criminals like those Nazi bastards in the SS and Gestapo, and the *Goldfasanen.*"

Brooks looked at him questioningly. It was a word he didn't know. "*Goldfasanen? Was ist das?*"

"Party officials. Golden pheasants," Jung explained, moving his arms up and down like wings. "In the Wehrmacht we hate their guts. With all those trimmings and decorations on their brown uniforms they look like golden pheasants."

Brooks glanced aside to smile at Sergeant Blumberg who, besides jotting down notes, stared at Jung with the kind of intensity that might have made another man nervous or irritable. Blumberg nodded to his CO, but didn't return the smile; this was too serious a business for him. He found nothing amusing about being this close to German soldiers without taking a shot at them to assuage the private rage that seethed in his gut. He had cautioned Brooks to be wary of new and phony anti-Nazi fervor, which was why Dan had turned to smile at him.

"We don't much care for them ourselves!" Blumberg mouthed to Jung in German. "It is admirable that you volunteer now, but where were you ten or twenty years ago, *Oberfeldwebel?*"

Jung felt both anger and embarrassment as he met the stare of the antagonistic man who spoke excellent German. "As I told you...sir..." He didn't know how else to address the man. "I was in the army. I was not a politician then, I am not one now. In the beginning I didn't like the Nazis, but I didn't hate them. I thought they were a joke and I didn't put much stock in them. Few of us in the Wehrmacht did. That is a mistake which I would now like to correct. I was told that we might fight against the Nazis and help rid Germany of Hitler and his bunch. That is why I have volunteered."

It was the standard answer Brooks was getting from most of them. "You've still not told me *why*," he insisted. "What happened to make you change your mind, Jung?"

"There are many reasons, *Herr Hauptmann*," Jung shot back at him, and Dan was glad to hear passion in his voice rather than the cool, calculating whine of a toady. "Hamburg is now sixty percent rubble, destroyed by British and American bombers. I saw it with my own eyes. I was there on leave earlier in the year, before I was taken prisoner. But I am not mad at you Americans and British. I know who is responsible. Hitler and his criminals. They are the real enemies of the Reich. That fat pig Göring who boasted about his air defenses. That bullshit artist Goebbels. That slimy bastard Himmler and all his SS and Gestapo. Not only do they have to be stopped but they must be made to answer for their crimes against Germany and..." Here he faltered slightly, choked up with long contained rage he could hardly get out. "...and against me and my family."

Blumberg looked at him dubiously, despite the unexpected outburst. "Against *you*? What did they do to you, *Oberfeldwebel*? It seems to me they treated you pretty good."

Jung spoke in a low, tight voice as he fought to contain the mixture of sorrow and rage he had been carrying with him since his last visit home. "My father was taken away by the Gestapo," he said. "My mother was beside herself with grief when she told me. It was not enough that they already had been bombed out of their home and living like rats amidst the rubble."

"Why did the Gestapo arrest him?" Brooks asked with renewed interest.

Jung's shoulders sagged for a moment, then he leaned toward his interrogators and spoke in a flood of embittered words, as if this were the first moment he had been able to talk freely in decades: "Hitler...to cover up his stupidity and his losses...always seeking scapegoats, that son-of-a-bitch. He decided to crack down on what was left of the labor unions. My father was a minor functionary in the stevedores' union. This is a man who loved Germany. He was a patriot and a hard worker...and I do not know what has become of him...if he is dead or alive."

Brooks classified Jung as above average and earmarked him as a possible platoon leader. "Are you sure you want to join us?" he asked.

"There is more I would like to know, *Herr Hauptmann*."

"What?"

"The purpose for which you intend to use German soldiers and the place where you will send us."

It was not an unreasonable question, and others had asked it—and been refused answers. While his recruits were still confined in the POW cages with tens of thousands of other German prisoners, many of them unregenerate Nazis, Brooks did not want them to know.

"You will be told more during your training," Brooks answered. "If you don't make the grade you will be returned to one of the prison camps. If you ever decide that what we want you to do is dishonorable or in violation of your principles and beliefs, you will be permitted to drop out without prejudice, which is more than the Nazis ever did for you."

"I would like to be a member of your group, *Herr Hauptmann*," Jung said firmly.

Brooks looked at him appraisingly. Who knew how many Allied soldiers had died at his hand or under his orders? Yet this was the kind of man he had hoped to find. If he could fill the roster of his company with men like him he would have a formidable force. "Be prepared to move out of here in about ten days," Dan told him. "Meanwhile, keep your mouth shut and stay out of trouble. You'll receive your orders."

From Lyon to Montélimar to Marseilles to Carcassonne to Toulouse, Brooks and his recruitment team were a week on the road, driving through the south of France, presenting at each prisoner of war camp the proper authorizations from the French Ministry of Defense and interviewing the men on Dietrich's lists and others referred to them. By the time they reached Carcassonne, Brooks had accepted 127 candidates. The recruiting team had taken all who appeared in good physical condition and responded well to the question of *why*.

At Carcassonne, before entering the prisoner of war camp, Brooks found himself unexpectedly spellbound by the medieval battlements and turreted walls of the city. The age of the place! He conjured up the vivid feeling of a clash of arms long silent, a time long gone. What might it have been like to fight a war when those fortifications had been built? He would have been a warrior then, too. He knew it to be so.

With a pang of remembered love, the image of his grandfather rose in his mind. He had been the man he most revered in his boyhood. His father had died before he was a year old, and his mother's father had come to live with them in Yorkville. The dignified, gray-haired gentleman had been a general in the Russian Czar's imperial army. A fairly wealthy man, he had sold his investments and property in Russia and emigrated to America years earlier with his daughter, Dan's future mother, to try to lessen his deep brooding and sadness over the death of his beloved young wife. He spoke many languages, as did Dan's mother, who had been educated at home by tutors and then in Switzerland.

The stories the old general had told. Particularly when his friend Baron Fittinggoff, also a retired Russian general, visited. The old warriors had recounted their tales to Dan in German, which his mother had preferred him to learn along with French rather than Russian. The baron's war stories were even more daring, gory and spiked with hyperbole than his grandfather's.

Dan still remembered the day his grandfather had showed him his medals. The old general had really treasured one in particular. The heroic deed for which it had been awarded had made a deep, indelible impression on the boy. The event had occurred long ago.

He had never lost the vision of his grandfather on horseback riding into the massed Turkish ranks, thrusting and slashing with his sword, cutting down those around him, and then, when his horse was shot out from under him, leaping off and, undaunted, leading the assault on foot.

"Grandfather, weren't you scared?"

"No. I was determined to press forward. That desire dominated my mind."

"But even when your horse was shot out from under you and you were fighting on foot?"

"We had to destroy the enemy. I was totally dedicated to that mission."

36

"Even if you could be killed?"

"It was a sacred duty. I had to inspire my men, for whom I was responsible."

Did he himself long for a heroic moment like that? Sometimes Brooks wondered.

The prisoner of war camp was a stark and depressing contrast to the old city which had induced in Brooks a lofty epic mood. The chain link fence that encircled the camp, topped by barbed wire, moved people to refer to it as a cage. At intervals along the circumference were wood towers where guards stood watch, some manning machine guns, others carrying rifles and carbines.

Contained within the fencing were approximately 20,000 of the hundreds of thousands of Germans, Austrians and other nationals who fought with them, who had been captured since the Allied landings in Normandy and on the Mediterranean coast. They were housed in one- and two-story wood barracks and squad tents that reminded Dan of hastily built military posts at home. Mostly, except for their own rotating services and clean-up assignments within the enclosure, the prisoners had nothing to do except wait for the war to end so they might be repatriated to their homelands.

The camp commandant had been expecting Brooks and his team and received them courteously in his office. "If I may be permitted," he said, "there is one name I would like to add to your list."

"Someone you're eager to get rid of?" Captain LeGrange asked warily. "A troublemaker?"

"No, no," the commandant insisted. "Though he *is* different from the others. He is a man who seems to attract hostility from everyone. I do not believe he is a Nazi. He seems to hold everyone in contempt—Nazis, communists, socialists, even we French and you Americans."

LeGrange was about to reject the suggestion when Dan interrupted. "Why not? If he's above the rank of *Gefreiter* I'll talk to him myself."

"He is only a private. But see for yourselves, gentlemen." The commandant took up a pen and added a name to the list.

He was perhaps twenty-seven or twenty-eight, Brooks thought, although he might have been younger. He had the slender, blond good looks that Hitler and the ugly bastards around him had ludicrously decreed to be Aryan and eminently desirable, thereby ironically excluding themselves from ever being part of that spurious ideal. They were the sort of boyish good looks that some men retained all their lives, but there were now dark circles under this one's eyes and the beginnings of unexpected crow's feet at the outer corners of his eyes and sensual mouth. Long stretches of intensive combat and deprivation could do that to a man.

37

Schütze Kurt von Hassell had presented himself formally and correctly, waiting at attention before Brooks' interview table in the day room that had been made available to the recruiting team.

"*Rühr dich, Schütze von Hassell*...At ease Private von Hassell," Dan said. "*Ich bin Amerikaner...Ich heisse Hauptmann Brooks.*"

Von Hassell, who had been summoned for the interview without knowing the reason why, as the others did, seemed amused. He bowed his head slightly, clicked his heels and said, "*Es freut mich sehr, Sie kennenzulernen, Herr Hauptmann!*" And then, with a clipped British accent, he repeated it in English, "Pleased to meet you, Captain. Your attire had me fooled."

Dan had not been prepared for a POW who spoke English. He saw now that despite the anguish and fatigue in his eyes and face, there was an aristocratic bearing about the man, a superior air of confidence. It stopped just short of arrogance. But perhaps it was difficult for a soldier wearing the insignia of the lowest rank to be arrogant. This was not a military man in the way that many of the Wehrmacht veterans were. He smiled pleasantly as he stood at ease and waited for Dan to continue.

Brooks continued to speak to him in German. "I'm putting together a unit of German soldiers to fight against the Nazis. Are you interested?"

The prisoner's eyes widened in surprise, but Dan also saw his expression brighten and some of the languor drain away. Von Hassell responded reflexively and cautiously, "*Ich weiss nicht, Herr Hauptmann*...I don't know, Captain." Then he switched to English again. "Excuse me, sir, but there is no need to practice your bad German on me," he said haughtily. "I speak English quite well."

Brooks was not offended by the effrontery. It was the kind of subtle impudence he understood and had used often enough himself. "I hope you also speak American, von Hassell," he retorted. "But how come you're only a buck-assed private?"

Von Hassell smiled. "In my opinion, sir, that is the most important assignment. It is the one I preferred to do in defense of my country. I did not wish to work for the Nazis. Any higher rank—which I was offered, of course—would have meant that I would have had to collaborate with them and condone their policies. I do not."

Dan looked at him appraisingly. "Where did you learn to speak English?"

"First at boarding school in Switzerland, then at the university. Heidelberg. Also a few summers in England."

"What were you, a spy?"

Von Hassell cracked his first genuine smile. "No, Captain, I stayed with friends of my father."

"And what does your father do?"

"He is a banker."

"Where?"

"In Berlin."

"And you? What did you do in civilian life?"

"I was a junior executive in my father's bank until I was called up for service."

"Are you a Nazi?"

"No, sir. Which should be obvious to you. Otherwise I would not be what you insultingly call a lowly private in the infantry."

Brooks found himself unexpectedly apologizing, for he didn't want the man to think that he approved of snobbery. "It was not meant as an insult, Private. It was merely a comment of fact. At least an attempt to establish the facts in your case. Nazi officers have been known to divest themselves of their identities in the moments before capture."

"In which case I would have changed my name to Schultz or Schmidt, not von Hassell," the prisoner commented acerbically.

Dan laughed. "What about your father?" he asked. "Is *he* a Nazi?"

Von Hassell hesitated. "It is a complicated matter."

"Go ahead. Enlighten me. But only if you're interested in volunteering for my group. It will be a demanding assignment physically and emotionally."

"Yes, Captain. I am interested."

"Then please tell me more about yourself."

Kurt von Hassell, as the camp commandant had suggested, was indeed quite different from the men with whom he was confined. He was also very different from the men who had been recruited earlier as candidates for Brooks's company. The others came from working and middle class backgrounds. Kurt was a member of a distinguished Prussian family which for generations had owned an extensive estate in East Prussia, but resided mainly at their city home in a fashionable section of Berlin.

Speaking in English, he revealed to Brooks that his father was the chief stockholder and director of their bank. Though the senior von Hassell had a lukewarm attitude toward the Nazis in their early years he nevertheless had donated money to them and had given them political support and credibility, like most bankers and industrialists did. "It was a matter of self-preservation," Kurt insisted.

"In American that translates as 'saving your own ass,'" Brooks commented without rancor.

"Very well, sir, I will add that to my American vocabulary. May I continue or have I told you enough?"

"Please continue."

Von Hassell gave the standard apologia which, regrettably, was true. Brooks had been there to see some of it himself. Germany had been going through terrible times of economic stagnation, inflation, political upheaval, military revolution and civil fighting in the aftermath of defeat in World War I. Hitler had claimed that he would be a bulwark against Bolshevism. The bankers, industrialists and aristocrats supported him and didn't pay much attention to the rest.

"I do not blame my father," said von Hassell. "However, when I was old enough to understand what was going on I realized that the Nazis were no better than the communists and in many ways they were worse. I hated their brutality, their violence, the way they were persecuting Jews and others."

"What did you do about it?" Dan demanded.

"Nothing," the prisoner replied without apology. "I lived my life as best I could. I never participated in Nazi activities."

Brooks suddenly realized he was giving this man more time than he had intended. He had already decided he wanted von Hassell in his outfit, though he wasn't sure if he would fit in or how he would use him.

"Tell me about your military service," he directed.

"I was drafted in 1942. I declined officer candidate school which, as you might imagine, upset my father very much. Afterward I refused all opportunities to advance beyond the rank of private. It was my own small way to fight against the Nazis but still defend my country."

Brooks believed him, at least for the present. "With those sentiments, would you work for the Americans in order to help defeat Hitler?"

The prisoner stared at him intently. "Shall we say rather that I'd volunteer to fight the Nazis to destroy Hitler if you Americans afford me the opportunity."

Brooks disapproved of his arrogance, but it was not the moment to reprimand him for it. Perhaps it would be a useful trait if guided in the right direction. "Very well. I'll accept you as a candidate," Dan told him. "However, there's one thing we'll have to change. Your name. The 'von' may not sit well with the rest of the volunteers. They'd be suspicious that I was sneaking in an undercover officer."

"It didn't seem to make any difference to the men I served with in Russia and France," von Hassell said. "With respect, sir, I must decline that aspect of your offer."

Dan thought it over for a few moments. The man was an unknown quantity, but so were the others. This one was stubborn and stuck by his principles.

"Okay, von Hassell," he said, meeting the man's intense gaze. "We'll do it your way and hope it works. Since you speak English so well, maybe you can help me improve my German. How's your French?"

"*Pauvre, mon capitaine.*"

"Too bad. Your Russian?"

"Just a little I picked up there. Is it something you will need in your unit?"

"I hope not. Just curious as to how clever a fellow you are," Brooks told

40

him. "Within a week or so you'll be transported to my training base. Keep your mouth shut regarding what we've talked about. And *viel Glück!*"

"Thank you, Captain," the prisoner replied. There was a new look of vitality in his face. He stood to attention, saluted, did an about face and strode out smartly.

Brooks turned toward Sergeant Blumberg, who was still looking uncomfortable in his too snug civilian outfit and uneasy about the parade of enemy soldiers he had been forced to observe and listen to for days. He had remained to one side, absolutely silent and inconspicuous during the entire interview. "What do you think, Freddy?"

"I don't trust a one of them," answered Blumberg. "That one least of all. All that bullshit about how he didn't like the way the Nazis persecuted Jews. He comes from a class that could have squashed Hitler like a bug in the beginning, but they didn't. Prussian Junkers. The worst sort of Germans, in my opinion. Feudal barons. Militarists. Pricks who think they can run roughshod over anybody. And bankers, no less. They liked what was happening. For them it meant increased personal wealth when the Nazis came to power and cranked up their economy based on war and plunder. The only reason I'd say take him is to see the *Landser* tear him apart. If he's devoured by those he's helped deceive, I would enjoy the sight of it."

By the end of the week, when they had finished their interviews in the POW camp at Toulouse, Brooks and his recruiting team had 162 former Wehrmacht soldiers on their list of candidates to be transferred to St. Germain. In theory, there was not an SS man or Nazi among them. He was especially glad to have been able to recruit the higher grade noncoms: three *Stabsfeldwebel*—sergeant majors; one *Oberfeldwebel*—master sergeant; two *Unteroffiziere*—buck sergeants; four *Gefreite*—corporals; and the rest *Oberschützen, Obergrenadiere, Schützen* and *Grenadiere*—privates first class and privates. Among them were a few who had served in Alpine units and would know the uniforms, weapons and equipment used by a *Gebirgsjäger Einheit*. All of the volunteers were well trained and combat experienced.

There would be time enough during their preparation for the mission to weed out the phonies, the malingerers, the inept and the Nazis.

Seven

✠ "We *are* allies, you know," said Major Schepilov softly as he reclined into the corner of Ann Jordan's sofa.

It was their fourth date in three weeks and he had decided it was time to drop his pose of being the very reserved, always solicitous, very proper escort, enjoying her company for its own sake but wanting nothing more.

"In fact it is we who have been carrying the major burden in fighting and casualties so far. Wasn't it the Soviet army that delivered the fatal blow at Stalingrad in 1943? Yes, we softened them up for your armies. Certainly that deserves some appreciation," he continued, patting the cushion beside him and motioning her to join him.

Actually it had been Colonel Lazovsky, his superior officer, who had decided for him. "*Results, Schepilov,*" the colonel had urged that afternoon with a crude smirk. "*It is time for results. We do not intend to continue to finance your London social life indefinitely. You know enough now to attack, Schepilov. Go for the target. I assume you know how to find it. Think of it as a mission, perhaps one more pleasant than your others.*"

In a way, Schepilov felt that the assignment was beneath his dignity, although Ann was a very appealing woman and there was no doubt about the seductive signals she had been sending him. He could even feel genuine passion, he thought. Still, he was bothered that as one of the most decorated *Spetsnaz* officers, combat veteran of many missions behind enemy lines, he now played the role of a languorous, drawing room dilettante, a seducer.

Perhaps GRU thought they were rewarding him for all the blood he had shed, the enemy's and his own. The assignment to the Soviet Military Mission in London had been described to him in Moscow as rest and recreation.

After meeting Ann Jordan, Major Schepilov had written the required report on new contacts that might be susceptible to recruitment. He had listed her as an American employed by one of the U.S. government

42

agencies in London. But, adhering strictly to procedures designed to avoid scaring off potentials, he also had reported that he had not pressed her yet for specific identification of the agency she worked for or her function there.

Schepilov had given Ann's name, phone number, address and description, and the fact that she appeared interested in furthering his acquaintance. This had been checked in the files of the GRU—the Registrational Directorate of the Field Staff of the Republic—the Soviet military intelligence organization for which he worked under cover as an operative while ostensibly employed in a more prosaic role with the Soviet Military Mission in London. The files had revealed that Ann Jordan was an employee of the American Office of Strategic Services.

Curiously enough, the role of *Spetsnaz* resembled the unconventional warfare functions of the American OSS. Major Schepilov wondered at the possibility that Ann, if she was an agent, was doing to him what he was doing to her.

She kicked off her high-heeled, slender evening pumps, glided across the room and curled herself onto the sofa against him. She wore a simple black cocktail dress with thin straps at the shoulders and enticing dècolletage. The press of her body excited him. She looked and smelled very different from the Russian and German women he had known. She seemed all glowing, polished smoothness. There was a soft pink tone to her flesh where she had dusted it with scented powder. The mere fact that she was an American beauty, so very distinctive from his prior experience, roused his hunter's instincts.

He embraced her, she tilted her head up and he kissed her. She responded eagerly, wrapping her arms around his neck and pressing her lips against his with a sigh of pleasure. He held her, feeling the warmth and passion. He understood how lonely and yearning she must have been these last months since she had been widowed. He was glad that it was he whom she had selected, for whatever reasons of interest, attraction or intrigue.

Ann drew her lips away slowly and stared into his eyes. "Were you there, Mikhail...at Stalingrad?" she asked.

"Yes...and I have the wounds to show for it."

"Show me."

Schepilov was still not comfortable in his role as ardent lover. He squirmed a bit and asked, "You wish me to disrobe?"

Ann laughed. "You put it so bluntly, Mikhail," she teased, eyeing him up and down. "When I was a child we had a game. I'll show mine if you'll show yours. A primitive form of sex education. Do Russian children do the same thing?"

"No," he said, forcing a solemn expression onto his face. "Russian children are interested only in Marx, Engels and tractors. We do not believe in sex. It is the opiate of the masses."

"I'll say it is," Ann concurred heartily, running her tongue over her lips.

"But for this game we must trust each other," he said. He tried to look melancholy. "Yet, when I ask you about the agency you work for and what your duties are, you refuse to answer me. That is not trust, Ann. I have told you freely about myself."

"It's not that I refuse you personally, Mikhail. It's that I am forbidden to speak to anyone about it. Surely you, as a Soviet officer, must understand."

Schepilov continued to stare at her with that same downcast look and then he suddenly grinned. "I will tell you a secret. Ann. I have already guessed who you work for. If it is true, I must tell you that I admire you very much because of it. It makes you, in my eyes, the sort of very rare and brave woman whom I had thought you were."

"You flatter me, sir," said Ann in a nervous voice. Then she narrowed her eyes and challenged him. "Go ahead. Tell me who I work for."

Schepilov decided to be cute and clever. "SOS", he said triumphantly.

It had exactly the effect he wanted it to. Ann burst into uninhibited laughter and, when she finally stopped, she said, "OSS, my dear Mikhail. Not SOS. I'm not a ship in distress."

Schepilov feigned embarrassment at his mistake. "Yes, of course. Forgive my stupidity. It is OSS not SOS. It is, nevertheless, an organization whose work I admire."

"Oh, Mikhail, I'm just a secretary. I'm not involved in any of that cloak-and-dagger business."

"Then you are not Mata Hari?" he said with mock disappointment. "You do not jump by parachute into enemy territory to kill fascists?"

"No, of course not," Ann said, still laughing.

"That is too bad," Schepilov said with a sigh. "I thought that finally we would be able to tell brave war stories to each other. All those clandestine operations we have participated in or know about."

Ann realized he was no longer joking. "I couldn't do that, Mikhail," she said softly.

"But you wouldn't be betraying your country," Major Schepilov assured her. "We could make it like the children's game you spoke about. You tell me. I'll tell you. In fact, I'll tell you first. Ask me anything you want to know about me and I will answer you honestly."

"I'd be breaking faith disclosing classified information," Ann said pensively. "I'd feel guilty."

"Why should you have a feeling of guilt? We are allies. You have expressed sympathy for the suffering of my country and an understanding of our ideology. There must be complete trust between us or we cannot really be friends. It might even be helpful in preventing duplication of effort."

44

"I agree, Mikhail. There must be complete trust. I like you very much... you must know that."

Major Schepilov removed his arms from around her and stood up. "Excuse me, dear Ann, but perhaps I have taken liberties with you that offend you. Please forgive my prying. I ought to be going. It's very late."

Ann did not want him to leave. She stood up, wrapped her arms around his waist and stood on her toes to kiss him again. The fervor of his response was not that of a man who wanted to go. Ann leaned her head back so that she could look into his eyes. "It's not too late for *us*, is it Mikhail?"

"It is entirely up to you, lovely lady," said Schepilov softly. "In Moscow I was warned by my superior officers that I was always to behave like a complete gentlemen in London. What would you like this gentleman to do, Ann?"

"Show me your wounds..." she replied, taking his hand and leading him toward her bedroom, ".. and show me what you'd like me to do to soothe them and make you happy. All the rest is talk...and very unimportant."

Counting heads, quickly taking in the size of the full American operations staff of Knight's Cross, it struck Captain Dan Brooks how few there were. Nine of them, including himself, met in the main salon of the manor house in St. Germain on Friday evening, December 1, 1944. Nine to train, motivate, control and lead almost two hundred German and Austrian soldiers and civilians.

Lieutenant Chadwick and his OSS housekeeping staff would not be part of the training cadre or privy to operations. Captain LeGrange, based in Paris, would be limited to liaison and expediting supplies and equipment, and would be briefed on operations matters only when there was an absolute need for him to know.

The operations staff sat in a semicircle of comfortable chairs facing Brooks, who stood in front of a table and chair. Appraising them for a few moments, he was struck by the fact that each of this group of Americans was of German lineage. If their ancestors or parents hadn't left the old country they might have been fighting for Hitler. He had asked for an operations staff fluent in German, no matter their ethnic backgrounds, and this was the way it had turned out. Any one of them might have changed places with the Wehrmacht soldiers he had interviewed in the French POW cages.

"I trust that all of you are satisfied with your quarters and have been well fed this past week," Dan said affably. He was pleased by the way they had taken up their duties and started training the civilians at the holding compound while he had been on the recruiting trip.

"Best duty station I've ever had," Lieutenant Becker said.

Each of the noncoms agreed heartily that the mess was sumptuous and their accommodations superb.

Sergeant Blumberg, who had returned with Brooks just that afternoon, had been amazed by the splendor of the manor house and the lavish first dinner he had been served there. "Captain, you said we were going on vacation," he spoke up. "Now I believe you. I've never had it so good."

Brooks laughed. "Freddy and I have been in some tight places together, so he's easy to please. But we're all gong to have to work our tails off to earn our keep here. I'd like to start by getting acquainted. Speak in German." He sat against the edge of the table behind him and folded his arms in a casual stance. "Lieutenant Becker?"

Rudy Becker stood up. He was a big man, six feet two, broad-shouldered and deep chested. He had trained and competed in crew and swimming in an Ivy League college, and that was where he had perfected his high school German. That had been only a few years earlier and his army and OSS service had maintained him in the pink of condition physically and linguistically. His speech was more grammatical than Dan's and better accented. His basic branch was also infantry.

"I've been on the OSS 3rd Army Detachment, training German defectors and running them behind the lines," he concluded and sat down.

"Let's hear from our medic now," Brooks prompted.

A man of medium height with a scar on his dark-complexioned face stood up. He wore a Purple Heart among his badges and ribbons. "I'm Sergeant Peter Paulsen, sir. SO trained with specialized OSS medical training. I've not yet been on an OSS mission, but had combat experience with the 101st Airborne Division as a squad leader."

Paulsen was in his mid-twenties, as were the rest of them. Sergeant Blumberg was next, then the second radio operator, whom Freddy had recommended in London. He was of medium build, a bit on the heavy side, with a full, expressive face.

"Sergeant George Fischbein, sir. SO trained, but no OSS operational experience yet. Combat service as a mortar section leader with 82nd Airborne Division. OSS trained in radio communications."

A big, powerful, heavy-set man stood up next; he also wore the Purple Heart. "Sergeant Michael Maurer, sir. SO trained. Before that I was a platoon sergeant in combat with the 1st Division." He sat down, having said nothing about the ribbon for the coveted Silver Star Medal that he wore. Brooks figured he was a man who had seen plenty of action. He wondered how Maurer would feel about leading enemy soldiers that might include the one who shot him.

Another big man, Sergeant Ralph Brunner, followed him. Brunner was SO trained and had been in combat before that as a pathfinder with the 101st Airborne Division. His jaw jutted out of a determined face and he had a confident air about him. He also wore the ribbon for the Bronze Star Medal with V for valor.

Sergeant Robert Mangold, a short, stocky man who also wore the Bronze Star with V, had operated in Yugoslavia with one of OSS's Operational Groups. He had done the same sort of behind-the-lines work with guerrillas that Brooks had performed as a Jedburgh in France. He appeared composed and sure of himself and spoke deliberately and slowly.

Last of the operations team was Sergeant Walter Schafer, a short man with sharp features and a tendency to gesture as he spoke with assurance. "I was on an OSS intelligence mission in France, sir, but I'm also SO trained."

Dan took in the fact that he wore only one decoration, the Distinguished Service Cross. Schafer probably had a hair-raiser to tell, for the DSC was a rare decoration for OSS personnel, who usually performed their heroics unheralded and unsung.

"I guess you speak both French and German," Dan said.

"Yes, sir. I'm of Alsatian descent and we spoke both languages at home."

Brooks unfolded his arms, pressed himself off the edge of the table where he'd been leaning, and stood almost at attention as he switched the dialogue to English.

"Not a word about Knight's Cross is ever to be revealed to anyone. Now and in the future. Your lives will depend on that."

They stared at him with interest and courtesy. They had heard that warning before, but he knew they had never heard a reason like the one he was giving them now.

"We will conduct our mission somewhere in the German Reich," Brooks divulged. "You will not be told exactly where until the appropriate time. We will conduct the full range of unconventional warfare behind enemy lines—ambushes, raids, destroy lines of communications, commit sabotage, gather intelligence, induce subversion, capture ranking Nazis and generally harass the enemy."

All eight faces became animated. He really had their attention now, and he had managed nicely at the same time to both tell and conceal from them the singular purpose of the mission. There was no way, however, to hide the next part of what he had to tell them, nor was there any reason to do so as long as the secrecy of what they would be doing and the security of the unit itself were maintained.

"Our unit will be composed of a company-size group of German defectors, mostly prisoners of war. We'll operate in German uniforms with enemy weapons and equipment and pose as a *Gebirgsjäger Einheit*, a mountain infantry company."

He stopped. Every man's attention was unwaveringly fixed on him as he continued his briefing.

* * *

Watching the high, white Tyrolean peaks rush up out of the darkness to meet him, Karl Bergen knew a few minutes of fear on that first night when he and Willy Hupnagel dropped out of the belly of a Liberator bomber flying over Austria. He didn't know whether to pray to God or curse Adolf Hitler in what might be his last moments of life but, being a pragmatic man, he conjured up the voice of his instructor at the jump school in England. He let the remembered lessons coach him to touchdown in the deep snow of the high gap of the *Lüsener Ferner.*

It was a struggle for him to gain his feet on the loose powder and to gather in the parachute and unbuckle it. He kept sinking and falling and fighting to stand upright. Only when he was stabilized and free of the drag of the chute did he look around in the moonlight for his radioman and see, with relief, that Willy had landed safely about one-hundred yards away and was going through the same struggle with the snow and his parachute.

They were fortunate that weather reports from the area had been correct and forecasting good for this night. Unfavorable weather had delayed their flight almost two weeks. Though they had left England on the night Lieutenant Commander Cassidy had told them they would, they had been kept in France since then, held back at the OSS staging area in Dijon, waiting for the right combination of weather and moon.

The drop zone was more than five-thousand feet in altitude, surrounded by towering Alpine peaks. It was very cold. But it was the right place, Willy told him when they staggered together. In his boyhood he had come up here to ski in the winter and hike in the summer. They were approximately twenty-five kilometers from his aunt's *Gasthaus* on the south side of Innsbruck.

This first night was a good test of their physical stamina. Still wearing jump coveralls and boots, it took them several hours to plow around in the snow until they recovered their equipment canisters. Then, bathed in sweat despite the freezing temperature, they dragged the canisters, wrapped in parachutes, into the nearest treeline. They bedded down there for the rest of the night in their sleeping bags on top of the parachutes. In the morning they divested themselves of their jump clothes and double-checked each other to be certain that they were wearing only clothing and carrying only items that would be worn and carried by a local man—except for the suitcase radio. Nothing could be done about that, though the case itself was old and beat-up, tied with straps and rope to make it less likely that anybody would want to look into it.

They repacked their clothes and gear from the canisters into rucksacks, then buried the canisters and parachutes. They made an effort to restore the surface to look untouched, but it would need another snowfall for that. Then, slowly, constantly checking the terrain for observers, they descended the mountain to the Inn Valley below.

Karl Bergen was exhilarated to return at last in this way. He was not yet in Germany where he wanted to be, but he was within the Third Reich. Willy Hupnagel was nervous, hungry and thirsty, but he too felt exhilaration at coming home.

It was slow going, even after they reached the valley road where they began to see vehicles, horses and carts, sleighs and pedestrians trudging along as they were. No one paid them any special attention. Their route hugged the foothills, skirted the airport and did not bring them into the urban center of Innsbruck. They came up on the *Gasthaus zum Hirschen* from the southwest, in a sparsely populated area on the edge of the city.

Willy stopped and stared. He turned and spoke to Karl with unexpected emotion. "My God! I never expected to see this again," he said, crossing himself. "How beautiful!"

It was a lovely building with the typical, heavy Tyrolean roof overhanging it, balconies where flower boxes waited for spring, and bright murals painted on the exterior walls. Willy's appreciation, however, was cut short by the bark of Karl Bergen's voice:

"*Sprich deutsch, Dummkopf!*"

Willy's hand flew to his mouth and he stared around anxiously. He was glad no one else was close by to have overheard him. In English, he thought first: *I am sorry.* Then he forced his mind to think only in German and his lips to speak it. "*Es tut mir leid*...I am sorry," he murmured abjectly.

"So help me, I'll kill you myself if you fuck us up." Karl muttered angrily in German.

"No damage was done. And I said I was sorry," Willy snapped in German. He was locked into the language now and knew he wouldn't slip, but he was fed up with Bergen's superior attitude about everything.

They entered the building, went into the *Bierstube* and dumped their rucksacks and suitcase at a table close to the huge stone fireplace whose crackling flames kept the taproom comfortable. There were few patrons. A girl behind the bar had just poured a beer and was wiping suds off the counter. Willy's heart leaped as he recognized his cousin, a young woman his own age whom he had not seen in almost seven years. He stood up, walked to an empty section of the bar, and sat down and placed his elbows on the counter in such a way that one arm and hand partially hid his face.

Only when he felt her presence across from him and heard her voice asking what he wanted, did he speak to her softly, with his face still averted. "Trude, you must listen to me very carefully," he whispered. "Do not look startled and you must not give any sign of recognition, whatsoever. I am your cousin, Willy Hupnagel."

Then he lowered his arm and stared at her full on. Her chin trembled and her eyes moistened and she quickly looked away and busied herself with the bar mop.

"Is your mother in?" Willy asked softly.

"Yes. She's in the kitchen. Go right in," Trude replied, straining to control the emotion she felt. As children they had played together, even had a crush on each other.

"No. You go, and speak to her quietly so that no one overhears you," Willy instructed. "Tell her I must speak to her, but she is not to call me by my name. As long as there are other people around, she is to give no indication that she knows me. After you have warned her, come over to our table with two lagers and a menu and let me know if I can see her now. Otherwise, when."

Trude smiled at him as if he were a stranger who had just placed an order and said something complimentary. Then she disappeared into the kitchen and Willy returned to the table.

Speaking in an ordinary voice, just in case anyone was eavesdropping, Willy said to Karl, "The girl has gone to see what's available now for a meal. She will bring a couple of steins with her after she talks to the cook."

A few minutes later, Trude returned to their table with the foaming lagers. "The cook would like to speak to you," she told him softly. "She said you are most welcome to go into the kitchen." Then she moved quickly back to the bar to tend to other customers.

Willy drank a full, satisfying mouthful of the beer. He began a sound of exquisite pleasure and then cut it short, realizing that a local man would be used to it. It had been a long time since he'd had any beer as good as this local brew. Then he nodded stiffly to Karl, stood up and walked into the kitchen.

His Aunt Anna, a stout, rosy-checked woman, stood transfixed, watching the doorway for him, but made no move toward him and said nothing as he came in. She gestured to the stairway that led up to the family's apartment and Willy followed her. Only in the privacy of her home did his mother's sister turn and sweep him into her arms. She could hardly get out all the words that rushed to be spoken:

"My God, how you've grown! I never thought to see you again. Your mother? Your father? What in the world are you doing here? You must have dropped out of the sky."

"Exactly" said Willy, trying to control his own welling emotion. "By parachute."

The joy in her face was replaced by wonder and fear. "*Ach, mein Gott*... then it's dangerous for you here. *Liebchen*... you do not know how bad it is."

She explained that Gestapo informants dropped by occasionally, checking for foreigners and suspicious persons. However, she went on, the general attitude of the populace was strongly anti-Nazi. Most of the people of the Tyrol had had more than enough of their own homegrown variety of Nazis and too much of the kind that had come strutting across the border from Bavaria and the rest of Germany since the *Anschluss*.

It was what Lieutenant Commander Cassidy and his intelligence analysts had told Willy before he and Bergen had left London.

"Is there an underground organization?" he asked.

Anna looked around nervously even though they were alone together in her own living room. "I know nothing about such things, Willy...but I hear stories."

He took her hands again. "It is imperative that I be put in touch with these people," he said, careful to keep his voice as soft as hers.

To make contact with the Austrian underground, perhaps even with units of guerrilla fighters, had been among their orders from Cassidy, though the SI chief had not told them where to find such people or the identity of the agents already on the ground dispatching information from the Tyrol. If he or Karl were caught, it was best that they know nothing about others like themselves.

"I will do what I can," his aunt replied

"How is Uncle Franz?"

Anna shook her head. "God knows. They took him for the army. A man his age. It was not enough that he was in the First War. They said he was a man of experience, needed to defend the Fatherland. That's how bad things are, that they took your poor uncle."

Willy was disappointed. He had hoped Franz would be there to help him defend the Fatherland in a better way, one that he was sure would be more to his liking, for he remembered that his uncle had been against the *Anschluss* and had feared its consequences for the people of his beloved Tyrol.

"You don't know where he is?"

His aunt shook her head again and began to weep. "I hope he gave himself up to the Americans. To your friends. Then we will see him again, *Gott sei dank.*"

"I'm sorry. I too hope that he is well and will come home safely," Willy said. Then he turned to more immediate and practical matters. "Where can we stay? We need a safe house. Not just for tonight, but for an extended period." When he saw her hand go to her mouth in apprehension, he added, "It won't be much longer before you're free again, but I don't want to risk getting you into trouble."

Anna thought a few moments. "There is a place, a man I know, a farmer who will give you shelter, who will welcome you as if you were Jesus himself coming to save us. It is only five kilometers from here. I will take you there myself."

"There is another man with me."

"It is a big farm. A barn, stables for the animals, huts for workers. There will be room. He is a man to be trusted."

Willy hugged his aunt.

"Willy... Willy," she murmured. "How good to have you here. It is almost as if I touch my sister. How is she? How is your father? They know you are here?"

Willy smiled. "When I last heard from them they were both well. Happy and prosperous in St. Louis, but also very worried about you and the family and the war. No, they don't know I'm here. If they did, they'd faint."

"What you are doing is very dangerous, I know," Anna whispered. "Go now, *Liebchen*, into the *Bierstube* and eat and drink like everybody else."

"How long before we can leave?"

"We must not go to the farm until after dark." His aunt looked at him the way his mother used to. "But first I will give you such a meal as you have not had in years. You are so tall, but also so skinny. Do they not have good food in America? We are lucky still to have our own good food and drink here. But how long, God help us, before Hitler and his Nazis come from Berlin to take it away from us? There are rumors that some of the *Goldfasanen* are here already, that they will..."

"*Goldfasanen?*" Willy repeated. "*Was ist das?*"

"Party officials. Golden pheasants," she explained, wiggling her extended elbows up and down. "Nazi bureaucrats and crooks and bigwigs." Then she smiled at a private memory. "Your Uncle Franz taught me that when he was home on leave. It is a new word he learned in the army."

"What are these *Goldfasanen* doing here?" Willy asked with new and excited interest. It was the very thing that Cassidy wanted to know most of all. Who and where?

"People say they will turn Innsbruck and all of the Tyrol into a hell. *Walpurgisnacht. Götterdämmerung!* They want to take everyone with them." Her voice became softer, secretive. "But there are men and women who will fight to see that this does not happen."

"Those are the people I must be put in touch with, Aunt Anna."

"I will do what I can, *Liebchen*. First you will eat and try to relax in the *Bierstube*. After dark, leave the inn and I will meet you and your friend behind the barn and take you to the farm."

"You must have Trude give us a bill for our food and beer, just like anybody else," Willy cautioned.

"*Ach,* of course not."

"Please do not be insulted, *Tante*. We have brought money with us. We must behave as others do. You must give no sign of special treatment. It would look suspicious to your customers, especially if any of those Gestapo informants you spoke about turn up."

* * *

The meal was superb. Afterward, they made their way back to the barn where Willy's aunt was anxiously waiting for them.

"We must walk," she said. "A car, or even a horse and wagon, might attract attention."

They walked in silence along a country road for an hour, going southeast of Innsbruck. When they became aware of anyone else moving on the dark road, whether in vehicles or on foot, they scurried into hiding. When they reached the farm, Anna went in without them to explain the situation to the owner. Karl and Willy hid themselves in a stand of trees.

"I remember this place," Willy whispered to Karl. "When I was a boy I was sent here sometimes to buy fresh milk and butter and other produce."

"Can the owner be trusted?"

"He was a good man then, but who knows if it is the same one?"

In fifteen minutes, Anna reappeared in a circle of lantern light at the edge of the copse. The man who held the lantern was stocky, middle-aged, with a dark mustache. He wore thick wool trousers tucked into boots, a dark jacket with embroidered piping, and a floppy felt hat with a feather in the band.

Speaking in a solemn voice, Willy's aunt introduced the farm owner as *Herr* Josef Kayser. He greeted them with exuberance.

"I remember you when you were a little boy," he said, grasping Willy's hand. "And your dear mother and father. You and your friend are very welcome here and have nothing to fear. It is a privilege to give you shelter and I will help you all that I can."

Karl, asserting himself as team leader, addressed the farm owner formally: "Thank you, *mein Herr*. Your help will be acknowledged to my superiors. I assume that the police or the Gestapo are not in the habit of investigating your property."

"No. They have never been interested in me, nor have I given them reason to be," said the farmer. "Except for the dairy, there is not much activity here now. The land is dormant for the winter."

"God bless you," Anna intoned. "I must go now."

"I'll walk you back home," Willy said solicitously.

"*Grosser Gott*, you will do no such thing! You will stay here," she ordered. "Do not expose yourselves to unnecessary risks. Do not come to the *Gasthaus*. I will come here. Herr Kayser will act as go-between when it is necessary."

She kissed her nephew, shook hands warmly with Karl and the farmer and began walking quickly back along the road they had come.

Kayser led Karl and Willy to his barn and up into the hayloft. "You will be safe here," he told them. "I will bring you breakfast in the morning and we will make what arrangements you wish to make."

"We will be sending radio signals from here. Does that distress you, *Herr* Kayser?" Karl asked.

"Only if you are caught," the farmer replied. "I thank Jesus and praise God that you are here and that we will all soon be free again." He hesitated a moment, as if weighing something of great portent, then said, "May I tell you something of military interest?"

Karl wondered what this man could possibly know, but he replied politely, "Of course, *Herr* Kayser."

"Please call me Josef. When you radio your superiors, tell them that the Nazis are moving a lot of munitions and soldiers on trains through Innsbruck and the Brenner Pass into Italy. It would be a good thing for them to bomb the railroad marshalling yards in Innsbruck."

The possibility of immediate results excited Karl. "Thank you, Josef," he said effusively. "That is important. Are you with the Resistance?"

"No, not actively, *mein Herr*. But I am against the Nazis. Anna told me that you wish to contact the leaders of the Resistance. I will try to help you."

Willy opened his mouth to express his gratitude, but Karl leaped in ahead of him, as if he were dispensing royal favors. "I am indebted to you, Josef. At the proper time, you will be remembered."

Herr Kayser climbed down from the hayloft and left the barn.

"You sure know how to lay on the bullshit, don't you, Karl," Willy muttered. "Just remember that these are *my* people and I don't want you jerking them around."

"*You* remember that I'm the team leader, Hupnagel," Karl shot back at him angrily. "Set up the radio and we'll get a message off that we're in business."

He would try it on the batteries tonight and hope for the best, Willy thought as he ran the antenna wire out to the loft opening. Tomorrow he would ask Josef about plugging into the farm's electricity. Ten minutes later he was on the key, tapping out his message in Morse code to London. The first five-letter bracket of the transmission was his secret identification. They would know it was Willy Hupnagel sending, not an enemy operator, and that he was not under duress.

Karl Bergen went outside to listen, look around and take a piss. If the air corps actually bombed the marshalling yards, it would be a great beginning for him. Also in tonight's signal would be the intelligence that Willy had passed on to him from his aunt, that Nazi big shots were already gathering in the Tyrol. How he longed to get his hands on some of those he remembered from the early days. The radio transmission alone, if it got through, would strengthen his hand both in London and here with the Resistance.

What he wanted most of all was complete control of the Inn Valley, the entire Tyrol, before that wise guy captain and his Knight's Cross mission arrived on the scene.

54

Eight

✠ *Unteroffizier* Otto Würster watched with grudging respect as the American captain easily scaled the front façade of the manor house, using a climbing rope with great agility. Brooks had not lied when he told them in the beginning that he would do everything they were required to do, and that those who would not try or could not accomplish these athletic feats would be returned to a prisoner of war camp. Even after only the first week of training some of the German soldiers and German civilians—communists, weaklings and traitors, all of them, Würster had decided—who had not demonstrated sufficient strength, endurance and proficiency had already been expelled from the company and taken away.

Würster was impressed by Brooks. He found the captain's military bearing admirable and his knowledge of German customs, history and language commendable, despite shortcomings in grammar and pronunciation. His ability to assume the almost cultural role of a German officer was uncanny—not an aristocratic fop like that snotnose *Schütze* Kurt von Hassell, but a tough guy up from the ranks.

Even now, Brooks—a wiry man of average height, well muscled and obviously an experienced physical culturist—was putting them to shame with a demonstration of his agility.

"Why is it necessary for me to climb ropes?" *Stabsfeldwebel* Gunther Ferber had dared to ask earlier. "After all, *Herr Hauptmann*, I am no longer a child who is able to play such games with ease."

"Because it might be the only way you will be able to reach the bedroom of your girlfriend," Brooks had retorted slyly, before flinging the grappling hook over the balcony railing and telling them they would all have to do what he was about to do. "Or maybe...less important to you, of course, Sergeant...it will be a place where I will order you to go on our mission."

Würster had already marked Ferber as the oldest of the three *Stabsfeldwebels* in the company and the one with the longest years of service in the Wehrmacht. He was right to complain. A sergeant major, after all, had his dignity and his position to preserve, even in captivity; he should convey orders from their captors, demonstrate military skills when necessary and if not in violation of his oath to Adolf Hitler and the Third Reich, and also plan secretly to escape. But he should not be expected to jump around like a boy of eighteen.

Not that Würster gave a damn about Ferber personally. He just liked the idea that one of their own had spoken up to the showoff American captain instead of meekly performing disciplines and tricks for him. Yet Würster also believed that Ferber, and maybe even all the others—if they were speaking the truth now and not pretending like himself since the POW camp—were traitors to the Reich. For all he cared, let Ferber and Jung and all the rest above and below him in rank suffer all the pain, exhaustion and embarrassment *Hauptmann* Brooks cared to inflict upon them. Let him fall from the rope and kill himself. The man had dishonored his rank of *Stabsfeldwebel*. He and the others should be shot. If Würster had a loaded weapon in his hand, what a temptation it would be to shoot the American captain as he climbed to the balcony.

Würster continued to savor the exceptional gullibility of the Americans, their naïve innocence and their eagerness to believe in him. In the prisoner of war camp at Toulouse he had managed to keep mostly to himself. He had not identified himself with either the staunch Nazis or the smaller number of those who declared themselves against *der Führer*. But when he had heard about the interviews with the Americans he had arranged to talk to them, merely in the hope that they would improve his lot by taking him from that *verfluchten* cage.

And so they had. Except that he never had been subjected to so rigorous a training schedule. Würster also had felt fear clutch his belly when he had watched carpenters raise the posts and crossbeams of the exercise and training apparatus. The high poles and transverse bars had reminded him of German scaffolds he had helped erect all over Europe— and of the men and women he had helped to hang from them.

Kurt von Hassell remained a loner. He had to interact with the other men during training, but when he went to the day room in the evening to read and listen to the radio, he kept to himself. Most of the company considered him a snob. Some of them mockingly referred to him as "the baron."

When the opportunity presented itself, Kurt spoke to Captain Brooks in English. It particularly infuriated Helmut Jung. Once, when they were away from the Americans, Jung had shouted at von Hassell, "Speak in German like the rest of us, you goddamned aristocrat shit! If you had spoken English to Hitler twenty years ago instead of kissing his ass we wouldn't be in this pickle we're in now!"

But Jung failed to intimidate von Hassell. Kurt had responded calmly, "Twenty years ago I was not even eight years old, *Herr Oberfeldwebel.* Too young to influence the affairs of state even for a Prussian."

Nor did von Hassell pay much attention to the harassment of the others. Mostly they left him alone and he liked it that way. He sometimes thought that if he'd had the chance to develop a more normal life, even the traditional life of a wealthy aristocrat, he might have been different. But detachment had been his only defense, sometimes his only attack, against the Nazis when he was a civilian, and certainly since he had been called up by the army.

Sunday evening, December 17, 1944, the radio in the day room tent was playing pleasantly in the background. It was dialed to the American Armed Forces Radio network in Paris. They played mostly American swing music; occasionally an announcer delivered a personal message to some unit or soldier or broadcast the news. The volume was just loud enough to hear.

Von Hassell sat nearby, reading a copy of *Stars and Stripes* which Sergeant Maurer, the American on duty, had given him. The war news was good for the Allies. Kurt was glad, except for the specter of Russian hordes pouring in from the east and taking over his ancestral lands.

Elsewhere in the tent, about thirty of the company, wearing their American o.d.'s, clustered around tables and benches and played skat. Card games were their favorite off-duty activity, though a few had dared to ask Captain Brooks for permission to visit a bordello. Brooks had refused, of course, yet in such a tactful way as to hold out the possibility at a later time.

The shouts of the men as they placed their bets and played their cards, their cursing as they won or lost, and their insulting remarks to each other, were not unpleasant to Kurt. He wondered if maybe the rigorous training toward a worthwhile goal and the feeling of comfortable tired-ness that it brought him made him mellower.

Then he heard words from the radio that forced him to turn away from the newspaper and listen attentively. It was a news bulletin spoken by the American announcer in a grim and solemn voice. Von Hassell felt a chill come over him. Sergeant Maurer, who actually had been playing skat with his charges, stood up and moved closer to the radio.

"Sonofabitch!" he muttered angrily in English.

"What is it?" Helmut Jung called out in German.

Maurer did not respond. He leaned close to the speaker until the music came on again. He didn't know if he should mention it to the Germans or not.

"Don't any of you guys dare move from here until I get back!" he ordered in the most authoritative German he could muster. He ran from the tent toward the headquarters building, wondering if the CO had heard the news. It would be better for the captain to handle it his own way.

Jung turned to von Hassell, the only other man in the room who might be able to tell him the contents of the broadcast that had so upset Sergeant Maurer. He did not mock him now, but spoke to him properly. "*Schütze* von Hassell, would you explain to us please what disturbed Sergeant Maurer? What has happened?"

They had all stopped playing cards now and were staring at Kurt. He, too, just like Sergeant Maurer, did not want to tell them. But he didn't see how he could avoid it.

"The Wehrmacht has launched a massive new attack in the Ardennes," he said in a soft voice. "There is a terrible battle in the snow. German soldiers wearing American uniforms, speaking like Americans have infiltrated American positions."

Every man in the room, except *Unteroffizier* Otto Würster, stared at him in consternation.

Würster cried out, excitedly, "*Fallschirmjäger*! Paratroopers! No...Brandenburger division! That is *their* technique! *Wunderbar*! *Herrlich*! Those boys will show them now!"

Every man in the room turned to stare at Würster, then looked back to von Hassell as he continued to tell them what he had heard on the broadcast.

"Panzer divisions have broken through the American lines in Belgium," he related in a dull voice. "They are moving toward St. Vith and Bastogne. It is very bad. They are heading for Brussels and Antwerp again just like in 1940."

Würster stood up. The moment had possessed him. "Very *bad*!" he said angrily. "When the German army has such a success, you say that it is very *bad*. You are a traitor, von Hassell! Germany will now win the war. *Der Führer* is infallible."

Kurt von Hassell leaped to his feet and moved toward Würster, but Helmut Jung was a few steps ahead of him. Every man in the room now stared at the *Unteroffizier* with disbelief and anger.

Würster immediately realized his mistake. He started to laugh. "I am joking, of course!" he shouted.

Seeing Jung coming at him from the other side of the table, he dropped back down onto the bench in a gesture of submission. Jung grabbed a handful of his shirt and tie. "You Nazi bastard!" he exploded.

"No, *Herr Oberfeldwebel*," Würster squeezed out. "I am only fooling. Can you not take a joke? Do you think I am one of those fucking Nazis? I am here with you to fight them. A volunteer just like you."

Jung pulled back his clenched right hand so he could smash it into Würster's face. Sergeant Maurer returned at that moment and grabbed his fist from behind.

"What the hell's the matter, Jung?" he demanded. "You catch him cheating at cards?"

Jung's chest heaved with the fury he felt. "*Ja*, he was cheating all right." He looked up to see von Hassell close by, shaking his head, the expression on his face urging Jung to say no more. He released his grip and looked around at the others. They too stared grimly, indicating by their silent demeanor that they wanted him to say nothing against Würster.

The American noncom looked at Würster with disgust. "Cheating your buddies, Otto," he muttered, shaking his head and clucking his tongue. "You're banned from the day room from now on. Don't let me see your ass in here or I'll let them tear you apart."

"It is a private matter, Sergeant," Jung insisted. "I would appreciate it . . . we would all appreciate it . . . if you would take no disciplinary action against the *Unteroffizier*. Keep him out of the day room. That is okay. But, as for the rest, we understand his type now. Isn't that true?" he asked, sweeping his gaze over the other men in the room.

They answered in chorus, "*Jawohl, Herr Oberfeldwebel!*"

Nine

✠   In London, Major Alan Blakely of Plans and Operations was feeling peevish and horny. He shadowed Ann Jordan when she left OSS headquarters and followed her to her three-story apartment house in Knightsbridge. Then he waited in another building entry nearby. Several people went in and out of her building and he was able to scrutinize them closely. There was still plenty of light due to double daylight saving time which the British had instituted early in the war.

Blakely took particular note of a tall, robust man with a swarthy, somewhat Asiatic appearance, who wore a Burberry coat over civilian clothes. A short time after entering the building he and Ann came out together and went up the street arm in arm. Blakely figured they were going to dinner. Rather than follow, he went to a nearby Red Cross servicemen's center and ordered some sandwiches. By the time he returned to the street, it was dusk and the light had begun to fade. He positioned himself on the steps leading to the basement of an adjoining brownstone residence.

Around eight-thirty, despite the gloom of the blackout, he spotted them on their return. He hoped the bitch didn't keep the man in bed all night. He was determined to follow him. It was not just a matter of jealousy, Blakely convinced himself, though that was certainly what had prompted him originally. There was the matter of OSS security. Ann Jordan had access to extremely sensitive material and he felt he should know whom she was sleeping with.

Crossing the street, Blakely went back into the hallway opposite Ann's building. It was a long, cold wait, and he glanced often at the luminous dial of his wristwatch and felt the fool just for being there. Not until a few minutes after eleven was he rewarded for his patience when the tall, swarthy man exited to the street.

Blakely followed. He trailed him to the Knightsbridge station, took the same train in an adjoining car and got off at the same station he did at

60

Marble Arch. But now the man started to take precautions, the sort of security measures that an operative might use. He would duck into hallways and wait before reentering the street. several times he emerged from a hallway and reversed his direction. It was getting difficult to hang on to him. Finally, Blakely saw the man enter a building and the diffused light from the vestibule disclosed a sign alongside the entrance. Blakely watched for a few minutes. The street was empty. He walked over and shined his penlight on the sign. Printed in small letters it read: *Soviet Military Mission.*

In St. Germain, the men who shared a tent with *Unteroffizier* Otto Würster ostracized him, even as he continued to make excuses for his Nazi outburst. All the Wehrmacht POWs in the company refused to have anything to do with him during their hours off and barely tolerated him during training. But no one put forward what further action should be taken.

Kurt von Hassell finally did. He went to Jung's tent one night and requested that they speak in private about Würster. Previously, the master sergeant would have bawled out Kurt for daring to disturb him, then would have berated him merely for the fact of his birth and tossed him out without hearing what he wanted to say. Now he looked at him, nodded, put on his GI overcoat and garrison cap and they went outside into the chill, damp darkness. The nightly bed check by the American sergeants would take place in about fifteen minutes, so they walked back and forth between the latrines and tents, talking very softly.

"*Herr Oberfeldwebel...*" Kurt began.

"Forget the damned formality," snapped Jung. "We've got a real problem on our hands, von Hassell."

"Then you accept that it is *our* problem and we must not tell the Americans?"

"Without question. I knew it the moment you gestured to me in the day room. I was about to strangle that Nazi shit and then I would have gladly explained the reasons for it to Sergeant Maurer and..."

Kurt interrupted. "And after him to Captain Brooks, who will think that if there is one rat among us there might very well be more. Maybe he would punish all of us for it, send us back to the POW cages and we would never have this opportunity to help rid Germany of the Nazis."

"How do I know that *you* also are not a Nazi at heart, von Hassell?" demanded Jung. He paused in his stride and turned to stare at Kurt through the darkness.

"And I *you*," Kurt retorted. "But at some point we are going to have to start trusting each other, just the way we have put our trust in the Americans. I believe that point is now, Sergeant."

"What do you want to do?"

"I am not sure," Kurt replied. "We must consider our actions very carefully. Würster must be watched closely, his every word must be listened to. It is correct to ostracize him. But, in another way, he must also be put at ease and given the opportunity to make a mistake again and reveal his true self."

"It must remain a strictly military matter," Jung said. "The civilian platoon will not be brought into it and certainly not the Americans. Only we of the Wehrmacht have the duty to act."

"Agreed. What do *you* want to do?"

Jung bent his head closer so that they saw each other's faces. His expression was anguished. "I am a fair man," he said. "We must first of all be absolutely positive that Würster is what we now think he is. We cannot behave like Nazis."

"Of course," von Hassell said. "I will see if I can get him to reveal himself again."

"What will you do?" Jung demanded.

"Pose as one of them, an agent provocateur," Kurt told him. "A favorite trick of both the Nazis and communists. It will be simple to do. Why, you yourself, *Herr Oberfeldwebel*, have already accused me many times before the other men of being a Nazi. I suggest you continue to behave the same way toward me. Our Otto will be more likely to accept me as one of his own. I'll bring you confirmation that he's an unregenerate Nazi who would betray us and see us all killed when we return to Germany. Then we must take a democratic vote as to his fate."

Jung look at von Hassell with a new feeling of respect. "What do you propose?" he asked.

"If he is found guilty, an 'accident,'" Kurt said calmly.

Brooks invited the German field sergeants to his quarters for a friendly chat on a Sunday night late in January. He served them mugs of cold beer, charged to his own account at the PX.

Gunther Ferber, Willy Hartmann, Hans Zweiger and Joseph Werner were pleased to have been made platoon leaders under the command of their American counterparts. Helmut Jung was not happy to have been made their ersatz company commander with the rank of *Oberleutnant*. He had never wanted to be an officer.

During these last couple of weeks, whenever the company had worn their *Jäger* uniforms for close order drill and certain training exercises, Brooks and his staff had disappeared into the ranks. Dan had worn the insignia of a *Gefreiter*, his cadre posed as *Schützen*. The *Oberleutnant* and *Feldwebels* had functioned very well as ersatz commanders. This evening, however, they sat in Brooks's luxurious quarters, spruced up in their GI uniforms.

"Relax, gentlemen," Dan said.

They stirred around on the couch and chairs but still looked ill at ease. Jung commented, "We are not used to drinking and socializing with officers in the Wehrmacht, *Herr Hauptmann.*"

Brooks wanted them to trust him to the extent that they would drop a hint of what was troubling their platoons. "Up to now I've made the decisions as to who stays with the company and who is transferred out," he told them in an amiable voice. "Now I'm going to leave the decision entirely up to you. Something is bothering you and your men and I think it's that card-cheating incident in the day room many weeks back. Sergeant Maurer told me about it right away, but he said you didn't want him to take any disciplinary action against Würster beyond barring him from the day room. Is that correct?"

"Yes, *Herr Hauptmann,*" replied *Stabsfeldwebel* Gunther Ferber, the senior Wehrmacht noncom. Ferber, a solemn, thoughtful man, had not felt slighted at all when Brooks promoted Helmut Jung over him to be the German commanding officer.

"Are you sure you don't want me to kick him out of the outfit?"

"No, sir. But thank you for your concern," Jung spoke up. "We don't want to make trouble for Würster. It is a matter we have resolved among ourselves. We do not believe it will happen again."

"Anything else troubling you or your men?"

Ferber nodded to Jung to speak for them.

"We continue to wonder what all this training means," said the new *Oberleutnant,* "and where we will be going. You told us it will be in the Reich, but everybody wants to know *where*, and how you Americans intend to make use of us. Some of them think we are going to do something crazy like jump into Berlin. All these exercises in blocking streets and clearing houses makes the idea seem plausible."

"Would you be against that?"

"No, sir. We trust you, *Herr Hauptmann.* You can rely on us," Jung replied.

Brooks smiled and said, "Thank you. How do you rate the local beer?"

"Not too bad," answered the *Oberleutnant.* He picked up his mug, drained it, then added, "But not nearly as good as the German brews. *That* is beer."

Lawrence Dillard, the civilian chief of Special Operations, stared at Major Alan Blakely with barely suppressed rage. They were in Dillard's handsomely furnished office on the second floor of OSS's Grosvenor Street headquarters. Blakely had never imagined that Dillard, generally a reserved and conservative gentleman, could feel and speak in this way.

"Major, your conduct is indefensible," Dillard accused, his tone seething. "For the gratification of your cock, you've compromised Knight's Cross."

"We don't know that that's so, Larry. We have no way of knowing yet whether or not the mission has been jeopardized," Blakely responded weakly.

"We'd better find out pretty damned quick, hadn't we. Have you notified the security people?"

"No, you're the first one I've told. And don't try to place the blame on me," Blakely insisted, forcing the dialogue back to a rational analysis. "I haven't been sleeping with the goddamned Russian. Ann Jordan's been doing it."

"But before that it was you who was sleeping with her. And that's against all regulations. It was you who protected her job when we didn't really need her and granted her access to classified material. Lord only knows what you told her when you were in your cups or in the sack with her."

"Nothing, Larry, that she hadn't already learned by typing up my plans, reports and correspondence. We didn't talk shop after hours. In fact, I haven't seen her socially in six or seven weeks."

"Which was why you followed her last night?"

"Yes, I was upset. Now I'm glad I did or we might never have found out who she's been seeing."

"Let us hope, Alan, that it's only seeing, or screwing, or whatever the current euphemism is. If it's anything more, we're all in big trouble."

The following morning, Ann Jordan was brought to Lawrence Dillard's office. She and Major Schepilov had been arrested in her apartment the night before and grilled separately for hours. The security team had got nothing out of the major and, not wanting to create a messy incident with the Russians, finally had to let him go. They couldn't bring espionage charges against him merely for having an affair with an OSS employee.

In the early stages of the questioning, Ann had only admitted dating Schepilov. But hours into it, after some phone calls and legwork by security, they had been able to break her with tidbits about the Russian that sent her into an absolute fury. OSS and MI-5, the British intelligence service, had reports of Schepilov having seduced other women employed by various military headquarters and intelligence agencies.

Alone with Dillard in his office, looking rather bedraggled from her night's ordeal, Ann Jordan mumbled responses to the gentle questioning of the Special Operations chief.

"You must help us," Dillard said.

"They're on our side, aren't they...the Russians?" she protested feebly.

"In this war, yes. That's quite true. But secret information can be used even by our Allies in ways that are bad for American fighting forces.."

"I don't know anything about politics," Ann said defensively.

"But you do know how misuse of information can get our people killed," Dillard commented, twisting his figurative knife a little bit, wanting to be harder if not crueler. "You were duped, my dear. There's no question about it. I know that you would never intentionally betray your country. After all, you've already lost your husband in the war. You're certainly not a spy for the Russians or anybody else and I would never think of charging you with violation of the Espionage Act. But only you know if you revealed information about Knight's Cross to Major Schepilov. That is what we're most concerned about."

"He played me for a fool," Ann murmured, unable to look at Dillard, her head lowered. "I hope you hang the sonofabitch!"

"I'm afraid not," Dillard said. "There can be no charges brought against him. But he'll be useless to his intelligence service in London from now on. The British government will declare him *persona non grata*. He'll be shipped home and they'll do with him whatever they do with their failed operatives. Please tell me, Ann, in as great detail as possible, what you told the major about the Knight's Cross mission."

Ann raised her head and stared at Dillard for a moment, pushing her hair aside with one had. "We were lovers," she said softly. "I thought he cared for me. He said to me it would make no difference. We were allies and we could tell each other our war stories. He even told me some of his. Perhaps they could be of use to you."

"Maybe. What did you *tell* him, Mrs. Jordan?" Dillard repeated.

"Everything, Mr. Dillard," she finally said. "Everything that came across my desk from Major Blakely's office in regard to the mission. Not all at once. Bit by bit. He wormed little pieces of it out of me, week after week, and then one night...last night too when your men were questioning me...I realized he knew it all."

"The name of the commanding officer?"

"Yes."

"The German personnel?"

"Yes."

"The zone of operations?"

"Austria. The Tyrol. The Inn Valley. The Last Redoubt."

"Kidnapping the Nazi leaders?" Dillard asked apprehensively. He wouldn't let himself speak the name "Hitler." She couldn't know that unless she had guessed. Even Blakely hadn't been told specifically that Hitler was the true target of the mission, though he might have inferred it, as Captain Brooks surely did.

"Yes. He was particularly pleased by that."

Dillard slammed his fist down on his desk. The Russian major would already have passed all he knew to his superiors. Would OSS have to scratch the mission?

That whole area of the Tyrol, it had been agreed by the highest levels of Allied command, including the Russians, was to be exclusively an

American sector of operations. No one else was supposed to maneuver military forces in there or try to carry out covert operations. Though they might know about Knight's Cross now, what could the Russians possibly do about it?

Dillard glanced over at Ann and felt genuinely sorry for her. She would have to be confined to an OSS detention center until Knight's Cross was completed. Then she would be sent home under the severest orders to keep her mouth shut or face prosecution and imprisonment in a federal penitentiary.

More immediately, Dillard would have to tell his boss, Colonel Hoose, commander of all the agency's European operations, what had happened. Together they would have to evaluate the political and military damage. After that, he would have to go to St. Germain to tell Dan Brooks. Maybe Brooks would want to make changes in the plan, take additional precautions. It was Brooks, in the end, who would have to deal with it.

Ten

✠ On a cold, snowy day early in February, Karl Bergen wended his way through the streets of Innsbruck toward one of the city's administrative buildings. He was wearing a decent suit and tie, an overcoat and fedora, rather than his usual Alpine clothes. The contact he was about to make was the most dangerous for him yet.

Bergen entered the Police Department and asked to see, *"Kriminalinspektor Bernard Klung, bitte!* I am expected."

He forced himself to appear calm as the desk officer wrote his name in a visitors' ledger and telephoned Klung. He listened, alert to anything that hinted of danger, but heard nothing.

"You may go up now, *Herr* Bergen," the desk officer told him respectfully, hanging up the telephone. "Do you know the room?"

"No, please direct me," Karl responded, laughing. "I am not used to being in a police department."

Bergen moved through the building cautiously, taking in everything, reading signs on doors, fixing the locations of corridors, rooms and stairways and filing it away for possible future use. Uppermost in his mind these many weeks had been the question of what would happen to him if the Allies never made it, if Germany, in the end, won the war.

In the middle of a corridor on the second floor a tall, slender man about forty-five years old, stood in a doorway. He had his right hand in the pocket of his jacket and Bergen thought it might easily be wrapped around the handle of a pistol.

"Herr Bergen?" he asked. His voice was open and pleasant, his appearance friendly.

"Yes, sir. Thank you for seeing me, Inspector."

"Of course. Please come in," Klung said, moving into the small, private room while closing the door behind them. *"Herr* Weisskirch told me you had a confidential matter you wished to discuss. Do you know him long? I thought I knew most of Werner's friends. They are mostly the same as mine, from childhood on."

"No, sir. We only met some weeks ago through acquaintances," Karl replied, sitting down in the chair Klung gestured to beside his desk.

It had been through Werner Weisskirch, an Innsbruck schoolteacher and member of the Resistance, that Karl had heard about the anti-Nazi activities of Inspector Klung of Kripo, the criminal police department. He had put off contacting him until now. During the Nazi offensive in Belgium he had felt abandoned in a resurgent Third Reich that might have another chance to finish him off. Hitler and his treacherous cronies had almost done so in 1934 when they had killed his friend, Ernst Röhm, leader of the *Sturmabteilung* Brownshirts, and others Bergen had worked with before fleeing for his life to America.

"What can I do for you, *mein Herr?*" asked Inspector Klung, relaxing back into this desk chair. His right hand was still in his jacket pocket.

"Mainly, I wished only to make your acquaintance, sir," Bergen replied softly, "and ask your advice about a personal matter."

"Of course. Please go ahead."

It was then that Bergen reminded himself why he was really there. Klung's criminal police branch was allied to the Gestapo and SS through a chain of command that rose all the way to the Reich Central Security Office in Berlin and Heinrich Himmler himself. When the first American soldiers turned up he wanted to be sure it was he who received credit for gathering and transmitting intelligence vital to them, no matter how many other unknown agent teams might be operating in the Tyrol. He wanted credit too for organizing guerrilla forces that would pave the way to victory and for having the government infrastructure under his control. With these accomplishments, how could the Americans refuse the request he would make to place him in political charge of the region?

Bergen leaned forward, pointed to a pen and notepad on Klung's desk and made gestures to indicate that he wished to write something. He was relieved to see the inspector take his right hand from his pocket to hand him the items. Bergen wrote: *Are we free to talk here? Are you positive that there are no listening devices in the room and that nobody else can hear what we say?*

Klung read the note, looked up at him warily and said, "Yes. Please continue."

Even in this moment Bergen was not sure what he would say. But then he said it—"I am an American agent"—in a subdued voice, watching Klung's expression closely.

"And I am Adolf Hitler," Klung responded angrily. "What do you take me for, a fool, *Herr* Bergen? This is a favorite trick of the Gestapo's, to send *agents provocateurs* to try to trick honest citizens and policemen."

"I assure you, Inspector, that I am not a *provocateur.*"

"Perhaps not. But you are also not an American. You are a German.

68

Your accent is Bavarian. Lord knows we have heard enough of *that* in these parts for many years."

"You are correct, *Herr* Klung. I *was* a German. But I have lived in the United States for ten years. I am an American citizen and an agent with the Secret Intelligence branch of the Office of Strategic Services."

"In that case, *mein Herr*, you are already a candidate for the gallows."

Bergen suddenly found himself staring into the barrel of a Walther .38 automatic, which Klung had yanked from the jacket pocket where Bergen had suspected it was cached. "Let me see your papers," the inspector ordered. "Move very slowly and try no funny business."

Despite the pistol, Karl was less frightened than he had been. He sensed that it was the policeman who was now afraid. The way Klung spat out the name of Adolf Hitler and the contemptuous tone he had used in reference to Bergen's Bavarian accent had subtly revealed his true feelings. Nevertheless, Karl opened his jacket wide with very careful movements, extracted his wallet and handed it to the inspector. "If I am a candidate for the gallows, *mein Herr*, your friend Weisskirch and you are also candidates," he said confidently. "You will also be very gratified by the authenticity of the documents prepared for me in London."

Klung quickly scanned the documents. Various papers identified Karl as a munitions factory worker, exempted from military service, who had been transferred to Austria to help set up new underground factories in the mountains of the Tyrol. He even had the correct, current pass permitting him to leave the Ruhr, where his former home and place of work had been bombed out.

"Very impressive, *Herr* Bergen," said Inspector Klung finally, smiling at him. "I find nothing out of order in your papers and I wish you good fortune in your new work in Austria. Your little joke is amusing, but I have work to do now and I must bid you good day." He shoved the pistol back into his pocket and stood up, indicating that, no matter what Karl had in mind to discuss, their first contact was over for now. "It has been a pleasure to make your acquaintance. Perhaps you, Werner and I can take a beer together soon. Where may I communicate with you?"

"Through Werner. He will know how to reach me."

Each of them was being cautious and correct. Neither bothered with the *Heil Hitlers*.

Unteroffizier Otto Würster stood back against the wall of the bombed-out apartment building in St. Germain and waited for something to happen. He hated all this play-acting in the night. The only thing good about it was that he wore again the uniform of a German soldier and carried in his hands a Schmeisser machine pistol, one of his favorites, though the Schmeisser and all the other weapons issued that night were loaded only with blank cartridges.

"You are transferred to the SS for the night's activities," *Stabsfeldwebel*

Gunther Ferber had said to him in a surprisingly jovial mood that afternoon. "Pick ten men, Würster, any ten you want in the platoon. You will act as an SS detail to guard a Gestapo headquarters where Nazi dignitaries are visiting. You must be prepared to defend the building against a surprise attack by an enemy raiding party who intend to kill or capture the big shots."

He disliked these night exercises even more than the drills and maneuvers they were forced to participate in during the day. It was an insult to a sergeant of the Wehrmacht to go through all this crap as if he were a raw recruit. And with this bunch of traitors, no less, working for the Americans.

Würster and his squad had been driven in a truck from the base to this block of apartments in St. Germain that *Luftwaffe* bombers had severely damaged. It was a familiar place where Captain Brooks occasionally brought them to demonstrate tactics and perform various exercises. Arrangements were always made with the local police to block the roads and keep curious civilians away. Two trucks and two jeeps parked in front of the building were specified as belonging to his SS guard unit and were therefore also his responsibility to protect. He had placed himself far off to one side of the entrance, hidden in the darkness away from any position of first danger, a habit that had helped him survive when in combat with his unit of the Wehrmacht.

Würster intended to discover before they left France precisely what the Americans were up to with all this special training. He would escape and reveal their plans to the highest authorities the moment the *Jäger Einheit* arrived in the Third Reich. Rumor had it that they might even parachute into Berlin itself!

Suddenly he stiffened. He had heard his name whispered. The words came again, softly but urgently... "*Unteroffizier* Würster!"

He turned behind him, recognized *Schütze* von Hassell in the darkness and was startled by his ability to have moved this close to him unseen and silent. Von Hassell's attitude was neither threatening nor jubilant; he gave no indication that he was a member of the raiding party. Though he was armed with a Schmeisser, dagger and hand grenades, he made no attempt to put any of his weapons into mock play.

Würster aimed his Schmeisser at him and said, "You are my prisoner!" He did not think it necessary or even desirable yet to pull the trigger of his machine pistol and begin a mock fire fight that might cover the moves of the rest of the attacking unit.

"No, no, *Herr Unteroffizier*," von Hassell insisted in a pleading whisper. "You do not understand. I am here to warn you about *Oberfeld-webel* Jung."

"What do you mean?" demanded Würster, trying to keep his voice low. "Where is he?"

70

"He will be here in a few moments. He is in charge of the raiders," von Hassell blurted out quickly. "Do not trust him. He will pretend to be friendly, even if you take him prisoner. But while he is talking to you his men will be placing demolitions charges in the vehicles you are guarding."

Würster narrowed his eyes and spoke harshly. "Why do you tell me this?"

"It is his intention to make you look bad, *Herr Unteroffizier*, so that you will be dismissed from the company by *Hauptman* Brooks and be returned to a POW cage like the other rejects were."

"So? It seems to me that is what you and all the others would like too. Why do you tell me this, von Hassell?"

"Because I have been ashamed and a coward. When you revealed your true allegiance to *der Führer* and the Reich I did not have the courage to agree with you in public, to tell them proudly that I am a Nazi like you."

Würster leaned closer and demanded, "Why did you not approach me before, von Hassell, during all these weeks that I have been treated so badly by everybody? Why did you wait until now, during the middle of an exercise?"

"I was afraid. I dared not be seen talking to you," Kurt replied hurriedly. "But this exercise tonight, alone in the dark, has given me the first moment to reveal the truth to you. Now you must shoot me, *Herr Unteroffizier*."

"Shoot you?"

"Yes. By firing your Schmeisser you will show that you were alert and have begun to repel the attack upon 'Gestapo headquarters.'"

Otto Würster actually felt a moment of pleasure when he squeezed the trigger of his machine pistol, heard the staccato explosions of the blank cartridges and watched *Schütze* von Hassell fall to the ground and pretend to be dead. He swung the weapon around just in time to bring it to bear upon *Oberfeldwebel* Helmut Jung running low from the direction of the parked vehicles, coming directly at him. He squeezed the trigger and fired another burst of blanks.

"Oh, Otto, you're real sharp," Jung said in a subdued voice.

Eleven

✠ During his private hours of the night, when he could no longer stand all the idiotic ranting of *Mein Kampf,* all the skewed reasoning of Adolf Hitler writing twenty years earlier in Landsberg Prison, Captain Brooks put the book aside and engrossed himself in photographs of the Nazi leaders of Germany.

He sat at his desk studying pictures of *der Führer,* Göring, Goebbels, Himmler, Bormann, Kaltenbrunner and others. He practiced with erasable pencil on the pictures to see if beards and different hair grooming would serve to render them unrecognizable. In a closet in his room he had a small supply of theatrical beards, mustaches, wigs and makeup to disguise their identities. But it was the hoods to go over their heads that would be the quickest. London had been very good about providing him with all he needed, plus profiles on each of the Nazi leaders.

Adolf Hitler was believed to be still living and working in the *Reichskanzlei* in Berlin, despite major bomb damage to the building. He was also known to travel occasionally by train or car to visit the eastern and western fronts where he conferred with his generals, gave speeches to his deteriorating forces and bestowed medals on his heroes.

Hermann Göring, field marshal of the battered, depleted *Luftwaffe* and still deputy commander of the government despite his seeming disgrace, was usually at Karinhall, his castle estate northwest of Berlin, but met sometimes with *der Führer* in the *Reichskanzlei.* He also was known to leave Berlin occasionally to go to his private retreat in the Obersalzburg, the Bavarian mountain range on the border of Austria where his wife and daughter lived not far from Hitler's vacation chalet at Berchtesgaden.

Joseph Goebbels continued to wage war from his Propaganda Ministry on Wilhelmstrasse in Berlin. Martin Bormann hovered close to Hitler, winning more and more influence with him, to the detriment of Göring,

Goebbels and Heinrich Himmler. Himmler, the hated chief of the entire Reich Central Security Office, which included the Gestapo and Kripo, had recently been named head of Army Group Vistula, though he had no soldiering experience whatsoever. It was a last ditch army thrown together to try to hold back the Russians on the northeastern front.

However, there was still a corridor from Berlin open to the south between the pressing Allied armies of the east and west, an escape route to the mountains of Bavaria, the Austrian Tyrol and the *Alpenfestung* of the Last Redoubt. Brooks eagerly hoped that Hitler and his cronies would flee through that corridor soon and then take refuge in the Inn Valley when he and his unit reached there.

Larry Dillard and Lieutenant Colonel Pearson, in nominal charge of the operation, came to St. Germain in mid-February to review progress of the *Jäger Einheit*. They were enormously impressed. Brooks expected that meant they would, at last, brief him on specific drop zones, targets and the latest intelligence from the area of operations. After a fine dinner in the manor house dining room, they settled into his quarters upstairs, holding snifters of cognac Dan poured for them.

Dillard looked at him unhappily, then dropped his bombshell. "The Russians know about Knight's Cross."

Brooks almost gagged on a sip of cognac. He felt a rush of anger and frustration. "Was the leak here?" he asked brusquely.

"No, it was with us in London," Dillard admitted. He went on to divulge the details of the hapless involvement of Major Alan Blakely with Ann Jordan and the duped and culpable involvement of Ann with the beguiling Major Mikhail Schepilov.

Brooks gave momentary thought to Alan Blakely's miserable position and considered that he himself might have had a narrow escape, that he could have become involved with the very alluring Ann. He had limited his pleasures, however, to a few visits to popular Paris bistros he'd known since before the war and had always managed to find a girl who desired what he did.

Dillard opened his briefcase. "Here are some pictures of the Russian Romeo," he said. "Add them to your rogue's gallery."

Dillard explained the pictures were eight-by-ten enlargements of photos that OSS operatives had taken unobtrusively with minicameras. One showed Major Schepilov in a street snapshot, wearing civilian clothes. Another showed him in military uniform, a picture taken at one of the diplomatic parties he frequently attended in order to pick up vulnerable women in key jobs.

I'd like to meet the son of a bitch face to face some day," Brooks muttered darkly.

"Major Schepilov is out of our reach now, made *persona non grata* by

73

the British, at our request," Dillard told him. "Probably shipped back to Moscow in disgrace. We think he's a *Spetsnaz* operative."

"When did this happen?" Dan asked.

"A month ago. There didn't seem any point in rushing the news to you. We wanted to see first what the Russians would do, if anything. No matter what we ultimately decided, I didn't want anything to interfere with your work here getting your unit ready."

"Have the Russians done anything yet?"

"Nothing that we're onto. As far as I'm concerned our operation goes."

"The Tyrol is *our* zone of operations," Pearson interjected. "I don't think they'd dare go in there."

"We should go on as before," Dan insisted, "but be alert for their possible interference."

"How about jump training for your men?" Pearson asked.

Earlier in the day, they had watched the *Soldaten* run through exit procedures from the C-47 mock-up on the estate and leap from high platforms to glide to earth in parachute harness on cables.

"There won't be any," Brooks told him. "It would take too long and complicate our security if we moved the company to a parachute training center. I've known agents to go in with less preparation than I've given these men. Their first real jump was their combat mission and my men are willing to do the same."

"Very well. I've brought the drop zone intelligence," Dillard said. He removed aerial reconnaissance photos from his briefcase and laid them out on Brooks's desk. "Special Operations Wing has suggested two possibilities."

Dan studied the aerial photos through a stereoscopic device that enlarged the details and gave greater depth and definition to the panoramas. Both sites were poor DZs, he decided. They were small, snow-covered gaps between Alpine peaks, at elevations of more than 4,500 feet. The one above Schwaz had a canyon at one end into which men and canisters could tumble. But the one closer to Innsbruck, near a town called Solbad Hall, was perhaps 250 yards longer and without any steep slopes at either end. It also afforded more room for the aircraft to maneuver between peaks.

"I'm for this one, though it isn't one I'd ordinarily relish," Brooks said. "I think it best that I jump in with a pilot team to check it out first, then bring in the rest by platoons."

"That's rather foolhardy, isn't it Dan?" Dillard questioned. "You're the only one in the company who knows what the mission is really about. If you're lost before it starts, that will be the end of it."

"I'll make provision for that," Brooks said in a tone that left no room for argument on this point. From the beginning, everyone in the chain of command had agreed that he would be in complete charge of the details of the operation and its personnel and, so far, there had been no conflicts.

"I've brought the cover stories and documents for you, your cadre, the *Soldaten* and civilian agents, as requested," Dillard said, extracting the papers from his briefcase.

Dan glanced quickly at only a few of the documents. Among them were almost two hundred of the thin, green little paybooks that looked like passports, *Soldbücher* that every German soldier carried as his primary I.D. Each POW's own *Soldbuch* had been revised and updated. The forgers and artists of the OSS documentation section were topnotch people and he didn't think it necessary to examine their handiwork personally now, though he would require each of his men to double-check his own and have it inspected again by one or more of his buddies.

Brooks's new cover story and documents, which he had helped to create, identified him as a corporal, *Gefreiter* Paul Halle, in the *Jäger Einheit*. He was supposed to be a physical education teacher of French-German parentage who had grown up on the Caribbean island of Martinique, had been caught in Europe by the war and had joined the Wehrmacht because he admired German culture. Dan didn't think he could pass as a native German or Frenchman because of his accent in each language. But, if it were ever necessary for him to prove his false identity to military or civilian authorities in the Reich, he figured no Nazi bureaucrat would know what a man from Martinique was supposed to sound like.

In the documents for his OSS cadre, the men had opted to retain their own German family names, but each would now have a *Soldbuch* and new personal history to memorize.

"How much time do we have left?" Brooks asked.

"Three weeks," Dillard said.

It would be more than enough time, Dan thought, for the men to learn their cover stories and for him to fine tune the outfit and complete his training of the civilian agents who would jump with them.

Helmut Jung was as proud of the *Jäger Einheit* as he had been of any unit he'd ever served with in the Wehrmacht. It was Kurt von Hassell who first whispered to him his suspicions about who the main targets of their mission might be. That day Brooks gave them very critical instructions regarding the use of hand grenades during house-clearing raids. The captain warned that whenever high-ranking Nazis were present in a room no grenades were to be used. They were to expose themselves to the additional risk.

Kurt spoke to Helmut alone after that day's instruction. "Now I know why we have been given such magnificent treatment and extensive training all these weeks," he said. "I think that *Hauptmann* Brooks is preparing us to capture *die grossen Kanonen*. Göring, Goebbels, Himmler and the rest of that lot. But best of all, I think perhaps *der Führer* himself—Adolf Hitler!"

Jung repeated the name in a seething voice that sounded as if he were rending Hitler limb from limb. "If that were possible I would follow him into hell itself!" he said.

"Consider it, Helmut," Kurt advised. "But do not speak of it to anyone else. If Brooks wanted us to know he would tell us. However, if I were he I would want no one to know at this stage."

It made sense, Jung thought, and the idea of being part of such an undertaking felt exhilarating. "If I could kill the monster myself," he said, "what a fulfillment for my life!"

"You and a hundred eighty other Germans and Austrians in this outfit," von Hassell declared. "Minus one. Leave out that swine Würster. But don't think the Americans are going to let any of us kill our great *Führer*. They want him alive and secretly, for whatever reasons of their own. Perhaps even they would not know what to do with him."

Jung sensed, as did the others, that the company would be leaving soon on its mission. There was not much time left to do what had to be done regarding *Unteroffizier* Otto Würster. If he didn't act, he was almost certain that von Hassell would take matters into his own hands, and it was not Kurt's position to do so. It was Jung's responsibility, or perhaps *Stabsfeldwebel* Gunther Ferber's. But Ferber already had admitted he had no stomach for it.

Difficult as it had been, a vote finally had been taken among the POWs, though there was not one among them who did not feel nervous about the result.

Jung waited until after bedcheck one night, then slipped out of his tent, awoke von Hassell with a whisper and told him to come to the empty, darkened tent of the day room where they could talk. He often sought Kurt's counsel now. He enjoyed his companionship and found it surprisingly comfortable to talk to him about this and other matters that concerned them. For a Prussian aristocrat he was not such a bad guy after all.

"Time is growing very short," Jung told him. "We must end the Würster business now, once and for all."

"I will do it if you would like."

"No. It is not your responsibility."

"Will you?"

"Yes."

"How?"

"There will be more firing of live ammunition, grenades, demolitions during these final days of training. I will find a way."

"Will you tell me?"

"No one. I will just do it so that it looks like an accident, as you suggested."

* * *

Each time they returned from the field with Würster still walking upright and cocky, Jung faced the questioning glances of the other men and the challenging stare of Kurt von Hassell.

The throwing line on the grenade practice range had four pits, twenty feet apart, four feet deep. They practiced with the *Stielhandgranate 24* stick grenade and the egg-shaped *Eihandgranate 39*. Mostly the egg grenade because it was smaller, weighed half as much, was easier to throw and many more could be carried comfortably into combat by the individual soldier.

Three men were able to throw at a time at marked targets in the near distance. The fourth pit was for the trainer to leap into to get out of the way. The duty of the trainer was to check out the readiness of each man by getting down into the pit with him. Then, when satisfied, he climbed out, ran for shelter, shouted "*Werf!*" and the grenades were thrown.

One afternoon, a hand grenade with a short fuse went off prematurely. Everyone, including the thrower and trainer, had taken proper cover except for *Hauptmann* Brooks who liked to position himself close enough to observe their work. The captain had just turned away to find shelter behind a broken wall when the early explosion came. Shards of shrapnel whizzed past his helmet. Jung heard him shout, "Son of a bitch! *Scheisse!*"

Yet Brooks took the incident in stride. He held no one responsible. It had been an accident. The cycle of repeated live-ammunition training quickened to simulate the frequent action and fire fights the captain told them to expect when they jumped into their area of operations. He had them moving on the double from the firing range to the combat course to the demolitions site to the grenade range. Everybody was exhausted.

The light was fading fast one day by the time they reached the grenade range. Jung made sure he was the trainer when *Unteroffizier* Otto Würster took his place in one of the throwing pits. Helmut jumped in after him, inspected the grenade Würster would throw and handed it back to him. Then he ran through the oral instructions again while Würster gave him his usual contemptuous stare.

"I have perhaps not thrown as many little eggs as an old fart like you, *Herr Oberfeldwebel*," Würster muttered scornfully. "But what do you take me for, an amateur? I know what I'm doing."

He tossed the grenade up and down in his hand a few times, as if playing with Jung, trying to frighten him. But Jung saw that the blue metal safety cap had not been unscrewed.

"One day, after we return to *das Vaterland*, this will be for you, Helmut," said Würster, sneering, "and for the *Hauptmann* and all his traitors and Jews."

As the grenade rose in the air again above Würster's hand, Jung darted his own hand under it and caught it.

"*Viel Glück*, Otto," he muttered.

He kneed him in the balls and as the man fell back in pain Jung leaped from the pit, pretended to stumble at the rim, shielded the grenade against his body, unscrewed the cap, aimed himself at his safety pit twenty feet away, yanked the ring, dropped the grenade into the hole with Würster and raced away.

He'd barely taken refuge and had not yet had time to shout "*Werf!*" when the grenade exploded behind him.

Twelve

✠   Brooks summoned Helmut Jung to his quarters. The *"Oberleutnant"* stood at rigid attention and looked stoic. His dark brown eyes stared straight ahead at a point beyond Brooks's head, seeing something that was in his mind, not in the room. His field gray *Jäger* uniform still had the stains of the earth and blood on it. He had rushed back to Würster after the grenade exploded and helped lift the man's torn body from the throwing pit.

Brooks hated accidents. There had been a few firing range mishaps during these months of training. He tended to seek cause and effect, if only to prevent the next accident from happening.

"Rühr dich, Oberfeldwebel," he said to Jung. Then quickly corrected himself to, *"Oberleutnant."*

Jung brought his eyes down to look at the captain. "Sergeant will do nicely, sir," he said respectfully. "I told you, *Herr Hauptmann*, that I was not good officer material and I'm not comfortable in the role."

"Are you suggesting that Würster would be alive if you had not been made *Oberleutnant*?"

"No, sir."

"Or had not just happened to be his instructor this afternoon? It could have been anybody, you know."

"No, sir," Jung answered. He was not lying, though he was avoiding the truth. He knew that somebody else would have killed Würster if *he* hadn't. Probably von Hassell. Or maybe somebody else would have botched it.

"Was there bad blood between you?" Brooks asked, and thought he saw a flicker of undefined emotion cross the master sergeant's face.

"Yes. We didn't like each other," Jung replied. He decided in this moment, if he was indeed *Oberleutnant*, to take full responsibility for his decisions and action. "Würster was a Nazi," he said bluntly. "He deceived you and was going to betray us all."

79

Brooks accepted that. "The only one among you?" he asked.

Jung shrugged. "I think so. We took a vote about what to do. Very democratic. If there had been even one vote in his favor, maybe we would have reconsidered. But we could never have trusted him to go into Germany as a soldier in this company."

Brooks nodded. He was not certain what he had seen on the grenade range, but he could piece it together now. He didn't want to know any more. "Thank you, *Oberleutnant*," he said. "You're dismissed."

"*Danke, Herr Hauptmann*," Jung responded softly. He did an about face, head held high and marched out.

Brooks thought he might have done the deed himself if he had known about Würster.

Hans Zimmer and Walter Freiherr arrived at the St. Germain base from England wearing GI uniforms without insignia, as Brooks had requested.

"A pleasure to see you again, *mon capitaine*," Hans's voice boomed out warmly, as he and Walter lowered their duffels and packs to the parquet floor of the entry hall.

To Brooks, the two agents still looked like an assassin and a con man, good images considering the roles they were going to play. To get them out of sight of the rest of the company and give them the proper instructions, he had them bring their gear to his quarters.

"*Wein oder Bier?*" he asked, startling them by his suggestion at this early hour in the afternoon.

"Wine, please, sir," Walter replied in a deferential voice.

"How about you, Zimmer?"

"Whatever is easiest, sir. That would be very nice. I thank you," Hans ventured in a humble tone.

"You've just made your first mistakes as Gestapo agents," Brooks told them. "They are imperious sons of bitches who demand what they want and expect to get it."

"Sorry," Zimmer said.

"No. You are never sorry if you're going to work as a Gestapo agent for me, Hans. Do you want a beer or a glass of wine?"

"I *want* a beer, Captain," Zimmer snapped with gruff emphasis.

When they had each sipped from their glasses, Brooks said, "Now, gentlemen, what's the name of Himmler's doctor's dog?"

They each looked at him and then at each other in bemusement. The eyes of the pale, blond, bull-necked Hans Zimmer narrowed in frustration. The slender Walter Freiherr, darker in hair and complexion and more engaging in personality, smiled ingratiatingly and shrugged.

"I don't know," he replied. "We were not taught this." Then he wiped the grin from his face, narrowed his eyes and spoke in a curt voice that challenged his listeners to doubt him. "However, as you must know, *Herr Hauptmann*, our beloved *Führer*, Adolf Hitler, has an Alsatian bitch named Blondi, from whom he is inseparable."

Brooks said, "I didn't know that before, Walter. Now I do. Thank you."

Freiherr's manner relaxed again. "Is Himmler's doctor's dog important?" he asked.

"Everything is important."

He had them put on their Gestapo costumes, which included the ubiquitous leather coats and black felt hats with brims pulled low. He asked them about their training and questioned them about the Gestapo and Reich Central Security in general. They responded with ease and precision. He interrogated them on their personal cover stories and was unable to trap them in errors. Then he checked their credentials, identification disks, Lugers and shoulder holsters.

"You guys will do just fine," Brooks complimented, then told them to repack all their gear. "Wear your GI clothes. You'll be assigned a room and will participate in physical training until we leave. But I don't want you talking to any of the men in the company. As far as you're concerned, they don't exist."

"When do we leave, Captain?" Walter asked.

"Soon. You two will be going in with me as part of the pilot team."

The frequent sound of arriving and departing aircraft could be heard in the distance as Brooks, his pathfinders and two platoons of the *Jäger Einheit* settled into the OSS staging compound Wednesday, March 7. They were a short drive from the Dijon air base.

Dan and his radioman wore their American uniforms. German uniforms and gear were to be dropped separately in canisters. The two agents, Hans Zimmer and Walter Freiherr, wore American uniforms without insignia. They would change into civilian clothes, topped by jump coveralls, just before take-off. But the mere presence of ninety fully uniformed and armed German troops debarking from a truck convoy stirred up more curiosity and comments than Brooks would have wanted.

Just before sundown, a courier plane from Paris brought Larry Dillard, the civilian Special Operations chief in London; Lieutenant Colonel Pearson, head of OSS's Paris office, who had been in on the initial planning; and Captain LeGrange, the mission's liaison officer, to the flying field, each with a briefcase chained to his wrist. Brooks waited for them beside the tarmac.

"Are we go?" he yelled above the roar of engines.

Dillard gestured to the twilight sky as the four men strode to a car and driver waiting for them. "Up to the weatherman," he shouted back.

It was clear and crisp, which made Dan optimistic about the forecast for the drop zone. Weather in the Austrian mountains was more critical than here. Data would be updated to flight time. If conditions in the Inn Valley changed for the worse they could even be recalled after takeoff.

The four men were driven the short distance to a Quonset hut in the OSS guarded isolation area. Inside the sparsely furnished shelter, LeGrange issued the operational funds in money belts and Brooks signed for them. Then LeGrange left. Despite his involvement with Knight's Cross all these months and his feelings of closeness to Dan and his men, he was excluded from knowing the drop zones, the area of operations and the true goals of the mission.

"What's the latest enemy strength there?" Brooks asked.

Lieutenant Colonel Pearson placed a German map on a table and, while Brooks studied it, Pearson pointed and elaborated: "The latest intelligence from Bluenose and other agents is marked. Disposition of enemy units, fortifications, underground factories. I've also brought you five copies of the same map unmarked, one for each of your platoons and one for your command post. They're what German units in the area would be using. Don't get caught with the marked map on you. It would be too incriminating. You know what that would lead to."

"Probably summary execution," Dan acknowledged, "if I couldn't think of a good reason for having it."

"Fortunately, the enemy buildup in the Redoubt is less than we had anticipated," Dillard interjected. "Your company should be able to blend right into the scenery and have room to maneuver. You're also heading into an area fertile in anti-Nazi sentiment among the Austrians."

"We'll need contact points and passwords for my agents to rendezvous with Bluenose."

"I've got them for you," Dillard said. "I must tell you, though, that Lieutenant Commander Cassidy in London..."

"My favorite nemesis," Brooks cracked.

Dillard looked askance at him for a moment. "He speaks equally well of you," he said with a quick smile. "One might think you two were on opposite sides of the war. Cassidy is worried that you and your people will blow the cover of any of his Secret Intelligence agents you tie up with."

Brooks bristled at that. "It's more likely to happen the other way around," he said, thinking of Karl Bergen. "What in hell is Cassidy doing, fighting a private war!"

"He's being cooperative, if reluctantly," Dillard conceded. "Though he keeps trying to pry information about Knight's Cross out of me."

"You haven't told him anything, have you, Larry?"

"Of course not," the Special Operations chief responded in an injured tone.

He gestured to Pearson to leave the Quonset hut. There were aspects of Knight's Cross that Pearson wasn't privy to and dialogue that he shouldn't hear, even though the idea of using the anti-Nazi German civilians and

POW's for an OSS mission had originated in his Paris branch. When they were alone, Dillard told Dan how to reach Karl Bergen and Willy Hupnagel and the passwords and countersigns that were to be used.

Then the SO chief stared at Brooks intently and spoke with rare fervor: "First and foremost, get Hitler. That's the gist of it. We've beaten around the bush before, but that's what we really want. Nothing you might do in your area of operations is as important as that one assignment."

"Do you know he'll be there?"

"No. But intelligence indicates he might be and we assume that he will. That's the primary reason that you and your unit are being dropped there."

"Do we sit on our duffs and wait for him to come down the road?" Dan challenged.

"Of course not," Dillard replied brusquely. "But we know your penchant for action, Captain. Don't sacrifice men and matériel or yourself just to get another crack at the German army or the SS. There are lots of other people taking care of that, but nobody's got the assignment you've got or the resources backing you up." He paused a moment, then added, less reprovingly. "I don't want to hogtie you. Just use discretion, Dan. That's all we're asking. Avoid fights that are there just because they're there. Keep your eye on the main prize."

"Agreed, sir," Brooks responded prudently.

"Have you determined how you're going to keep the identity of your captives secret from your own men, both the Americans and the Germans?"

"Mostly yes. However, there might be a few who will, of necessity, come face to face with them during the snatch itself," Brooks told him. "There is no way I can think of to prevent it. But if I can arrange it so that I'm the only one to know, I will. In any event, every one of us knows he must keep his mouth shut about what he sees and hears, until released from that vow by higher authorities—or suffer certain irreversible consequences."

The SO chief smiled at the euphemism. "Handle it as you see fit, Dan," he acceded. "We're going to have to play a lot of this by ear. Once we turn you loose, you're on your own, except for whatever aerial support and resupply you'll need."

"As few of my people as possible will be allowed to see or know who we grab."

"Yes, that part of it is good, and we're in agreement," Dillard acknowledged.

"The only way to be sure that nobody is left to talk," Dan quipped, "is to make sure we're all killed after the Nazi leaders we kidnap are in your hands. Maybe we can accommodate you by leaping off an Alpine peak together."

Yet even as he joked, watching the innocent face of his superior, Brooks felt a chill run up his spine. He remembered a conversation he'd had once with another OSS executive early in his career: *No agent was ever recruited to work for the agency without thought being given to the possibility of having to dispose of him, if necessary, after his usefulness had ended.*

"You're beginning to sound more German than the Germans, Dan," Dillard commented insouciantly.

Brooks stared at him searchingly another moment, then asked, in a normal voice, "What are the procedures for our extraction when the mission is accomplished?"

Dillard removed two one-time code pads from his briefcase and handed one to Dan. "These are the only two written in this cipher," he explained. "Our radiomen will not know what they're sending and receiving. You and I will encode and decode our own messages. When you've completed the mission, you're to radio me in code, '*The fox is bagged.*'"

"Is that only for Hitler?"

"For any of them. In fact for anyone you want us to pick up, no matter how high or low in the Nazi hierarchy. It's your decision, Dan. We'll have planes standing by. The moment an airfield near you is liberated and secured I'll send the planes in to bring you all out. Your captives are to be thoroughly disguised by then so that nobody can recognize them. None of us at headquarters—whether radio operators, cipher clerks or top brass, including me—will know who you've got until you're ready to let us have him. There will be no danger of another leak like the one with Blakely, Ann Jordan and the Russian major."

Dillard looked away now, nervous and embarrassed as he reached into his brief case. "There's one more thing," he said softly. "I have cyanide pills for you and your Americans. If you're captured and faced with torture."

"I was only joking about jumping off the Alps, Larry," Dan said lightly. "Keep the pills. We'll take our chances. All we need now is a favorable weather forecast for the Inn Valley tonight and we'll be on our way."

Dillard nodded gravely, went to the phone and rang the base meteorologist.

Thirteen

✠   Until this week in March, Major Mikhail Schepilov had thought he might never again be given anything important to do, that he might never again see combat, even if it was only to be thrown into battle as cannon fodder and be permitted a soldier's death. The fighting front was now nine hundred miles to the west of Moscow where he had been stationed these past three months. Soviet armies were on the verge of breaking through to Vienna and Berlin, meeting the Allied armies coming from the west and ending the war without him.

Ever since Colonel Lazovsky had sent him home from London in disgrace, Schepilov had been relegated to paper shuffling and translations, working in the secret compound of the GRU—the Registrational Directorate of the Field Staff of the Republic—located in a group of secret buildings adjacent to Khodinka Field, Moscow's main airport. There was no war here. Only plotting, planning and scheming.

During these three months he had been trying to convince his superiors to allow him to mount a *Spetsnaz* action to duplicate and shadow the American Knight's Cross operation he had told them about. It seemed nobody paid attention, nobody cared.

Then General Merkulov himself, chief of the GRU, had called him in. That in itself was unheard of in the chain of command of the bureaucratic and compartmented military intelligence service. It was a great honor.

"Do you understand what this will mean if you succeed, Schepilov?" the general had asked. Smoke from the cigarette dangling in the corner of his mouth had trailed up to his narrowed eyes.

"Yes, General," the major had answered, still standing stiffly at attention.

The broad-chested general in the high-necked, beribboned tunic, sitting behind his desk, had not had the courtesy to invite him to stand at ease. A peasant without manners, Schepilov had thought. But a very dangerous man to cross.

"The war will end," Schepilov had continued, trying to perceive what Merkulov wanted to hear. "We will have possession of the criminal responsible for the devastation of our nation and the suffering of our people. The Soviet Union will be able to exact vengeance, retribution and justice for all the world to see."

Listening closely, General Merkulov had let a length of ash from his cigarette drop onto his tunic before pulling the stub from his mouth and mashing it angrily in an ash tray. "That is right, Schepilov," he had agreed. "And, by following my orders, you will be a hero of the Soviet Union such as no other man before you. Your name will be remembered for all time. You may stand at ease now, Major."

"Yes, thank you, sir." Schepilov had let his muscles and bones untense, but he could never feel truly at ease before a man with Merkulov's power and reputation. "I will merely be doing my duty, sir."

Merkulov had smiled, a most unusual occurrence in itself. "And loving every moment of it, won't you, Schepilov? A much better assignment than playing Casanova in London. Yes?"

"It is one I prefer, sir."

"Do you realize what it will mean if you fail, Schepilov?"

The major had hesitated. There were so many possible answers to that question. He could not respond.

Merkulov had answered for him. "If you fail, your action may well provoke the next stage of our war against the imperialists, a consequence that we do not want yet. As far as we are concerned, not only will you be disowned and dishonored, but if you somehow manage to survive and return to Moscow without the subject of your exercise, I assure you, Schepilov, that despite all your heroics and accomplishments of the past you will not be given the opportunity for an easy and painless death."

Major Schepilov had been given a secure office of his own in which to work in one of the heavily guarded GRU buildings, plus top priority access to aides, communications, equipment and personnel. But now he had suddenly come up against a snag. The *Spetsnaz* staff company he wanted—parachutists, linguists and killers all—were in Hungary. They were temporarily attached to the 6th Guards Tank Army, which had helped to encircle Budapest, then crossed the Danube and was fighting its way closer to the Austrian border and ultimately Vienna, which was still 140 miles to their west. There were few parachute operations called for by the GRU these days and the unit had been sent into the line just to keep them in fighting trim.

These, however, were men specially trained to kidnap or assassinate high-ranking officials and military commanders of the enemy. Among them were officers and enlisted men fluent in German and English. They were experienced in the wearing of enemy uniforms and using enemy weapons and were prepared to disguise themselves with the uniforms and equipment of any of the Allied armies if it should become necessary.

A direct phone link to the front had been patched together for Major Schepilov. Orderlies were in the process of trying to locate Captain Viktor Astakhov for him, when the officer holding the line brought Schepilov up sharply with a hurriedly spoken report that the Germans were counterattacking strongly in that very sector. Schepilov was suddenly concerned that the men he wanted might no longer be available to him. He could actually hear the explosions of the German rounds and the answering fire of Russian batteries.

Then Viktor came on the line with his usual eruption of comradely and disrespectful profanity, his way of showing his delight at reestablishing contact with the man with whom he had experienced many battles, shared many perilous situations and years of professional and personal friendship.

"Are you coming to the rescue, Mikhail?" he taunted. "We are under fire. In Moscow you have forgotten what that sounds like."

"I hear, Viktor. I hear." Schepilov responded and he did indeed continue to hear the roars and blasts of the heavy guns of both sides, including now the distinctive whoosh of the "Stalin organ" rockets flying off their launchers toward the attacking Germans. Viktor was certainly in the middle of things and for just a moment Schepilov actually envied him. But then he began to speak openly on the wire in plain talk, in prearranged code words and phrases, shorthand communication that they each understood and had developed over the years. The enemy would never know what they were talking about if they tapped into the line.

"I have something more entertaining for you," Schepilov said. "Mother is having a birthday party. You are invited to bring your entire company, but certainly no less than fifty of your favorites. Half will be expected to sing for mother in German and half in English with American accents. You know mother's strange, bourgeois tastes. Your men must, of course, be prepared to dress appropriately for such a party. We will be able to help them with their change of attire, naturally."

"Yes, I understand you, Major, and I appreciate the invitation," said Captain Astakhov over the crackling phone line. "When are we expected?"

"Immediately. Air transport is standing by to fly into the airfield nearest your position and bring you home for the party. You are all probably overdue for leave anyway."

"Can you give me a few days until this new situation settles down?" Astakhov shouted into the telephone.

"No, Captain. This is an order directly from the top. You and your men must present yourselves at mother's party."

* * *

Karl Bergen had not yet grown to feel at home in the Third Reich or its Austrian Tyrol, nor had he permitted himself to relax his vigilance or slow his obsessive drive during these three months of building his networks of agents and gathering intelligence. In one of the crowded, noisy *Bierlokale* where they met from time to time in Innsbruck, he sat speaking uneasily with *Kriminalinspektor* Bernard Klung and Werner Weisskirch, the teacher who was an Underground leader. Bergen spoke so softly that they had to lean forward to hear him above the clamor around them.

"Remember, Klung," said Bergen, the imperious tone still in his voice despite his anxiety, "if you do everything now as I tell you, you will be placed in charge of the Kripo as soon as our army arrives in the Inn Valley."

"And when will that be, Herr Bergen?" the police inspector asked with a subtle note of derision in his voice. He had noticed for many weeks now how Bergen no longer addressed him with deference and respect. He was like the Nazis in his manner, domineering, offensive, giving orders as if he and not the people themselves should be in charge of their lives.

"It cannot be too much longer, *mein Herr*," Bergen answered. He had discerned the displeasure in the policeman's voice and had decided it was necessary to sound more humble.

But, overall, Bergen was frustrated and angry that he was still not sufficiently in charge of the Underground networks and partisan bands in the Inn Valley. In fact, though he had been feeding information to Cassidy's Secret Intelligence desk to support the Last Redoubt idea, he had begun to suspect that, aside from some token construction, a few crack units and a lot of talk, maybe there was no such reality as an *Alpenfestung* except in the minds and hearts of diehard Nazis and Allied intelligence.

Bergen looked around the tavern to see if anyone was paying any special attention to him and his companions. No one seemed to be. The room was filled with civilians and soldiers. The SS uniforms made Karl feel uncomfortable, but he worried it would be the Gestapo or some innocuous informant who could be his downfall. Willy Hupnagel hardly ever had to face what he did. He was with their radio, waiting for word about the arrival of Knight's Cross.

Bergen looked back at his companions and tried to sound as if he were really in command: "I want you each to inform me immediately of any unusual Allied agent activity. I'm expecting assistance very soon."

Weisskirch looked around carefully before speaking. "Will they bring guns, ammunition and explosives?"

"Yes, Werner, I assure you. These things will come."

Actually, Bergen had been signaled by Lieutenant Commander Cassidy that no arms and supplies would be dropped to him for partisan bands. The Secret Intelligence chief had implied it was not his decision, though he personally approved all Bluenose was trying to do. He had advised Karl to apply himself strictly to the collection of intelligence and warned that getting enmeshed in a guerrilla movement was dangerous and could blow their mission. Knight's Cross was on the way and would take care of operations.

Bergen still did not know what Knight's Cross consisted of, except for Captain Brooks and that Jewish sergeant he had hassled with at OSS headquarters. But how many more were there, how and where would they arrive?

"Be wary of any so-called 'agents' who approach you," Bergen cautioned. "Do not reveal anything to them until you have reported to me who they are and where they can be found."

Weisskirch drained the last of the beer from his stein and said, "You are not our commander, Karl. Though we welcome you here and appreciate all you have tried to do for us, please understand that we have our own chain of command and are not willing to defer to you."

Bergen smiled. "As it should be," he agreed reluctantly. "Please do me the courtesy, however, of letting me know if any of these strangers turn up."

Captain Brooks stood up as quickly as he could manage in the grasp of the deep snow. He released the harness, rolled up the parachute and slung his rucksack over his shoulders. Quickly, he turned a full circle all around him and peered through the shadowed moonscape to be certain there were no unwanted observers of the drop. Dragging the chute with him, he waded through the snow looking for the others and softly calling out their names. He picked out a darker blotch on the white landscape, heard Blumberg's muted response and joined him as he was rolling up his chute. Freddy spotted a canister which they opened immediately, hoping it would contain the snowshoes that would make the going easier, but they were disappointed.

The temperature was very cold but the wind was light and the deep snow created a mantle of quiet. The reality of being behind enemy lines again, hunter as well as hunted, stirred Brooks's blood and sharpened his senses. He took a flashlight with a red plastic covering from the map pocket of his jump coveralls. He blinked it a few times in the direction Hans and Walter should have landed and then heard a call. A few minutes later the two shadowy figures appeared, dragging their chutes.

"Freddy, stay put and hold the light," Brooks said. "We'll go looking for our stuff."

It was exhausting work to move through the waist deep snow searching for the other bundles and canisters. Blumberg blinked the light intermittently to keep them oriented. The bundles and canisters, including the vital radio and hand-cranked generator, were found at one side of the DZ where the mountain slope began. Some distance down the incline, the silhouetted dark mass of a patch of woods could be seen. For more than an hour they pulled bundles and canisters under cover there. By 0300 they were exhausted.

"Let's camp here for the rest of the night," Dan said.

Blumberg eyed him with a whimsical expression. "You want to tell me where I am, Captain, or is that still breaking security?"

Brooks stifled a laugh. He had never told them during the flight, just in case they had to turn back. "Welcome to Austria," he said. "You're in the Tyrol, a few miles from Innsbruck."

"*Österreich!*" Hans exclaimed. "*Wir sind in dem Tirol? Innsbruck?*"

"*Wir sind in Österreich. Nicht in Deutschland,*" Walter said in amazement. To Hans, he murmured, "Just think—Austria. We're home."

"How about the safe-landing signal, Captain?" Blumberg asked.

"It can wait till morning. First watch is mine," Brooks said. "One hour. Then you, Hans, then Walter. Freddy, you take the last. We want to be up before dawn."

Stabsfeldwebel Hartmann took careful aim and adjusted the rear V-sight of the *Gewehr 98* to 150 meters, but held his fire. The men with him stared uneasily down the slope at his target and seemed to hold their collective breaths waiting for him to squeeze the trigger.

Their part of the platoon had been moving down the slope with *Gefreiter* Paul Halle—the cover name and rank by which the captain was now known—to establish a new bivouac in a larger forested area when they had spotted the three men in Wehrmacht uniforms and overcoats in the distance.

"We can't let them get away!" *Gefreiter* Halle had said urgently, summoning Hartmann to his side. "But don't shoot them. Place a couple of rounds in the snow ahead of them just to stop them."

The trio were descending the mountain on foot, trudging slowly through the heavy snow. The *Jägers* had moved faster, some on skis, some on snowshoes. Equipment and supplies from the bundles and canisters had been repacked into smaller loads, the heaviest on sleds made from skis. Their American platoon leader, Sergeant Maurer, had stayed behind near the DZ with one squad, to serve as the reception committee for the next platoon that night.

Hartmann, the son of a game warden on a private hunting preserve in Bavaria, was an experienced hunter and woodsman, adept with many weapons and a crack shot. The *Gewehr 98* was more suited to the task than his Schmeisser and he had borrowed the rifle from one of his men. But it was not a good moment for shooting. The early morning was gray and cold and the wind whipped snow from the mountainside in powdery gusts that obscured vision.

Before the jump the night before, some of the *Soldaten* had thought

90

they were going to Berlin and were surprised to have come down into the deep snow of the Tyrol; but Hartmann had been glad to be back in his own element, and as exhilarated as his men had been for having actually made their first parachute jump.

Yet now, aiming his rifle, he felt as emotionally confused as he had thought he might feel the first time he would have to put Wehrmacht uniforms in his sights. He had ordered three of his men also to aim at the fleeing soldiers, but absolutely not to shoot. If necessary, they could box them in with rounds on either side. Praying that he would not inadvertently hit them, he squeezed off one round, then a second. The explosions reverberated through the high valley and the three distant soldiers flung themselves into the snow. There was no need for follow-up shots. They didn't move.

"Hans. Walter. Ski down there in a hurry and question them," *Gefreiter* Halle ordered the two civilian agents. "We'll cover you from here. Don't hurt them or scare them with your I.D.'s. Tell them you're a couple of guides from near the Brenner Pass, trying to escort this unit around the local mountains. Tell them we fired to halt them, not to hit them."

Hans and Walter kicked up powder as they schussed down the slope. The three soldiers were just picking themselves up and brushing the snow off their coats. The moment Walter saw them he recognized the haggard, hungry and bedraggled appearance. They varied in ages, one perhaps as young as seventeen, the second in his mid-twenties, the third at least fifty. They looked totally defenseless and frightened.

"Sorry about the shooting," Walter called out. "We only wanted to talk to you."

The older man spoke up. "You frightened us. We are lost."

Walter felt they were deserters, fearful of being taken back and executed, if not shot on sight. "Ach," he commiserated. "I thought maybe you could help us. What outfit are you with?"

He saw that their dark gray overcoats and winter field caps had no insignia. He could make out the outlines of places where emblems had been removed.

Quite far from here," the spokesman said. "We are on leave."

Walter looked at them slyly but not threateningly. "It's not much fun wandering the mountains in the cold and snow," he said. In a jocular tone, he added, "Is this the best you can do on leave, well paid soldiers in the Wehrmacht, defending the glorious Fatherland?" He hoped his remark held the proper note of irony to put them at ease and indicate he was a potential ally if they were indeed what he thought they were.

The soldier in his mid-twenties spit into the snow. "These days we're lucky to find enough to eat," he muttered.

"I haven't heard there was starvation in Austria," Hans challenged, trying to inject the right note of offended patriotism into his voice.

"Depends who you are," said the older soldier, "and where you're stationed. Who are those troops you're with? What are you doing here?"

"Hundred and sixth *Jäger* Regiment," Walter replied. "They're based near the Brenner Pass. This platoon was sent out to locate deserters and guerrillas. Stupid bastards. We talked ourselves into a job as their guides, and we know less then they do about this stretch of the mountains."

"You sound as if you are against them," ventured the old one.

"The sooner this war is over and we get rid of them, the better," Walter said brashly. Then, apologetically, "But forgive me, *Mein Herr*. You are their countrymen and I do not mean to insult you."

"Countrymen, shit!" muttered the second youngest. "We're Austrians just like you."

"So is Adolf Hitler," retorted Hans sourly. "That is no recommendation."

The three soldiers laughed.

Walter hoped he could build on the friendly mood. "It seems to me, just looking at you three, that you might be AWOL from your outfit and need help," he risked saying in his most affable manner.

"How do we know we can trust you?" demanded the angry one. "You're a real smooth talker."

"Shut up, you fool!" warned his older companion. He turned to Hans and Walter and implored, "Please excuse my comrade. He is tired, cold and hungry and doesn't realize what he is saying."

"I understand. That's all right," Walter said kindly. "But you still have not explained who you are, where you are stationed and what you are doing here." He nodded up the hill. "I have to give the sergeant up there some kind of reasonable answer. He ordered us to question you. Are you with the Innsbruck garrison or from somewhere else? Give me a unit and a place, please. Something that will make sense to those blockheads. We do not want them to hurt you."

"Our company was in reserve near Kufstein," the old one finally admitted. "We cannot go back."

He and his companions huddled together shivering, their backs to the cold blasts of air sweeping across the slope, faces averted from gusts of snow. Everyone had to speak loudly to be heard in the wind.

"Then you are looking for shelter and food?" Walter suggested.

"Yes."

"Where did you expect to find it? Surely not up here in the high mountains where no one lives," Walter said skeptically.

Shelter was one of the first things he and Hans had to find for the *Jäger Einheit*.

"No. Down below," the oldest one continued. He scrutinized Hans and Walter closely, then made his decision. "I will take a chance with you. I think you also are not happy with the situation in our country, that you are not Nazis."

"No, we are not," Hans declared angrily.

"Nor are we. We were drafted into the Wehrmacht against our wishes. For the greater glory of *der Führer* and the Third Reich," the old soldier said with bitter contempt. "There are farmers in the valley who are sympathetic to us. They have put us up in the past, but only for short periods. They too are afraid."

"That does not explain why you are wandering around up here on the mountain," Walter coaxed, trying not to make it sound like a challenge.

"Trying to find a hut that was open. Maybe food," the second youngest said. "Two nights ago and again last night we heard planes circling and saw lights blinking high up. I said to these two let's go up there... maybe there has been a clandestine parachute drop. Maybe the Americans have come. But then we saw the German soldiers and tried to get away."

Walter pondered whether to tell them the truth or let Brooks do it. These deserters could guide them to the friendly farmers they were talking about. There would be barns and outbuildings where sections of the company could stay, and perhaps food that could be bought to supplement their rations.

"Are there others in this area who feel as you do?" he asked.

"Many. But it is still dangerous for them to declare themselves or take action."

"How far are we from Innsbruck?" Hans asked.

The boy spoke for the first time. "Six kilometers."

"Solbad Hall?"

The boy smiled. "Just fall off the mountain and you will hit it."

Walter laughed. "You sound like a native."

"I am, *mein Herr.*"

"Do you know if any bigwigs have come here from Berlin lately?"

"We hear rumors. But I do not know."

"Come with us, please," Walter said gently, trying to make it sound like an invitation not an order. "Do not be afraid. We will help you. What you hoped to be true last night really is true. We are an American unit. We will protect you and we need your help."

Fourteen

✠   Helmut Jung stayed close behind the Wehrmacht deserter leading their scouting party down the mountainside. He'd hardly had a few hours to become used to the fact that he was again breathing the air of the Third Reich when "*Gefreiter* Paul Halle"—*Hauptmann* Brooks—had sent him out with Kurt von Hassell and the civilian agents, Martin Herz and Franz Scholl, who had trained with them at St. Germain.

Their assignment was to find secure places in the valley to base the *Soldaten* who were bivouacked in a forest up on the mountain and those who would jump in during the next two nights. Jung knew there was a second pair of agents who had come in with the pilot team, but the CO had been secretive about their function.

"While you're looking for quarters," he had told Herz and Scholl, "start building your network of informants. Party leaders and government officials will be headed this way from Berlin. Find out where they are."

"Hitler?" Martin Herz had joked.

He was a blond man of thirty-five with sunken cheeks, known more for his anti-military stance than his sense of humor. At St. Germain, Brooks had personally drilled him and Franz Scholl in procedures for collecting information, setting up networks with cutouts, establishing safe houses, live and dead letter drops, tailing and shaking a tail and other covert activities such as subverting enemy personnel and inducing defections.

"It's possible," the captain had replied offhandedly. "But whoever you locate, you're to report it only to me. You're not even to tell each other."

Hearing that, Jung and von Hassell had felt a new surge of excitement which they kept to themselves, as they had kept their earlier speculations about the true purpose of Knight's Cross.

Behind him now, Helmut heard Kurt, Martin and Franz chattering away happily as if they were tourists on holiday. Though Kurt had come to Innsbruck before the war to ski, he did not know the area well. Franz, however—a sinewy man of average height, in his late twenties, with a thin, well-tended, black mustache—was elated to be back in the Tyrol, which he kept telling his companions he knew well. Like his friend Martin, Franz was another civilian who held the army in low esteem, though Jung remembered he had trained as well as any of the *Jägers*, in addition to his instruction as an agent. He apparently recognized every mountain within their view.

Jung was glad for that, because he still did not fully trust Egon, their guide, one of the three Wehrmacht deserters who had been found on the mountain the day before. An Austrian of about twenty-five, he had a furtive look.

On a narrow dirt road below the snow line, they paused to remove their snowshoes and strap them to their backs, then proceeded northeast of Solbad Hall. The early afternoon sky was overcast, the air cold. The rutted mud of the road was dry and hard-packed. Before long, Jung saw a farm in the near distance. There was a large stucco main house, framed by heavy, protruding wood beams and topped by a steeply pitched shingle roof. There was also a barn and some outbuildings.

"That is Jupp Schmidler's place," Egon told him. "I have stayed there a couple of times and he has always been very kind to men in my situation. There is also a pretty daughter," he added with a grin. "But I advise you to keep your hands off. Schmidler is a big man and very protective of her. He is against the Nazis, but he is also against soldiers screwing around with Lisa."

Jung would not let Egon go to the door alone. The entire party, on the alert for instant treachery, moved with him. Jung himself knocked on the door. It was opened by a strikingly pretty young woman who drew the same reaction from each of the men who stared at her. They gaped and were tongue-tied for a moment. Her blond hair was shoulder length and tied back with a remnant of the same cloth that made up the patterned dirndl she wore. Her eyes were large and of a radiant blue color. She held in her hand a pot holder and towel, as if she had just been interrupted in the kitchen. But she looked startled at the sight of the tall, husky *Jäger* lieutenant staring down at her. Then she glanced beyond Jung, saw Egon and fear crept into her eyes.

"It's all right, Lisa," Egon called out. "These are friends."

The girl's gaze shifted to the two men in civilian clothes, then back to Jung and again to Egon, and the look of consternation grew stronger on her face.

"No, no. It is really all right," Egon said again. "I am not their prisoner. They are friends. We would like to speak to your father, please."

Kurt von Hassell looked at the girl with admiration. She reminded him of the pretty girls pictured in all the vacation brochures that had lured him to the Tyrol years before. Her skin was pale and clear. She radiated good health. If anything, a little too buxom for his taste. He still preferred the slender, elegant women of his class, who used to go to spas for their figures and to Paris for their clothes.

"He is out in the fields with his helpers," Lisa said nervously. "Preparing for the spring planting, God willing. Do you want me to get him?"

"No, no, *Fräulein*. Thank you," Jung said gently. "Please just direct us. We will find him. I assure you there is nothing to worry about."

Jung took the lead now and followed the girl's directions. They left her standing in the doorway, staring worriedly after them as the scouting party moved away from the farmhouse along wagon tracks and paths through the fields. Jung saw horses and carts and men working in the middle distance.

"The girl is frightened," von Hassell said, walking beside him.

"So am I," Jung admitted. "Who the hell knows who is loyal to whom these days. Look at us."

As the group approached the men working in the fields, a burly, bearded man walked toward them. Egon greeted him, "*Guten Tag, Herr Schmidler!*"

Schmidler stared at him as if uncertain whether to acknowledge that he had ever seen him before. Finally he said, grimly, "You are on leave again, *Soldat?*" Then he turned warily behind him to make certain that the two old farmhands a short distance away were working instead of eavesdropping on the conversation.

Egon smiled. "It is all right, *mein Herr*. These men are friends."

"What kind of friends?" Schmidler asked suspiciously. "Also looking for a handout and a place to stay? I am not a rich man, soldier. I suggest you take your friends elsewhere. Let the government pay for their meals and a bed."

Egon realized the man was still afraid to say anything that could be used against him. "These are men whom the authorities would arrest. Like me," said the deserter. "They need help."

Schmidler stared at Jung and von Hassell, who looked well fed, assured and intimidating in their *Jäger* uniforms. They appeared to be the quintessence of Nazi soldiery. The two civilians with them also did not look as if they were on the run. They, like the soldiers, seemed more like hunters than hunted.

"What kind of help? I am a farmer. I know nothing about military or political things."

Egon turned with a helpless look to Jung, who deferred to the civilian agents, as Brooks had instructed him to do in matters like this. They were trained for it and had worked with the Resistance in France.

Martin Herz stepped up close to the burly man and spoke very softly and courteously: "Please listen closely, *mein Herr*. We are not here to hurt you. Though we ask for help now, it is we who actually have risked much to come here to help *you*."

"What do you mean?" Schmidler asked, baffled.

There was no use carrying on with tact and guile anymore, Martin decided. "*Herr* Schmidler, we are the advance party of an American undercover unit," he said. "We need quarters and a base from which we can operate secretly against the Nazis.

Schmidler's eyes bulged out. "*Mein Gott!*"

"Our comrades are dressed in the uniforms of an Alpine infantry company," Herz continued. "Everything from equipment to *Soldbücher* are in perfect order. You yourself were fooled."

Schmidler scrutinized each closely again, asked for their identification papers which he examined with care, then finally spoke. "At last, *Gott sei dank*, we can do something against the damned Nazis," he said. His dark, bearded face was radiant.

Walter Freiherr and Hans Zimmer placed their valises next to the table they had selected and settled themselves importantly before the fireplace in the *Bierstube* of the *Gasthaus zum Hirschen*. Walter noticed immediately the looks of contempt and fear that appeared on the faces of the few patrons in the middle of the afternoon. That pleased him very much. In their black leather coats and black felt hats, which they removed almost ceremoniously before sitting down, they had been taken as they hoped for Gestapo agents. The dark gray conservative suits they wore had been appropriated by OSS in captured German cities and altered to fit them.

A girl was serving patrons at the bar. When she did not rush to their table, Hans was tempted to shout for service, but decided not to overdo the Gestapo act. Brooks had taught them that it was really best for an agent to do his work as inconspicuously as possible. The barmaid finally walked toward them nervously and asked if she might bring them something.

The slender, affable Walter, less intimidating in appearance than his companion, spoke to her with disarming courtesy. "You are too young and pretty to be the owner of this establishment, *Fräulein*," he said.

"My father is away in the Wehrmacht," Trude replied, hoping that simple statement would make a good impression on the two Gestapo men.

"Who is in charge?" Hans asked.

"My mother is here," Trude said uneasily.

"May we speak to her, please?" Walter asked pleasantly.

"I will see, *mein Herr*."

"Please do not worry," Walter tried to cheer her, smiling. "It is nothing bad, I assure you."

Anna came from the kitchen a few minutes later, nervously wiping her hands on a towel. Her daughter had prepared her for the sight of the two Gestapo men, but she was not more inclined to deal with them. Having entertained her American nephew in this very room, she had already committed a crime in the eyes of the authorities. Could they possibly know anything about Willy and his friend Karl?

Then she heard Walter Freiherr speak the words, "Wilhelm sends his regards." Her first thought was that they knew everything. Willy had told her that American operatives seeking to make contact with him or Karl would use that phrase. But surely not from the mouth of a Gestapo agent!

Anna remained speechless, staring at them boldly. "Wilhelm who?" she asked.

Walter realized that in this instance their deception was too good. He glanced around the room to be certain that no one could overhear him. "Please, dear lady," he whispered. "We are not who we appear to be. Wilhelm sends his regards."

Torn by doubt, Anna felt she had to let the exchange go to the next step and suffer the consequences if there were to be any. She prayed that she would have the strength to protect Willy and his comrade. Haltingly, she whispered, "Can I ever forget him."

"Thank you, Aunt Anna," Walter said reassuringly.

She drew back, surprised that he knew her name.

"Behave absolutely normally," Walter coached, "but speak softly. Can you reach Karl Bergen?"

Anna nodded. "I will try."

Hans Zimmer and Walter Freiherr, wearing Alpine clothes instead of their Gestapo costumes, took the funicular from its base close to the Inn River and rode up to the Hungerburg Plateau, then switched to the cable car that carried them 7,500 feet high into the snow mass on Hafelekar Mountain. Puffy white clouds scudded across an otherwise blue and sunny sky. Men and women, cheerful and robust, rode with them. There were skiers, mountaineers and tourists, a few in military uniforms. Walter marveled that, with the war about to burst into their country, they were still able to seek their pleasures in the mountains as if nothing else were important.

"This Karl Bergen must be a cautious man," Hans muttered to Walter in disgust. He leaned close so that their conversation could not be overheard. "Why does he put us to all this trouble? We could have met him in a *Bierlokal* or anywhere else in the city."

"Security, I suppose, as you say," Walter agreed, though he too had wondered why it was necessary to have such a difficult and time-consuming rendezvous.

When they debarked from the cable car at the mountain station and began to walk they felt a strong, cold wind blowing across the ridgelines and down through the open spaces. Brooks had given them a description of Karl Bergen. Bergen's message through Anna had been that he would approach them somewhere along the trail near the lodge at 1330 hours. Walter had asked Anna to convey a description of them, wearing Alpine clothes. It was important, he had made clear, that she not reveal they had the capacity to act as Gestapo agents.

They walked along the level trail a few minutes, stepping aside for cross-country skiers, when they spotted a solitary man in dark, heavy mountaineer's clothes walking toward them. He wore a cap with the earflaps pulled down, obscuring a good part of his head. He glanced toward them, murmured, "*Guten Tag!*" then looked away and kept walking.

Walter took a chance. "Karl," he called out.

The man stopped and turned. Walter could see the enlarged cheekbone, the uneven eye sockets out of which he stared at them challengingly. Walter gave his most ingratiating smile. "We were just talking about you." He spoke the recognition phrase, "Wilhelm sends his regards."

Bergen stared a few moments longer, sizing them up. Then scowling rather than returning a smile, he muttered, "Can I ever forget him."

Walter waited for him to say something more, but he didn't. He just continued to inspect them, on edge as if he would bolt or attack them any moment. "It is all right," Walter said. "We are who you think we are. Knight's Cross has landed."

"So what," Bergen snapped with disdain. "I have been here for three months, doing quite well without you. How many are you?"

Now it was Walter who became suspicious. He did not like this man at all. There was no joy at seeing them, no feeling of camaraderie. "Whether there are two of us or twenty thousand is none of your business," he answered. "You should know better than that, *Herr* Bergen."

Skiers and hikers passed around them while they talked in low voices, as if they were old friends who had met by chance on the mountain. "Where is your Captain Brooks?" Bergen insisted.

"Quite safe and secure, thank you," Walter replied pleasantly.

"What is it you want from me?" Karl demanded. "You endanger me just by asking for this meeting."

"Ask?" retorted Walter, incredulous. "What in hell do you think we're here for? The skiing?"

Hans Zimmer also now stared at Bergen angrily. He didn't understand the man's hostile attitude. "We are here representing Captain Brooks," he said brusquely. "You are ordered to convey intelligence to us and to help us contact the leaders of the Underground and partisan bands. In addition we must have news of any party leaders and high government officials who have crossed the border into the Inn Valley from Germany."

"I take my orders from Lieutenant Commander Cassidy of SI," Karl declared. "I don't work for Brooks or SO."

Walter smiled at Bergen, though he felt anger. "You are partly correct, *mein Herr*," he said soothingly. "But, please, let us not stand out here in the cold any longer. We will go into the lodge, drink something hot and have a nice, quiet chat."

"Your names?"

"Of course. Forgive me. I am Walter Freiherr. My companion is Hans Zimmer."

"Code names?"

"No. Quite real. Just as in your case, it was felt by our superiors that there was no need for additional complexity."

In the lodge, they sat at a table near the window overlooking the stupendous vistas of snow-covered peaks, forests and deep gorges. They were able to speak privately, without fear of being overheard by people at other tables, and they were careful to say nothing suspicious whenever the waiter came to serve them. They drank rich, creamy *Schlagobers*. The whipped cream topping was thick and quite real, though the coffee in them was ersatz. And they ate sausages and fried mushrooms. Walter insisted that the treat was on him and Karl ate then with even greater relish.

"Please believe me, *Herr* Bergen," Walter began cheerfully, then paused. "May I call you Karl?"

Bergen stopped chewing for a second, tipped his head and mumbled, "*Ja.*"

"Please believe me when I say that Special Operations and Secret Intelligence are working together in this operation," Walter continued. "In London you are thought of with the greatest admiration and respect. Captain Brooks himself has often said how he wished you were one of his personal agents instead of us *Dummköpfe.*"

Karl was taken aback by the compliment. In London, Brooks had seemed only superficially cordial. Cassidy had told him afterward that the captain was snooping into his records and that had angered him. If Brooks ever found out he had been a Nazi party member and Storm-trooper (until Hitler and his SS cronies had started, in 1934, to murder factions of the very same Brown Shirts, the *Sturmabteilung*, who had helped him to power) that surely would be the end of his career as an American agent and his dreams for a new rise to personal power.

"You must help us, Karl," Walter said urgently. "We will see that you get credit for everything you tell us."

Karl liked the deferential tone. He was appeased to hear that he had made a strong impression on London after all, though Cassidy hadn't provided him with all the air drops he had requested.

"Did you bring guns, ammunition, explosives?" Bergen demanded. "My people are waiting."

100

"Yes, we have brought everything," Walter answered truthfully. "All in good time, Karl."

Bergen forced a smile, unaware that on him it never looked right, and he shined it on Hans Zimmer and Walter Freiherr. To get ahead in this world—as that fool Hitler had done until he botched it and destroyed Germany—one had to take chances.

"To whom do you owe your basic loyalty?" he asked. "To Brooks? To OSS? To America? To Germany? Or perhaps to something else?"

"We are against Adolf Hitler and his Nazis," Hans replied, staring coldly at Bergen.

"To Brooks," Walter said, "and to the rebirth of a free and independent Austria and Germany."

"Which loyalty is more important to you?"

"They are of equal importance."

"Brooks is an American. I am a German. Give me the basic loyalty that you now give him and we will share in the rebirth of Germany and Austria. All elements of the Resistance here in the Inn Valley now come together in me. It is to me that they look for orders and supplies," Bergen lied. "When the war is over, we will use what we have done for the Allies here to build a political career for ourselves in the new Germany."

Bergen sounded like Hitler, thought Walter. He wondered how a man like that ever had managed to worm his way into OSS.

"I'm an Austrian," stated Hans forcefully. "I have no interest in Germany, except that they mind their own business about Austria. And I promise not to go to Germany, like Adolf Hitler did, to tell them *their* business."

"I have already made contacts at the highest levels of the anti-Nazi movement," Karl said fervently. Then, realizing that his voice had risen higher in volume than was prudent, he looked around to reassure himself again that their conversation could not be heard and that nobody in the lodge was paying special attention to them.

"That is wonderful, Karl," Walter said, leaning toward him and speaking in an enthusiastic undertone. "I'll think about what you've said. However, there is information you must give us before we leave."

"Let's stroll outside," Bergen said, standing up.

They stopped at an open place on the path and the usually stolid Hans allowed himself a few moments to gaze with pleasure northwest at the tiers of mountains that climbed to the white peak of the Zugspitze more than fifteen miles away and almost 10,000 feet high. As a boy he had skied up there.

"Before I tell you anything, or even listen to your questions, I must know the purpose of Knight's Cross," Bergen told them.

"Forgive me, Karl, but that is none of your business," Walter insisted.

"Then why should I reveal to you what I know?"

"Because, *Herr* Bergen," Hans spoke up harshly, "that is what you are paid to do. We were told about this ridiculous rivalry between SO and SI. It is bullshit. For us it doesn't exist. It is Nazi business."

Karl again forced one of his perverse smiles. "I was just testing you," he lied. "I will answer your questions now."

Fifteen

✠   Sergeant Robert Mangold stared through his field glasses at the building and grounds of the resort hotel. He had seen the sign—*Hotel Edelweiss*—at an intersection eight kilometers back down the narrow, winding road through the mountains between Wattens and Walchen. He and his patrol were screened now within a stand of firs on a snow-covered rise about 150 yards from the building.

The captain's orders had been, "Find the roads leading to hotels and ski resorts. I want you to mark on your map as many of these places as you can find tucked back up in the mountains off the main roads. They must still exist. The signs that advertised them in peacetime might still be intact."

Brooks had begun to send patrols through the Inn Valley even before the last of the *Jäger Einheit's* platoons—almost 190 men altogether—had been brought down from the mountain bivouac to their present dispersed quarters. Using Wehrmacht maps they had carried in with them, the patrols were ranging from the outskirts of Innsbruck on the west to as far east as Rattenberg, approximately fifty kilometers away, and probing north to south through an area approximately thirty kilometers deep.

The building Sergeant Mangold scrutinized was typical of the chalet style architecture of the Tyrol: a colorfully decorated white stucco exterior with steeply pitched, shingle roof and wood balconies. There were flower boxes on the balconies and outside the windows, waiting for spring to burst into color. It was a fine-looking hostelry, but not a huge building. Mangold estimated it might have fifteen or twenty rooms. He saw neither fortifications nor soldiers.

He passed the field glasses to *Stabsfeldwebel* Gunther Ferber. "It appears deserted," he said.

Mangold, wearing the insignia of an *Oberschütze*, a private first class, on his gray mountain trooper's uniform, felt very comfortable having Ferber as his nominal superior in case they came upon enemy troops and had to have a dialogue with them. There was never any doubt between them that it was the American who was in charge, as he had been during the three months they had trained together. Nor did Mangold feel any threat from the six *Soldaten* with them. Though there was still a certain reserve on his part toward German soldiers who looked like others he had killed on sight only months before when he had fought as an OSS agent with the partisans in Yugoslavia, he trusted these men completely. The patrol already had passed German units marching along the road and there had been only the usual shouts of greeting and waving of hands. Nobody had challenged them.

"There is somebody coming around the side of the building," Ferber said softly as he continued to stare through the glasses.

"A soldier?" Mangold asked.

"No. A civilian. An old man with a shovel in his hand. Maybe it is a caretaker."

He extended the glasses to Mangold who reexamined the scene through them. "Let's go down there and talk to him," he said. "Remember, all of you, we are searching for deserters."

For days, Kurt von Hassell had been watching in fascination as the situation map on the wall of Jupp Schmidler's hayloft sprouted with new locations, notes and a symbol table marked on the clear acetate overlay. The symbols indicated vital road and rail crossings, potential ambush sites, observed enemy installations and troop deployments, and the locations of isolated mountain chalets, hotels and resorts.

Two platoons—approximately ninety men—were billeted in Schmidler's barn and outbuildings. A third platoon was dispersed three kilometers east to a farm owned by a friend of Schmidler, and the fourth was quartered in a bomb-damaged warehouse less than a kilometer from there. While out patrolling, the men studied the terrain carefully. There were farmlands on both sides of the main east-west road. On the north the fields climbed slopes to steep, high forests, tiers of granite and towering mountains of snow; south of the road the fields extended to the dark, narrow Inn River. Here and there were access roads to chalets of farm families and roads climbing into the mountains to secluded hotels and ski resorts where Nazi leaders might go to ground.

There were also clear views of the railway on this side of the river. Trains loaded with troops and war matériel had been observed on the way to Innsbruck, from where they would go south through the Brenner Pass to the Nazi army in Italy. Across the river the patterns of terrain repeated, rising again to lofty heights that confined the valley in its deep gorge.

In the flexible table of organization of the *Jäger Einheit*, Kurt von Hassell had fallen into the function of being *Oberleutnant* Jung's orderly and the company runner. He found it amusing and ironical to remember that Corporal Adolf Hitler also had served as a runner in the First World War. Captain Brooks, Lieutenant Becker and *Oberleutnant* Jung used Kurt to convey messages to the platoon sergeants and to carry out minor administrative duties.

The platoons were operating under field conditions. Latrines had been dug in a clump of trees on Schmidler's property. Crude washing and showering facilities had been set up nearby; water was piped from the farm's wells and hauled from the river. Outdoor fire pits were used for cooking. However, men on rotating KP found it desirable to make trips to the farmhouse on the pretext of borrowing large cauldrons but actually to fill their eyes with Schmidler's beautiful daughter Lisa, who was delighted to have so many men flirting with her, Kurt among them. Brooks had warned them to keep hands off.

Schmidler and his farmer neighbors had agreed to supplement the company's rations when necessary and were helping to build a network of Underground contacts. If questioned about the troops billeted at their farms, they were to reply that the Wehrmacht had temporarily requisitioned the barns and outbuildings and there had been no way they could refuse.

By Saturday afternoon, March 17—ten days after Brooks and his pilot team had jumped in—all the patrols were back from their first probings of the Inn Valley and had been debriefed by Brooks, Lieutenant Becker and *Oberleutnant* Jung. Von Hassell, in his role as aide and sidekick to Jung, had been privy to many of the debriefings. Only the two agents, Walter Freiherr and Hans Zimmer, had not returned, and Kurt could tell that the captain was worried.

The patrols had told a very interested Brooks about secluded chalets and vacation resorts in the mountains, presently unoccupied. Sergeant Mangold's patrol, for example, had returned with news of a hotel that Brooks thought would bear further surveillance. The Hotel Edelweiss was on the other side of the Inn River, in the mountains between Wattens and Walchen, about fifteen kilometers from Schmidler's farm.

"There was only a caretaker there, but he was beginning to get the place in shape for occupancy," Mangold had reported. "He didn't know who was coming. There was just the old guy and he was griping about having to do all the work himself. He said he'd been told to start preparing the place for important guests and he'd have help in a few days. I told him we were looking for deserters and he allowed us access to the building and showed us around."

"How big a place is it?" Brooks had asked.

"Fifteen good-sized bedrooms. Most with private baths," Mangold had elaborated. "Public rooms downstairs off the lobby...a lounge, a dining room and kitchen and a separate bar. The guy even poured us all a schnapps, he was so glad to have company. I told him we'd be coming around again while hunting for deserters. He said he hadn't seen any up there, but we'd be welcome anytime."

Mangold, *Stabsfeldwebel* Ferber and their patrol had pooled their recollections of the layout of the building and grounds and had made a few diagrams for the captain. Then they had returned to their billet at the second farm.

Despite his Wehrmacht training and years in combat, Kurt had never considered himself a military man. It was a revelation for him to observe how "Corporal Halle" put into operation the many separate aspects of their mission. The parts were coalescing with a slow, careful and what seemed inexorable pace.

But toward what special goal, Kurt still could not be certain, though he continued to have the same suspicion he and Jung had talked about privately, that they were going after *die grossen Kanonen*, maybe Hitler himself. Did Brooks really expect *der Führer* to fall into their hands here in Austria?

Why not? Kurt reasoned. It was probably the most remote and secure place left for him to hide in the shrinking Third Reich, and Hitler was by birth an Austrian. Not that he would want to stay. There would be plans for a getaway made in advance, an escape route organized, sanctuaries in faraway parts of the world already prepared by accomplices and sympathizers, and vast sums of money and matériel made available for the scheme.

Kurt thought that if he could reason this out for himself, then surely Hitler could too, and so could the Allied commanders who had sent Brooks and the Knight's Cross mission into action. He wanted very much to do something important before the war was over, something extraordinary to finish off the Nazis, wipe the shame of them from his heart and help to liberate and rebuild Germany. He craved action now, which he had never wanted before. He hoped that Brooks would lead them into it.

Walter Freiherr worried that they might have overdone it when he saw the look of fear and hatred appear on *Kriminalinspektor* Bernard Klung's face. He hadn't expected two men in Gestapo attire, but he quickly covered his fright and waited for them to say something.

"There is much snow on the Zugspitze," Hans Zimmer recited.

The police inspector stared at him. Then, assuming that his prearranged countersign could hardly be deemed incriminating by the Gestapo, he acknowledged, "There always is at this time of the year." Still unwilling to commit himself on the basis of so banal an exchange, he added, "I don't usually have much business with the Gestapo. This is an unexpected visit."

Walter put his finger to his mouth, gestured to his ears and waved his hand around the room.

"There are no secret microphones," Klung assured him. "In any event, why should agents of the Gestapo have anything to fear from the Austrian police?"

"Our friend Karl Bergen has talked to you?" Walter said. There was just the slightest uncertainty in his voice, despite the recognition sign and countersign that had passed between them.

"Yes. He gave me your names and said you would call on me, but he said nothing about the Gestapo."

"It is our wish that he continue to know nothing about this little subterfuge of ours."

"He also told me to be wary of you."

"These days everybody must be wary of everybody else," Walter said gravely. "However, we are not what we appear to be. Did Bergen tell you whom we represent?"

"Yes, but that is a standard Gestapo trick, gentlemen." Klung studied them as if they were suspects in a crime. Then, aware that he would have been compromised already by his association with Bergen, he made his decision. "I'll take a chance with you, as I did with Karl," he said. "Though, so far, it has not been a fruitful arrangement. He has not delivered on certain promises he made in the beginning."

"May I ask what?" Walter inquired benignly.

"Arms, ammunition and explosives for partisan bands."

"We promise nothing," Hans spoke up, "except that we are who we tell you we are. Our reason for being here is to collect information, not deliver guns and supplies to the Resistance. That *may* result from the intelligence we gather, but it is someone else's function."

The inspector looked at them thoughtfully. "Is it possible to be put in touch with this 'someone else'?"

"It is possible," Walter told him. "You must be aware, though, that our armies are fighting their way closer to where we are now. It will not be long, *Herr* Klung. A month or two at most and it will all be over. I am sure you would wish to make your true feelings known before then and reap the rewards later of whatever help you can give us now."

Klung smiled. "That is what *Herr* Bergen tells me, except that he says it can only be done through him."

"That is not true," Hans insisted.

Klung raised a finger to his mouth, stood up and walked to his door. He opened it and looked up and down the hallway, then closed the door and returned to his desk. "If you two can get in here as Gestapo men, God knows what else might be going on in this building," he said. "Fortunately there has never been any suspicion regarding me, but..." He left the sentence unfinished. "What, exactly, do you want of me?" he asked.

"We have a few questions," Walter said, "but first a practical matter. We need a car. Not an official one. Something inconspicuous."

"It can be done," Klung agreed readily. "We have in our garage a number of vehicles impounded for various reasons. I will arrange for you to drive away in one."

"That's very good of you, *Herr Kriminalinspektor*," Hans acknowledged, feeling better about the cop.

But Klung was unwilling to linger over pleasantries. "Quickly now. What is it you want to know?" he rushed on. "Your presence here is neither desirable nor comfortable for me. If anyone were to barge in here, perhaps even the Gestapo, I don't think your identifications, as good as they might be, would hold up in the Reich Central Security Office. Hereafter, I would prefer that we meet elsewhere."

Walter agreed, then asked the inspector pointedly, "Do you have any information about high Nazi party leaders or government officials from Germany who have recently come into the Tyrol or are expected soon?"

"I don't believe any of the top leaders are here now, but I was alerted recently that Heinrich Himmler and staff will be coming to the Inn Valley soon."

"Will you know when?" Walter asked.

"Yes. I will keep you informed."

"Any others?"

"Kaltenbrunner comes to the Tyrol often. Supposedly, he . . ."

"Chief of the Reich Central Security Office?" Walter interrupted.

"Yes. He is overall head of security services, including Kripo and Gestapo."

"But Heinrich Müller runs the Gestapo, doesn't he? And they are both under the command of *Reichsführer* Heinrich Himmler, leader of the SS."

The police inspector looked at him with approval. "I see you have done your homework well," he complimented. "Kaltenbrunner comes supposedly in regard to the building of the *Alpenfestung*. He is very much in favor of it."

"Is there such a thing?" Hans asked. "A Last Redoubt?"

"There are small indications of it, but nothing on the vast scale that would be required to make it effective. I don't think the Germans have the men or resources anymore to undertake such a task. Also, I pray to God that they will not try it. I have no wish to see this old and beautiful city I love destroyed in a Nazi *Götterdämmerung*."

"And where is Göring these days?"

"Take your pick. Berlin. Karinhall. Or even withdrawn already to his stronghold in the Obersalzburg, not far from Hitler's retreat at Berchtesgaden. Goebbels still broadcasts from Berlin."

"*Der Führer*?" Hans asked in an offhanded way, as if it were of minor importance.

"Only rumors. One says he is holed up in the *Reichskanzlei* directing what's left of his armies from there. Another story says he is at OKW headquarters with the general staff in the west or OKH headquarters with the general staff in the east. And there is always the possibility that he is already in the Obersalzburg with the others, defended by fifteen to twenty-five divisions which may or may not be a figment of somebody's imagination. But all of whom, if they are real and are not slaughtered beforehand, might very well fall back upon Innsbruck and the Tyrol. It is this that we must prevent," Klung declared fervently. "How can I contact you, if it is necessary?"

"You can't. We will have to contact you."

"Not even through Bergen?"

"No," Walter told him. "But do not be concerned. We will be in touch with you by phone in two days and will arrange a way for you to contact us quickly. Please do not have one of your cops follow the car you lend us. It will make 'somebody else' very nervous."

$\mathfrak{Sixteen}$

✠   Brooks felt a new sense of urgency now while he waited for Hans and Walter to bring in the intelligence that would guide him to Hitler and the Nazi leaders. He had expected his ersatz Gestapo agents to be out two or three days; they'd been gone five. He and Lieutenant Becker stood in front of the situation map in Schmidler's barn loft, working up plans for secondary objectives.

"This area south of Innsbruck on the way to the Brenner Pass is ripe for picking," the exec said. "I could take one platoon down there and..."

Brooks interrupted, shaking his head. "I can't let you go anywhere yet, Rudy. I need you here at the command post when I'm away."

He had finally divulged to Becker the most secret aspects of Knight's Cross. His exec understood why he had been operating very cautiously, moving his men around like chess pieces probing a way to the king.

"Whoever goes south," Becker continued, "should take Egon or one of his pals along to round up more deserters, then try to tie up with the guerrillas who are supposed to be down there. Get them to start blowing up tracks and trains near the pass. Maybe block it off altogether."

Brooks agreed readily. Their patrols had observed loaded trains still moving south from Germany to Innsbruck, then through the pass into Italy, despite earlier air raids on the marshalling yards. No enemy units had been spotted guarding tracks. On vehicle and pedestrian roads, traffic was mainly small, scattered troop and supply convoys. Some might have been SS, but it was hard to tell because in the field they wore the same uniforms as the Wehrmacht. None of the *Jäger* patrols had been challenged.

"If enemy units are sent south in response to guerrilla actions," Dan concurred, "it would take the heat off us up here when we start operating."

His eagerness to go after secondary targets was impelled by the swift progress of the war elsewhere. They had been receiving news each night on Armed Forces Radio Network and BBC. On the day he had jumped in, units of U.S. 1st Army in Germany had captured a bridge at Remagen and crossed the Rhine. Third and 7th Armies were fighting to get across at points further south and would likely be east of the Rhine in a matter of days. He expected divisions of the 7th to turn south into Bavaria and then force their way through the mountain passes into the Austrian Tyrol. He intended to make the way into the Inn Valley easier for them by creating havoc behind German lines.

Yet, if there was to be any success in his primary mission, it had to be accomplished before the American army reached Innsbruck. The very presence of U.S. units would be a hindrance to the search for Hitler and his cohorts. OSS didn't want the kidnappings to be a public event. He would have one hell of a time explaining to any regular army mind what he and his eight American cadre were doing there in German uniforms leading a company of enemy soldiers—provided they didn't get wiped out by friendly elements in an unexpected initial contact.

"Let's dispatch only a small team south," Brooks told his exec. "We don't want to dilute our force. We'll send Sergeant Schafer and six of the men who fought with the French maquis. And Sergeant Fischbein with a radio for scheduled communications. We can still retain the ability to assemble rapidly for an assault in force on a Nazi refuge."

Darkness fell and the evening meal had been eaten. In the middle of Brooks's briefing of Schafer and his team, a warning came over the Command Post walkie-talkie from one of the outlying sentries: "Vehicle coming!"

Dan snapped a command and the men dispersed. Becker, Jung and von Hassell sped down the ladder and through the barn and outbuildings relaying his orders. Lights were turned off and the two platoons took up prearranged defensive positions inside and out. Brooks grabbed his Schmeisser and the walkie-talkie, swept aside the tarp covering the loft opening and saw the headlights of the vehicle already moving closer on the dirt access road. The fact that it was only one small car lessened his concern.

He called over his shoulder, "Jung, go out there and deal with it."

He watched as Jung and von Hassell, their weapons at the ready, approached the car—an old Volkswagen—as it braked to a stop in the barnyard. Moments later, with great relief, Brooks made out the figures of Hans Zimmer and Walter Freiherr, dressed in their Alpine clothes, stepping from the car.

Their debriefing proved enlightening. They had done more than Brooks expected and were quite pleased with themselves. With Lieutenant Becker present, the four sat on benches and bales of hay in a corner of the loft while the agents divulged details with relish. Their news about the expected arrival of Himmler was encouraging.

"Klung will pass the word to us," Walter said confidently.

"Anybody else of importance?" Brooks asked with quickening excitement.

Walter told him what the policeman had said about the frequent visits of the chief of Reich Central Security, Ernst Kaltenbrunner, and his personal interest in the *Alpenfestung*.

"Have you seen evidence of it?"

"No. The inspector and Bergen too have seen very little in the way of heavy construction and large troop concentrations, though I think Karl would like to make it a thing of great importance."

"Maybe he already has," Hans suggested. "Maybe Karl is the source of all the intelligence regarding it."

"No, there was information about the Last Redoubt before Bluenose jumped in," Dan told them. "What did you think of Bergen personally?"

"He does not instill immediate confidence and friendliness," Walter replied. "I can't quite put my finger on it, but I don't trust him completely. The odd thing is that Inspector Klung also gave that opinion. He too thinks there is something not quite right with Bergen. To us, Karl was antagonistic one minute and then tried to butter us up the next."

"There was some funny business about loyalty," Hans spoke up.

He related how Bergen wanted them to switch primary loyalties to him and some private, unexplained agenda he had for Germany after the war, though he had never specified what would be expected of them to fulfill this new fealty.

"He told us that all elements of the Resistance in the Inn Valley looked to him for orders and supplies," Hans continued, shaking his head, "and that he had exclusive control. He wanted guns, ammunition and explosives. He said he had bands of partisans waiting for the stuff so they could go into action."

"That son of a bitch is not supposed to butt into operations," Brooks said angrily. He was thinking of Cassidy as well as Bergen.

"Well, sir, I don't think you ought to worry about it," Hans ventured. "I think the man's full of shit. Inspector Klung doesn't look to him for leadership and I doubt whether anybody else in the Resistance does either. I think Bergen wants everybody to believe he's the top man, then maybe it will happen."

"Did you hear anything about Hitler?" Dan asked nonchalantly.

"Only rumors. He could be anywhere between Berlin, the Russian front and Berchtesgaden."

Brooks already had given thought to switching the focus to Berchtesgaden, Hitler's mountain stronghold 120 kilometers to the northeast. He had no orders to extend his operations that far, but he would go after Hitler there, too, he vowed, if he knew he was there. More immediately, with another extravagant idea occurring to him, he turned his attention back to getting Sergeant Schafer's team on the road.

"What's the driving situation like?" he asked the agents. "Any road-blocks and check points?"

"No. It's been easier getting around than I thought it would be," Walter told him. "We've even got a couple of jerry cans of extra fuel from the Kripo garage. If we're ever stopped we've got our Gestapo I.D.'s and all the proper papers from Klung for the car."

Brooks ordered the Volkswagen into service as a troop carrier. Taking turns during the next couple of hours, Hans and Walter drove Schafer's team through Innsbruck and across the river south of the city. En route, Hans picked up Sergeant Fischbein and a radio at the warehouse billet. They left him, Schafer, Egon and six *Soldaten* close to Igls to make camp in the woods and begin their search for deserters and guerrillas next day as they hiked south toward the Brenner Pass.

At his headquarters in Moscow, Major Mikhail Schepilov and Captain Victor Astakhov studied the latest map they had been able to obtain of the Inn Valley. It was marked with enemy installations and troop deployment reported by underground Communist Party members in Austria whose names were in the files of the Ministry of State Security, the NKGB.

The NKGB was fiercely jealous and unbelievably narrow-minded regarding its resources. They looked upon the Soviet military intelligence organization for which Schepilov worked, the GRU—the Registrational Directorate of the Field Staff of the Republic—as if it were an enemy rather than an agency fighting for the same cause. It had been extremely difficult for Schepilov to obtain the names and find out how to make contact with the Austrians. But he had succeeded. The feat finally had been accomplished through the highest levels of authority, perhaps even with Comrade Stalin himself issuing the orders. Schepilov felt a great sense of pride that the importance of his assignment had forced such a resolution.

Yet, why not? It had been he who had uncovered the information about the American Knight's Cross operation and the names of the Special Operations Chief, Dillard; the OSS European chief, Hoose; the planning officer, Blakely; and, most important, the Knight's Cross leader, Brooks. Plus their operational sector in the Austrian Tyrol and their main objective: to capture high ranking Nazis, maybe Adolf Hitler himself.

The voice of Captain Astakhov interrupted his musing. "Have you selected the drop zone for the agents yet, Major?"

"Yes. Though I will consider any arguments you might make for other sites, Viktor. Are your two teams ready?"

"Yes, ready and eager to go. Two men in each team, one of them a radio operator. They will wear Alpine clothing and concealed weapons for the jump. Radio packs, rations, changes of clothing, skis and other mountain gear will be dropped with them in canisters. Each is a combat-experienced *Spetsnaz* operative, fluent in German."

Schepilov's mind drifted from the task at hand. He could not escape from the vivid images of those delightful nights of intimate duties in London when he had enticed the Knight's Cross intelligence from Ann Jordan. He felt a stirring in his loins. Drawing the relevant bits from Ann had been a long, slow adventure in lovemaking. Before the unfortunate finale she had been marvelous in bed. Schepilov had conjured up her face and body often these last three months. There had been no opportunity for women since he had been ordered back to Moscow.

He had never told Captain Astakhov or anybody else he worked with about his duties in London or about Ann Jordan. He would have been ashamed. There were only a few in the GRU who knew about it because it was their job to know these things. Fortunately, it was also part of their jobs to keep their mouths shut. No one, in any event, had dared to ridicule him about it, except for that one slightly amused comment by General Merkulov the day the GRU chief had finally acceded to his requests and directed him to mount the operation to shadow Knight's Cross.

"One pair of agents will parachute here, about twenty-five kilometers southwest of Innsbruck," said Schepilov, tapping the map. "*Lüsener Ferner*. It is high in the mountains, but there seems to be a wide, level snowfield there. They can descend to Oberperfuss and Innsbruck from there. The second pair should go in here, east and north of Innsbruck, beyond Schwaz. A drop zone at much lower altitude in the Ziller Valley."

Schepilov had wanted to go himself as one of the first agents, to stalk both the Nazi quarry and the Americans, making contacts among the populace and planning the next steps of the operation in accurate detail. But Victor had pointed out how foolhardy that would be, to risk losing the commander of the operation in its earliest stage.

"I like this idea, Mikhail," Astakhov said now. "It will give us separate intelligence on two very different types of drop zones for the operational group when we go in."

"Yes. Each team will have room to range, independent of the other. There is also this business about a so-called National Redoubt," Schepilov cited. "A refuge where Nazi fanatics will make their last stand. If it is there, our agents will find it."

There was still the unresolved matter of how to deal with the Americans if contact could not be avoided. Schepilov and his superiors justified their intrusion into an American operations zone with the rationalization that no one had a better right to capture the highest Nazi oppressors than the Soviet Union, the nation that had suffered the most.

"Let us assume that all goes well, Mikhail, and one or more of our quarry is sighted," Captain Astakhov speculated. "What then?"

"Then you will not be able to hold me back, Viktor. You and I will take in a group of..."

"How large?"

114

"Not many. An overstrength squad in American uniforms. Let us say fifteen of your best men who speak English. Our cover will be that we are a U.S. 7th Army long-range reconnaissance patrol. That small a unit can disappear into the scenery. A larger group would be hard to pass off as merely a patrol."

"It seems hardly enough!" Astakhov complained. "You said Knight's Cross has almost two hundred."

"One hundred and eighty-nine at full strength, according to Captain Brooks's projection of the Table of Organization when he was planning the unit. Most of them German defectors."

"How do you know these things, Mikhail?"

The major smiled confidently. "I had a superb briefing."

There was a blizzard the first day of spring and Sergeant Walter Schafer, leading Knight's Cross's long-range patrol south of Innsbruck toward the Brenner Pass, took his men down out of the high mountains and woods east of Steinach where they'd been looking for deserters and guerrillas to tie up with. He found shelter for his men in the late afternoon by breaking into a railroad shed beside a track embankment outside the town. They were about twenty-two kilometers south of Innsbruck and somewhat east of the Brenner Road.

Schafer's short, wiry frame still shivered from the cold. The storm had brought him abruptly back to reality. During these past few days, while futilely searching the Alpine forest for deserters and guerrillas, he had become enamored of the peace and quiet of the evergreen woods and the majesty of the mountains and had nearly drifted into a mood of contentment. Nobody had shot at them and the war had almost left his mind. The terrain and trees reminded him of wooded mountains in his native Pennsylvania.

Sergeant Fischbein made radio contact with the command post forty kilometers northeast of them and they were, at last, given instructions for a potential guerrilla rendezvous the next morning. It had been arranged through their civilian agents' growing network in the Austrian Underground.

The contact was a boy who led them on a foot trail back up into the mountains to a high valley and an isolated farm.

"Wait here for me, please," he told Schafer when they came within sight of the cluster of outbuildings, barn and main house.

From the forest, the sergeant watched the youth disappear into one of the outbuildings, then reappear a few minutes later and wave to him. Schafer ordered Egon and another man to accompany him as far as the entrance, weapons ready. "Take up positions on either side of the doorway where you can see the interior and hear what's being said," he told them. "If there's any sign of treachery, move in shooting."

They left Fischbein and the rest of the team in the woods and walked to where the boy was waiting. Schafer looped his thumb under the sling of his Schmeisser so he could bring it around quickly into firing position.

"Come in, please," said the youth. "They are expecting you."

Schafer and the guide entered a storage building that had been remade into a bunkhouse with sleeping tiers along the walls. Egon and the *Soldat* positioned themselves outside as instructed. In the room, ten men of varying ages, wearing ski clothes, stared at Schafer's *Jäger* uniform with hard eyes. The guide introduced the leader, an older man named Seppl. He was a powerful-looking fellow with broad shoulders.

"Who are you?" he demanded.

Schafer thought there was no point in dilly-dallying. If he had been tricked, his life was already lost. "I'm with a company of defectors operating under American command," he said. "My patrol was sent to this area to make contact with deserters and guerrillas."

Seppl moved closer to him, glowering. The man was more than a head higher and a lot wider than Schafer, but he didn't intimidate him. "To what purpose?" Seppl prodded.

"We want men willing to start sabotaging the railroad and harassing the Nazis."

"Partisans?"

"Yes. Real ones. Fighters." Schafer looked around the room at the men still staring at him with angry suspicion. "Not a bunch of guys who just hide out in the hills until the war is over."

Seppl eyed him uncertainly, not sure if he had been insulted. "We need guns, ammunition, explosives. All we have is old hunting rifles and shotguns," he said angrily.

"For men who are sincere, who show courage and ability, supply drops can be arranged."

"How do I know you are not here to trick us?" Seppl demanded. "From what I see, you are a German private in a *Jäger* unit."

"Shit, fellow," Schafer said. "I don't have time for games. You either want our help or you don't. If you don't, I'm moving on."

Seppl softened somewhat. "Tell me, please, who you are. It doesn't make sense, your suddenly appearing here in German uniform."

"My radioman and I are Americans."

"Your German is too good for that," Seppl argued.

"I'll take that as a compliment," Schafer said. "Wait until you hear the rest of them. The bulk of our force are former soldiers in the Wehrmacht."

"What is your name?"

"Walter Schafer."

"Very well, Mr. American Schafer," Seppl said. "What can you do for us?"

Seventeen

✠   Summoned hurriedly to a *Bierstube* meeting by *Kriminalinspektor* Bernard Klung, Karl Bergen looked forward to receiving important new intelligence which his radioman would dispatch to Cassidy in London within hours. Instead, the police inspector greeted Karl angrily and stared at him as if he were guilty of some terrible crime. Seated at the table with Klung, wearing the same wrathful expression, was the Underground leader, Werner Weisskirch, who had arranged the first contact between Bergen and the anti-Nazi cop many weeks earlier.

Klung gazed around quickly to make certain they were isolated from others in the room, then he leaned close to Karl and demanded, "Are you responsible for what happened on the railroad near Steinach last night?"

Bergen opened his mouth to defend himself, but Klung was not finished.

"You must never again conduct such an operation without permission," the inspector commanded.

"I don't know what you're talking about, Bernard," Karl whispered back sharply.

"Tracks were blown up. A German munitions train was derailed. Two Austrian National Railways men were killed. Others were injured, including personnel in the military guard detail."

Knight's Cross! thought Bergen. He forced himself to keep an impassive face, but his mind raced, trying to figure out the best position to take—other than the truth.

Werner Weisskirch leaned closer and spoke angrily. "The fireman on the locomotive was ours. He never had a chance."

Bergen looked properly sympathetic and shook his head. If he let them believe he had foreknowledge of the incident or lied that he had participated, they would find him culpable for what they obviously considered bad. If he told them he knew absolutely nothing, they would consider him a fool, inadequate for his job. Either way he would lose. He had to find a middle ground that shifted blame but at the same time led them to believe that there was new power in the Resistance because of him.

"They are moving faster than I expected," he said.

"Who is?" demanded Werner.

"Be quiet now," Klung said quickly.

Bergen saw the waitress approaching their table. He picked up the menu and studied it.

"*Mein herr?*" the waitress asked.

"*Leberknödlsuppe, bitte,*" Karl said. He wasn't hungry, but the meat broth with liver dumplings would invigorate him if he had to spend hours out in the cold again after he left here. He also ordered a stein of beer, as the others did.

When the waitress left, Weisskirch repeated, "*Who* is moving faster than you expected them to?"

"The two American agents I sent to Bernard last week," Karl declared. "I did it only to get rid of them, so that they wouldn't interfere with our own network. They must have intercepted an air drop intended for me, as I have been promising you. However, they were supposed to report back to me before undertaking any action."

"Then perhaps I am more at fault than you," the inspector continued in a bitter tone. "I helped them and later put them in touch with Werner."

"And I with others," said Weisskirch irately. "It would have been quite easy for them to make connections with guerrillas in the mountains through the contacts I gave them."

"So much for cooperation with those bastards," Karl muttered darkly. "You can't trust them. You must understand, Bernard, and you too, Werner, that to them you are still the enemy. It is only I who know that you aren't."

Karl couldn't tell if Klung and Weisskirch believed what he had just said. They remained silent while the waitress brought steins of beer and their food.

When he was free to speak again, the police inspector asked, "Do you have a way to reach the two agents, Hans and Walter?"

"No. But they make contact with me every two or three days. They know how to reach me, then I communicate with them according to the instructions given and we arrange to meet."

"Then a message given to you to be delivered to them will reach them?"

"Absolutely. Is there such a message?"

"They must consult with us before undertaking any more sabotage. It is my job to protect Innsbruck and its citizens—from the Allies as well as the Nazies."

"Of course, Bernard. I understand your position very well."

When the bill came, it was the police inspector who reached for it and insisted upon paying. Karl saw that as a good omen.

Two of Seppl's scouts returned to the bunkhouse at mid-morning after a new reconnaissance of the tracks north of Steinach.

"A repair crew is there, guarded by a military detail," one reported. "They've brought in a big crane to clear the right of way and are trying to patch up the engine and overturned cars and get them back on the rails."

"If you want to go, we're with you," Sergeant Schafer told Seppl.

He had to keep reminding himself it was their operation not his. It was the same restriction under which he had worked with the Resistance in France. The leadership and deeds had to come from the guerrillas themselves.

"We have to try out our new weapons," Seppl said, smiling.

The previous night, while Schafer, Seppl and the men on the demolitions team had slept, Sergeant Fischbein had gone with a fresh detail of guerrillas summoned earlier by their leader, plus two *Jägers*, to the prearranged drop zone higher up the mountain. Fischbein had taught them the procedures for receiving an arms drop. The guerrillas had witnessed the miracle of cargo chutes drifting down to them and Fischbein had been relieved that OSS air support, dispatched by Captain LeGrange from Dijon, had actually followed his radioed instructions.

Sergeant Schafer let Seppl's partisans take the lead as they worked their way through the forest back down the mountain in the early afternoon toward the site of the train derailment caused by their having blown the tracks. As the guerrillas neared the location of their previous night's attack they could hear the sounds of men and equipment at work. Schafer and Seppl crept forward alone with field glasses.

From behind brush they observed that a civilian repair crew had already replaced the blown tracks and ties. Using a crane, they were still attempting to set upright on the rails the toppled locomotive and lead freight cars. There was only half a military squad guarding them. Schafer couldn't tell if they were SS or Wehrmacht. The soldiers were standing around chatting and smoking, their weapons slung casually over their shoulders, not expecting any attack in broad daylight.

The noncom in charge was a *Feldwebel*. His face was shadowed by his deep steel helmet, but Schafer noted the sullen line of his thin lips and the pugnacious thrust of his jaw. Staring at him through the field glasses, trying not to see him as a man, Schafer knew that it was he who would have to kill him.

Schafer and Seppl returned to their men and explained the plan of attack. Each man deployed through the edge of the woods slightly above the railroad, with a clear field of fire. The *Jägers* were not to move beyond the tree line; they were to remain under cover to prevent enemy soldiers and civilian workers from seeing their uniforms.

Schafer raised his Schmeisser to his shoulder and took careful aim at the *Feldwebel*. He steadied the machine pistol with his left hand gripping the long, vertical magazine. He would have preferred a rifle or carbine for accuracy. Even as he leveled his sights, he wondered if now—their first time having to shoot German soldiers—his own team of *Soldaten* would fail to fire or turn on him.

He held his breath and squeezed off a burst. The *Feldwebel* jerked backward and slumped to the ground. The partisans opened fire with a devastating salvo. Schafer stopped shooting and quickly turned his head to observe what his own men were doing. He was relieved to see them also firing. He looked toward their targets again and saw the entire German guard detail sprawled on the ground, apparently all dead. Firing ceased.

The repair crew cowered behind whatever large equipment they had been closest to. Schafer and Seppl had instructed their men not to shoot them. They didn't want to anger the local people and turn them against the guerrillas.

From his place of concealment, Schafer shouted, "All you civilian workers, get the hell out of here. Don't be afraid. There will be no more shooting."

One of the civilians found his courage, rose and took off running in the direction of Steinach. When no shots were fired after him, the other workmen appeared from behind the locomotive, freight cars and crane, began to back away from the scene, still unable to catch sight of the attackers hiding in the woods, then turned as one man and raced toward the town.

In the new silence, the partisans went down out of the forest while Schafer and his team continued to cover them from hiding. The demolitions men applied their charges to the heavy crane and the boiler of the locomotive. Another section of the band stripped the dead soldiers of weapons, papers and any item of clothing and equipment that had not been torn and bloodied in the attack.

When Seppl saw that everything was done he gave the order to withdraw. The entire group was well on its way up the mountain when the valley resounded to the new explosions.

On Sunday, the 25th of March, Dan Brooks traveled into Innsbruck in the guise of *Gefreiter* Paul Halle. *Oberleutnant* Jung, *Schütze* von Hassell, Walter Freiherr and Hans Zimmer accompanied him in the Volkswagen.

As Hans drove south on Kaiserjägerstrasse, he turned into various side streets and dropped passengers who continued to make their way on foot toward the *Hofkirche*. He circled the block and returned to the main thoroughfare after each drop-off, always scrutinizing the pedestrians. When he was finally alone in the car, he drove all the streets around the square until he spotted Karl Bergen, dressed in a decent suit and Fedora, coming out of the Ottoburg tavern. Hans pulled to the curb, opened the passenger door and called to him. It took Bergen a moment to recognize Hans, who was wearing a cheap brown suit and hat he'd bought in a used clothing store.

"Where's Brooks?" asked Karl, getting into the car.

"Please do not call him that," Hans corrected sharply. "He is Corporal Paul Halle of the 106th *Jäger* Regiment. He has gone to the *Hofkirche* to meet Inspector Klung."

"He probably should have been a corporal to start with. Just like Hitler," Bergen cracked. "Taking orders instead of giving them."

Hans shrugged philosophically. "We must all take orders, including our commanding officer. But please remember, *Herr* Bergen, that here *Gefreiter* Halle is in charge and you must always follow his orders to the letter. *Verstehen Sie?*"

He found a place to park on Universitätsstrasse, from where they could observe the Folkloric Museum and the Court Church.

"What now?" asked Karl.

"We observe the entrance to the museum and the activity in the street to make certain that nobody else is taking an unusual interest."

"And then?"

"We enjoy this mild, clear afternoon in Innsbruck until we are summoned to join our friends."

Brooks gazed across the marble floor at the sarcophagus of Emperor Maximilian I of the Holy Roman Empire. He had been dead for four hundred years but his funeral was still in progress. Maximilian himself was there as a kneeling statue; attending him around the perimeter of the chamber was a cortege of twenty-eight giant bronze statues of his relatives and ancestors, men and women beautifully sculpted in the magnificent robes and headgear of their times and stations.

Walking and pausing among the statues were citizens and tourists, civilians and military of the Third Reich. Brooks wondered if the dead would envy or scorn them in this dire moment of their history.

"Inspector Klung is there," whispered Walter, leaning close to Brooks's ear, "just passing in front of the statue of that fellow in the high pointed hat with the wide, rolled brim."

"The tall, slim man?"

"Yes. I told him you would try to approach him when he paused at the tomb of Andreas Hofer."

The great Andreas had not been a nobleman but, having led the army that saved his generation from Napoleon in 1809, he too had been buried within this noble *Hofkirche*. Brooks wondered what the revered leader would have done about Hitler.

"Remember the passwords," Walter said softly. "Otherwise Klung will not acknowledge you."

Brooks smiled and tapped his temple. He began to walk past the figures of the funeral cortege. Walter placed himself so that he could watch his CO and at the same time have a broader security view of the church. Quick glances around the room corroborated that Jung and von Hassell were both on duty, observing the statuary and tombs and at the same time fully cognizant of the whereabouts of *Gefreiter* Halle and the movements of others in the church.

Walking slowly, Dan kept Inspector Klung in sight as he followed him from statue to statue, ten meters behind. At the tomb of Andreas Hofer he saw that they could be alone together and he stepped beside him and spoke. "How much we need a man like this today in the Tyrol."

The tall, slim man turned in the direction of the voice. His eyes rose in surprise at sight of the *Jäger* corporal. He had expected someone different. Yet he had to remind himself this was just a guise. *Gefreiter* Halle could be anybody, any rank. He was supposed to be an American intelligence officer.

Klung looked away for a moment, his eyes quickly surveying the room. There was a mustiness in the chamber, a gloomy silence appropriate to clandestine activities. People there gave their attention to the dead, not to each other. Whispered dialogue remained private.

"We have many men like this today in the Tyrol," said the police inspector, giving the countersign. He looked around again to be doubly sure they were unobserved. Then he realized, with an initial shock, that they actually were being watched closely by men who knew their jobs well. He saw the agent Walter Freiherr observing them from beside a statue of Archduke Leopold III of Habsburg. Elsewhere a private and a lieutenant dressed in the same Alpine uniform as the man beside him pretended interest in the bronze gowns of the ladies and gentlemen of Maximilian's cortege. They were doing a creditable job of keeping their leader and the occupants of the room under surveillance.

Almost angrily, resentful at the thought of not being in control in his own bailiwick, Klung discarded the propriety of a polite beginning. "You are creating more havoc in the Inn Valley than is desirable now," he whispered harshly to the *Jäger* corporal. "Wasn't the derailment Thursday night enough for you? Why did you have your men go back the next day to attack the repair crew and kill the army security detail? It has infuriated the local military commanders. They have dispatched troops from Innsbruck down to the south to find the perpetrators."

"Exactly what I had in mind, Inspector," Brooks replied softly. "The actions were conducted by Austrian partisans who, according to my men who helped them, can take good care of themselves. Aren't you with us on this?"

"Actions must be approved by leaders of the Resistance," Klung insisted.

"If there were one command we'd work with them," Brooks said, "but there isn't. Until then, we'll train and supply every legitimate band of partisans who will help get rid of the Nazis."

"And afterward?" the inspector demanded. "Will you treat us as defeated enemies or liberated friends?"

Brooks didn't know how to answer that, but an answer was required. "We will remember that when the SS and Wehrmacht went after guerrillas south of us, there were less of them to interfere with what my men and I have to do up here," he stated calmly. "And that when German soldiers were chasing partisans near the Brenner Pass there were fewer of them to shoot at American soldiers coming into the Tyrol from the north which they will be doing very soon now."

Klung nodded. He seemed to accept that as the best answer he could get. Dan looked around and exchanged glances with his watching men. He was beginning to feel confined by the mausoleum now. "Do you know the quickest way out of here, *Herr* Klung?"

The police inspector led them to an exit that brought them out into the square. At the north end, Brooks saw the gleam of the steep, tiled *Goldenes Dachl* over the balcony from which royalty once watched knights jousting in the courtyard.

"What shall I call you?" Klung asked, as they began to stroll about like tourists.

"*Gefreiter*," answered Dan. "Or Paul, if you prefer."

He turned around and saw that his three men had entered the square and were following him. He hoped that Hans was nearby with the car and that he had already found Karl Bergen.

"I am Bernard," said Klung, no longer angry. "I am glad that you and your men are here, Paul, and that we will soon be free of these Nazi bastards. But please understand, conducting guerrilla operations your way nobody knows what is about to happen. Thursday night, one of our railroad men, an important member of the Resistance, was killed in the train wreck. The same sort of tragic mistake can happen again."

"I'm sorry. This is the first I've heard of it," Brooks said with genuine sympathy.

"Karl Bergen was told about it," Klung said.

"He hasn't passed the information to us yet."

"I met with him Friday, before there was the second attack. I thought he might have been responsible."

"Bergen is not an operations man. You understand that, don't you? You can convey information to him and he is supposed to see that it reaches us, but don't look to him for weapons and supplies or to plan and carry out actions."

"I understand that very well now," said the inspector. "It is you who must prevent Austrian patriots from becoming victims of your operations."

"We will cooperate as much as we can, but there is no way to keep you informed about every action," Brooks retorted sharply. "I have a number of missions to carry out before the American army gets here. I can't wait until it's convenient for you."

"Am I permitted to know what those missions are?" the inspector asked.

"Primarily guerrilla operations," Brooks lied. "To smooth the way for our army. If possible, to convince enemy forces to lay down their arms."

"That is my purpose, too," Klung said fervently. He waved his hand around at the magnificent old buildings on the square. "To keep Innsbruck from becoming a battlefield, to prevent the destruction of this beautiful, historic city."

"I need your help. You need mine," Brooks said. "Do we work together or not?"

"How can I help you?" Klung asked as they strolled past St. Jacob's Cathedral and turned the square toward the *Goldenes Dachl*.

"One aspect of our mission," Dan said, "is to take into custody any of the top Nazis who come across the border from Germany seeking refuge. If they're high enough up, we believe we can get them to use their influence to stop the war."

"Yes. That would be very good."

"Would you recognize them even if they disguised themselves?"

"I don't know."

"We've heard that they're going to fight in the Tyrol, defended by as many as twenty-five SS divisions."

"Hah," Klung scoffed. "I doubt there are that many crack troops left to them. They are scraping the bottom of the barrel. One SS division, parts of which are already spread around the Tyrol... maybe. Two or three divisions are less likely. Twenty-five? Ridiculous."

"You don't think there's a Last Redoubt in place?"

"No, I don't think there is any such thing. But there are enough Waffen SS and Wehrmacht units around to force a terrible battle, believe me. Also, Himmler is coming soon, as I told your agents. Maybe he is going to take charge of this *Götterdämmerung* we are all worried about."

"Where will he be staying?"

"I don't know. But I don't think it will be in Innsbruck itself. He would be too boxed in here. There is no room for units to maneuver, if that is what he intends to do."

"How about one of those secluded hotels in the mountains?"

"A good possibility," the inspector acknowledged. "It is also conceivable that other high Nazis will come to the Inn Valley too, whether there is an *Alpenfestung* or not. There will be those who take refuge here temporarily but plan to escape Europe altogether. They will travel secretly and incognito."

"Those are the Nazis who interest me," Brooks said. "When they turn up you must get the information to one of my agents immediately."

"Agreed. And I will pass your request along to everyone it is possible for me to reach in the Underground," Klung said. "I assume that you do not wish to tell me how I can reach you directly. Or how many men you have in your command. Or where they are."

"It's better that you don't know," Brooks said. "Not that I don't trust you. But, if you're uncovered, the less you know the better for all of us."

As they passed near the Ottoburg tavern, Dan paused as if to gaze at yet another monument there. Between the buildings, he caught sight of the river and, just across it, the mountains that climbed quickly and steeply to the north. Trying to make it look inconspicuous, like the gesture of one tourist showing another something of mild interest, he drew an envelope from beneath his tunic and handed the police inspector a photo.

"Do you know this one?" he asked.

Klung studied the picture a few moments and replied, "No, I've never seen him before. Is he German?"

"No, Russian. An intelligence officer. Major Mikhail Schepilov. Do you keep track of Russians who wander into your jurisdiction, Bernard?"

"I know that Austrian Communists remain in touch with their Russian friends. But that is a Gestapo matter, not Kripo business. I keep clear of that. For now, I don't have anything against the Communists. If they fight for Austria to get rid of the Nazis, fine. But if they betray us to a new tyranny, I will fight against them as I have the Nazis."

"I have a personal interest in this one, Bernard," Brooks said, placing the photo back into the envelope that held his rogue's gallery pictures. "Do you think you can remember the face?"

"Not as well as Hitler's," Klung said archly, "but I'm trained to observe and remember."

"You'll let me know of any Russian agent activity in the area?"

"Of course. What else can I do for you?"

"Join me for a beer at the *Goldener Adler*," Brooks said. The old hotel with its variety of restaurants and taverns, dating back hundreds of years, was in sight on the square.

"You know it?"

"Yes, from before the war. The *Goethe Stube* is one of my favorites."

"You continue to amaze me, *Gefreiter*."

"I would prefer trust and cooperation, *Herr Kriminalinspektor.*"

"You have it."

"Good. My men will follow us there and take another table. Karl Bergen will join us shortly. We will straighten out whatever needs to be straightened out regarding the chain of command and our separate functions."

Eighteen

✠   Three days later, from his vantage point in the forest, Brooks watched SS troops 150 yards away digging emplacements on the grounds outside the Hotel Edelweiss. Sergeant Mangold had been back here twice during the past two weeks and had reconnoitered other isolated hotels tucked up in the mountains, but none displayed the same kind of activity going on as this one. Brooks had come out with a nine-man patrol to see for himself.

"There's someone new," Mangold said. "The officer who's just come outside."

Brooks fixed his field glasses on the black-uniformed popinjay in the long, elegant officer's coat, black gloves, white scarf and gold-braided hat who, by his sudden appearance among the soldiers and noncoms, had interrupted their tasks and prompted a series of calls to attention and saluting. He continued to stride around importantly, carrying on a rapid inspection of the field fortifications.

"That one's got to be at least a *Sturmbannführer*," Brooks said derisively.

It was another piece of evidence that indicated his speculations were sound. Whatever the Nazis were planning at the Hotel Edelweiss, it had to be important. It was unusual to have an SS major trouble himself with the mundane duties of what appeared to be only a reduced-strength company. An SS lieutenant, an *Obersturmführer*, hovered close by, taking some heat from the major.

"As soon as the officers leave, I'll go down there with Ferber and three of the men," Brooks told Mangold. "You and the others cover us from here." His eyes fixed on random patches of bare ground in the snow cover. "How about mines?" he asked. "It's the kind of setup where they'd bury them on the approaches."

"I don't know," Mangold answered.

"Maybe we've been lucky. I'll get Ferber to find out."

Fifteen minutes later, the *Sturmbannführer* entered a staff car and was driven away on the access road that descended the mountain. Brooks saw the *Obersturmführer* make a quick, rude gesture toward the vehicle carrying his superior, then order his men back to work. Many of them were digging in the hard ground, filling sacks with dirt and carrying the sacks to build chest-high bulwarks around their gun emplacements. The *Obersturmführer* watched for a few minutes, then spoke to one of the noncoms and entered the building.

Brooks briefed *Stabsfeldwebel* Gunther Ferber on what he wanted him to find out from the SS men they were observing.

"*Ich verstehe, Gefreiter Halle,*" the sergeant major replied. "I recognize the noncom. I talked to him last time we were here."

Brooks cautioned him. "Don't try to be too damn clever or ask questions that will make them suspicious. Remember, basically we're on patrol looking for deserters."

"*Jawohl, Gefreiter.* I will be very subtle," Ferber assured him.

He took the lead, with *Gefreiter* Halle right behind him, and the five men strode out of the tree line in a file and moved across the snowy, open ground toward where the SS troops were working.

Brooks noted that there were two machine gun sites, one on either side of the snow-covered, open grounds in front of the building. They would have an excellent interlocking field of fire. Two pits for mortars and trenches for riflemen were also being dug and sandbagged half way between the machine guns and the hotel.

He saw an *Unterscharführer* turn away from the men he was supervising, spot the approaching *Jäger* patrol and wave a sign of recognition to Gunther Ferber.

"Hello, Max! You're still here," Ferber called out cheerfully. "Your vacation turned out to be longer than you thought, huh?"

"Vacation, shit! Does this look like a vacation to you? Still hunting, I see."

"*Ja.* Also a lousy job. Everything is falling apart. Deserters are running for the hills and we're running after them. What in hell is going on here? Are you expecting an attack?"

"Orders from the top," Max confided, leaning close. "But I have no idea what it means. There is no headquarters to defend. Nobody is living here except us."

"Looks like you are lolling in luxury," Ferber kidded, pointing to the hotel. "Plush quarters for you and your men."

"Luxury? *Scheisse.* We're bunking in servants' rooms, utility buildings and tents in back and eating lousy rations," griped the *Unterscharführer.* He looked around, dropped his voice, and Brooks could barely hear him say, "Only the *Sturmbannführer* is enjoying himself, and he's crazy."

"They're *all* crazy. All the officers on both sides," Ferber declared. He

128

darted a mischievous glance at Brooks, whose eyes rolled upward in a silent plea that the *Stabsfeldwebel* not carry the banter too far.

"I agree with you. Gunther, isn't it?"

"Yes."

"I agree with you completely, Gunther. Otherwise we wouldn't be in the fix we're in. Our crazy *Sturmbannführer* is obsessed by the empty guest accommodations and these useless field fortifications. Maybe this is the famous *Alpenfestung* I keep hearing about."

"Maybe he is planning to go into the hotel business after the war," Ferber joked.

"*Ja, vielleicht...* maybe," the SS sergeant concurred, laughing. "*Sturmbannführer* Jürgen is especially concerned about the comforts in one suite. He comes from Innsbruck a couple of times a week to check up on us. Then he locks himself in those rooms alone overnight. Not even with a girl. Just to sleep there and test it out himself. In the morning he comes out like he has had an interview with God. Crazy!"

Not so crazy, thought Brooks as he eavesdropped, if Jürgen was the advance man for Heinrich Himmler. He would give the major's name to his network of agents to find out more about him.

"Well, we have to get going, Max," Ferber said. "Nice to talk to you. We will probably be through here again soon. *Auf Wiedersehen!*"

"*Auef Wiedersehen*, Gunther. Good hunting," said the SS sergeant jovially. "Since there are no Americans or Russians to shoot at yet, you might as well shoot our own bad ones, eh?"

Brooks watched Ferber turn away quickly and saw his face contort, but couldn't tell if it was with anger or laughter. He took a step to block the sergeant's way, caught his eye and silently mouthed the words, "*Minen gelegt?*"

Ferber's eyes went wide and his mouth dropped open, but he quickly recovered and turned back to the SS man. "Achh, I think I'm getting too old for this job, Max. I forgot something important. You tricky fellows haven't planted any mines in the area, have you? I would hate to lose one of my men or end my career in such a stupid way."

The *Unterscharführer* assured him that there were none. "Not a good idea if we have to go into the woods quickly."

"*Danke,*" Ferber said and turned resolutely back to the forest with *Gefreiter* Halle and the men following closely in a column.

By April 2, when Wehrmacht troops moved into their area to flush out guerrillas and deserters, Russian *Spetsnaz* agents Pyotr Kostin and Nikolai Rozhko had been reconnoitering successfully for two weeks in the western sector of the Inn Valley and Sill River Valley south of Innsbruck. Captain Astakhov himself had been their jumpmaster the night they parachuted to the Drop Zone on the *Lüsener Ferner*. Sixty kilometers to the northeast, another *Spetsnaz* team had jumped from the same aircraft near Schlitters in the Ziller Valley.

Pyotr and Nikolai, dressed in Alpine costumes, had made their way down from the high mountains using skis, snowshoes and ropes. Nikolai carried their radio in his rucksack. They had rendezvoused the next day in the village of Oberperfuss with underground Communist Party members who were expecting them.

The two Russians spoke German fluently and carried false identification as Austrians. They expected their appearance and demeanor would get them by; being very blond, fair-skinned and blue-eyed, they each had the Aryan look so exalted by the Nazis. If that didn't work, they were armed with an array of concealed weapons. If that didn't work, they had been equipped with cyanide pills and ordered to commit suicide rather than be captured and risk revealing the nature of their mission.

During the two weeks they had ranged through the Tyrol, Pyotr and Nikolai had kept in touch with Major Schepilov by radio. In code tapped out on his Morse key, Nikolai had reported the active presence of a *Jäger Einheit* they believed to be the Americans' ersatz unit, plus the location of the company's various billets and the nature of those activities that had been observed so far. They also had relayed news of guerrilla attacks on the railroad, though Schepilov didn't really care about that. They were tracking bigger game for him and he expected the Americans to lead them to it.

Their operations group was poised now at a newly captured airfield near Szombathely at the western edge of Hungary. Five armies of the 2d and 3d Ukrainian Fronts had just crossed into Austria and were fighting their way toward Vienna.

The mission of Pyotr and Nikolai might have continued to go well except for the increased guerrilla activities that had brought enemy troops out of their barracks in Innsbruck to find the perpetrators of the outrages against the railroad and Wehrmacht. The *Spetsnaz* team had the misfortune to take shelter this night in a ski hut above the village of Trins, five kilometers west of Steinach, when two squads of German soldiers were sweeping the sector.

Nikolai was tapping out his evening transmission to Major Schepilov's radioman in Szombathely when Pyotr, glancing out a window, thought he caught sight of movements outside in the darkness. "Kill the light," he yelled to his partner. "There is somebody sneaking up on us."

Nikolai stopped sending, turned down the wick of the lantern on the table, then got up and extinguished the second one across the room. There was still some light from the fireplace. Pyotr rubbed his fingers quickly on the fogged windowpane to clear it and made out the forms of soldiers surrounding the hut.

The first rush of apprehension and anger threw him out of character and he spit out obscenities in Russian, followed by orders to Nikolai, "Tell Comrade Schepilov we're under attack! Then stop sending and pack up to get out of here."

He rushed away from the windows to pack his gear and grab his weapons. He wished they hadn't built a fire and lit the lamps. If they had elected to remain in the cold and darkness through the night instead of succumbing to creature comforts, maybe it wouldn't have become apparent to whoever was outside that the hut was occupied.

Steel-helmeted heads and the barrels of guns rose up over the outside window sills and eyes quickly surveyed the firelit interior. Pyotr realized they must have spotted the radio Nikolai was stuffing into his rucksack. There was no way to get out of this except fight.

There was a loud banging on the door and a voice shouted, "*Machen Sie die Tür auf!*... Open the door!"

Pyotr ducked behind a chair so the soldiers at the windows wouldn't see what he was doing. He grabbed the separated stock and barrel of his machine pistol from his pack, snapped them together and rammed in a magazine. He also had a Luger in a shoulder holster. From his cover, he quickly scanned the windows, the one door, the confined parameters of the hopeless place in which they had been trapped. The banging at the door came again, and the voice demanding it be opened. Pyotr knew what had to be done. He was the team leader and it was his responsibility. There was no question of meekly surrendering.

Nikolai ducked down beside him, his knapsack and radio pack on his back, his machine pistol in his hands. "What do we do?" he asked anxiously.

The banging continued and any moment Pyotr expected the sound of breaking glass, shots to be fired through the windows, perhaps a hand grenade to be thrown in. "You must escape with the radio and continue the mission, Nikolai," he said quickly. With whispers and hand gestures, he told him what they must each do in the next seconds.

Pyotr began the fire fight. Glass exploded into clattering shards as he sprayed a burst through each window and then the heavy wood door. The helmeted heads disappeared from the windows. He heard cries of pain that told him his bullets had hit some of the soldiers. Volleys were returned through the windows and door, but he was sure the enemy couldn't see targets. Bullets struck furniture, walls and floor.

Pyotr and Nikolai each fired new fusillades through the windows and door to clear the way on the other side. Then they yanked the partially spent magazines from their guns and shoved in full ones. Pyotr rose up, strode to the door, undid the lock and turned to Nikolai with a nod. The radioman stepped quickly to the window on the left, closest to the woods, peered out and saw the slumped figure of a German soldier under the sill and no one else. He gestured to Pyotr that he was ready.

Pyotr pulled the door open, crouched and ran outside, weaving from side to side, firing his machine pistol in short bursts that swept a semicircle before him. If the Germans concentrated on him then Nikolai might get away. That was the thought that propelled him. That and the exhilaration of the battle itself. Then he was down, floundering in the snow before he even knew he was hit and that he was in pain.

The stabbing waves pushed him one more time onto his back. He no longer had his gun. It had flown away from him and he didn't know where it was . He struggled to reach his Luger but his hand wouldn't respond. In the darkness, growing darker still, he stared at helmeted heads that prodded him with gun barrels and boots as if afraid he might explode.

In his last moments, Russian invectives burbled from Pyotr Kostin's mouth along with his blood.

Two days later, Knight's Cross agent Walter Freiherr returned from the field to the command post in Jupp Schmidler's barn. He brought with him a sealed letter from *Kriminalinspektor* Klung for *Gefreiter* Paul Halle.

Walter had been ordered by Klung not to read the letter and to destroy it instantly if he was apprehended before reaching his commanding officer. This order annoyed Walter, who would have preferred to deliver the message orally and who didn't like the idea of being endangered by secrets to which he wasn't privy. Nevertheless, he followed his orders explicitly, hoping Brooks would reveal to him what was in the message and why it was so special.

Brooks didn't.

The message reported that two strangers had been killed in an action with the Wehrmacht, who had been looking for deserters and guerrillas near Trins. The account of the incident had been related to Klung by the Gestapo, who were conducting an investigation after being brought into the matter by the army. One of the strangers, before dying, had been babbling in Russian. Their radio was of Russian manufacture. The Gestapo had taken pictures of the dead, which they had showed the police inspector.

Neither of them, Klung reported, resembled the photograph of the Russian that the *Gefreiter* had showed him in Innsbruck nine days earlier.

Nineteen

✠   "The bridge itself will not be hard to blow," agreed Knight's Cross's *Oberleutnant* Helmut Jung. He stared out of the tree line toward the railroad trestle that spanned the narrow gorge of the Sill River near Stafflach. "To do it without alerting the guards beforehand is another matter."

"Does that bother you?" Sergeant Walter Schafer, his American superior, asked.

Schafer was thinking again of Wehrmacht soldiers killing Wehrmacht soldiers. He could see the enemy guard detail's pup tents and truck in a bivouac about thirty yards from the beginning of the bridge on this side of the river. He had no worry about the *Soldaten* who had been with him these past weeks. They had already been blooded. If they felt remorse, they kept it to themselves. But now there was Helmut Jung and Kurt von Hassell and three more men from the *Jäger Einheit* whom Brooks had dispatched to help him with the increased tempo and number of guerrilla operations, and Schafer had no way of knowing how they would react in combat.

Jung heard the challenge in the American sergeant's voice. He put down his field glasses and turned to him. "No," he replied.

Two nights later, Kurt von Hassell crouched in the darkness near the trestle they were going to blow up. He had crossed the Sill on an unguarded road bridge fifty meters north. Waiting for the signal to go, von Hassell reached down to the scabbard tied around his leg and grasped the haft of the stiletto. It was Sergeant Schafer's own knife. "Specially designed for the job," Schafer had said with cold detachment when he handed him the weapon.

Kurt had volunteered to be one of the sentry killers: *Move in silence, strike stealthily, grapple the sentry from behind with one hand over his mouth, press a knee into the small of his back and bend him backward while plunging the stiletto between his ribs.*

Schafer, Fischbein and a newly acquired partisan leader named Maxl had chosen a mixed group of raiders. Sergeant Fischbein had insisted on being included in the action this time and had led von Hassell's team across the river.

Oberleutnant Jung had wanted to be a sentry killer, but Schafer had ordered him to stay back with Maxl's larger security element to engage the enemy reserve if the raiders were discovered. Jung was to take charge of the operation and withdrawal if Schafer and Fischbein became casualties. Fischbein had left his pack radio with him.

Hours earlier, before leaving the guerrillas' base camp, the leaders had checked each man to make sure he had nothing loose on him that would rattle. The C-3 plastic charges, linked by primer cord, were tied around the waists under the jackets of the demolitionists. The security men had their Schmeissers hidden under baggy windbreakers so they could move through Stafflach without alarming anyone.

Except for the rushing stream and pounding of his heart, Kurt heard no other sounds. The men beside him were silent, their eyes fixed on the barely perceived silhouette of the sentry they were to kill.

"Will you actually be able to plunge a knife into another German or slit his throat?" Sergeant Schafer had challenged each of them.

Kurt von Hassell, the cultured Prussian aristocrat, had felt the pain of the knife in his own guts. There was a difference between shooting a vaguely defined fellow countryman from the distance and engaging in direct physical contact to kill him.

"There can be no turning back at the last moment," the sergeant had warned. *"You will have to go through with it or compromise the entire operation. If the other side doesn't shoot you, I will."*

Kurt felt Sergeant Fischbein tap his shoulder and he started forward, the stiletto clutched firmly in his right hand. He and his backups inched out ahead of their security men, creeping and crawling out of the trees and brush, moving closer to the stationary sentinel standing just off the end of the trestle. Fischbein moved with them until they paused twenty feet from their target. Kurt's heart thumped hard and his mouth suddenly went dry. All his senses were alert. For the first time, he heard, above the sound of rushing water, the footsteps of the middle sentry walking his beat out on the trestle. That man was his too. But to reach him he had to kill the first one!

Fischbein tapped Kurt again. It was 0130 hours.

He rose in a half crouch, the two backup men following him. He darted forward and closed with the sentry from behind. Kurt's left hand clamped over the man's mouth and the sentry had but a moment to struggle and emit a strangled gasp as von Hassell bent him brutally back over his knee and plunged the stiletto between his ribs into his heart. The body was

134

eased to the ground as one backup man grabbed the rifle and the other the helmet.

Alongside him now, Fischbein whispered, *"Fein, gut gemacht*... Fine, well done."

They held still until they could no longer hear the footsteps of the sentry on the platform of the trestle, then Kurt yanked the stiletto from the corpse and wiped it clean on the dead man's uniform. The others carried the body into the brush. One of the backup men donned the sentry's helmet, took his rifle and belt with ammo pouches and assumed the post he'd stood. Demolitions men climbed over the railings and started down the rungs on the closest pilings while Kurt and the others squatted low beside the tracks and began to slink toward their second target.

The sentry was walking ahead of him. Kurt's heart pounded less this time, his mouth was not as dry. He and his team moved their feet in synchronized steps so as not to shake the span. The rushing water of the river covered the tiny padding sounds they made. He knew the point at which the guard would turn and begin to pace toward him. A moment before this could happen, Kurt rose up, closed with him and killed him as he had the first man. His backup grabbed the rifle and helmet, put on the dead man's gear and continued to pace the trestle. His silhouette would be visible if one of the enemy reserve left his tent and glanced this way. Fischbein and a security man carried the corpse off the trestle and hid it in the brush with the other dead sentry.

Von Hassell moved stealthily across the rest of the trestle and was intercepted by Sergeant Schafer. Schafer was crouched down with two demolitions men who were waiting to descend the middle pilings to plant explosives. Kurt's voice came out in panting breaths. "It's all clear, Sergeant. They can go."

"We got the one on this side," Schafer whispered. "Egon's replaced him." He stared into Kurt's wild eyes, then at the bloody stiletto clutched in his hand. "Wipe it off and put it away, von Hassell," he ordered. "Jung has your Schmeisser. Go get it. If the reserves wake up you'll need it."

Kurt moved quickly off the trestle, nodding dully at Egon as he went past. His job was done and he refused to let himself feel anything, neither pride nor revulsion. He eyed the German bivouac thirty yards off to one side where a truck was parked and tents set up. All was quiet. He ran to the trees where Jung, Maxl and the others waited.

On the far end of the trestle, Sergeant Fischbein inspected one of the taped fuse connections a *Jäger* had just completed. He leaned over the edge of the platform, his leg wrapped around a post, his body half dangling toward the rushing river below, when he heard the sounds of a train approaching through Stafflach. "Son of a bitch! Ten more minutes and we'd have hit the jackpot!" he muttered.

Everybody along the trestle took cover on the pilings. The bridge vibrated and strained as the locomotive and rolling stock began their slow journey across. The train took three minutes to rattle past and when it was gone it left behind once again a deep silence, except for the sound of the rushing water beneath them. Fischbein climbed to the platform again and glanced in the direction of the Wehrmacht truck and tents. No one had come out.

A few minutes later, Fischbein and Schafer gave synchronized orders to light the fuses and the raiders began to move off the trestle. They had ten minutes before the charges went up, but they still had to slip past the Wehrmacht bivouac and out of Stafflach without being seen or heard. Then, one of Fischbein's team tripped on a rail tie and went flying. He shouted an obscenity as the rifle and helmet he had taken from the dead sentry banged against the rails with a great clatter. The noise was amplified as the man groped to retrieve the equipment. The disruption broke the ordinary pattern of sounds and roused someone in the guard reserve. Shots rang out and the whipsnap of bullets came close.

Fischbein's security men returned fire toward the Wehrmacht bivouac, but he realized his group had to reverse field. If they crossed the trestle, they would become more exposed. If they stayed where they were they would be blown up in about eight and a half minutes. Bullets chewed the flooring around them as Fischbein crawled to each man, pointed him back in the direction from which they'd just come and barked, "Move off fast. Cross on the road bridge."

They left one by one and Fischbein rose to a kneeling position for better aim and fired a burst from his Schmeisser toward figures he saw crouched near the German truck on the far side of the river. Then the crescendo of shooting increased and he realized that Maxl's security element had come out of the woods and were engaging the enemy.

On his side of the trestle, Sergeant Schafer stared at the place where Egon lay sprawled on the ground between him and the Wehrmacht bivouac. At the first sound of firing, the Austrian had dropped his pose of being one of the sentries and shot the Wehrmacht soldier who had started the fire fight. Then one of the tents had been ripped away, a machine gun revealed and a stream of bullets had caught Egon and dropped him to the ground.

Schafer sent Jung and three *Jägers* on a traverse path up the hill to get above the Wehrmacht encampment and try to take it out. Glancing toward the road bridge, Schafer caught sight of some of Fischbein's group crossing one by one, running at a crouch into the protection of Maxl's position. In less than four minutes the trestle would explode.

Fischbein, still in the middle of the trestle, let go one more burst from his Schmeisser toward the Wehrmacht bivouac, then rose to follow his men. Ahead, one still on the span fell.

"I'm hit!" he roared.

Fischbein bent over the thrashing man and saw blood gush from his thigh. "Lie still," he ordered as he tore away the fabric and examined the wound. He took a field dressing from his pocket, ripped open the packet, sprinkled sulfa powder, applied the compress and tied it tightly with gauze.

"Hold onto your gun and I'll help you stand," he said. He placed the *Jäger's* arm around his shoulder and eased him up.

"Thanks, Sergeant," the man muttered through clenched teeth. "I can move. Let's go."

They were the last words Fischbein heard. The Wehrmacht machine gunner across the river, swiveled his gun to enfilade the two raiders he saw left on the trestle and his burst cut through them, slammed them lifeless against the railing and over the side into the rushing water below.

Willy Hupnagel had just started to transmit to London on Monday evening, April 9, from a *Gasthof* that was their safe house in Ampass, when a knock sounded at the door.

Karl Bergen who had joined him in the room only half an hour earlier, immediately disconnected the antenna wire and tucked it above the flue in the fireplace chimney while Willy closed the suitcase radio, repacked it swiftly under clothes in his rucksack and placed it in a closet.

The knock came again. Karl signaled Willy to position himself where he would be hidden behind the door when it was opened. Willy pulled his Luger from his shoulder holster. Karl opened the door. The *Gasthof* porter stood there with a folded piece of paper in his hand. He was a man who could be trusted, as could his employers.

"There has been a telephone call for you, *Herr* Bergen, and this is the message the man wanted delivered," the porter said, extending the paper.

Karl did not immediately open it. "Did he not ask to speak to me personally?"

"No, *mein Herr*. He wished only for the message to be delivered."

Karl thanked the porter and gave him *Trinkgeld*. The tip elicited a slight bow and he closed the door.

Willy placed his Luger back in its holster, thankful that he hadn't had to use it, that he'd never had to use it in the five months they had been operating in the Third Reich. He had long believed that once he had to pull the trigger then he himself would soon be a dead man. Yet the tension and anxiety couldn't go on much longer. He varied the time he transmitted to London, though he thought the early evening, as now, was best because the airwaves were still cluttered with everybody else's signals and the German monitoring patrols theoretically would have a harder time locking onto his frequency and finding him.

Bergen opened the message and read it. "Inspector Klung wants to see me," he told Willy. "I must go right away. I'll return here immediately afterward. Maybe there will be something new to send to London."

It took him half an hour to pedal through the chill, dark evening to the *Bierstube* where Klung had said he would wait for him between seven and nine. It filled him with anger to think again of Walter Freiherr and Hans Zimmer driving about in the Volkswagen that the police inspector had arranged for them. He had not seen the two Knight's Cross agents since a fortnight earlier with Klung at the *Goethe Stube*, when Captain Brooks had been present in the uniform of a *Jäger* corporal.

That patronizing son of a bitch had laid down the law to him about how to gather intelligence and *not* conduct operations. Klung had affirmed that was the way he wanted it too. The two agents had then left the table and joined a tall, husky lieutenant and slender, blond private in *Jäger* uniforms sitting at another table. They had looked like the real thing, those two, like Nazis, and the sight of them had worried Karl.

There had been reasons to meet with Bernard a couple of times since, information to be conveyed back and forth, but those men and that earlier meeting had not been discussed. It seemed to Bergen that the status he thought he had achieved with *Kriminalinspektor* Klung no longer existed.

The inspector was waiting for him when he entered the *Bierstube*. "*Grüss Gott!*" they greeted each other. Klung ordered another beer for himself and one for Bergen. Karl was hungry, but didn't order any food. He hoped Bernard would also invite him to eat.

After the steins were brought to their table and the waitress left, Klung leaned close and said in a resigned, quiet voice, "Your friends have been very active again."

Karl looked at him with narrowed eyes. "What do you mean?"

"Guerrillas blew up a railroad trestle near the Brenner Pass three nights ago," Klung whispered.

"That is news to me. I swear to you that I knew nothing."

"I believe you," Klung conceded. "I didn't call you here to scold you. Obviously, as *Gefreiter* Halle said, you are not part of operations. The news has been suppressed, but I've had a report from the Gestapo." There was a look of dread on his face as he continued. "Three sentries were knifed to death before anyone even knew they were under attack. There was a battle when the saboteurs were discovered placing their explosives. Soldiers from the Innsbruck detachment were killed and wounded."

Karl felt his heart pounding. "To me, it sounds like much more than just guerrillas."

"Yes. It sounds like well-trained killers. Allied commandos. You know whom I mean. Your friends."

"Do not call them my friends," Karl snapped. "They are not."

Klung was again surprised by Bergen's vehemence against people he

138

should have viewed as comrades. "They were successful, at least temporarily, in cutting off German shipments by rail to their forces in Italy," he said. "However, I fear they will now bring the Wehrmacht and SS down on their heads."

"Will they take hostages for revenge?" Karl asked with apprehension. It would be a crazy twist of fate to be picked up in a random sweep of citizens to be shot in reprisal.

"I don't think so," Klung replied. "It's too close to the end. Even those in the Gestapo know that the situation will change here very soon. The pursued will become the pursuers. Political prisoners will be freed and jailers condemned. There will be vengeance as well as justice. Which brings me to the main reason I sent for you. There is a message which you must deliver to *Gefreiter* Halle as quickly as possible."

"I can only reach him by radio," Bergen said. They finally had exchanged frequencies during their meeting in Innsbruck, so that Willy could contact their radioman. "I still don't know where he and his men are staying."

Klung looked around the room again to check for eavesdroppers and then said, "Himmler is coming on Friday."

"Here to Innsbruck?" Karl whispered, covering his mouth to contain his excitement. It presented the possibility of ferreting out the first highly placed Nazi he had learned about during all these months in the Tyrol.

"Whether he comes into the city or not I do not know," Klung continued. "However, he will be staying not far away, at a little place in the mountains between Wattens and Walchen. The Hotel Edelweiss. Do you know it?"

"No."

"Half way between Innsbruck and Schwaz. There is a connecting byway at Wattens. The Edelweiss is eight kilometers up a winding mountain road. Secluded, but not difficult to find. Himmler and his staff are expected there in the afternoon. They will be in a motor convoy leaving from Munich that morning."

"How big a convoy?" Karl pressed, his mind already taking flight.

Why pass this information to Brooks? he thought. Why not use it himself? Surely among the Underground leaders with whom he had conspired these many months there were men who would join him in trying to capture Heinrich Himmler! What a coup it would be!

"I don't know exactly," the police inspector replied, "but usually it is a couple of limousines, four or five command cars and a complement of SS guards. In these times, he might travel with heavier security. At the hotel, I understand there is almost a full company of SS making preparations for the *Reichsführer's* arrival."

"What route will he use to get there?"

"From the northeast. The convoy will enter Austria at Kufstein, then proceed southwest through Wörgl and Schwaz until the turnoff at Wattens. The journey from Munich should take approximately two-and-a-half to three hours, if all goes well. Though perhaps they will make stops along the way."

"Are you involved in the security, Bernard?"

"No. The information was merely related to me in a general briefing to Kripo by the Gestapo."

"Do you know why he is coming?"

"Only rumors," replied Klung with bitter sarcasm. "One says that he is coming to take charge of our famous *Alpenfestung*, which I pray to God is not true. Another rumor says he comes to prepare the way for his great *Führer*."

"Prepare the way to do what?"

"To get the hell out of here, of course. To escape to enjoy the hundreds of millions of *Reichsmarks* in secret bank accounts and hidden loot that I am sure he and his Nazi friends have stashed away in neutral countries like Switzerland and Spain."

"I heard South America," Bergen whispered.

"Who knows?" Klung commented dryly. "There is yet another rumor that cancels the previous ones. This one says that Himmler is coming to negotiate secretly with Allied representatives for the surrender of the Third Reich."

Bergen couldn't decide which rumor he liked best. But it was time for action. He had four days in which to plan something and carry it out. He drained his stein of beer.

"Do you want another, Karl, and perhaps something to eat?" Klung asked solicitously.

"No, thank you, Bernard." He had lost any interest in food. "As you said, I mut get your message to *Gefreiter* Halle quickly."

Bergen smiled, thinking of Captain Brooks, Corporal Hitler and *Reichsführer* Himmler and how he might be able to put something over on all of them and earn the kind of kudos and gratitude from the Americans that would make them eager to reward him with the high political appointment he wanted in Germany after the war.

Willy Hupnagel was just finishing his dinner in the *Gasthof's* dining room when Karl Bergen returned and signaled to him from the doorway that he wanted him to go up to their room. Willy had planned to linger over the *Schlagober* that he had ordered to top off his meal, but he gulped it down quickly, paid the bill and followed Karl upstairs.

When the door closed behind them, Karl asked, "Can you raise London again tonight?"

"Yes. They're probably wondering what happened to us a couple of hours ago when I stopped transmitting so abruptly. I figured I'd better wait until you got back before contacting them again, just in case you had something important."

"I do," Karl told him excitedly."

Willy waited for him to say something more, but he didn't. "How about letting me in on it," Willy finally spoke up.

"I'll write it out for you just the way I want you to send it. Then you encode it and tap it out."

A few minutes later, as he prepared to put the message in code, Willy read it over: *For Cassidy only. My guerrillas blew railroad bridge Stafflach. Line to Brenner cut. Can capture Himmler here Friday. Need weapons, supplies for fifty men to set road ambush. Must have immediate reply. Will give new coordinates for air drop.*

"You're out of your mind, Bergen," Willy said. "I'm not going to send this. It isn't true."

"Yes it is," Karl insisted. "That railroad bridge was taken out. Klung told me. If not for me... for you too, Willy... making the first contacts with the Underground, it wouldn't have happened. I'll be damned if I'm going to let somebody else get the credit."

"How about this Himmler bullshit?"

"It's true. If Cassidy sends guns, ammo and supplies, I can put together a guerrilla ambush just as well as Knight's Cross. It's time they gave me a chance to prove it."

"You're not supposed to," Willy insisted. "I know our orders. Even Cassidy told you to knock it off."

"But Himmler is something else. Something special. Cassidy wouldn't want to miss the chance. I'm the team leader. Not you. Send the goddamn message!"

"Are you going to inform Knight's Cross also?"

"No."

"What the hell are you doing, Bergen, fighting your own private war?"

"I've got old scores to settle."

Twenty

✠ Sergeant Blumberg heard the coded signal coming in and for a moment thought of George Fischbein on the other end. Then he felt a lump rise in his throat: George was dead and there wasn't even a body to send home or bury. Sergeant Schafer had used Fischbein's radio himself to report the action and casualties at Stafflach.

Blumberg now identified the I.D. bracket and key touch as Willy Hupnagel of the Bluenose team. He and Willy had already tested contact procedures since the captain exchanged code frequencies with Bergen in Innsbruck, but so far Bluenose had not reported anything of interest.

Freddy acknowledged Hupnagel and told him to go ahead with his message. The dah-dit-dahs came in a steady stream of coded letters. He quickly wrote them down and went to his duplicate of the one-time pad Bluenose was using. The message read:

"Alert Knight's Cross leader. Bluenose leader thinks I'm transmitting this message to London. Quote. For Cassidy only. My guerrillas blew railroad bridge Stafflach. Line to Brenner cut. Can capture Himmler here Friday. Need weapons, supplies for fifty men to set road ambush. Must have immediate reply. Will give new coordinates for air drop. End quote. Acknowledge receipt. More to come."

Blumberg told Hupnagel to stand by and he shouted down into the barn for Lieutenant Becker to come up. Captain Brooks wasn't due back until later that night. He had gone out, wearing civvies, with Walter and Hans to scout isolated hotels marked on the situation map in the Jenbach-Schlitters area.

Rudy Becker climbed the ladder to the loft CP. "Read this, Lieutenant," Blumberg said, handing him the message. "Willy needs a reply pronto."

The exec read it and exploded, "Lying son of a bitch!"

"I never trusted Bergen," Blumberg said, "and neither does the CO. Obviously his radioman doesn't either now."

142

"What about this Himmler business?"

"If it's true, he's ours, not Bergen's."

Becker pulled a stool close. "Let's assume Bergen is with him. Make believe you're London responding," he directed. "Find out more about Himmler. Tap out some questions. Why does it have to be Friday? Is Himmler here now or is he arriving then? If he's coming from somewhere else, where? How will he be traveling? Where will he be staying? Who will be with him? What's he supposed to be doing here? And, most important, what's the source of the intelligence?"

Hupnagel had answers to each of the questions. When he had responded fully, he tapped out a request of his own: "Send message to show Bergen. Quote. Do absolutely nothing till you hear from me. Cassidy. Unquote."

Lying in wait for him at the ambush site near Heiligkreuz, Brooks wondered if *Reichsführer* Heinrich Himmler was superstitious about this being Friday the 13th. The rites, rituals and dogmas of Nazism were rank with ancient myths, fears, malevolence and sorcery. So why not that bit of silliness too? He doubted, though, that the infamous chief of the *Schutzstaffel* could possibly be inspired by the fact it was also Good Friday.

Brooks had taken note of it wistfully early that morning as he passed with one of his squads through the forest near Pill and, looking down from their vantage point, had noted parishioners flocking to the church. If any of his men would rather have been in church, they kept it to themselves. They seemed inspired by the possibilities in the assignment they had this day. Brooks had been compelled to tell them they were going to intercept a convoy in which Heinrich Himmler was supposed to be a passenger. He had stressed his order not to kill the man, but to preserve his life at peril to their own.

More than sixty *Jägers,* their two American officers, two American sergeants and two German *Feldwebels*—dressed now in a motley array of civilian clothes gathered up by the agent networks during the past three days—were positioned at two sites above the road, well camouflaged within the wooded edge of the slope. They had left their German uniforms, rucksacks, rations and sleeping gear in the mountains seven kilometers southwest of the ambush site in charge of Sergeant Paulsen, the medic, and a security squad at a bivouac where they had slept the night before.

Sergeant Mangold's three squads were located above the curve of the road. Their job was to stop the lead vehicle. Rudy Becker had positioned himself with them. It was he who would start the action. The lieutenant prided himself on having a good baseball arm and had taken charge of two British gammon grenades, cloth bags filled with about a pound and a half of C-3 plastic explosive.

On Mangold's left flank a light machine gun was positioned so it would enfilade both sides of the convoy. Beyond the gun the rest of Mangold's men were placed to block passage by anyone who tried to break through.

Brooks had placed himself with Brunner's three squads, who held the right flank of the extended ambuscade. Both the lead and rear vehicles would pass their position before Becker threw the grenades. Then Brunner's men, with another light machine gun, would close the trap behind them. The only way for anyone in the convoy to outflank the bushwhackers would be to go into the river.

One squad of *Jägers* on the operation had not disguised themselves as guerrillas. *Stabsfeldwebel* Hans Zweiger and his squad had marched further northeast than the rest of the company and bivouacked in the woods south of Schwaz. Zweiger was in touch with Brooks by radio through a chain of lookouts.

As he waited anxiously for the first signal, Dan thought with satisfaction that he no longer had to be concerned about Karl Bergen interfering. Before they had left base for the ambush site, Walter Freiherr had brought news from Klung that Bergen and Willy Hupnagel were safely in custody in a Kripo jail on a trumped-up charge that would keep them there for a while and also out of the hands of the Nazis. He wondered what Lieutenant Commander Francis Cassidy in London might have done if Karl Bergen's message had been sent to him instead of to Freddy Blumberg? Would Cassidy have tried to follow through in support of his agent?

It was 1500 hours before the radio crackled with a message from the furthermost lookout: "This looks like them now. One armored car leading, followed by a scout car, two limousines and two command cars. There are Nazi party standards on one limo. The convoy is moving at about forty to fifty kilometers an hour."

Brooks felt a sense of relief and anticipation. He was well over strength for the convoy. The combined vehicles wouldn't be carrying more than twenty men. He sent a runner to Becker's post to alert him that the motorcade would reach them in approximately ten to fifteen minutes.

When the next signal was relayed from the lookouts, the observer reported more passengers riding in the second limousine than the first. He had not been able to spot Himmler, but the car was flying the standard of a *Reichsführer*. Brooks dispatched a runner to inform Lieutenant Becker. A few minutes later when the third alert came, Dan still couldn't be positive which vehicle contained Himmler. He passed the word along the ambush line: "Don't shoot into the two limos. Himmler may be in one of them. Shoot out the tires to stop them, but don't fire at anyone in those cars."

Lieutenant Becker felt the adrenaline hit his bloodstream as he spotted the convoy approaching. The potent-looking armored car was in front.

The long snout of a 20-mm automatic cannon protruded through the plate of its turret and a heavy machine gun peeked from an open hatch. The commander of the armored car had his head and shoulders jutting out of the turret. He wore a black, wedge-shaped garrison cap and black tunic and kept his eyes fixed on the road ahead.

Becker knew he would have the advantage of surprise only in the first seconds and after that the armored car's weaponry could blow him away. He muttered "*Auf Wiedersehen!*" under his breath as he picked up one of the gammons. He waited until the armored car was almost even with him, then hurled it. The grenade blew the hood apart, throwing particles of metal into the open slits of the driver's aperture. Becker followed up immediately with the second grenade, which blew out the left front wheel and destroyed the front undercarriage. The armored car swerved broadside and stopped dead, blocking the vehicles behind it. The commander's head had snapped back and disappeared as his body slumped into the interior.

A fusillade of machine gun, Schmeisser and rifle fire sprayed the convoy except for the two limousines in the middle. A flurry of black SS uniforms burst from the opposite doors of all vehicles except the armored car. Guards and passengers who had not been hit in the first fusillade used the cars for cover and began to return fire with machine pistols, rifles and handguns, shooting blindly into the woods on the slope above them. Brooks's men directed heavy volleys at their targets. He heard the cries of SS men who were hit and watched them topple into the road and lie still.

Then the armored car erupted into flames and heavy black smoke spread back through the column. Dan could no longer see what was happening to the passengers in the limousines.

"*Hört das schiessen auf!* . . . Stop firing!" he shouted to his men.

The shooting slowly stopped. Above the silence was the crackle of flames from the burning armored car. Becker's voice yelled from the distance, "Some of them are making a run for it!"

Brooks spotted SS uniforms darting for the river and jumping in, jackboots and all. The water was about five hundred feet wide and he could see them thrashing toward the other side as the current swept them downstream. He doubted the *Reichsführer* would throw himself in, so he shouted, "Pick off the ones in the water! Don't let them get away!"

Jägers armed with Mauser rifles sited on the swimming figures and fired with great accuracy until the river was dotted with bloody swirls on the dark water and floating lumps of black-clad corpses. One officer made it to the other side and was dropped as he clambered up the bank.

Then Brooks heard shouts of surrender from behind the screen of smoke . . . "*Wir geben auf!*" . . . and he made out white handkerchiefs waving above the roofs of the limousines.

Again, he shouted to his men, *"Hört das schiessen auf!"*—and the shooting ceased. To the SS personnel, he commanded, "Drop your weapons and move out into the road with your hands above your heads. Stand where we can see you."

Three officers in dress uniform stepped cautiously around the limousines with their arms raised and took tentative steps toward the wooded slope.

"Take a few men and we'll check them out," Brooks directed Sergeant Brunner.

"Doesn't look like Himmler from here," Brunner observed. He called three of his men and they followed him and Brooks down the slope. They held their Schmeissers ready to fire at the slightest hostile move.

Becker, Mangold and some of their men also descended toward the burning armored car and vehicles. The three SS officers with their hands raised darted worried glances from one approaching group to the other. Brooks reached them first and identified the insignias of their ranks: one *Standartenführer* and two *Obersturmbannführer*, a colonel and two lieutenant colonels.

The colonel was very tall, with a long, sunken face that looked like a death's head. He reminded Brooks of one of the photos in his rogue's gallery of top Nazis. The dark eyes fixed on him. There was arrogance in the stare, but also new and unaccustomed fear. Dan had to look up at him to meet his eyes. "Are you Kaltenbrunner?" he demanded.

The colonel looked startled. Then his thin lips twisted into a malignant little grin, not certain whether to be amused by the error. *"Ich...Kaltenbrunner? Nein. Kaltenbrunner ist ein Gruppenführer. Ich bin einzig ein Standartenführer."*

The two lieutenant colonels—one flush-faced and pudgy, the other silver-blond and slick—grinned at the stupidity of the Tyrolean peasant.

"Where is *Reichsführer* Himmler?" asked Brooks softly. He pointed his Schmeisser toward the two limos close by. "Is he hiding in one of those cars?"

The colonel's expression was puzzled. "The *Reichsführer* is not with us," he replied.

"That's a *Reichsführer's* standard flying on the fenders," Dan stated. "None of you look like a *Reichsführer* to me."

"The cars were loaned to us," said the colonel. "The standards came with them."

"Where is Himmler?" Dan demanded.

"I do not know," replied the colonel stiffly. "The *Reichsführer* does not confide in me. We were ordered to use these vehicles for an inspection today."

"Where?"

"The garrison at Innsbruck."

146

"You're a liar, Colonel."

Rage leaped into the *Standartenführer's* face. He was not a man accustomed to being spoken to in this way, nor to being ambushed and almost killed by a band of Austrian partisans. He turned his head slightly and saw that more of them had come down out of the woods. What an ignominious end, he thought. Better to have been captured by the Americans, who were said to treat prisoners quite well. He was thankful, at least, that these were not Russians. With them it would go very badly.

Brooks kept the Schmeisser aimed at the three officers and stared them up and down. Their pistol holsters were empty. Perhaps they had dropped their guns in the road, or they might have hidden them on their persons. "Frisk them, Brunner," he ordered.

The sergeant patted each of them down and found the Lugers tucked into their trousers waistbands, covered by their tunics.

"You were ordered to drop your weapons, not hide them," Dan told the SS officers angrily.

He accepted only the colonel's pistol from Brunner and jammed it into his jacket pocket. He told Brunner to keep one and give one to Becker. The three SS officers followed the transactions balefully.

"Check the limos for strays," the sergeant called out to his men.

Three of them went to the first car and peered in. It was empty. Beyond them, at the head of the column, Brooks saw Becker, Mangold and their men pass the burning armored car and check the scout car, where the dead driver was draped over the wheel and two bullet-riddled SS noncoms were sprawled in the back.

"Look them over fast," Dan shouted. "We've got to start moving out."

Suddenly there were two pistol shots overlapped by a burst of Schmeisser fire. Brooks's head whirled toward the second limousine. One of his men staggered back from the open rear door and crumpled to his knees on the road. Blood oozed at two places through the dark, coarse fabric of his borrowed Tyrolean jacket. Dan ran past him, his finger on the trigger of his own machine pistol, ready to fire.

There was no need to. The vacant eyes of an SS *Brigadeführer* stared back at him. The salvo from the wounded *Jäger's* machine pistol had slammed the general back onto the floor where he'd been hiding. His hand still clutched the Luger he had fired.

As Brooks turned away to tend to his wounded man, he heard Sergeant Brunner shout, *"Nein! Tuen Sie das nicht!* . . . No! Don't do that!"—and in that second he saw the slumped, bleeding man use all his strength to raise the barrel of his machine pistol and rake the three standing SS officers. Dan had to halt in mid-stride to stay out of the line of fire. The *Standartenführer* and two *Obersturmbannführer* twisted around screaming as they took bullet after bullet, collapsed to the ground, thrashed a few seconds and lay still.

When the magazine in his Schmeisser had emptied, the *Jäger* lowered the barrel and looked toward Brooks as if seeking forgiveness. He and Brunner reached the man just as he rolled over. Dan eased the Schmeisser from his fingers. The man stared up at him with glazed eyes and murmured, "I kept my promise. I did not shoot *Reichsführer* Himmler."

Then he lost consciousness. Brooks checked him for vital signs. He doubted the man would live long enough to reach their base. "Fix up a litter for him, Brunner," he said. He looked around and called out, "Any other casualties?"

"A few wounded," Becker reported. "All ambulatory."

"No sign of Himmler?"

"No, sir. I'm sorry."

"The son of a bitch must have bugged out at the last minute. Start the men back to the reassembly area, Rudy. I'll follow in a couple of minutes. Mangold!"

"Yes, sir!"

"Check every vehicle for Himmler just to be sure. Pick up any I.D.'s, papers and weapons you find on the dead ones."

By the time the next part of Brooks's ambush plan was put into action, as prearranged, the perpetrators of the attack were gone. *Stabsfeldwebel* Hans Zweiger's squad of Knight's Cross *Soldaten*, dressed in their *Jäger* uniforms, delayed their arrival until the optimum moment. They marched down the road from the direction of Schwaz and made their way past shocked people from the nearby hamlet of Heiligkreuz who were fearfully viewing the scene of carnage.

The villagers had been drawn to the place by the heavy firing and smoke from the burning armored car, but had held back until it was safe to inch closer. A local *Schutzmann* moved among the wreckage and dead, writing his official police report.

"A terrible thing," he said to Zweiger. "Not one survived. Even their papers have been taken. One of the limousines carries the flag of a *Reichsführer.* Who might it have been? I do not know how to report something like this."

"Just do your job," Zweiger advised with a pretense of anger.

He and his men examined each of the corpses and vehicles, though they knew from the last radio exchange with *Gefreiter* Halle what they would find. They made a great show of examining the ground and nearby slopes looking for footprints and clues they might use to pursue their quarry. As he and his men left the area on their pretended hunting mission, Zweiger muttered darkly to the *Schutzmann*, "We will find these fucking shits and blow them to hell!"

In four days he was to pass through Heiligkreuz again and tell the

Schutzmann that his patrol and a larger group of the *Jäger Einheit* had caught up with the guerrillas in a remote mountain gorge and wiped them out. The *Jäger Einheit* would be elevated in the esteem of enemy units still operating in the Inn Valley.

Sergeant Blumberg greeted Brooks with a look of deep sorrow when he made it back to Schmidler's farm on Easter Sunday, April 15. Dan and his squad had forged their own trail through the mountains from the reassembly area after the ambush, staying out of sight of the enemy and maintaining radio silence. The men who had come in before him stood around talking softly with those who had not been on the raid.

"Have you heard the news, Captain?" Blumberg asked.

"What news?"

"President Roosevelt is dead. Harry Truman is President."

Brooks felt a terrible sense of loss.

"When?"

"Three days ago. We heard it on the radio after you left."

Oberleutnant Jung came to him later and extended the deep condolences of all the Germans in the *Jäger Einheit.* "If only he could have lived to the day of our victory," he said solemnly.

Brooks understood that they genuinely shared his feelings of personal bereavement. But the death of Roosevelt would not affect the imminence of victory, he knew; nor would he let it hinder the completion of his mission.

In one of the isolated *Schihütte* they used in the eastern sector of the Inn Valley, *Spetsnaz* radioman Vladimir Butakov decoded the new signal from Major Mikhail Schepilov:

"The time is very close. Intensify your efforts regarding Knight's Cross. Sniff right up the asses of the American *Jägers.*"

The major, Captain Astakhov and their *Spetsnaz* group—though still 350 kilometers to the east—were closer to their ultimate target than they had been two weeks earlier. Schepilov's headquarters was now in Vienna.

"The great hero speaks," scoffed Feodor Kalinin, the team leader, when he read the message.

He and Vladimir considered themselves lucky to be still alive five and a half weeks after their jump into the Schlitters area of the Zillertal. Not only alive but continuing to transmit excellent intelligence about both the Germans and the Americans' ersatz *Jäger Einheit.*

Their comrades, however, Pyotr Kostin and Nikolai Rozhko, who had parachuted sixty kilometers farther west on the same night and from the same aircraft in which they had flown, had aborted their last transmission to Schepilov while under attack on the night of April 2. There had been no further word from them in three and a half weeks. Vladimir had been monitoring their signal that night. He and Feodor assumed that Pyotr and Nikolai had been killed by the Germans. Rumors regarding their deaths had been communicated by underground Austrian Communists.

"Sniff their asses indeed! What the hell does Schepilov think we're doing here, having a ski holiday?" Feodor muttered. "If we'd been any closer to their ambush two weeks ago we would have been killed."

They had witnessed it from farther up the slope after tracking one of the *Jäger* squads for two days, seeing them rendezvous with the others at the forest bivouac and change into guerrilla clothes. After the ambush, the Russians had mingled with the frightened civilians of Heiligkreuz viewing the scene.

Feodor had been surprised by the murderous efficiency of the American undercover company, so like the tactics of *Spetsnaz*. He knew that, except for two American officers and a few noncoms, the rest of the group were German defectors. Yet not one German in the motorcade had been permitted to survive. Feodor had observed the shocked *Schutzmann* writing his report, and the *Jäger* squad that had turned up to pursue the guerrillas—though he had considered that they too might have been part of the Knight's Cross operation.

He also still had no information about who the American undercover company had expected to find in the convoy that day. Merely to engage an SS unit in a fire fight had made no sense. That was not Knight's Cross's mission, as Major Schepilov had explained before dispatching his teams on their tracking assignments. Feodor believed the Americans had thought there would be a high-ranking Nazi in one of the cars and then had been disappointed to find none. The *Brigadeführer* and lesser ranks they had killed hadn't been important enough to warrant mounting such an attack.

Could it have been Hitler himself they had been expecting, as Major Schepilov had said? Perhaps. But obviously they hadn't caught him. If they had, there would have been news about it. Soviet intelligence believed the lunatic *Führer* was still in Berlin.

However, since the day of the ambush, Feodor realized that if Hitler or anyone of importance had been in that convoy and Knight's Cross had captured him, there would have been nothing that he and Vladimir could have done about taking him away from them. It was time for Major Schepilov, Captain Astakhov and their group to jump into the Inn Valley and take over the operation.

Feodor was positive the Nazis were not building their rumored Last Redoubt here. There were various transplanted war industries functioning in the Tyrol, and strong defensive installations and units of the SS and Wehrmacht that could make the Americans pay dearly when they began fighting their way in. But there was no vast and impregnable *Alpenfestung*.

The SS company at the Hotel Edelweiss, however, was of greater interest to Feodor than more formidable installations elsewhere. Major Schepilov had reacted similarly after Feodor reported Knight's Cross patrols had the hotel under constant surveillance.

The American *Jägers*, fortunately, seemed unaware that they were being followed by *Spetsnaz* agents.

To Vladimir, his radioman, Feodor now said, "Please encode for Major Schepilov the following message: 'Agree time close. Asses too. Drop zone prepared. Reception committee ready at your pleasure.'"

Twenty-one

✠   Kurt von Hassell was drunk and Helmut Jung was amused by it. They sat alone on the ground against a shed on Schmidler's farm, huddled in their *Jäger* coats as they passed a bottle of brandy between them. It was the last night of April, still a chill in the mountain air.

"What a fine night, Helmut," mumbled Kurt, staring at the star-filled sky.

"Agreed," Jung said, handing over the bottle.

"The war will be over in weeks. Maybe days. Mark my words, Helmut," Kurt declared.

"It would be hard to disagree with you, *mein Freund.*"

They had listened regularly to news from the American Armed Forces Radio Network, BBC and German High Command. Berlin was burning, almost completely overrun by the Russians. Forward elements of the American army had met Russian soldiers on the Elbe at Torgau, cutting the Third Reich through the middle.

Kurt tipped the bottle to his mouth again, dribbling a little of the liquid down his chin onto his coat. "Aachh, we should have fine goblets for this stuff. It is too good to be drunk like cheap Russian rotgut."

"My apologies, *Baron.*"

"*Baron?...Scheisse!* I was never a baron, *Herr Oberleutnant.* Of that you may be sure."

It had been a week since *Gefreiter* Halle had recalled them to base. He had withdrawn Sergeant Schafer and all the *Jägers* from the Sill Valley, leaving the guerrillas to continue on their own. Their wounded had been left in the care of Underground doctors. The dead had been buried secretly in the mountains, except for Sergeant Fischbein and the *Jäger* who had been lost in the river.

Jung and von Hassell had sensed since returning to the farm that another important operation was imminent. But *Gefreiter* Halle had assigned them nothing except one overnight patrol to the road between

152

Wattens and Walchen to observe the layout of the Hotel Edelweiss and the activities of an SS company there.

This evening, Jung, von Hassell and two of their comrades had been privileged to dine in the farmhouse with Herr and Frau Schmidler and the beautiful Lisa. Jupp Schmidler, in an outpouring of gratitude and *Gemütlichkeit*, had taken Jung aside as they were leaving and presented him with this extraordinary bottle of prewar Asbach Urhalt that he shared now in private with von Hassell.

Kurt gripped the long, slim bottle with the fingers and palms of both hands and held it toward the heavens as if it were a chalice. "I have never been a particularly religious man before, Helmut. But now, in this moment, I want to drink to *them*. And ask God to look after their souls."

"Who?"

"The poor bastards I killed at Stafflach."

Jung had known for more than three weeks that von Hassell was haunted by what he had done that night at the bridge. He had tried to ease Kurt's conscience by sharing the blame, by talking about the men he had killed in battle himself and reminding Kurt he had done the same thing for years merely by aiming his rifle toward masses of enemy and pulling the trigger. But Kurt had not accepted this attempt at absolution.

"A religious man, Kurt?" Helmut scoffed now in mock seriousness. "It is perhaps the final step in your degradation. What I think is that you need to get laid."

"Is that an order, *Herr Oberleutnant*?"

"*Jawohl!*"

Von Hassell gulped another mouthful of brandy from his imagined chalice, then handed the bottle to Jung with a silly little smile. He had a fatalistic feeling about his mortality. He had wished these last three weeks that he had a wife at home and a son.

"Not such a bad idea," he murmured. "I must confess, Helmut, that I have given this very matter some thought. But...where to go?" He giggled. "More important...who to do?"

"A logistical problem easily solved," Jung answered readily. "We have within easy range the most delectable of possibilities—Miss Lisa Schmidler. She of the golden hair and magnificent bosoms."

"*Aachh, Gott.* It is very dangerous, *Herr Oberleutnant*. That father of hers will kill me if he finds me there. And if not him, then *Hauptmann* Brooks. *Verzeihen Sie bitte*...Excuse me please. I mean *Gefreiter* Halle."

"Are you a man or not, von Hassell?" Jung asked, wiping his mouth after swallowing another slug of brandy.

"How can you ask a question like that, Helmut, after what I did in Stafflach?"

Jung stared appraisingly at his companion. "I agree. *Verzeihen Sie*

153

bitte," he said deferentially. "Oh, but she had her eye on you tonight, Kurt. Of all the men in our company, I think that it is you she would love to take to her bed."

"*Unsinn*...Nonsense. She has been flirting with every man in the company at every opportunity."

"Then, *mein lieber Baron,* you must do it for the honor of the company. Before we leave here—and, as you say, it will be soon—one of us must make Lisa happy! Otherwise, we will be remembered with shame."

For a full month, Klaus Bartels, a retired trackwalker for the Austrian National Railways and a member of Franz Scholl's branch of the Knight's Cross network, had been charged with the early morning surveillance of the emergency landing field west of Innsbruck, near Kematen.

On Tuesday morning, May 1, from his post in the doorway of a storage shed, he saw a limousine approach along the access road an hour after dawn and park close to the control shack. He had noticed a small personnel carrier there earlier and lights showing in the structure's windows, which indicated an aircraft was expected.

Klaus raised his binoculars and saw an elegantly dressed SS *Sturmbannführer* leave the limousine, enter the shack and return outside in a few minutes. He heard the aircraft before he saw it. Scanning the sky, he fixed his binoculars on a low-flying Fieseler Storch weaving its way out of the mountain passes to the north. He marveled at the skill of the pilot, who barely cleared peaks and outcroppings, turned into the wider valley of the Inn and descended on a direct path to a landing.

When the plane stopped he saw the pilot and a man in SS officer's uniform help a third man from the aircraft. This third man wore civilian clothes, moved feebly and the most notable thing about him was that his head and hands were swathed in bandages.

The limousine was driven close to the Fieseler Storch. The *Sturmbannführer* and driver, also in SS uniform, leaped out and there was an exchange of stiff-armed salutes with the officer who had arrived on the plane. Klaus picked out his rank insignia through the binoculars and identified him as an *Obersturmbannführer.* The injured man just hung there limply and did not participate in the greetings. The others helped him into the back seat of the car. The pilot and driver transferred valises from the plane and locked them in the trunk. Both SS officers entered the vehicle and it was driven away toward Innsbruck. Before it was out of range, Klaus remembered to get its license number.

A few minutes later, the pilot took off again, heading at low altitude toward the main Innsbruck airport. Two Luftwaffe men who had been in the control shack drove away in the personnel carrier. Klaus did not wait until his relief arrived. This was the most intriguing event that had occurred at his station during the many weeks of his watch and he felt compelled to convey what he had seen to his contact immediately. His bicycle was hidden close by and he retrieved it and pedaled toward the nearest *Gasthaus* where there was a public telephone.

When he finished reporting his news in guarded language to the American agent Franz Scholl, he pedaled his bicycle to Oberperfuss. There he reported the same information to the leader of the underground Communist cell he had been part of for more than twenty-five years.

Obersturmbannfürer Dietrich Reiter breathed a little easier once he and *Herr* Siegfried Schmidt arrived at the Hotel Edelweiss. The contrast between the inferno of Berlin the night before and the quiet, beautiful mountains and woods of the Austrian Tyrol this morning began to soothe his jangled nerves.

The SS lieutenant colonel glanced only briefly at the defense emplace-ments when the limousine was driven past them on the approach to the front door. He declined the invitation of *Sturmbannführer* Jürgen to inspect the trenches and gun pits or to review the honor guard drawn up to welcome them.

Reiter said, "The less contact with anyone the better."

He would have preferred a less conspicuous means of security than to have this Waffen SS unit inflicted on the place. Its mere presence announced there was something or someone of importance here.

Herr Schmidt had not been consulted about the specifics of the arrangements beforehand. He merely answered with a croaking *"Bitte!"* when Jürgen had asked him if he was comfortable during the limousine ride from the flying field; and then, *"Danke, nein,"* every time he had been asked if he wanted anything. Reiter was amazed that his charge had not complained during the entire, long, fearful flight. He seemed content to let Reiter handle everything.

"I have installed a maitre d'hôtel and staff to look after your needs and desires, *Herr Obersturmbannführer,*" said Major Jürgen as the limousine approached the hotel's entry. "I hope you will find the suite I selected for you and *Herr* Schmidt satisfactory. I have slept in it myself and found it most comfortable."

"Whatever you have done to make our stay here more comfortable, *Herr Sturmbannführer,* is much appreciated," Reiter commended with-out enthusiasm.

But Jürgen, regrettably, felt it necessary to make an additional revelation about his important services to the hierarchy of the Third Reich. "It is the very suite that I ordered prepared for *Reichsführer* Himmler when he was expected three weeks ago."

At mention of Himmler's name, *Herr* Schmidt's arms and body went tense. It was one of the few indications of an emotional response that Reiter had noticed since the Russian artillery almost killed them in

Berlin less than twelve hours earlier. Schmidt seemed about to speak but then changed his mind. He merely stared at Jürgen through the eye slits in his head bandage. It seemed an angry look.

"We were disappointed that he did not come," the major continued to relate, unaware of the displeasure he had fostered in *Herr* Schmidt, "but it was also fortunate that he changed his plans that day."

"Oh? Why is that, *Herr Sturmbannführer?*" asked Reiter with forbearance.

"There was an ambush of the convoy with which he was supposed to be traveling."

The angry, strained voice of *Herr* Schmidt spoke at last from behind the mouth hole of his bandages. "Patriots or traitors?"

Major Jürgen thought that a rather curious, perhaps even dangerous remark and he wasn't sure what was meant by it or how he might be expected to respond. Reiter, however, had no trouble understanding Schmidt's meaning. There had been reports during these last weeks that Himmler had been trying to negotiate a separate surrender to the Western Allies without the knowledge of *der Führer,* which infuriated many in the inner circle.

"Traitors, *mein Herr,*" Jürgen answered with appropriate outrage. "It grieves me to report that not one man in the convoy survived. However, the guerrillas also paid for it with their lives. Those responsible for the attack were pursued into the mountains by a *Jäger* company and were caught and wiped out."

There was a moment's strained silence, Reiter waiting to see if *Herr* Schmidt would have further comment. When he made none, Reiter filled the vacuum. "I sincerely hope, Jürgen, that your security will be much more effective for us. To retaliate against guerrillas after the fact is already too late."

"Of course, *Herr Obersturmbannführer,*" replied the major.

The driver brought the limousine to a stop at the building's entrance and leapt out to open the rear door for his three passengers. Gliding down the short, wide stairway at that moment was a man in a dark suit, white shirt and tie, whom Reiter took to be the heralded maître d'hôtel. The man preened on the bottom step, as if he were receiving guests at the Grand Hotel in Berlin, while they assisted *Herr* Schmidt from the vehicle.

The greeter raised his arm and spoke the formal *"Heil Hitler"* to the arrivals.

Only *Sturmbannführer* Jürgen responded with alacrity. Reiter raised his arm and repeated the phrase without vigor. *Herr* Schmidt seemed rather startled by it, half raised his arm and flipped his wrist back without saying anything.

Major Jürgen began to make the introductions, then realized he was about to get into a moment of confusion, though there was nothing to do but go ahead. "May I present...also *Herr* Schmidt," he said. "*Herr* Luther Schmidt who is in charge of the hotel staff."

From behind the head bandage of Siegfried Schmidt there came what sounded like an approving cackle and then an outpouring of what his aide was pleased to see were newly vigorous and delighted words. "You see, Reiter, I told you we would not go far before meeting another Schmidt." He extended his bandaged hand, which trembled slightly, and the hotel man touched it gently and sympathetically. "I congratulate you on your family name," said Siegfried Schmidt. "It is one that I share, though I doubt that we are related."

Luther Schmidt bowed deeply. "It shall be my great pleasure to make your stay with us comfortable, *Herr* Schmidt."

Lieutenant Colonel Reiter felt the compulsion to laugh at this meeting of Schmidts, but he settled for a friendly, open smile and extended hand. "*Obersturmbannführer* Dietrich Reiter," he said crisply as the hotel man's soft palm touched his for a moment. "Please show us immediately to our quarters."

"At your service, *Herr Obersturmbannführer.* There will be no need to register."

Of course not, you stupid little shit, Reiter thought. Did the man think they had come here on vacation? "See to the luggage, Jürgen," he ordered. "You said there was a staff, didn't you? Have it brought right up. None of it is to be opened. We will tend to that ourselves."

The major wasn't pleased to receive so demeaning a command. Yet, not knowing who these two new arrivals really were—except that they had come in by special plane, a rarity these days, and his instructions by radio from Berlin had said they were very important—he was prepared to do almost anything to cater to them.

"*Jawohl, Herr Obersturmbannführer,*" he replied with feigned humility and gestured to the driver to open the trunk of the limousine.

The maître d'hôtel glided up the stairway to the wide front entry. Reiter tried to place a supporting hand under *Herr* Siegfried Schmidt's arm, but it was pushed away. "It is all right, Reiter," he said. "I will manage on my own. Just to be here in the mountains has invigorated me."

The voice did indeed sound a little stronger, Reiter thought, though still muffled by the layers of gauze.

The maître d'hôtel preceded them into the small lobby where he instructed the porter, an old man wearing a colorful Alpine costume, to go to the car and fetch the luggage. Then he led his guests up two flights of carpeted, dark wood stairs to the top floor, the third story of the building. Reiter was gratified to see that his charge moved along well now, if a little slowly. The additional codeine tablets he had urged upon

157

him aboard the plane were still doing their pain-killing work; but he stayed one step behind *Herr* Schmidt, ready to assist if he faltered.

They were shown to a suite that consisted of a living room, one bedroom with twin beds and a private bathroom. Glass paneled doors opened onto separate balconies outside the living room and bedroom. The drapes were open, allowing the bright, even light of late morning to flood the rooms. *Herr* Schmidt gravitated immediately to the doors in the living room. He removed his fedora and pressed his bandaged face close to the glass panels to admire the view of nearby forest and snow-covered high mountains in the middle distance. Reiter realized that unless he asked for another bedroom or used the sofa in the living room he would have to sleep in the same room as his charge, a degree of intimacy he had not considered. Yet, he supposed the arrangement would also enable him to maintain a higher degree of security.

"Sir, I understand you will only be with us a short time," the maître d'hôtel said, addressing Reiter.

"Yes. Just a few days. We will relax and stay in our suite. My companion is still suffering from burns received in a bombing raid and needs rest and quiet, so we do not wish to be disturbed."

"Then I'll have one of the staff serve your meals here, if that will be satisfactory." Luther Schmidt glanced with sympathy at his silent guest still standing at the balcony door, engrossed by the view. "Just pick up the phone and it will buzz downstairs on the switchboard in the office. Someone will always be close enough to respond."

Herr Schmidt—who had been listening, though he appeared not to be—turned away from the balcony door, drifted past them, murmured, "*Dankeschön*," and went into the bedroom.

The maître d'hôtel began backing away from Reiter toward the open hall door, bowing at the same time, and almost collided with Major Jürgen carrying a valise. He was leading a procession of the hotel porter and the SS chauffeur, each heavily laden with baggage.

"One moment," said Reiter, striding to the bedroom. He peered in and saw that Schmidt had opened the balcony door and stepped outside. He was fixed on the view again, inhaling and exhaling deep breaths of fresh air through the nostril and mouth holes in his head wrappings. Reiter wished he hadn't stepped outside, but didn't want to reprimand him in front of the others. "Put everything on the floor in the bedroom," Reiter told them.

When they had done so and were leaving the suite, he asked the *Sturmbannführer* to stay a few moments. "Is the phone to the outside working, Jürgen?" he demanded. "Long distance?"

"Yes, sir. But connections are irregular and some areas have been cut off. Berlin is difficult, though I believe the main exchange there is still operating."

"We are expecting important calls. Instruct your hotel staff to put them through to this room immediately. It might also be necessary for us to telephone out from here through the switchboard. The security of these calls must be absolute. No one is permitted to listen in, Jürgen."

"*Jawohl, Herr Obersturmbannführer.*"

"What about radio communications? Have you arranged it, as instructed?"

"Of course, *mein Herr*. We are equipped with long-range transmitter and receiver and there is a code man who will maintain absolute secrecy about messages he handles."

"It will be Greek to him, Jürgen. He will not be able to decipher. We have our own code book. Just make certain that any signals intended for *Herr* Schmidt or myself are brought to us immediately."

"*Ja, natürlich, mein Herr,*" Jürgen replied. Then, in a hesitant voice, he ventured to ask what had been on his mind ever since he had received notification from Berlin to be at the emergency flying field that morning to meet the plane and take the two passengers under his protection. "Is it permitted, sir, to ask who *Herr* Schmidt is? I thought I knew the names of all the important men in the government and party. But, I confess, I cannot place the name 'Siegfried Schmidt.'"

Reiter favored him with a smile. "*Herr* Schmidt is a scientist, Jürgen. A rocket scientist whose importance to Germany is the equal of ten SS divisions," he explained, glad for the opportunity to let this be known. "He is a man close to our *Führer*. His survival and escape is very important to the future of Germany. You already see how badly he was wounded in the service of the Third Reich and how bravely he conducts himself. If he were a military man he would surely be awarded the Knight's Cross with diamonds."

"Is he to be addressed, then, as *Herr Doktor?*" asked Jürgen, quite impressed.

"No. He prefers a simple *Herr* Schmidt."

Reports of the arrival of the bandaged man and his SS escort reached Captain Brooks periodically during the day and evening of May 1. The men were tracked by separate informants, agents and patrols of the Knight's Cross network from the time of their arrival at the emergency flying field, during their journey by limousine through Innsbruck, past Solbad Hall to the Wattens-Walchen road and the Hotel Edelweiss.

That day's patrol near the resort, observing through binoculars from vantage points in the woods, spotted the arrival of the limousine and its passengers and then the eerily bandaged man staring out from behind the French doors and standing on the balcony on the third floor. The *Jäger* with the radio reported the sighting.

A mummy-like bandage around the head was daunting in itself, Brooks contemplated. It had the effect of suggesting horrible wounds, beseeching sympathy for the wearer and discouraging further investigation, though it might also serve no purpose other than disguise.

"Let's put two additional squads on stakeout at the Edelweiss right away, Rudy," he ordered his exec. "They're to hold onto the patrol that's there now, but they're to lay low and not make any moves against enemy personnel or the hotel's occupants. If our quarry leaves, they're to radio us immediately and track them. If we mount a raid, they'll be part of it."

Becker heard the "if" and it disappointed him. "You're not sure we're going in?" he pressed.

"Not yet," Dan said. "I want more surveillance before we move, more intelligence from our agents and Inspector Klung about the identities of the new arrivals and the function of *Sturmbannführer* Jürgen."

Yet if they were going to do a snatch, he knew it had better be that night or the next. They had heard the latest broadcasts that American forces had captured Munich, fought through southern Bavaria and were already in the western Tyrol. Seventh Army was expected to reach Innsbruck in two or three days. That would be the end of it for Knight's Cross, with no prize to show for their efforts.

It was soon after dark, 1800 hours, when the two squads led by Sergeant Schafer and *Stabsfeldwebel* Zweiger were ready to leave for the Edelweiss. They would have to force march the fifteen kilometers. The Volkswagen was unavailable. Hans Zimmer and Walter Freiherr were meeting with Inspector Klung in Innsbruck and Underground leaders throughout the region, planning actions to neutralize SS and Wehrmacht units in the path of the American advance. Brooks estimated it would take his squads four hours to reach the hotel.

The twenty-six men formed in a semi-circle around him outside the barn and listened intently as he briefed them. Beyond them, Jung, von Hassell and large numbers of their comrades also heard what was being said. The *Oberleutnant* and *Schütze* had been dragging ass most of the day, Dan had noticed, with what appeared to be a hangover. It was a most unusual condition for any of the men to be in, but he hadn't challenged them about it. He assumed they had overdone the drinking during their turn as dinner guests at the Schmidler house.

"Any questions?" he asked the squads about to leave.

"Who do you think is holed up there?" Sergeant Schafer spoke up.

Every one of the men within earshot became alert. "I don't know," Dan answered honestly. Yet he didn't want to just leave it at that. He felt he had to give them some kind of logical answer to stress the importance of the target. "But I believe it might be someone high up in the Nazi government. Perhaps someone as important as Heinrich Himmler or Martin Bormann."

Minutes later, the two squads left and they seemed inspired by what he'd said. Brooks returned to the command post in the barn loft. He ordered Blumberg to send messages to the outlying platoons at the other farm and the warehouse to get ready to move at a moment's notice with all their equipment and supplies.

Despite their eagerness regarding what was brewing that night, *Oberleutnant* Jung and *Schütze* von Hassell had resolved that for these next few hours while they were off duty their private mission was more important than the war mission of the *Jäger Einheit*.

By 2030 hours they had hidden themselves in a grove of trees on the north side of the Schmidler farmhouse. A half moon bathed the stucco walls, steep roof, timbers and balconies of the structure in what Kurt chose to think of as romantic light. He and Helmut each sipped prudently from the small amount of brandy Jung had saved from the previous night.

"To keep us warm," the *Oberleutnant* whispered.

"To give me courage," the *Schütze* murmured honestly.

During the next half hour, they observed through night glasses the target bedroom beyond the balcony on the second floor. They saw a lamp come on, then the lovely Miss Lisa moving about beyond the glass-paned French doors, shedding her dirndl and blouse. Each drew a long inward gasp when Lisa opened the doors and stepped out onto the balcony. She threw her arms wide, as if to embrace the moon in a charming gesture of invocation and breathed deeply of the cool night air. The radiance of the moonlight was drawn to her bright blond hair, white face, bare throat and the alluring breasts that pushed above her undergarment. The ritual seemed one to which she was accustomed. The scene made Kurt think of sensual poems about the secret yearnings of country girls and boys. He wanted to call out to her, but didn't dare.

Lisa turned then, went inside and drew the drapes. Kurt watched the faint penumbra of light barely perceptible around the edge of the French doors. When it was gone he knew she had turned off the lamp and gone to bed. Helmut allowed them each one more small sip of the brandy, then he shoved the bottle of Asbach Urhalt into his coat pocket.

"Now," he said softly, hefting the padded grappling iron and coil of climbing rope in his hands.

Von Hassell put out his hand and stayed him. "What if she has locked the balcony door?"

Jung looked at him with disappointment. "That is not an obstacle, *Herr Baron*. Our captain taught us what to do in such a circumstance. Here, take these." He handed von Hassell a roll of wide black tape and a glass cutter. "We practiced the procedure at St. Germain. I have seen you do it yourself. Tape the pane nearest the door latch. Cut it and tap it out. The tape will keep it from shattering. Reach inside to unlock the door. After that, proceed swiftly, courageously and with joy to the bedside of your intended beloved."

"How eloquent you are, Helmut," quipped Kurt. "I did not think you had it in you."

"In truth, I have the soul of a poet," Jung retorted grandly in a soft voice, "but life has thwarted me."

Jung yanked von Hassell after him before he could get cold feet. They stood under the balcony and Helmut tossed the padded grappling iron expertly so that it wrapped around the top railing and gripped against the wood. He pulled on the line and it held. He went up hand over hand a few feet to test it and it still held. He slid down lightly and handed the rope to Kurt.

"I trust that you will know what to say and do," Helmut whispered. "I believe with all my heart that she will welcome you. I will wait in the trees if you need me. *Viel Glück!*"

"How long may I stay?"

"Let nature be your guide. But I assure you, Kurt, I will not remain on sentry duty in these circumstances for longer than two hours. I will comfort myself with the remains of *Herr* Schmidler's brandy and that will not last very long," Jung made a pretense of grumbling. "So, be quick about it. But, of course, not too quick. Look to the obvious needs of the young lady. I have found, in my experience, *Herr Baron,* that if you take care of the needs of the woman, your own will also be well served."

Kurt grinned at Helmut and took his first grip high on the rope. "Not only a poet, *Herr Oberleutnant,* but a philosopher and a lover, too, eh?" he teased. "Would you like to go up in my stead?"

"Of course not, von Hassell," Jung hissed. "Get the hell up there immediately or I'll call the party off."

"*Jawohl, mein Führer,*" von Hassell muttered and started his smooth ascent to the second-story balcony, using his hands and legs in the proper climbing procedure as taught to him by *Hauptmann* Brooks.

As he swung himself over the balcony railing, Kurt was surprised to find that he had lost all fear. He was actually enjoying himself. He tried the door and was delighted to find that it was not locked. He eased himself through the opening and closed the door behind him. Now he was sandwiched between the French door and the heavy draperies. He felt along its folds until he parted the middle opening. Then he reached high along the seam and slowly, gently, so that it made no noise, pressed the fabric back along the rod to let moonlight enter the room. He stood rigidly and silently, letting his eyes become accustomed to the darkness and the placement of the furniture.

Diffused beams of moonlight touched the bed and Lisa Schmidler's blond hair on her pillow. Kurt tiptoed close to her, waiting with each footfall for the boards to creak, grateful that they did not. He took off his cap, knelt beside her and watched her a few moments. How peaceful she looked in sleep, how lovely and desirable. Did he dare disturb her? Would she scream? To roughly cover her mouth with his hand might be prudent but surely it would send the wrong message and frighten her. It was not what he wanted to do.

He whispered her name, "Lisa."

She stirred and rolled toward him still in her sleep, disarranging the thick comforter, revealing more of the long-sleeved, high-necked night-gown that covered her.

Softly again. "Lisa."

Her eyes flickered open and she stared toward the voice.

The voice thought he had best identify himself.

"It's Kurt, Lisa. Kurt von Hassell. I was here at dinner last night. The lowly *Schütze*."

She smiled. There was neither fear nor surprise in her expression. "I know you, Kurt," she said in the softest, sweetest voice. "You are not lowly. I was told that you are a baron."

"Who told you that?"

"The *Oberleutnant* confided it to me when I told him you were very nice...and very handsome. Are you real or am I dreaming?"

Kurt smiled at her with the gentlest, most unthreatening of smiles, though he was not sure she could discern it in the faint moonlight. "No. I'm real. I'm here. I wanted very much to be with you alone. But if you do not want me, Lisa, I will go, just as silently and quickly as I flew up here. And in the morning you will believe it was only a dream."

Lisa pulled aside the comforter and opened her arms to him in the same way she had raised them to the moon earlier. "Of all the men in your company, Kurt, it is you I have thought of most of all."

Still kneeling beside the bed, Kurt leaned closer and kissed her lips. He felt her arms wrap around him and squeeze him tightly against her breasts. The firm yet pliant feel of her body drove the last thoughts of soldierly things from his mind; her taste thrilled his mouth, her scent excited his nostrils. He withdrew his lips and moved to stand and undress. "Pardon me a moment," he mumbled.

"I have wanted this so much," Lisa whispered, her hand extended to draw him back to her.

As he took off his coat, shoes and clothes, Kurt wondered if she would have said that to any man who had had the courage to enter her bedroom as he had.

A few minutes after 2200 that night of May 1, 1945, Captain Brooks, Lieutenant Becker and Sergeant Blumberg gathered close to the small all-wave broadcast receiver in the command post and waited to hear a special German news bulletin that had been announced earlier. Dan wondered where Jung and von Hassell were. He hadn't seen them for a couple of hours. He surmised that, off duty, they might be asleep already or perhaps listening with the *Soldaten* gathered around another radio in one of the sleeping sections below in the barn.

A low, funereal roll of drums gave Dan a moment's forewarning, then the solemn voice of an announcer spoke:

"It is with profound regret that I announce the death of Adolf Hitler, *Führer* of the Third Reich, in his command bunker in Berlin yesterday. Grand Admiral Karl Doenitz has taken up his duties as president of Germany, according to the wishes of *der Führer*. Admiral Doenitz has begun negotiations with Allied commanders, seeking a cease fire. Further details will be broadcast as they become available."

Twenty-two

✠   *Stabsfeldwebel* Zweiger of Knight's Cross confirmed the sighting made earlier by one of his men. In the subdued light of an overcast morning he slowly swept his field glasses below a ridge in the middle distance. For just a moment he too spotted the unusual and unexpected cluster of soldiers in olive drab uniforms. They were traversing the upper face of a mountain west of the Hotel Edelweiss. They became visible only when they passed briefly through clearings in the woods.

"*Amerikanische Soldaten?*" he murmured in disbelief.

He had no doubt about the GI uniforms. He had worn one himself for three months at St. Germain and had seen more than enough of them coming at him with blazing guns before that. Even as he looked, they disappeared from view. They never came out of cover again. He didn't know whether to be elated that they had arrived at last or frightened that they might unwittingly attack him and his men. There weren't supposed to be any American troops in the area yet. If they hadn't done so already, they would surely spot the men of the *Jäger Einheit*. They might fire at them, even if their actual target was the SS company at the hotel. Or his comrades in the Knight's Cross company might have to shoot at the Americans, if only to defend themselves. What a tragedy that would be, since they now fought on the same side.

Zweiger went to Sergeant Schafer with his problem. For an American, this Schafer was a good German noncom. He would know what action to take.

"We'd better get out there quick as we can, Rudy!" Brooks exclaimed to his exec.

Even as he spoke, he realized he was being unusually testy. He had just talked on the radio to Schafer on patrol near the Edelweiss. He had ordered him to avoid physical contact with the intruders reported by Zweiger, but to keep watching for them and radio in if they were spotted again. If he was attacked, he and his men were to withdraw via Wattens toward the base and keep in frequent radio contact. The rest of the company would be moving up to support him.

Brooks had been depressed ever since the news of Hitler's death the night before. While cheers had rung out from other parts of the barn where men had heard the broadcast, he had felt keen disappointment, frustration and anger. He had been fueled for months on the hubris that he would be the captor of Adolf Hitler. Now the *Führer* had cheated him.

"Seventh Army is moving faster than we thought," Becker muttered, shaking his head. "They're liable to raid the hotel and grab whoever's there before we do."

"Or kill them," Brooks speculated. "Or kill our own men. Or us."

He forced the bitter disappointment of Hitler's suicide out of his mind and considered the radio conversation he'd just had with Schafer. A possibility teased at his mind. He had suspected—ever since Klung's message about the Russian agents killed near Trins a month earlier—that there was a *Spetsnaz* team in the Inn Valley. But he hadn't told anybody else about it.

A *Spetsnaz* unit might operate here as German soldiers, Tyrolean civilians or American soldiers. They were known to wear any uniform or apparel that suited their purpose, just as Knight's Cross was doing. Dan doubted that elements of 7th Army could be near the Hotel Edelweiss yet. The soldiers spotted might even be Germans. Skorzeny's men had worn U.S. uniforms during the Battle of the Bulge.

"Radio Mangold and Brunner," he directed Blumberg. "Tell them to bring their platoons and all equipment and supplies over here. They're to move out by squads at ten-minute intervals and take the most concealed routes to get here. I don't want them on the open road."

When Freddy had relayed his orders and received acknowledgment, Brooks told him to contact the commander of the OSS unit traveling with forward elements of 7th Army. "You've got the frequency, haven't you?"

"Yes, sir. Been looking forward to using it since we left France."

"Find out their exact position. I'm betting it's still somewhere west of Innsbruck."

Sleep the night before had been difficult for *Obersturmbannführer* Reiter. He had felt the suffocating presence of Siegfried Schmidt in the next bed, though his companion had slumbered like a man at peace with himself and the world. Perhaps it was the codeine pills and sedatives that had allowed him to rest for a change, like a person without troubles. Only the rumbling of his stomach and frequent passing of wind had indicated turmoil beneath his new outward calm. Few forced to be in his company, particularly during these last weeks in the *Führerbunker*, had the nerve to comment about his flatulence.

One opinion said it was because of his vegetarian diet; another that it was the stress of his responsibilities and the intolerable turn of events; another that it was because he rarely knew day from night and slept very little. Reiter attributed it to the tumult of his unpredictable disposition, a condition psychological as well as physiological. A man like him, Reiter had finally come to realize since being selected to be his aide, digested neither food nor mental input properly. During the night, therefore, Reiter had been grateful—despite his security concerns—for Schmidt's insistence that the French doors to the balcony be kept open a few inches to allow in the fresh mountain air he craved.

The day before, alone at last with the door locked and two SS guards in the hallway, Reiter had given Schmidt another potent pain-killing pill and slowly unwrapped his bandages to examine his burns. Much of his hair and all of his mustache had been singed off and the skin underneath seared. His skull, face and hands were covered with ugly blisters, charred blotches and cauterized vesicles that gleamed with the remains of salve put on in Berlin. The man was a mess; he looked like nobody Reiter had ever seen before. He felt sympathy for his charge's wounds, but the reality of the disguise was most effective.

Schmidt had insisted upon going into the bathroom to look at himself in the mirror. He had come out with an added look of shock on his face. "Even I do not recognize myself, Reiter," he had said. "God works in mysterious ways. I wonder only if everything will heal properly and I will be myself again."

Though hardly a believer himself, Reiter was startled to hear Schmidt refer to the deity as if he were one of His blessed. While he sat stoically, except for an occasional wince and moan, Reiter had cleaned his wounds with an antiseptic, replenished the ointment, wound new bandages and carefully cut holes for his eyes, ears and mouth.

Tending to him, Reiter had started to say, "I think, *mein...*" But he had caught himself quickly and gone on, "I think, *Herr* Schmidt, it will be all right to have a doctor look at your burns. I will have Jürgen summon the best he can find. With your permission, of course."

"You do not think he would recognize me?"

"No."

"Very well," Schmidt had agreed. With unexpected warmth, he had added, "You know, Reiter, I think it's not such a bad idea if you sometimes also call me by my first name—Siegfried. That way people will not be suspicious that I am too important a person, that I should always be addressed as *Herr* like a banker or a baron, or even like a general or *der Führer* himself." He laughed a pained little laugh. "Besides, you know how fond I am of the name Siegfried."

"Very well, *Herr*...very well, Siegfried," Reiter had replied.

A Wehrmacht doctor, summoned by *Sturmbannführer* Jürgen, had come in the late afternoon. The doctor was a burn specialist who had practiced for many years in Vienna. Jürgen had escorted him and enumerated his references to Reiter and Schmidt, trying again to win points for himself.

The physician had turned out to be quite good; an older man, a major in rank, taciturn and efficient in manner. He had disclosed little about himself except when pressed by Reiter. He admitted to having been called up only six months earlier when the need for army doctors had become critical. But he had made it known also that he had fought in the 1914–18 war before he was a doctor. That comment had animated *Herr* Schmidt who had declared—while Reiter kept hoping he would shut up before revealing too much history—that he too had been a soldier in the trenches in the First War, had been wounded and had been awarded the Iron Cross for heroism.

Reiter had hurried the physician along before Schmidt could take him further to heart and into his confidence. The man had recommended a hospital for the patient.

"That is impossible, *Herr Major*," Reiter had declared. "I want only your analysis of my companion's injuries, your recommendation for further treatments, which I will continue myself, and your prognosis regarding his recovery."

"Will I heal completely, Doctor? Will my hair grow again?" Schmidt had asked anxiously.

"I see no reason why not, *mein Herr*."

The doctor had left plenty of bandages, ointments and medications, including additional sedatives and pain-killers, and detailed instructions for treatments. Reiter was convinced he could take care of *Herr* Schmidt adequately himself as they moved along their escape route, and that in time he would recover, though it would be necessary to have him cultivate a full beard and mustache as his skin healed and his whiskers grew out, and to arrange the hair on his head differently and perhaps color it. Tinted glasses with heavy frames would be advisable too.

Reiter had eaten his meals in their room since their arrival—quite adequate fare considering the circumstances—but his companion had shown little interest in food. He had taken mostly liquid nourishment through a straw and small pieces of milk-softened bread that he had been able to pass through the mouth hole of his face bandages and chew slowly.

This morning Schmidt was out on the balcony again despite the cool air and overcast, doing his silly deep-breathing exercises. Reiter was from Frankfurt and preferred cities to the dubious glories of countryside and mountains. He didn't know this part of the Reich well at all. He wondered if it was too late in the spring to snow again. He hoped it would, to delay the advance of the Allied armies until he and *Herr* Schmidt could escape to a neutral country and avoid the ever-present danger of capture. They should not linger here for more than a day or two.

There was a knock at the door and Reiter called out, "One moment, please."

He went first to the balcony and said, "*Herr* Schmidt...Siegfried, please come in. I think it is dangerous to show yourself as much as you do, even with the bandages on. You can be spotted from the distance and it will make people wonder about you."

"But we are protected, are we not? Two SS guards at the door around the clock. A company dug in outside and patrolling the grounds. Is that not what you told me?"

"Yes, *mein Herr,* it is."

"I need air. Fresh mountain air," Schmidt continued in a tone of rebuke. He felt a little stronger, a little more optimistic after the doctor's visit. He was no longer concerned about events in Berlin that were beyond his influence. He now felt the need to take more control of his present situation and destiny. Reiter could only be a pawn. "It refreshes me and clears my mind"

"As you wish, Siegfried," Reiter acquiesced reluctantly. "There is someone at the door. Do you want to retire to the bedroom before I admit whoever it is, or shall I open it now?"

"See who it is, *Obersturmbannführer,*" Schmidt instructed.

Reiter opened the door to the maître d'hôtel, who extended an envelope in his hand. The two SS guards had stepped aside to allow him access to the door, but they kept their eyes on him.

"This radio message came for you a few minutes ago," he said, bowing obsequiously.

Reiter beckoned him into the room and closed the door so that the guards would hear nothing further.

From across the room, *Herr* Schmidt's voice called out, with a note of humor, "*Guten Tag,* cousin Schmidt."

Reiter wished his charge would shut up. The voice fortunately was still strained and unnatural. Whether the clever Siegfried forced it to be that way or whether the sound was related to his injuries, Reiter didn't know, but he felt it was sufficiently different not to be recognized.

"Not such a good day, *Herr* Schmidt, I am sorry to say," responded the maître d'hôtel. His face was drawn and sad as he handed the envelope to Reiter. "Have you heard the rumor that the *Führer* has committed suicide?"

He regretted immediately that he had spoken the words. He saw the terrible look of shock register on the *Obersturmbannführer's* face. Shifting his glance, the hotel manager found the eyes of his namesake boring at him through the eye slits in his bandages. It gave him a most uncomfortable feeling.

"Where did you hear such a thing?" Reiter demanded in a gruff voice.

"On the radio this morning, *Herr Obersturmbannführer,*" Luther Schmidt related. Suddenly realizing he might be suspected of listening to enemy propaganda, he emphasized, "It was a German broadcast. You have not heard it?"

"No, we haven't been listening to broadcasts," Reiter said calmly. "If it is true, then our *Führer*, Adolf Hitler, died for his people, fighting international Bolshevism. It was a final act of bravery."

"I regret being the bearer of this terrible news," the maître d'hôtel said gravely. "It apparently happened two days ago in Berlin. Admiral Doenitz has taken over as President of the Reich and has contacted the Allied leaders, asking for a cease fire."

"What terms?" Reiter demanded.

"They speak again of unconditional surrender."

"You may go now, Schmidt!" shouted the bandaged man in a strident voice.

When the hotel manager scurried out and pulled the door closed behind him, Reiter barely had time to lock it before he heard the explosion of epithets from his companion:

"It didn't take that turncoat Doenitz long! Unconditional surrender! Disgraceful! With such traitors like him and the treacherous, bungling general staff of the Wehrmacht, Nazis such as you and I, Reiter, never had a chance. They should all have been exterminated after their monstrous bomb plot last year!"

Reiter tried to mollify him. "Spreading the news of Hitler's death can only work in our favor, *Herr* Schmidt. We must thank Doenitz for that."

Schmidt's right hand trembled in heightened agitation, always a sign of the volcano about to erupt. The angry tirade continued to spew from the mouth hole of the bandaged head:

"Have no fear, Reiter! We will rise from the ashes of today's Germany! Next time the leaders will be true Nazis, faithful to the *Führer* and the cause, brave men who will not renege on their oath of allegiance."

Reiter found himself becoming annoyed, but dared not show it. Couldn't Schmidt see the irrationality of his ranting? Had he not witnessed with his own eyes the horror and inferno of Berlin in those last hours? Couldn't he fathom that it was the very policies and actions of the Nazi tyranny that had brought Germany to utter ruin? Even he, *Obersturmbannführer* Reiter, who had embraced the vilest of those philosophies and acts himself, had come to realize the futility, evil and basic flaws Schmidt espoused.

He tore open the envelope with a movement more violent than he might otherwise have employed, and read the radio signal. He looked up and saw that his companion had come out of his tantrum and was watching him expectantly.

"Who is it from?" he asked calmly.

"A moment, please, and I will decipher it," Reiter replied. He took the private code book and a pen and paper from his pocket and worked silently for a few minutes. *"Reichsminister* Speer," he said finally with satisfaction.

"Ahh. Speer. A good man. One of the few I could consider a personal friend. He will help."

"He has already helped greatly, *Herr*...Siegfried, as you are aware," Reiter reminded, "and now he has responded well again."

The *Obersturmbannführer* suddenly realized he had spoken almost curtly to his companion. He had to be more careful. Some of the motivation for his conscientious attendance upon Schmidt was still the old, lingering feelings of duty and homage. But he also wanted to be sure to be cut in for the monetary gratitude his charge and those who helped him might dispense for Reiter's assistance.

He had turned to Albert Speer, the *Führer's* favorite architect and Minister of Armaments and Munitions, for financial aid to abet the basic plan put in place earlier by the SS. He had told the *Reichsminister* that he had been placed in charge of a scientist working on a secret weapon project, a man who had to be spirited out of Germany. Reiter knew that Speer could be trusted not to disclose the flight in the event he saw through the ploy. His trust had been substantiated when Speer advanced him the funds they had now.

"Additional arrangements for our escape route and more funds will be completed later today," Reiter said, handing over his decoded copy of the signal. "We are to expect another message."

"I know Herr Speer will continue to serve me well, as long as he's able," Schmidt said. "Once we're in a neutral country, I won't have to worry."

"I've been wondering what final escape route he will arrange for us and where we can tap the account he has set up," Reiter mused out loud. He let the last part of his remark drop in with seeming nonchalance.

"Account?" Schmidt repeated with a note of smugness in his voice. "Believe me, Reiter, when I assure you it is much more than one account. I'm not concerned about finances. The funds we've got with us should last until we reach a haven. If we run short I can take care of that quite easily. A secure escape route is what we need primarily. I've been aware the SS established underground routes into many countries." In that instant his erratic temperament changed again and he vented his spleen. "It would take a *verfluchte* son of a bitch like Himmler to set up such a system."

Reiter winced at the vehemence of Schmidt's denunciation of the leader of the SS, a man to whom Reiter still owed nominal allegiance. If this was Schmidt's feeling about the man who, after *Reichsmarschall* Göring's fall from grace, had been Hitler's choice for Number Two Nazi, then Reiter didn't think anyone, even himself, could depend on retaining Schmidt's faithfulness.

What interested Reiter, however—more than his willingness to perform his duty to a successful conclusion—was the capability Schmidt spoke of to draw on financial accounts. The *Obersturmbannführer* knew that the upper Nazi hierarchy had been accumulating fantastic sums and secreting them in foreign accounts. Adolf Hitler himself must have amassed a huge fortune during the years he had been in power. He not only had mesmerized the German people, he had robbed them.

In order to profit himself, Reiter resolved to continue to coddle *Herr* Schmidt, no matter the man's frequent irrational outbursts and the negative feelings he had begun to have about him.

Major Mikhail Schepilov stared forlornly out the window of the isolated *Schihütte* north of Kolsassberg where he and his *Spetsnaz* team had been for two days.

He wore an American lieutenant's gold bars on his field jacket and shirt collar and carried papers identifying him as Second Lieutenant Michael Shell. Captain Viktor Astakhov, who was fluent in German but not English, had become Staff Sergeant Victor Albertson. Sergeant Igor Petrofsky, also with a cover name, wore corporal's stripes on his American uniform; he knew enough English and German to get by. Three of the squad were junior sergeants fluent in English. The rest made up in combat skills what they lacked in English or German.

It was not so much the gray Tyrolean morning that depressed Schepilov, as the possibility that he and his mission were now redundant. Only yesterday he had been optimistic that he was really onto something. One of his scouts had brought back encouraging news:

"SS officers and a civilian with his head wrapped in bandages arrived at the hotel this morning in a limousine. The bandaged man was treated as if he is a very important person."

Schepilov had been elated. His command post was only three kilometers from the Wattental, the valley up which the road led to the hotel. All intelligence indicated that of the many possibilities for a secluded, temporary refuge for escaping Nazi leaders, the Edelweiss was the only site where an SS company was dug in to protect someone of importance.

"Where are the Americans? Their German mountain unit?" Schepilov had pressed. "Did you observe them too?"

"Yes, Comrade Major," the scout had reported. "Through my field glasses I saw two of them moving through the forest, keeping the building and activities under surveillance. They used their radio after the limousine arrived."

"And the SS company on duty there?"

"No change. Still dug in as if expecting an attack. They seem bored, though, indifferent in performing their duties."

"They must know it is all up with them soon," Schepilov had declared with satisfaction.

But that had been yesterday when the major still had felt a passion and obsession to be the captor of Adolf Hitler. Now he wondered if it was even worth continuing the mission to see who else they might capture. He had received no orders to the contrary yet. But according to broadcasts he had listened to the night before on the German band and then on the American and BBC stations, the reason for the operation no longer existed. Adolf Hitler was dead in Berlin while he and his *Spetsnaz* unit were here in the Inn Valley looking for him, just as the Americans' ersatz *Jäger Einheit* was doing.

All through a restless night, Schepilov had felt the heavy frustration of failure for reasons beyond his control. Unless it was a hoax. That was his one remaining hope: that the broadcasts were in error, a deception perpetrated by the Nazis.

His scouts were still on patrol near the Edelweiss. Schepilov himself had gone with them twice. He loved being on the move in enemy country again. He savored the stimulation of spotting, tracking and hiding from enemy SS troops and the Americans' ersatz *Jäger Einheit*. He didn't know if he or any of his men had been seen yet, but they had not been fired on. He believed they might continue to operate as cleverly. He had great confidence in his own skills and those of Captain Astakhov and their team of fifteen men.

It was later on the second day that Schepilov was stirred from the gloom induced by the broadcasts of Hitler's death. His scouts reported they had seen once again, on an upper balcony of the hotel, the mysterious figure with his head wrapped in bandages.

"The American undercover unit has increased its strength in the vicinity," the scout leader related. "Usually there are only two or three. This morning we observed more than twenty-five."

"Then they are going forward," Schepilov said excitedly, "and we must also."

He glanced toward Captain Astakhov—a big man, bulkier than he but not as tall, a man with broad cheekbones and a square, determined jaw— and he saw his nod of approval.

Viktor recognized the familiar look of anticipation on Mikhail's face, the aspect of pleasure contemplated and the touch of cruelty. It was the Tatar in him, Viktor thought. Something bred in the genes. Ancestral memories of great hordes of mounted warriors galloping across the Steppes. Neither one of them gave a damn about ideology, though they were successful enough at feigning interest when political commissars were around. They agreed in private moments they couldn't care less whether Russia was ruled by an autocratic Czar or Soviet dictatorship, just as long as the army was unfettered and dominant.

"Whoever the bandaged man is, he must be someone important!" Captain Astakhov agreed emphatically. "How shall we proceed?"

173

Schepilov studied the sector map on the table. It would be suicidal for his small unit to attack anyone head on. His thinking, and a certain disquiet, were made more intense by his memory of the hideous death General Merkulov had promised if he blundered into a politically dangerous incident with the Americans and had the temerity to survive.

"We will let the Americans do the dirty work for us," the major said. "Let them capture whoever it is. We will follow them closely. When they least expect it, when they are fleeing with their prisoners, exhausted from their encounter with the Germans, we will ambush them and take their quarry away from them."

Twenty-three

✠   Innsbruck was in a state of turmoil.

As they walked through the streets early in the afternoon of May 2, picking up information wherever they could, agents Hans Zimmer and Walter Freiherr were glad they had the foresight to change into Alpine clothes instead of wearing the Gestapo costumes that had stood them well on other occasions. They had left the bogus attire and radio locked in the Volkswagen in the police garage on Kaiserjägerstrasse.

Nobody in the capital of the Tyrol seemed in complete control anymore, certainly not the Nazi power structure that had been in authority just the day before.

Elements of the American 103rd Infantry Division were little more than twenty miles to the west. SS and Wehrmacht troops who still had the stomach to fight were massing with heavy artillery and armor on the approach roads. Yet nobody knew if a battle for the city would take place. Hans and Walter had heard a broadcast by the Nazi Gauleiter of the Tyrol urging military and political forces to surrender Innsbruck without a fight.

Armed Resistance groups roamed the streets with impunity. The few German soldiers Hans and Walter noticed wore dazed expressions and made no threatening moves toward anyone. Some were being rounded up and disarmed by the Resistance. There was rumor of a mutiny in one of the Wehrmacht barracks.

The two Knight's Cross men made their way to the *Goethe Stube* of the *Goldener Adler*. There were only a few people in the room, none in uniform, all quietly eating, drinking and talking as if indifferent to the events taking place outside. Walter and Hans were too excited to eat or drink but felt obliged to ask for a couple of beers when a waitress came to their table. Within minutes, *Kriminalinspektor* Klung joined them. He had just come from the *Landhaus,* the seat of the provincial government,

175

a short distance away on Maria-Theresien-Strasse. He looked happier than they had ever seen him.

"The most incredible things are happening," Klung told them. "Everything we've worked for. I do not think there will be a battle for the city. You heard the Gauleiter's broadcast?"

"Yes," Walter responded, "and I was surprised that *verfluchte* Nazi had sense enough to do the right thing."

"It was not easy to get him to do it," Klung said. "It was not what he originally planned. At the *Landhaus* I heard that American OSS agents were responsible. Men I did not even know about are turning up all over the place and arranging the surrender of the city. One of them actually had been in custody of the Gestapo but escaped."

"It wasn't one of our two jailbirds, was it?" Hans asked, astounded. "Karl Bergen or Willy Hupnagel?"

"No, of course not," Klung assured him. "They're still in cells reserved for Kripo prisoners. I had one of my aides look in on them this morning. Hupnagel is quite relaxed. He has been kept informed. He knows it's almost over and is happy to be safe. I've left Bergen to stew in his own nasty juices. Like a Nazi, he threatens to have everybody shot when American forces arrive."

"Sounds like the happy Karl we all know," Walter observed sarcastically. "Our CO will take care of him when our work is done here. Do you have information about the SS?"

"Some units are still blocking the western approaches," Klung related, shaking his head. "Nobody at the *Landhaus* can tell what they will finally do, if they will listen to the Gauleiter and lay down their arms, or if the fanatics will incite a battle. However, most of the division has moved north of the Austrian border to deploy along the Inn River above Kufstein."

"How about the unit at the Hotel Edelweiss?" Walter asked pointedly.

"Still there. Only an understrength company. With no indication they intend to pull out with the others," the inspector reported. "This *Sturmbannführer* you asked me about... Jürgen... apparently has a free hand. He is ostensibly just another officer with the local Waffen SS, but we believe he conducts special assignments for the Nazi hierarchy. His communications bypass regular channels and go directly to Reich Central Security in Berlin. He has the authority to pull in as many SS elements as he wishes to use at the Edelweiss."

"Is it plausible, *Herr* Klung," asked Walter, "that he serves a function in the escape routes of high-ranking Nazis?"

"Yes. I now have the identities of the two men who arrived at the hotel yesterday, but they do not seem to fit the high profiles you're looking for."

"Who are they?" Walter asked eagerly.

"The SS *Obersturmbannführer* is Dietrich Reiter. His civilian companion, the one in the bandages, is Siegfried Schmidt, a rocket scientist who was badly injured in an air raid. They have just come from Berlin, so I surmise they are indeed trying to flee from the Allies. But neither one is known to me as a top Nazi."

"The bandaged one could be anybody," Hans declared. "Who told you their names?"

"I have a Kripo informant working there. The porter. If your people are planning an action at the Edelweiss, you will please inform *Gefreiter* Halle that my man is not to be harmed."

"Of course," Walter assured him.

"There is one other strange report," Inspector Klung continued. "Your army is moving on Innsbruck from the west. Yet my man at the Edelweiss informed me there have been glimpses of soldiers in American uniforms in the forest not far from the hotel. There has been no fighting, not even one shot fired by either side. They are seen, then they are not seen. But that's more than twenty kilometers east of here and forty kilometers beyond where your forward units are supposed to be at this moment. I doubt that they could have slipped through the German lines unnoticed. Have *Gefreiter* Halle and his men changed into American uniforms?"

"No," Hans replied. "To the best of my knowledge, there was no plan to do so. Maybe some paratroops have jumped in there ahead of the main forces. We will let the *Gefreiter* know about it. He also wants to know your assessment of the intentions of the Wehrmacht garrison here. We've heard a rumor about a mutiny in one barracks."

"It's true. You can forget about them. They're just playing skat until they can surrender. They'll never react to anything your people do."

"And Major Jürgen's SS troops at the Edelweiss?"

Out of habit, *Kriminalinspektor* Klung looked around the *Bierstube* and reassured himself no one was eavesdropping. It would not be long, he believed, before he would be liberated from the constant feeling of tightness in the guts and fear in the heart.

"They appear to be dug in for a fight," he replied. "I don't know why. I haven't been there to see for myself. I don't think the hotel is a command center of any importance, but *Sturmbannführer* Jürgen is staying there now. It is quite possible they will disregard the Gauleiter's broadcast to surrender."

Klung emphasized his next remark. He suspected what *Gefreiter* Halle might be planning to do, though he had no awareness of the number of men he had with him. "You know the SS mentality. They will even fight others wearing German uniforms."

Siegfried Schmidt stood just outside the French doors on the balcony and watched the Alpine peaks radiate the pinkish hue of the setting sun. The overcast had parted just in time for the display. How well he remembered scenes like this in better times at the Berghof in Berchtesgaden where everyone went out of their way to please him, where he had the entire retinue of men and women belonging to *der Führer's* staff to look after his needs. Who would have thought it could ever come to this? Now he had only Reiter. He seemed a good enough man and so far had served him well, but would the *Obersturmbannführer* be able to see them through to safety? Schmidt waited for the colors in the sky to fade, then went inside. He was actually feeling hungry. He hoped there might be spaghetti available, with a light sauce, and perhaps some vegetables, though he doubted there would be fresh ones in Austria this time of year.

Entering the room, Schmidt said in a pensive voice, "The scenery is so beautiful and peaceful, Reiter. Here I am able to relax. I almost forget that I'm a refugee."

Reiter looked up as he heard his charge's muffled voice. He was sitting at a desk decoding the transcript of the latest radio message delivered to him by the porter a few minutes earlier. He felt again an eerie sensation at the sight of the bandaged head and the sound of the odd voice coming out of it.

"I've never thought of it in that way, Siegfried," he said. "For your morale, I beg of you not to think that way yourself. Soon all will be well. I have a new message from *Herr* Speer."

"What does he say?"

"The numbers of various accounts at banks in Zurich, Switzerland."

"Let me have it," Schmidt ordered, extending his bandaged hand.

He studied the decoded words and numbers a few moments. "I wonder if Zurich is where we will be routed, even if only temporarily?" he asked. "It is actually a pleasing thought. I have never been to Switzerland, but I believe they are a decent, hard-working people. And there would be no language problem. Also, more important, it has been a scrupulously neutral and humane country. Its laws would give us sanctuary, as it has often given it to our enemies."

"I don't know where we will be going," answered Reiter. "The message said nothing about that. But I believe the accounts can be drawn upon from anywhere the banking system is still functioning internationally."

Schmidt spoke with irritation, his voice rising. "We must have an escape route and final destination quickly, Reiter. It is what we need more than bank accounts. I already have with me the numbers of secret accounts."

"Further instructions will come," Reiter stated confidently.

"I hope you are correct, Reiter," Schmidt said in a threatening voice. He handed the sheet of paper back to him. "Memorize the numbers, in case we lose the paper. I'll put it in my wallet with the others after you have studied it."

"Perhaps I should memorize the other numbers too," the *Obersturmbannführer* suggested in a voice seemingly without guile.

178

Schmidt stared at him through the eye slits in his bandage. His body went rigid, as if he were about to explode in anger again. After a few moments of silent staring, weighing his aide's words, he said, "A good idea. I will give them to you eventually. I would like to have my dinner now. Call downstairs." Schmidt told him what he wanted to eat.

Reiter went to the phone and ordered their meals. There had been a time when he would not have consumed meat in *Herr* Schmidt's presence, for he knew the man objected. But he had not observed that courtesy since arriving here and was pleased to hear from the maître d'hôtel that veal was available. Then Reiter sat down and read the Zurich account numbers again and again until they were implanted in his brain. He wouldn't forget them. Schmidt sat under a lamp across the room, holding a pair of reading glasses up to his eye slits and trying, with some difficulty, to scan old copies of the *Völkischer Beobachter* that had been brought to their suite. From time to time, he clucked his tongue and shook his head as if in wonderment at what had been going on in the world during these times.

Obersturmbannführer Reiter had a new feeling of power. His horizons had expanded. Opposite him was a modern Midas. Every time he called the right digits, enormous sums, denominated in any currency he chose, would gush forth. But not in the Reich.

That evening after dinner, anxious for the travel instructions that still had not arrived, Reiter tried to get through to Berlin by phone but learned that the main exchange no longer functioned. His calls could not be routed where he wanted them to go. Nor was there any response to the coded radio messages he sent via the guard detachment's long-range transmitter. The tight, secret cabal of contacts and cutouts in the inner circle of the SS who had helped arrange for him and Schmidt to come this far—without fully knowing exactly what it was they were doing—seemed now to have disappeared from the face of the earth, perhaps killed or captured or gone to ground in their separate ways. Even Speer did not reply.

"Skorzeny will come for me," Schmidt muttered when his aide reported he had been unable to get through to Germany to obtain additional escape instructions. Then his voice rose with hope. "Skorzeny will make our escape work, Reiter. He is already in Austria or the Obersalzburg with many of his best men. I knew this even before we left Berlin. Remember what he did for Mussolini two years ago? He took him from under the noses of his enemies."

But the mere mention of the Italian dictator's name suddenly chilled Schmidt's mood. "Poor man. What a terrible end," he whispered hoarsely. "Perhaps it would have gone better for Mussolini if Skorzeny had not saved him to meet a worse fate."

He had learned, as Reiter had, just three nights earlier while still in

Berlin, that the deposed fascist dictator of Italy had been captured again by Italian partisans, along with his mistress. They were then summarily executed with machine pistols and strung up by their heels outside a gas station in Milan.

Reiter sensed that it was a moment for reassurance. "If we do not hear something by tomorrow morning I will make arrangements myself. With the authority I have and the assistance of the SS, we will commandeer an aircraft and pilot to fly us out of here."

"To what destination?" Schmidt demanded.

Reiter thought quickly. There were only two countries in Europe where the Allies could not touch them. "It would depend on the aircraft available to us," he said, "and the supply of fuel that can be obtained. Switzerland would be the easiest to reach and there would be close access to the funds in Zurich. Spain would be more desirable for other reasons, but it might be more difficult to get there in one flight."

"In any event, after that, South America," Schmidt said eagerly, "where others have preceded us and still more will follow. Yes, Reiter, I know all about these things. National Socialism will rise again, perhaps in more fertile ground."

At dinner, Reiter tried to concentrate on his food and tune out *Herr* Schmidt's continuous monologue. Finally, when the dishes had been removed by the porter and one more futile attempt was made to get through to Berlin by telephone and radio, there was nothing left to do except go to bed early. He was pleased to follow his companion's instructions and leave the balcony door open a few inches.

Schmidt dropped off quickly. He had, surprisingly, shared a small carafe of local wine with his aide. Perhaps it was the wine added to his regular dose of sedative and pain-killer that put him out so quickly and deeply.

Reiter slept fitfully at first. He suffered through a batch of disjointed dreams. He heard the voice of Adolf Hitler screaming his fury at the treacherous, bungling army general staff. He heard *der Führer,* as he had sometimes listened to him in life, in the midst of a tirade about his magnificent vision of a Europe united under the control of the Third Reich—a Nazi empire—with the *Untermenschen* of Poland, Czechoslovakia, Hungary and the Soviet Union as the working slaves.

Interspersed with the sights and sounds of Adolf Hitler, Reiter dreamed of numbers...numbers of secret bank accounts that faded and weren't remembered. He did not fall into a deep sleep until after midnight.

Through his night binoculars, Captain Dan Brooks scanned the machine gun emplacements and mortar pits manned by Waffen SS troops in front of the Hotel Edelweiss. It was a clear, almost cloudless night with a crescent moon that gave dim visibility in open spaces but did not penetrate the forest. The enemy soldiers gave no sign they were aware the wooded slopes around them stirred with silent, hostile movement.

Every element of Brooks's *Jäger Einheit*, more than 160 men, was deployed to its position, led by the platoon sergeants and their *Feldwebels*. Each section hidden in the woods close to the Edelweiss kept in touch by radio. Lieutenant Becker, in command of the backup forces, had with him the stretcher details who would carry away the captives. Eight kilometers to the southwest, in the mountains above Tulfes, a security squad waited at a reassembly area under the command of Sergeant Paulsen, the medic.

The SS mortars Brooks observed in front of the hotel would pose no threat to his plan. Even in the unlikely event his raiders had to switch to their secondary strategy of a frontal assault, they would flank the guns quickly and enter the hotel itself. The machine guns too were placed for a set piece battle, a fight he did not intend to fall into. The enemy gunners did not look alert. They lounged on sandbags, talking and smoking, oblivious to what might be going on beyond their immediate perimeter.

There was enough distance between the entrenched positions and the building for his sentry-killer teams to slip behind the gun sites from the close woods on the flank and take out the two sentries marching stiffly back and forth under the balconies on the target side of the hotel. The fixed emplacements and bulk of the SS company would be no obstacle to the *Jäger Einheit* if silence and secrecy could be maintained. He had made allowance too for the possibility of a Russian *Spetsnaz* unit appearing.

"You're to fire at *anyone* who attacks you or tries to block the operation in any way, no matter what uniforms they're wearing!" he had told his exec and noncoms before leaving Schmidler's farm.

"Who else do you expect?" Rudy Becker had asked with a puzzled expression.

The American sergeants and German *Feldwebels* at the briefing also had looked confused. Yet Dan had not wanted to use the word *Russians*. He believed the truth would only baffle them further and inhibit their ability to respond instantly in a critical moment. Russians theoretically were allies to be embraced on meeting, not shot. His men would also hesitate to fire at other men in American uniforms, even if attacked by them, though he doubted they would be able to differentiate uniforms in the murky forest.

"There are others who might want the same captives," Brooks had replied brusquely. "Just follow orders. We don't have time to ask for I.D.s if somebody suddenly comes out of the darkness shooting at us. Pass the word to your men. They're to be alert for an attack from any quarter—not only from the SS we've been scouting. Kill anyone who gets in the way."

He had not divulged to his exec that he had names attached to his kidnap targets now. Walter and Hans had brought the names and other intelligence from Innsbruck just before the final briefing and had confirmed the location of the suite the men occupied. But the names had no significance and he had no way of knowing if they were true identities. With *Schmidt* and *Reiter* as the targets, instead of Himmler or Bormann, Brooks worried that his men's motivation might be diminished.

Lieutenant Becker had earlier pressed the subject of the bandaged man further. "Have you considered that the broadcast about Hitler's death could be a phony?" he had asked.

"Yes. That's why we've got to grab these guys," Dan had replied.

At their final briefing alone with him, the agents also had relayed the intelligence that *Sturmbannführer* Jürgen was now at the hotel with his troops and that Klung suspected him of having a function in the escape procedures of the Nazi hierarchy.

Hunkered down close to Brooks, merged with the night and the trees on the slope east of the building, were the three men he had chosen to go in with him as the snatch team: Sergeant Schafer, Helmut Jung and Kurt von Hassell. They held their grappling irons and ropes ready and were armed with Lugers, knives and grenades, though their strategy was to use none of the weapons unless absolutely necessary.

Schafer felt himself tightly poised to move. He had gone into combat so often these last weeks with the guerrillas that he hardly felt his heartbeat quicken. Even without binoculars, he could pick out the figures of enemy soldiers. Maurer's sentry-killer teams had moved out of sight somewhere below him, closer to their targets, but their action would be played out within his view.

Jung leaned close to von Hassell and whispered into his ear, "Too bad it is not Hitler in there, eh Kurt? Damn the bastard for killing himself before we could get our hands on him."

"At least we know what we trained for," von Hassell whispered. "Everything we practiced is coming up now, my friend. It is tonight or it will never be."

"*Viel Glück*, Kurt!"

"*Viel Glück*, Helmut!"

Stabsfeldwebel Hans Zweiger heard movement in the forest, the crackling of underbrush and leaves off to his right about fifty meters away, but he resisted the temptation to investigate. It was none of the twelve in his own squad. He had just finished moving along the line, whispering that night's American password, "Piston," and getting back the countersign, "Valve."

They were in a blocking position, one hundred meters back on the thickly wooded hillside. Zweiger couldn't see the Edelweiss from his location. His orders were to stay there until the snatch team and stretcher bearers carrying the prisoners came past. Then they were to fall in behind and act as rear guard and flankers. Another squad under *Unteroffizier* Joseph Werner, posted to Zweiger's left, would follow a few minutes later to serve as an additional rear guard.

Zweiger considered that the movement he heard was probably one of the other squads getting into position. But he also gave thought to the captain's warning to be alert for intruders other than the SS unit below them at the hotel. Could he have meant the *Amerikanische Soldaten* spotted that morning on a nearby mountain slope? Remembering the diagram Brooks had drawn of the planned deployment of his elements and the routes of approach and withdrawal, Zweiger knew there was enough room between the *Jäger Einheit's* separated squads and platoons to allow space for the intrusion of any foe that quietly came at them.

Major Mikhail Schepilov led his *Spetsnaz* squad through the dark, thick woods in single file behind their scout. Captain Viktor Astakhov held half the men back at a two-minute interval to avoid being trapped all together. They moved as silently as possible, yet almost blundered a number of times into elements of the Americans' undercover company.

Schepilov wondered how the Knight's Cross men wearing German uniforms would react in the first seconds to him and his men masquerading in American uniforms. Would they greet them as friends and contribute to their own doom? Or shoot at them? In the darkness, they might not even identify the uniforms immediately.

Working their way cautiously through the trees behind their scout, the two halves of the *Spetsnaz* squad reached the stakeout site where Sergeant Petrofsky had been hiding for many hours, surveying the east side of the hotel and surrounding area through binoculars.

Major Schepilov whispered in English, "They are all around us."

"I know, comrade Major," the sergeant whispered back.

"You are absolutely certain about the room of our quarry?"

"Yes, sir. They have gone to bed now. The lights are out, but I observed the bandaged one on the balcony before dark. I could see him and the SS officer in the lighted rooms before the drapes were drawn. The American unit has gathered in strength. I have heard them and caught glimpses of them."

"You've done well, Petrofsky. I'll take over the observation now. There is something else I want you to do quickly." He turned and whispered to Captain Astakhov. "You too, Viktor."

Schepilov glanced at his radium dial watch. It was 0050. The SS sentries had been changed at midnight and the next shift, according to his lookouts, was 0200. If he were running the American operation he would give the sentries on duty an hour to start slacking off, then begin whatever he was going to do at 0100.

"I'm convinced there will not be a frontal assault unless they are discovered," he continued softly. "They have climbing ropes and grappling irons and will attempt a silent, stealthy capture of the men we want."

"Then we ambush them in the forest and take the prisoners away," Astakhov murmured.

"Correct, Viktor," Schepilov acknowledged. "We must find the best place and moment to strike. Take a man—and Petrofsky you take a man—one team to the right, one to the left. Do a hundred meter sweep of the terrain and return here in ten minutes with a report of what you see. If you observe *Jägers*, count them and note their exact positions. I think the Americans will try to escape through this part of the forest. It's closest to our quarry's room. We must intercept them before the rest of their force joins them."

"What if they spot us, comrade Major?" asked the sergeant. "Shall we fire at them?"

"Of course not, Petrofsky. Fade into the trees, as *they* will. Until they've got their captives and are on their way out of here, the Americans will do nothing overt against us. They don't want to alert the Germans at the hotel and neither do we."

Twenty-four

✠ Having crept with his two sentry-killer teams to the closest concealing edge of brush, Sergeant Maurer watched the luminous hands of his watch ticking off the final seconds.

Thirty yards away, the two SS guards with rifles on their shoulders moved through the darkness toward each other from the corners of the building. It would take them two minutes to meet in the middle of the wall and do an about face under the overhanging balcony.

Maurer tensed as the minute hand reached 0100 and the captain's voice whispered through the walkie-talkie against his ear: "All elements are in place, Maurer. Go!"

Maurer tapped the killers and whispered, "*Zeit!* . . . Time!"

They waited the extra seconds until the sentries met, faced about and parted. Then the two men on each team, lightened of any burden but their knives, dashed out of cover, moving low, swift and silent. Each pair closed with their target before the SS men ever knew they were being attacked.

Jäger hands clasped firmly over mouths to stifle outcries; bodies were yanked back over knees; stilettos were plunged deeply between ribs into hearts. Each backup man grabbed rifle and helmet before they could clatter to the ground. He put them on and continued to walk the dark beat to the corner. The knife men lifted the dead sentries and carried them into the brush.

Dan Brooks shoved the binoculars under his tunic and buttoned it tight against his chest. The walkie-talkie fit snugly into his jacket pocket. Without elation or compassion he had watched the swift, ruthless killing of the sentries.

"Now!" he commanded the men beside him.

The snatch team rose up and dashed swiftly to the building. They halted under the middle tier of balconies. The lower one was fifteen feet high. Dan threw his padded grappling iron over its railing and it took hold as he drew back on the attached rope. Beside him, Schafer also hooked his grappling iron and rope onto the balcony with one toss. Each climbed swiftly and slipped over the railing and around the planters. They paused a moment to listen at the balcony door. When no sounds came from within, Dan signaled Jung and von Hassell to climb up the ropes. The balcony they had to reach was ten feet above them.

Brooks and Schafer stood on the shoulders of Jung and von Hassell. They hooked clamps and ropes to the railing overhead and pulled themselves to the next story. Jung and von Hassell followed, tied two more ropes to the railing and dropped the ends to the ground.

The two stretcher teams, dispatched from the wooded slope by Lieutenant Becker, took up their posts under the balconies. There were four men to a litter. Each carried a Schmeisser he could use with one hand. They flattened themselves into the darkness against the wall. The two *Jägers* impersonating the sentries paced past them.

On the top balcony, Brooks found the French doors to the bedroom ajar. The drapes were drawn back a couple of feet. He slipped through silently, his three men following. In the dim glimmer of ambient light from outside, he discerned the shape of the room, the layout of furniture. He and Jung moved stealthily to the furthest bed and Brooks saw the mummy-like head jutting out of the blankets. He flicked on a small flashlight, swept it over the two slumbering figures, then set it down on a chest so its beam hit the wall. The light reflected back and spread dimly through the room. Schafer and von Hassell approached the other bed and were the first to attack.

The sleeper was on his stomach. Schafer grabbed his head and pushed the pillow over it to keep him from crying out. Kurt yanked off the blankets, grabbed one arm and bent it up toward the man's shoulders, then sat on his back as he began to struggle. Schafer used one hand to take a morphine syrette from his pocket, but the quarry got his head out from under the pillow and cried out, "*Zu hilfe! Zu Hilfe!*... Help! Help!"

A moment later a knock came at the entry door of the suite's living room and a muffled voice called out, "*Was ist los? Herr Obersturmbann-führer! Was haben Sie? Machen Sie die Tür auf, Bitte!*"

Schafer put the pillow over the man's head to silence him while Kurt tied his wrists behind his back, though he continued to struggle. Then they stuffed wads of cotton into his mouth and taped them to his face. Schafer pulled the man's pajama shirt from his shoulder and plunged the morphine syrette into his arm. For good measure, he injected a second shot. Sergeant Paulsen had told him that one syrette would numb a man if he was in pain and two would knock him cold in a couple of minutes. As the prisoner's struggles weakened, Schafer pulled a cloth hood down over his head.

At the other bed, the quarry fought back with less strength. Jung tied his wrists behind him and pulled him into a sitting position. Brooks resisted the urge to rip away the bandages and see who was underneath. The prisoner was shouting, "Reiter! Reiter! *Helfen Sie mir! Wir sind unter Angriff!* . . . Help me! We're under attack!"

Dan shut him up by stuffing cotton wads through the opening in the gauze and into his mouth and taping them tightly in place. He drew a hood from his pocket and slid it over the man's head, then turned him over roughly, pulled his pajama pants down and injected two syrettes of morphine into his writhing buttocks.

The knocking at the suite's front door and the shouted questions of concern from the guards had ceased for a few minutes, but now Dan heard the banging of rifle butts against the panels and new German voices demanded entry.

"Colonel, this is Major Jürgen!" one of them yelled. "Please open the door! Is there something wrong? Do you need help?"

Brooks stepped into the living room and called out, hoping he sounded like one of the suite's occupants: "*Alles ist Wohl. Danke. Herr Schmidt hat einen Alptraum. Sie können abhauen* . . . Everything is all right. Thank you. Mr. Schmidt is having a nightmare. You can leave."

The knocking stopped. How fitting, Dan thought, that the enemy commander himself had been summoned to the other side of the door. He hoped Jürgen accepted his explanation and that he would heed his order to leave.

He dashed back into the bedroom. "Schafer," he directed, "you and von Hassell gather up all the clothing, wallets, luggage and papers you can find. Throw all the loose stuff into a blanket and bundle it up. Clean out every drawer and closet and take everything that looks as if it belongs to these guys. The living room, too. Jung, help me carry the prisoners to the balcony."

They moved quickly, tying the limp captives into rappelling slings and lowering them to the stretcher bearers. Dan tossed down blankets to cover them. As he and his men continued to execute their practiced maneuvers, he heard the banging of rifle butts again at the hall door. He heard *Sturmbannführer* Jürgen's voice shout, "Break down the door!" and the sounds of the panels being splintered.

Brooks stepped back into the living room, drew his Luger and fired several rounds through the door. There were yelps of pain, the scurrying of feet and the banging stopped. He rushed back into the bedroom.

"Toss all the stuff over the balcony now. Quick," he ordered. "Slide down fast, all of you. I'll cover."

His men threw down the luggage and bundled items and went over the side on the ropes. At that moment Brooks heard firing at both the front and rear of the hotel. He assumed the SS reserves had rushed to their battle positions and been met by a fusillade from Maurer's platoon at the rear and Mangold in front.

He grabbed his flashlight, flicked it off and jammed it into his pocket. He stepped to the threshold of the bedroom and faced the locked entry to the suite, listening to Jürgen screaming, "Break in, goddamn it! Get in there!"

Rifle butts smashed through the door and hands groped for the inside lock. Dan emptied his pistol through the wood, then reloaded. Screams and moans of casualties came from the other side, but now rifle barrels poked through and shots were fired, missing him by inches. The smashing sounds resumed, the door shook and he knew it would give way in a moment. He took a grenade from his pocket, pulled the pin and threw it into the opening as the door burst in. He was sliding down the rope when the grenade exploded. He assumed that *Sturmbannführer* Jürgen had been in the doorway and met the same fate as his men.

When Brooks touched ground, there was a tremendous blast from behind the hotel and flames erupted as the motor pool was blown up, lighting the area. The sounds of heavy fighting at the front and rear of the building were continuous but there was no shooting in his immediate vicinity. Dan saw Lieutenant Becker, Sergeant Blumberg and a squad of *Jägers* covering his side of the hotel. Brooks and the snatch team retrieved their Schmeissers from the men who'd been holding them. The stretcher bearers were already into the woods with the prisoners. Other men had carried away the luggage and bundles of items found in the suite.

Becker reported that they had the SS company blocked front and rear. Mangold's men had destroyed the machine guns and mortars. Maurer's platoon had the SS reserve pinned at the back. None of the action had reached Brunner's squads positioned out of sight on the wooded slopes a short distance away.

"You've got a clear path to withdraw with the prisoners through the forest, sir," Becker said confidently.

"Any casualties?"

"Two dead in Maurer's platoon, three wounded. Mangold reports one dead, two wounded but ambulatory."

Brooks ordered him to press the battle another fifteen minutes to give the snatch team and bearers a chance to get some distance behind them, then to break off and follow.

"We'll wait for you at the reassembly area. Carry your wounded out with you," Dan told his exec. "We'll come back for the dead tomorrow, if we can." To his radioman, he said, "Contact Paulsen. Tell him we should make it to the reassembly area in two-and-a-half to three hours."

Through his night vision binoculars, Major Mikhail Schepilov followed the action of the Knight's Cross company with admiration and excitement.

He had observed the movements of some of their raiding and blocking elements. Captain Astakhov and Sergeant Petrofsky had brought him sketchy reports about others. He had watched the silent, grisly knife work of the sentry-killers in awe, then the kidnappers climbing their ropes to the third-floor balcony and the litter bearers waiting below. He had wondered where Captain Brooks was, which job he had assigned himself, contemplating that if it were his own operation he would have led the team up the ropes. He had found himself silently cheering them on to success.

Then the shooting had begun and Schepilov had muttered a curse in Russian. If the Americans failed, then he would fail too. Only their success could bring him the quarry he wanted. He had watched anxiously while the captives were lowered to the ground, tied to the stretchers and carried up the wooded slope. Then he had seen their abductors escape and follow. He had become aware too that the dispersed elements of Knight's Cross were able to communicate with each other by radio. Regrettably, he could not eavesdrop on their frequencies.

Schepilov was able, however, to envision the direction the venture would most likely take. Astakhov and Petrofsky had seen *Jäger* reserve squads positioned nearby in the forest. The elements were deployed on the flanks of a corridor that would lead the abductors back on the route that had brought them there. They would escape west in the direction of their farm base near Solbad Hall. They would make their own pathway through the forest and mountains. He speculated that the other *Jäger* elements would keep pace with them, guarding the borders of the corridor but maintaining a wide distance from the section with the prisoners. If he could insert his *Spetsnaz* team into the escape corridor, he would be able to ambush them in the dark amidst the maze of trees.

"Petrofsky," he called out softly and the sergeant came to him. "They are carrying our quarry away on stretchers. Take one man with you and stalk them. Try to move ahead of them on the same track. They will not be able to move fast because of their burdens. We will follow a few minutes behind you. When you think you have them isolated and have found a good place to attack them, send your comrade back to inform us." He thought for a moment, then added, "Your password is 'Boston.' Ours is 'Texas.' Let us try to box them in, Petrofsky."

"Very well, Comrade Major," the sergeant said.

He selected one of the men eager to go with him and they disappeared into the dark forest moving uphill to the west. The shooting and explosions of a heavy battle still sounded from the front and rear of the Hotel Edelweiss, where the largest portions of the American undercover company kept the SS defenders engaged.

Schepilov wished now that he had more men in his unit, that he had kept with him his two excellent pathfinders, Kalinin and Butakov. But it had been necessary for them to stay behind at the ski hut so that somebody would be left to report to Moscow. If anything were to go wrong, he had ordered them to get out to the east to the Russian-occupied part of Austria.

If he did not succeed here tonight, he was confident that GRU would not give up pursuing the mission in other ways.

Kurt von Hassell thrashed his way uphill through the forest in a state of outward excitement and private uncertainty as he helped guide the litter bearers through the maze of trees in the darkness.

The things he had done this night! But more important—the *voice*! Something about the briefly heard voice of the bandaged captive had struck a chord of recognition in him. It was a voice he had heard before— yet not heard before. When the voice had cried out, *"Reiter! Reiter! Helfen Sie Mir! Wir sind unter Angriff!"* it had come from the depths of the man's soul and Kurt had felt a moment of unexpected pity.

There had been a familiar cadence and timbre to the voice, a passion that reminded him of a voice that had stirred millions to love and hate: Adolf Hitler!

But that couldn't be. *Der Führer* was dead.

Nor did anyone else appear to have reacted to the voice as he had. Certainly not the captain and sergeant. Unless they already *knew*.

Helmut Jung, who had been closer to the man when he'd cried out for help, who had actually had his hands on him...surely Helmut would have indicated by some look or word that he too had felt the same astonishment.

Yet they'd each had so much to do in this last hour. The speed with which they'd had to move and think. Their senses and nerves had been so overwhelmed. Their actions had taken all of their separate attentions. Helmut wouldn't have been able to indicate anything to him, even if there was something. He would talk to him later about it, when they were alone, when they paused to rest at the reassembly area.

They would make it safely. Of that he was certain. They had more protection now. *Stabsfeldwebel* Zweiger's squad had materialized out of the woods a few minutes into their escape...Zweiger softly calling "Piston!" and Kurt answering "Valve!" just as he was turning his Schmeisser toward him. The captain had sent Zweiger and two of his men ahead fifty meters to scout the compass track to the west and had deployed the others into a screening formation twenty meters away along the right flank and rear. Within minutes, *Unteroffizier* Werner's squad had arrived with the same nervous exchange of passwords. They had been deployed twenty meters out on the left flank, far enough to screen the snatch team from unexpected attackers, close enough to come to their immediate aid if intruders slipped through the blocking elements.

* * *

Sergeant Igor Petrofsky used his great stamina and strength to set a hectic pace to the west through the murky forest in pursuit of their quarry. His comrade kept close behind him. Cold, dim light from the stars and crescent moon faintly illuminated the clearings that Petrofsky's eyes groped for ahead of them.

The steep uphill climb away from the hotel had been brief and then their track had gone along ridgelines, vales and saddles, descending gradually to lower altitudes and requiring only an occasional uphill climb, grabbing at branches and tree trunks. The snow had melted but the ground was damp, the air chilly and their way slippery on rotting vegetation.

Less than two kilometers from the hotel, Petrofsky detected the sounds of crackling leaves and underbrush just ahead of them. The two *Spetsnaz* men veered north off the track, doubled their efforts to make headway to the west and soon left the sounds behind. The sergeant led his man higher on the slope to an outcropping that gave him a slight vantage into the dark maze of trees below and into the middle distance. Soon he heard the sounds again, this time approaching. When he used his binoculars, the dense trees massed together in the lenses, but he caught glimpses of the barely perceptible stretcher bearers as they passed through clearings. He did not become aware of the scouts and flanking squads, all of whom kept within the tree cover and deliberately stayed clear of the open spaces.

Petrofsky counted four men handling each litter, two men breaking trail ahead and two bringing up the rear. They were moving slowly and noisily. The men holding the litters struggled to carry them through tight spaces without dropping their burdens. Their route was constant to the west. Petrofsky was perhaps four minutes ahead of them now. He estimated Major Schepilov would be no more than three or four minutes behind.

The sergeant raised his field glasses, trying to pierce the darkness and pick a site in the middle distance that he might suggest to the major as the place for their attack. He saw the silhouette of a wooded saddle in the ridgeline, perhaps fifteen or more minutes further along their track. The American undercover unit would have to go that way for the most accessible crossing into the next canyon. He sent his comrade back to report to the major and guide him quickly to where he would be waiting.

All during the first fifteen minutes of their forced march, Brooks continued to hear the distant sounds of firing from the Hotel Edelweiss behind them. Then the shooting stopped, indicating the withdrawal of the rest of his company, and the noises of his own section thrashing through the forest became more apparent. He wished they could move silently and faster. The burden of carrying their captives made doing so impossible.

Dan let another fifteen minutes elapse—they had covered about two kilometers—before signaling to his screening elements on the radio and halting the formation to examine the prisoners. They were unconscious and breathing with difficulty because of the gags. He ripped the tape from their mouths, removed the cotton wadding and pulled the hoods back down. He resisted again the temptation to tear the bandages from the head of the man called Schmidt.

Before moving on, Brooks raised Lieutenant Becker on the radio. The exec reported the withdrawal of Mangold's and Maurer's platoons. He and Blumberg were with them. All elements of the company, including Sergeant Brunner's reserve squads, were following Brooks's track, pushing west at a good clip toward the reassembly area and would probably catch up to him along the way.

"Don't move too fast, Rudy," Dan told him. "I want you to stay about five minutes behind us just in case the SS company at the hotel sends elements in pursuit."

As Major Schepilov and his *Spetsnaz* team hurried forward through the dark forest to rendezvous with Sergeant Petrofsky, they skirted the slow-moving stretcher bearers by a wide margin.

"There are only twelve men in the group, eight of them occupied with the stretchers," the scout had reported after racing back to guide them to Petrofsky.

It was Schepilov's intention now to get ahead of them, to approve Petrofsky's ambush site or select another. Unwittingly, he led his men off the track so far to the north that he missed the two additional squads now furnishing security for the abductors.

"Fifteen of us against a dozen of them, plus the shock of surprise!" he had said to Captain Astakhov exuberantly. It would be impossible later, he knew, after Knight's Cross gathered together its separate elements.

They reached Sergeant Petrofsky in twenty minutes. He stood squarely in the middle of the ridgeline gap through which he believed their quarry had to pass. Schepilov approved the site.

"Viktor, pick four of your most powerful men to carry the captives away," he ordered Captain Astakhov. "They will fire at immediate targets when we attack, but then they must seize the stretchers and escape to the northeast on a direct line to our hut. They are not to stop. Their duty is the prisoners. The rest of us will continue the fight, then follow them."

Astakhov quickly named the men to grab the litters. Schepilov split the remainder of the squad. He, Petrofsky, three men and the litter bearers would take up ambush positions in the gap.

"Viktor, take the rest, go back fifty meters and hide on both sides of their track," he ordered. "We will box them in. As soon as you hear me shoot, attack them in the rear. Keep your fire above hip height. We don't want to hit the prisoners on the litters. Any questions?"

"No, Mikhail. It is done."

Stabsfeldwebel Hans Zweiger moved through the trees fifty meters ahead of the section carrying the prisoners. He listened carefully to the sounds of the forest. He sensed the presence of the two scouts he had dispersed to his left and right and occasionally heard their forward movements. But suddenly he detected the sounds of voices ahead of him and, still pushing on, tried to separate them from the louder noises of Captain Brooks's section coming up behind him. Their route was inclined upward now, still hidden in the woods but on a slight rise that led through a saddle in the ridgeline.

Then one voice, the words unclear, stood out from the others. Zweiger halted, hunkered down close to the ground with his Schmeisser extended ahead of him and called out, "Piston!"

From left and right he heard his men answer, "Valve!"

But no voice gave the countersign from out front!

Major Schepilov stopped in the middle of a sentence, alert to the close approach of his quarry. He saw somebody drop to the ground, but didn't see the men with the stretchers. He heard the word "Piston!" and the two responses of "Valve!" He thought of using the same countersign, but knew he would then have to advance and be recognized.

"Now!" he commanded his men.

Petrofsky and nine *Spetsnaz* attackers, submachine guns blazing, rushed forward in a blocking semi-circle. Schepilov aimed where he had seen the figure take cover and that burst brought an answering hail of bullets that missed him. The others fired blindly into the trees at targets that weren't there yet.

Kurt von Hassell, still moving as point man of the section carrying the prisoners, felt a sudden quickening of his heart when the shooting started up ahead. He halted his forward movement and brought his Schmeisser up into aiming position. Dark hulks rushed toward him and he hesitated, thinking it might be the flanking squads or scouts falling back. Then he heard the staccato of submachine guns at their rear and the answering fire of Schmeissers and small arms. He whirled in that direction but saw no attackers.

Captain Brooks was shouting, "Keep moving! Don't stop! Return fire as you go!"

Kurt turned forward, saw the rushing figures impossibly close and coming closer, flashes from their guns leaving no doubt whether they were friend or foe. He aimed his Schmeisser at the closest attacker, unable even to discern his uniform. He let fly a burst and saw the man fall. A moment later, before he could pick out another one, he felt a volley of bullets rake across his chest and slam him backward against a tree. He lost consciousness. Blood poured from his wounds and he stopped breathing.

Dan Brooks at first could hardly make out the enemy in the swirling melee.

Then he managed to pick out his rear guard and flankers, but only because their guns were aimed outward while they fell back toward the stretcher detail. A deadly fusillade from his men ripped into the attackers, but some broke through, heading for the captives. Brooks realized the stretcher bearers were the primary targets. He saw three topple to the ground, dropping their burdens. He faced his body toward assailants running in and fired quick bursts from the hip, hitting one and forcing another to take cover behind a tree.

Major Schepilov realized as he pushed through the first line of defenders that he had made a mistake. He had thought the captives would be right there in front of him, ready to be taken. He and his *Spetsnaz* team were now fighting their way through a larger security force than he had believed was in place.

The chatter of submachine guns and small arms exploded all around him. He heard, but still couldn't see, Astakhov's men coming at their quarry from the rear, provoking a fire fight of equal intensity. He had never become aware of how cleverly the *Jäger* squads were deployed. Petrofsky had miscounted the number of men protecting the stretcher bearers.

It would make no difference, the major vowed as he rushed into the close-quarters battle. The prize had to be his, not the Americans'. He had striven too long, come too far, to lose it now. He never saw *Unteroffizier* Joseph Werner and two of his flankers dart through the trees and trap him. He didn't see them aim their Schmeissers at him and fire. In the din of the battle he relished, he didn't differentiate the explosions of the rounds that cut a swath across his body and slammed him to the forest floor.

As he lay there dying, knowing it was the end, he wondered who the bandaged one really was. His last thought was that he would never have to face General Merkulov again and the hideous death he had promised.

Sergeant Schafer dove to the ground and melded into the black underbrush next to Reiter's fallen stretcher. Dark, hulking figures

194

disregarded him and reached for the handles. Schafer sprayed them with a burst from his machine pistol and they flew backward, arms flailing, and dropped to the ground.

Helmut Jung slammed another attacker across the face with his Schmeisser and tried to get to the second stretcher. Seconds earlier, he had emptied his weapon. He rammed in a new magazine, shot the man he had knocked down, then shot another heading for the litter of the bandaged man. Jung dropped prone beside it, ready to kill anyone who tried to take his captive.

In the frenzy of close-quarters combat in the dark woods, Sergeant Petrofsky emptied the rounds in his submachine gun. He could hardly tell who was an enemy, who a comrade. He no longer knew where his commander was or who to shoot at, but he knew he had made a terrible blunder. In fury he slung his submachine gun onto his left shoulder, yanked his fighting knife from its sheath with his right hand and looked for someone to kill.

Dan Brooks—shooting, twisting and turning in the close fury of the fight—fired the last round in his Schmeisser just as he saw the big attacker rush toward him, hand upraised. Too late to reload and fire, Dan saw the knife thrusting down toward his chest. In the instant, he dropped his gun and stopped the knife's plunge by blocking Petrofsky's arm with his crossed wrists. In one swift, smooth movement he clamped his assailant's wrist in both hands, swung around pressing his back against him and tossed him over his shoulder, twisting the man's wrist to make him release the knife. Two unexpected pistol shots exploded inches away from him and he saw his attacker's face disappear into bloody pulp and his body quiver and lie still.

"Son of a bitch!" muttered a familiar voice beside him.

Brooks turned his head and looked into the anxious face of Sergeant Ralph Brunner. He saw the Luger in his right hand.

"We heard the shooting and I ran like hell," Brunner blurted out. "Lieutenant's coming up with the rest. I don't know how these bastards got past us."

He whirled quickly to check behind him. He and Brooks stood back to back and reloaded their weapons. There were a last few scattered shots, then sudden silence.

"Brunner, take a couple of squads and sweep the area for any attackers who might be left," Dan ordered.

He rushed toward the place where he had last seen the litters. He passed crumpled *Jägers* and attackers. Three of his stretcher bearers were dead. Wounded men were calling out for help. He found Schafer hovering over Reiter and Jung over Schmidt.

"They're okay," Schafer reported. "Still unconscious, but neither one was shot."

"How about you, Jung?" Brooks asked, finally really seeing him in the darkness.

Helmut stood up unsteadily beside the stretcher of the bandaged man. A round had creased Jung's forehead, bloodying his face, leaving him with a throbbing head. "I am fine, sir," he replied.

Stabsfeldwebel Zweiger came staggering through the trees toward Brooks. He was holding a compress to a bloody wound in his left shoulder.

"I regret to report," he said, "that *Schütze* Kurt von Hassell is dead."

Helmut Jung heard the words and felt a pang of anguish. "Where is he?" he asked softly. He looked at Brooks challengingly. "I will carry him out on my back if I have to."

Zweiger wavered on his feet, pressing harder on the bloody compress. "I will show you," he said.

"Look after his wound first, Jung," Brooks ordered. "Schafer, assign men from your platoon to secure our captives here. Then take the rest and start sorting out the dead and wounded. Ours and theirs."

A few minutes later, Lieutenant Becker, Sergeant Blumberg and lead elements of platoons withdrawing from the Edelweiss came through the trees, guns ready. They stared at the carnage.

"SS?" Becker asked contritely. In the darkness, the differences in uniforms, weapons and equipment had not registered with him. "How the hell did they get around us?"

Brooks didn't want to reveal the truth, not even to his exec. "Yes, they're SS," he said, "but not from the hotel."

Schafer and his men, however—collecting the wounded and disentangling the dead—had begun to reveal to each other what they were finding. They had separated the casualties of the *Jäger Einheit* and their attackers and laid them out in rows apart from each other. There were nine dead Knight's Cross men and five wounded; thirteen attackers killed and four still alive but severely wounded. Schafer and his men, though, had begun to recognize the uniforms of the men they had shot, and they extracted I.D.'s from the pockets of some of the *Amerikanische Soldaten* that confirmed their worst fears.

Brooks and his lieutenant moved to the row of corpses. Dan illuminated the uniforms and faces with his flashlight so that they could finally identify them.

"Oh, my God," Lieutenant Becker murmured, distinguishing the uniforms. "They're Americans."

"No, they're not," Dan said forcefully as he looked at the lifeless face of Major Mikhail Schepilov. He turned away and spoke to the troubled OSS cadre and German *Soldaten* who stood close by. "Don't be fooled," he said. "These are Nazis disguised in American uniforms. Probably some of Skorzeny's commandos. I had an idea they might turn up, like the ones at the Battle of the Bulge last December. That's why I told you not to hesitate, to kill anyone who came at us, no matter what uniforms they wore."

The men passed the words on to those who had not heard them and they looked greatly relieved. Brooks turned back to shine his flashlight again on the face of Schepilov. They had played the same game. He could not help feeling some grudging respect toward so determined and cunning a foe.

"Do we carry out their wounded, Captain?" asked Becker.

"No. Just our own. If Jung wants to carry von Hassell, let him. Assign new bearers to the stretchers and take command of the company and captives, Lieutenant," Brooks ordered. "Head for the reassembly area as fast as you can. I don't think anyone else will be coming after us, but maintain your flanking squads and rear guard. I'll follow you in a few minutes."

"What about those?" Becker asked, pointing to the four wounded intruders in American uniforms bunched together on the ground.

They were all comatose except one. When Brooks shined his flashlight on him, he was struggling to rise and his eyes and ears seemed to be following everything with acute interest.

"That's my responsibility," Dan answered brusquely. "Clear the area now, Rudy. I want to be left here alone."

Becker stared at him somberly, as if he knew what the captain was going to do. Then he turned away, issued orders to the sergeants and *Feldwebels* and started the platoons moving through the forest again with their captives.

In a few minutes, Brooks was alone on the dark battleground amidst the dead and wounded. He felt he had no choice in what he was about to do, though it was a duty he abhorred. If he took these Russian wounded as prisoners, he would have to turn them over to 7th Army or OSS. Upon release to their own forces, the Soviets would learn that Knight's Cross had succeeded in kidnapping the two Germans from the Hotel Edelweiss, men whom they obviously also wanted, whoever they were. Dan couldn't let that intelligence get back to them.

The wounded Russian who had been struggling to rise had by now barely made it to his feet with great effort, concentrating his last strength with extraordinary determination. He pressed his hands over a gaping wound in his belly.

Brooks covered him with his Luger, uncertain what he was trying to do, why he had struggled so desperately to his feet. He wondered if the Russian thought he had a chance to escape or was going to produce a hidden weapon.

"*Spetsnaz?*" Dan asked, almost gently.

"*Da.* Yes," the wounded attacker gasped out, first in Russian then English, acknowledging he knew the nationality of his captor despite the German uniform Brooks wore. "I want to see my sergeant."

Dan showed the way with his flashlight as the man tottered along the row of dead Russians. He came to one and, though the bloody, torn face was hardly recognizable, Dan thought it was the man who had attacked him with a knife.

The wounded Russian pointed and uttered in a strained voice of contempt, "The great Sergeant Igor Petrofsky. That son of a bitch can't count." He spit in the open-mouthed face of the corpse. "Now you can shoot me," he added in resignation and toppled to the ground.

The man understood, which made it no easier. Dan shot him in the head, then dispatched the three other wounded who had been more dead than alive.

Twenty-Five

✠ After securing the unconscious, hooded captives in an upstairs bedroom of Schmidler's farmhouse, with guards inside and outside the room, Brooks had Sergeant Blumberg send out three urgent, coded radio signals.

The first went to the commander of the OSS detachment with 7th Army's advance elements. Dan reported his position and told his counterpart it was imperative to keep all U.S. units away from the area.

The second signal was to Captain LeGrange at the Dijon air base, requesting that the *Jäger Einheit's* American uniforms and I.D.'s be parachuted to the farm by 1100 that day. Exact coordinates and recognition signals were given and confirmation was received.

The third message was sent to Larry Dillard, the Special Operations chief in London: "Mission completed. A fox bagged. Details later. Must have air transports immediately to return all personnel and captives. Quick extraction vital. Now at great risk. Will signal landing site by 1600."

Helmut Jung lowered the body of Kurt von Hassell to the ground at the rear of the barn and placed two men as an honor guard. Then he went to the captain and asked if he might call on the Schmidler family.

"There is a special reason, regarding Kurt. The girl," he said awkwardly.

"The daughter?" Dan questioned in surprise.

"Yes, I helped him. She was interested in him."

Brooks tried to look at him severely. Von Hassell was her lover?"

"Lover?" Jung repeated bitterly. "Two joyful hours, Captain. Two nights ago. But who knows what might have been?"

Dan was silent a few moments. "He seemed such a lonely man," he finally said pensively. "It's all right, Jung. I"m glad he had his hours with her. Do the parents know?"

199

"I don't think so."

"I'm also glad you and he became friends. I know you hated him in the beginning."

"It was my own blockheadedness, *Herr Hauptmann.* Or must I still call you *Gefreiter* Halle?"

"No. *Gefreiter* Halle has served his purpose. He's been discharged. Go ahead, Jung. Tell the girl privately about Kurt, but don't tell the father and mother what happened between them. Tell them about all our dead. Ask Schmidler if he can arrange for burial in a local cemetery. I'm sending a detail back to retrieve them after our American uniforms are dropped to us. We'll commandeer some trucks. You can take charge of the detail and make the arrangements."

Soon after dawn, most of the men, except for those on watch, had fallen asleep in the barn and outbuildings.

Helmut Jung and Jupp Schmidler were commiserating over coffee and schnapps in the kitchen. Jung told the farmer only that there had been a terrible battle against the SS in the mountains and many casualties. He passed off as simple prisoners the two hooded men whom Schmidler had seen brought there on litters.

Mrs. Schmidler was consoling Lisa in her bedroom, surprised at the depth of her sorrow after Jung had reported the names of those killed in action.

Sergeant Paulsen was caring for the wounded.

The four civilian agents—Hans Zimmer, Walter Freiherr, Martin Herz and Franz Scholl—had checked in by radio and had been ordered back to base by Brooks. They were to be extracted with the *Jäger Einheit.* Nobody would be left behind to be interrogated by American military intelligence, to reveal anything about Knight's Cross.

Brooks isolated himself with his two captives in the spare bedroom of the farmhouse. The guards had been cleared from the room and were posted with the other sentries in the hallway, close enough to be available if needed, far enough away so they couldn't eavesdrop, which they had been warned not to do.

Reiter and Schmidt were still unconscious, which gave Dan more time to examine the clothes, wallets, luggage and personal papers that had been removed from the Hotel Edelweiss. They were still wearing the pajamas in which they were abducted, covered by blankets and the cloth hoods. Their hands had been retied in front so they were no longer lying in contorted positions. Just staring at them, watching the hoods rise and fall with their breathing, made Dan feel ill at ease. There was a rank, stuffy, latrine odor in the small room and he opened the window a few inches to let in some fresh air.

Brooks's expectations already had been quickened earlier by sight of his prisoners' money-stuffed wallets and the bundles of various national currencies and gold coins stashed in their valises. Even if there was not yet specific evidence that either of them was among the Nazi hierarchy, credibility had been added to his belief before the kidnapping that the two would have high-level Nazi connections. The large sums of money also added to the plausibility of his assumption that the men had been trying to escape the Third Reich on a ratline prepared in advance.

In the jacket of the SS uniform he had found the *Soldbuch* of *Obersturmbannführer* Dietrich Reiter, complete with photograph. He was in the *Sicherheitsdienst*, the elite Security Service of the SS. All Brooks would have to do was remove the man's hood and match him to his picture. He considered the document could be spurious, but really didn't think a war criminal fleeing Germany under a false identity would have selected so tainted an I.D.

There were indications that this lieutenant colonel was indeed highly connected. Among his papers, Dan found an address book containing familiar names such as Heinrich Himmler; Albert Speer, the *Führer's* architect and Minister of Armaments; Hjalmar Schacht, the Finance Minister; Colonel Otto Skorzeny, chief of the SS commando and subterfuge section; and various SS officers and government and party officials in Germany and Austria whose names were not as familiar. Contact addresses, phone numbers and radio communications I.D.'s were noted beside the entries. There was also what appeared to be a private code book.

The second captive's I.D. stated that his name was Siegfried Schmidt. He was described as a rocket scientist who served as liaison between the research and manufacturing center at Peenemünde and the control bureau in Berlin. Unlike Reiter's *Soldbuch* and other standard German I.D.'s, there was no photograph.

In addition to a large amount of Reichsmarks and Swiss francs in Schmidt's wallet, there were papers with long numbers and addresses in Zurich. His clothing contained no manufacturing or laundry labels. The fabrics of the two suits were dark gray and dark brown wool. The style was in keeping with clothes that might be worn by a middle-range bureaucrat, though his brown fedora and trench coat had a certain stylish flare.

Brooks was more intrigued, however, by the 7.65 caliber Walther pistol found in a pocket of the brown jacket that had been draped over a chair near Schmidt's bed. Few civilians were allowed to keep such weapons in Nazi Germany. Dan remembered reading that Adolf Hitler had carried a Walther pistol like this as far back as his Munich beer hall days.

He shook the nagging thoughts of Hitler from his mind. *Der Führer* was dead in Berlin and that was the end of it. He still indulged the hope that the bandaged one would turn out to be someone as significant as Heinrich Himmler or Martin Bormann.

He removed Reiter's hood first and stared at his face. It matched the

I.D. photo. Then he slipped off Schmidt's hood. There was something daunting about the totally bandaged head and neck, like a mummy just unearthed from the tomb. The captives began to stir, making little gurgling sounds.

While Schmidt was still unconscious, Brooks undid the pinned end of the wide bindings and began to remove them. He had to lift his head with one hand as he unwound the bandage with the other. Two layers came away before he reached the beginning of the third layer attached to pads of cotton and gauze sticky with yellow ointment, mucus, red stains and crusts of blood. It was not a disguise. The man's wounds were genuine.

"*Reiter...ist das Sie?*" Schmidt murmured. The voice was strained and frightened.

Brooks replied softly, in German, "Be quiet...save your strength."

In one abrupt movement he yanked away the bottom layer of bandage on the left side of Schmidt's face and a few encrusted pads came with it.

Schmidt screamed in pain.

From behind him, Dan heard Reiter shout, "Stop! What are you doing? He has been severely wounded. Leave him alone."

He turned in time to see the SS officer lurch off the bed and raise his bound hands. Dan sidestepped and pushed Reiter back onto the bed without trying to hurt him. "Don't move again," he ordered. "Remain silent unless a question is directed to you. *Verstanden?*"

The SS officer stayed put, silently seething, and Brooks continued his examination of Schmidt. The man had half risen on the bed and, despite his bound wrists and bandaged hands, had pulled the layer of bandage back across the lower portion of his face.

Dan recognized the complex trauma of burn injuries, the charred blotches, oozing and scabbed blisters and seared, polychrome flesh. But in the brief, partial unmasking he had not been able to identify the man or associate him with any of his photos of Nazi leaders.

Schmidt clutched the bandage to his lower face as if his life depended on it, and Dan felt the malevolence of the glare aimed at him through the eye slits he had not unwound.

"*Verzeihen Sie mir*...Forgive me," he said softly to Schmidt. "It was necessary to determine the extent of your wounds so that medical attention could be arranged."

"I am his medical attention," Reiter blurted out. "We do not need your help."

"Are you a doctor?" Brooks asked.

"I will deal only with an officer, which you obviously are not," Reiter responded stiffly.

"To relieve your concern about rank," Brooks said, "I am an American captain."

202

Reiter was stunned. *"Grosser Gott!* I thought you were a band of deserters!"

"Now you know the situation. Obey my orders," Dan admonished. "Neither of you are to disclose your identities to any of my men. Your safety depends on that. There are men here who would slit your throats. Do I have your word, Reiter, if that's your name?"

The *Obersturmbannführer* eyed him warily. It was Reiter's purpose to keep *Herr* Schmidt's identity secret. But he wondered what this American captain actually knew. "You have my word. Reiter *is* my name and my companion is Siegfried Schmidt. Obviously you have rifled through our papers." He saw their wallets, documents and money on top of a chest. "What do you want with us?"

"You are prisoners of war and will be treated as such."

"That category fits only me," Reiter protested. "I am a soldier. But Siegfried, as you see, is a civilian. He should be released."

"Herr Schmidt's identification is obviously false," Brooks said. "It is new and there is no photograph attached. Who is he, Reiter?"

"Of course his papers are new, *Herr Hauptmann,* if that's who you are," Reiter replied. "His original documents were destroyed in the bombing that wounded him. It was impossible to make new pictures. Siegfried suffered terribly, as he does now. What was the point of taking photographs of a man wrapped in bandages?"

"Your logic is good, *Obersturmbannführer,"* Brooks said, "and your effort to protect your companion is commendable. However, the SS does not send lieutenant colonels of the *Sicherheitsdienst* to protect a nobody named Siegfried Schmidt. Who is he?"

Reiter forced a bitter laugh. "Siegfried is not a nobody. As his papers have already informed you, he is a scientist connected to our rocket development program. He is certainly worth the efforts of a mere *Obersturmbannführer."*

"What was your place of departure before you landed in Innsbruck?" Dan demanded. "Before your reply, I advise you that our intelligence people have been tracking you."

"Then there is no point to this line of questioning, since you already know the answer," Reiter replied.

"The truth of your responses will determine our level of courtesy and consideration."

"Under the Geneva convention I am required to give you my name, rank and serial number. You already have those."

Brooks had no desire to continue playing cat and mouse with the man. He turned to Schmidt, who had been following the exchange avidly. He was sitting up, his feet on the floor, his bandaged hands still pressing the loose head bandage against his face.

"*Herr* Schmidt, perhaps you, as a civilian, will feel more comfortable responding to a few simple questions?" Dan asked in a friendly manner.

"I will not be interrogated," Schmidt declared angrily.

Dan tried to reassure him. "It will help us process you and perhaps let you go on to wherever you were heading."

Schmidt sighed. In a low voice, he said, "A few questions will be permitted."

The autocratic response indicated a person of authority, Brooks thought, whether he was Siegfried Schmidt, rocket scientist, or somebody else. "What was your eventual destination?" he asked.

"Exactly where I was when you kidnapped me," Schmidt replied petulantly. "I came to the Tyrol for rest and recuperation. You are an American, you say? Have I not suffered enough at the hands of you people? Look at what you have done to me. My face and head burned. God knows if I will ever be the same again. The pain is sometimes unbearable."

"I can help you with the pain immediately, *Herr* Schmidt," said Brooks, "and with proper medical attention. All I require is that you answer a few simple questions."

"You injected me with something at the Edelweiss. What was it?" Schmidt demanded.

"Morphine."

"I'm sure it was not your intention, *Hauptmann*, but it helped me. It was better than the pills Reiter has been giving me. It eased the pain greatly. It relaxed me. But the effect has worn off now."

"If you will answer a few questions, *Herr* Schmidt, I will send for my medical aide to examine your injuries thoroughly and administer to you."

"Morphine?"

"Of course, if it helps."

"I do not advise it, Siegfried!" Reiter blurted out.

"Do not concern yourself further, *Obersturmbannführer*!" Schmidt said brusquely.

To Brooks that sounded like a command from a man used to giving orders and having them obeyed. He opened the door and called two of the guards from the hallway. They were surprised to see the prisoners without hoods and startled at the sight of the bandaged man. The captives were astonished to see more men who looked and sounded like German soldiers.

"Are you Americans also?" Reiter asked.

"*Jawohl!*" the *Jägers* replied in unison. They didn't accord Reiter any of the courtesies of rank.

Dan put the hood back on him and said, "Take him into another room. Don't talk to him. If he opens his mouth, gag him. Send Sergeant Paulsen up. Tell him to bring his full medical kit."

When they left, Brooks turned back to the pathetic figure on the bed holding his face bandage in place. He was not fat enough to be Hermann Göring. He didn't have Joseph Goebbels' clubfoot. He was, though, about the right size for Heinrich Himmler, who had been expected for weeks. An even more intriguing possibility was that he could be Martin Bormann, Hitler's yes-man and confidant. Bormann's name was not in Reiter's address book and that suggested there was no need for it because the man was with him.

"Let me untie your hands," Dan said gently. "You will be more comfortable."

"*Danke!*"

The voice was hoarse and sometimes cracked, but there was something vaguely familiar about it, though not one he really knew. He untied the rope that bound the man's wrists and felt a creepy revulsion touching him, as he had when he had rammed the two morphine syrettes into his buttocks at the Edelweiss.

"Are you Martin Bormann?" Dan demanded.

The man was startled to hear the name. "No, of course not. I am Siegfried Schmidt," he replied. Then he coughed and gasped and looked to be in pain. He forced the spasm to stop by tensing his arms and body and rocking from side to side.

"Are you in pain, *Herr* Schmidt?"

"Of course I am in pain, *Herr Hauptmann*. As you would be too if you had suffered what I have suffered."

"Do you know Bormann?"

"I have heard of him, of course. He is said to be *der Führer's* closest friend and adviser. But I do not travel in such circles of high importance. I am a scientist, not a politician.

"There was talk at the Hotel Edelweiss that you were a man close to *der Führer.*"

Schmidt stared at him rigidly, then laughed caustically. "How do you hear such things?"

"By having someone there to listen."

"It was only *Geschwätz*...idle talk. Reiter gave them lots of big talk so they would give us the best treatment at the hotel."

"You were the only guests. Obviously it was opened only for your benefit."

"About this I know nothing. I have not been well. I do not pay attention to these things."

"Did that include the Waffen SS company stationed there to protect you?"

"I do not select billets for troops, nor am I responsible for where they stay," Schmidt answered angrily. "I am in great pain now, Captain ... Captain...What is your name?"

"Captain Dan Brooks, United States Army."

Schmidt was squirming in great discomfort. "I must have something to help the pain now, Brooks. Your morphine. When will the doctor come?"

"He is not a doctor. But he is a very proficient medical technician who will be able to help you. Are you Heinrich Himmler?"

The prisoner tensed and a great anger welled up in him. "That *verdammte* bastard of a *Dummkopf* cop! That you would even suggest such a thing to me, *Hauptmann*, is the greatest insult!"

Whoever he was, Brooks thought, the man apparently hated Himmler. Or was a good actor.

"One more question," Dan said.

"And that is all I will answer!" Schmidt responded indignantly. "Whether you provide medical help for me or not, *Hauptmann*. I am perfectly capable of bearing pain, as I have done all my life. You, however, will be reported to your superiors and the International Red Cross for your cruel behavior."

"Where did you take off from?" Brooks asked quickly. "Before you flew into the auxiliary landing field at Innsbruck?"

"Germany," Schmidt answered vaguely.

"Exactly where?" Dan insisted. "There's not much of Germany left from which Nazis can depart in their own aircraft."

"Berlin!" Schmidt shouted in furious resignation.

It was a good beginning, Dan thought.

Twenty-six

✝   Alone in his office at OSS headquarters in Grosvenor Street, Larry Dillard deciphered the radio signal. He was not trained in cryptography, so the process went painstakingly slow. Only he and Dan Brooks had copies of this one-time code pad. To the signalmen who had transmitted and received the message it had been gibberish.

But when he read, *A fox is bagged*, the SO chief murmured to himself, "It's not possible. There must be a mistake."

For three days he had accepted, as had all of the Allied command, that the *fox* was dead in Berlin. It was what the Germans had broadcast and the Russians acknowledged, though they hadn't come up with hard evidence yet.

Then Dillard realized the signal read *A fox* not *The fox*, and he pondered over that. He had given Brooks carte blanche to use the same signal for anyone he wanted extracted, and full discretion to keep the identity of his captive secret. To Dillard, that subtle difference meant the message did not refer to Hitler but to another Nazi leader, or perhaps more than one. Brooks's coded lines had used the plural word *captives*. The possibilities were tantalizing.

Goebbels, like Hitler, had been reported a suicide in Berlin, but Göring, Himmler, Bormann, Kaltenbrunner and many more were as yet unaccounted for. Germany had not yet officially surrendered; there were ceasefires only in certain sectors. It could be any one of them or none of them now in Brooks's hands.

Dillard understood the urgency in the captain's radio signal. Another message that morning, from the commander of the OSS unit with 7th Army in Innsbruck, had asked him to approve Knight's Cross's directive to keep regular army elements away from its location. Dillard had responded that doing so was imperative. Then LeGrange, the liaison officer at the Dijon air base, had notified him that American uniforms and I.D.'s for the company were already on the way.

The SO chief picked up his phone and asked to be connected to the commander of Special Operations Wing standing by at an air base north of London. There was no need for Dillard to confer with any of his superiors, for it had been long understood that they wanted no incriminating trace of Knight's Cross left behind.

In the upstairs bedroom at Schmidler's farm, Sergeant Paulsen applied medication to the prisoner's burns, bandaged him again like a mummy and eased his pain with another shot of morphine, enough to relax him and let him eat a light breakfast, but not enough to knock him out.

Brooks stayed in the room and got a better look at the man's face, but still couldn't identify him. When the guards were posted again and Dan and the medic were alone together in another room, Paulsen was unable to match Schmidt against any of the photos he showed him.

A few minutes later, Brooks entered the room where Reiter was held, dismissed the guards and began his interrogation. To put him at ease, he reassured him about the condition of his companion. The SS officer became extremely agitated to be told that the medic had examined and treated Schmidt out of his presence. He demanded that only he be permitted to tend the injured man.

"You're in no position to make demands, Reiter," Dan replied. "However, I'll allow you to do it if you cooperate with me."

"In what way?"

"To begin with, who is Siegfried Schmidt? Why your special concern?"

"He is a scientist engaged in rocket work, as we've each told you, *Herr Hauptmann*."

"Is he Martin Bormann?"

"That ass kisser!" Reiter exclaimed with glee. "Of course not."

"Heinrich Himmler?"

"An even worse choice."

"Schmidt seemed to think so too. It made him very upset."

The *Obersturmbannführer* leaned closer to Brooks and lowered his voice. "I will tell you something in confidence, *Herr Hauptmann*," he said.

"Go ahead," Dan urged. Momentarily, he thought something of importance might be revealed at last.

"Nobody liked those two. Himmler and Bormann."

Brooks wanted to slug the pompous bastard, but restrained himself. He continued the interrogation but was unable to get Reiter to change his story about Schmidt.

"Am I a prisoner of war or a political prisoner, that I have to answer such questions?" the *Obersturmbannführer* demanded.

Dan left him with a warning to ponder until his next grilling:

"As an SS lieutenant colonel, Reiter, you're in a different category than a Wehrmacht officer. You're not covered by the POW rules of the Geneva Convention. Furthermore, you will most likely be considered a war criminal and prosecuted."

The old Volkswagen drove into Schmidler's barnyard at 1300 on May 3. Dan Brooks, watching from the window of the command post loft, marveled that the little car could contain so many men. Out of it stepped his four civilian operatives—Walter Freiherr, Hans Zimmer, Martin Herz and Franz Scholl—and the two SI agents, Karl Bergen and Willy Hupnagel, who had been released into their custody by *Kriminalinspektor* Bernard Klung.

Brooks, wearing his American field uniform and captain's bars again, noted the look of astonishment on Bergen's face when he stepped out of the car and saw the area milling with a company of soldiers in U.S. uniforms without unit insignia. The air drop over Schmidler's farm had been executed with precision at 1100 and the *Jäger Einheit* was again dressed in the uniforms they had worn during training at St. Germain.

Sergeant Schafer and a guard detail waited to take charge of Bergen and Hupnagel. The SI agents were dressed in Alpine clothes.

"I want to see the officer in charge immediately!" Karl Bergen demanded, speaking English. His wrists were manacled and he sounded furious.

"He'll see you when he's good and ready," Schafer snapped. "Just do what you're told and keep your mouth shut."

The captain had ordered that these two men be held incommunicado under guard in the barn until the unit moved out that night.

"You have no right to hold me," Bergen responded angrily. "I'm an OSS agent who's been operating in this area for six months. I need a radio to contact my base in London."

"You'll have an opportunity to explain yourself later," Schafer said. The captain hadn't told him much, except that the big fellow who looked like a brawler was an untrustworthy son of a bitch and was to be held separately from his companion.

Hupnagel's wrists were in cuffs too, but he didn't protest. In fact he was relaxed about their imprisonment these past three weeks. Willy had been kept in a cell out of sight and sound of Karl. Inspector Klung had seen to it that he was well cared for and had even escorted him on a number of private visits to his Aunt Anna and Cousin Trude at the *Gasthaus zum Hirschen*. He liked being back now under the protection of a large American force. He didn't want Karl ever to know that it was he who had alerted the Knight's Cross commander to his intended treachery.

In the early afternoon, Brooks met with his four civilian operatives in the barn loft and pieced together what was happening in Innsbruck and throughout the Inn Valley. They talked softly, against the sounds of Blumberg's radio traffic in one corner.

"There are more OSS agents turning up in Innsbruck than I ever imagined could be operating here," Walter reported.

"Special Operations?" Dan asked, surprised. He had never been told that other SO groups were operating in the Inn Valley.

"No, Captain," Hans related. "I didn't talk to them myself, but Inspector Klung did. He says they're SI agents from Bari."

"I guess we had no need to know," Brooks commented wryly. "Lucky we never got into a hassle with them. How about the rest of you? Any contacts with these other agents?"

"No, sir. Only with our Austrian Underground people," Martin Herz answered.

"That's the way it's to remain," Brooks told them. "There is to be no record of our being here. We'll be returning to England tonight."

When Brooks entered the horse stall in the barn where Bergen was being held, Karl understood immediately the cause of his predicament.

He was sprawled out in a disrespectful posture and did not leap to his feet at one guard's order of, "*Achtung!*—though hearing it called out in German by a soldier in U.S. uniform confused him momentarily.

Dan, also speaking German, dismissed the guards, and told them to stand out of earshot until he summoned them back. Then he watched Bergen slowly rise to his feet, his broad, broken face seething with rage.

"You son of a bitch!" Karl spat out. "You're the one behind all this!"

"No, you are, Bergen," Dan responded coldly. "And I'm going to add 'son of a bitch' to the list of charges that will be brought against you at your court-martial."

"Court-martial? Me? You're the one that's going to be court-martialed, Brooks. Were you responsible for my being locked up?"

"I was informed by Inspector Klung that you and Hupnagel were arrested by the Gestapo. It was only because of his intercession that you're still alive."

"I never saw Klung when I was in jail."

"Of course not. He couldn't incriminate himself, but he was protecting you behind the scenes."

Having taken the onus off the police inspector, Dan phrased his next words so they would get Willy Hupnagel off the hook too.

"The inspector told me something that leads me to believe you committed treason," Dan accused. "You deliberately failed to convey vital intelligence he gave you for Knight's Cross. That's the work of a double agent."

"I don't know what the hell you're talking about," Bergen retorted angrily.

210

"Your treachery is also confirmed by a message your radioman sent to Cassidy in London," Dan went on. "Violating orders and interfering with another mission is bad enough, but betrayal is going to put you in front of a firing squad."

"If Willy sent an incriminating signal, maybe it was him that was responsible for it."

"Save it for your court-martial, Bergen. You're finished here, whatever it was you were planning to do. You're returning to England with us tonight. You will be turned over to OSS for further investigation and prosecution."

The smell of spring was in the air as Dan walked to the main farmhouse to check on his captives. Any hour he expected a broadcast that the war in Europe was really over. In the distance, Jupp Schmidler and his farmhands were at work in a field. He planned to give Schmidler a letter to show the American Military Government once it was installed, so that he and his neighbors would be secretly compensated. The letter would say that the farmers had given shelter and food to Allied personnel. It would not mention Knight's Cross.

Soon after dark, a convoy of civilian trucks and buses—to be supplied by *Kriminalinspektor* Klung as a gesture of gratitude to *Gefreiter* Halle— would arrive at the farm. They would convey the entire company and its captives to the auxiliary airfield where Reiter and Schmidt had landed two days earlier. According to one of Larry Dillard's signals, Special Operations Wing would have its ground control unit operating the flight tower and runway lights and there would be enough transports and converted bombers to fly them out in one operation. In the remaining hours before departure, Brooks intended to devote himself to Reiter and Schmidt.

The captives had been ordered to remove their pajamas and put on clothes, but their hands had been tied again and they remained under close guard in separate bedrooms of the farmhouse. Brooks entered Schmidt's room first and dismissed the guards to posts in the hallway. The prisoner was dressed in a gray suit. Sergeant Paulsen had cut slits for his eyes, nostrils and mouth in the black hood he had placed over his bandaged head again.

"For your own protection," the medic had told him astutely. "To help prevent infection."

Schmidt sat stiffly in a chair near the window, staring out at Schmidler's fields and the mountains in the middle distance. The window was open slightly and he was breathing deeply of the fresh air.

"Are you comfortable, *Herr* Schmidt?" Brooks asked politely.

The man turned away from the window and stared malevolently at him.

Dan couldn't see his expression, but it was the feeling he got, particularly from the eyes boring at him through the holes.

"Of course not," Schmidt answered, his voice raspy. He held up his arms, tied uncomfortably at the wrists. "Would you be in such circumstances, *Hauptmann?* I am also in pain again. The morphine your medic gave me this morning has worn off."

"I'll give you another. But let's talk first."

"About what?"

"You."

"I have told you all I am going to tell you, *Hauptmann*. If you are treating me as a military prisoner, I have complied with the terms of the Geneva Convention, except that I cannot give you a serial number because I do not have one. I am not a soldier. I am a scientist."

"Then may I ask you a scientific question, *mein Herr?*"

"If you wish, though I may not be able to answer it. After all, there are many special fields in science."

"I've always been curious about the famous formula of Professor Albert Einstein, $E = mc^2$. What does it mean?"

"Einstein? Einstein!" the captive muttered darkly. His bandaged hands clenched and he brought them up and down on his thighs in anger. His eyes blazed. "Einstein the Jew who ran away to America? What he says is of no importance."

"Perhaps you don't understand it either, Schmidt," Brooks said calmly. "In the States, the man is revered. Let me ask you something about the science of rockets. That ought to be easy for you."

"I will answer nothing, *Hauptmann*. Nothing! I will not reveal military secrets, even under torture. Of that I assure you!"

"Nobody's going to torture you, Schmidt. We're not Nazis. Let's try another subject. Money. Did you rob a bank or make off with part of the German treasury? I figure that all the currencies and gold coins you and your buddy have with you add up to more than one hundred thousand dollars American. Where did you get it?"

"None of your business!" Schmidt declared angrily. "If you wish to steal what is mine, I am powerless to stop you now. But one day you will answer for it, *Hauptmann!*"

"With this?" Brooks challenged, taking the Walther pistol from his pocket and displaying it flat on his left palm. "I suppose you're going to say this pistol is not yours."

"It is mine," Schmidt admitted.

"Why does a scientist need a gun?" Dan pressed.

"*You* are the obvious answer to that question," the prisoner retorted. "If I had been able to use it to protect myself I would not be here now."

"Did you know that Hitler had a gun like this?"

The prisoner was shocked into silence, but then recovered. "You must have been closer to him that I was to know such a thing, *Hauptmann*," he said calmly.

"Who are you really, Schmidt?" Brooks pressed in a confidential tone. "It might take a while to find out, but you Germans are noted for your conscientious record keeping. It will go easier for you if you tell me now. I promise you it will not go beyond this room. Not even to your friend Reiter."

"Reiter knows who I am and gives me respect."

"Okay. Who are you that you deserve such special respect and attendance from an *Obersturmbannführer* of the *Sicherheitsdienst?*"

"As you have been told again and again, *Hauptmann*, I am a scientist engaged in Germany's rocket development. Because of the present unsettled situation in Germany, that was reason enough for *Obersturmbannführer* Reiter to have been assigned as my aide. You know, of course, by now, the effectiveness of these new weapons."

"They're not worth a shit militarily. Terror weapons killing innocent civilians, that's all they are."

"That is *your* inferior opinion, *Hauptmann*, but it was not the opinion of Adolph Hitler!" Schmidt retorted angrily.

"You're no more a scientist than I am," Brooks said in exasperation. "A politician perhaps. Or a financial type. Maybe a bagman. But certainly no scientist."

Schmidt tilted his head in a questioning posture and Dan could almost picture the querulous expression on the burned face under the hood and bandages.

"What is this 'bagman'?" Schmidt demanded.

"A crook that carries illegal money between other crooks."

"How dare you speak to me like that!" the prisoner exploded.

"So far the evidence speaks for itself," Dan responded calmly. If he could get the man angry enough, he might inadvertently let something revealing slip out. "One more question for now."

"I will not be interrogated."

"What does this mean?" Dan asked. He took from his pocket one of the papers that had been in Schmidt's wallet and held it up in front of him. "A list of numbers...and addresses in Zurich."

Schmidt stared at the paper a few moments, then at Brooks. He tensed and raised his bandaged, tied hands to his head as if trying to soothe away a spasm of pain. "A private matter," he moaned. "I cannot speak of it."

In feigned resignation, Dan said, "You're a difficult man, Schmidt. Or whatever your name is. But I don't want you to suffer under my care and have reasons for complaint. I'll give you your shot."

Brooks untied his hands and helped him slip off his jacket and roll up the sleeve of his shirt to expose his upper arm. He took a morphine syrette from his pocket and jabbed it into the muscle. Again, he felt an unexplainable feeling of revulsion just touching the man.

"We'll be flying out later tonight. To England. I want you in good shape and relaxed," he continued calmly, as if it were not a matter of great importance.

"England!" the prisoner repeated in consternation. "Is Churchill expecting me?"

The remark, so unexpected, gave Brooks a moment's pause as he helped Schmidt button his shirt and put on his jacket. "No. Is there some reason he would be interested in you?" he asked casually.

"Merely a joke," Schmidt murmured as the morphine began to take effect. "I too have a sense of humor. Ahhh, that is good, *Hauptmann*. I thank you." Then he became expansive and confidential. "In Berlin or Munich, sometimes it happened that I had reason to see a doctor for one thing or another. I want you to know, *Hauptmann* Brooks, none of them ever administered anything that made me feel this good."

"They wouldn't."

"Why?"

"It puts a monkey on your back."

"What does that mean?"

"It's addictive. One day you'll have to shake the habit."

Brooks summoned the two guards to watch over Schmidt and he went to the room in which Dietrich Reiter was being held.

The man who stared uncertainly at him no longer looked like an *Obersturmbannführer.* He was a slender man of average height, with a strong physique. His features were handsome and his dark brown hair was fuller and more stylishly cut and combed than a short, military cut. According to his *Soldbuch,* his paybook I.D., he was 34.

Brooks had deemed the SS uniform too conspicuous for the next stage of the operation and had it taken away from him. Reiter had been issued, instead, the suit Dan had worn on his civilian forays. They were about the same size and it fit him adequately. It seemed to Brooks that some of the arrogance of the man had dissipated with the change of clothes.

"It feels rather strange," Reiter remarked, running his hands along the fabric of the gray jacket, "after years in uniform."

"You will be joining us on a trip tonight," Brooks said. "You will put the hood over your head before we leave here."

"Who am I supposed to be, *The Man in the Iron Mask?*"

"It's for your own protection, Reiter. I want no one to recognize you and no one who sees you now to remember what you look like."

"Where will we be going?"

"England."

Reiter looked shocked. "Siegfried, too?"

"Yes."

"What will you do with us there?" he asked, worried.

"Talk. Just as we have been doing here. You'll be thoroughly interrogated and investigated. You'll most likely be in custody for a hell of a long time. Or worse," Brooks said threateningly.

"There are no grounds for anything 'worse,' if by that you imply execution."

"The SS, as I told you, is different. Its war crimes are well documented."

"I am a soldier, that is all," Reiter insisted. "You cannot make me out to be anything else just by taking my uniform and identification away from me."

"We'll see. We'll talk and talk and talk until I've learned all I need to know from you," Brooks told him. "Where were you planning to go before we took you fron the Edelweiss?"

"I don't know," Reiter replied truthfully. "I was there expressly to await instructions concerning a means of travel and a route out of the Reich."

Dan nodded. "That's probably the first truthful thing you've said, except for your own I.D., Reiter. Perhaps we can now begin to make progress. Who is Siegfried Schmidt?"

Reiter smiled humorlessly. "He is not Heinrich Himmler. He is not Martin Bormann. He is Siegfried Schmidt, as he and I and his identification papers have told you."

"Why did you have all that money in your possession?"

"It was given to *Herr* Schmidt by his superiors to help him escape and continue his important work."

"For a Germany that no longer exists?"

"We did not expect it to come to this."

Brooks stared at him appraisingly. "I think, Reiter, that you have been too modest regarding yourself and your position in these last days of the Third Reich."

The *Obersturmbannführer*'s eyes narrowed. "What do you mean?"

There was a touch of mockery in Brooks's words now, hoping to goad the man into revealing something important. "How many men, even *Obersturmbannführers* in the *Sicherheitsdienst*, go around with the kind of address book that you have?" He took the small ledger from his pocket and began to turn the pages. "Himmler. Speer. Schacht. And so on. Otto Skorzeny. Now there's a man I've always wanted to meet. Perhaps you might arrange an introduction." He closed the book and slipped it back into his pocket. "What is your connection to these admirable gentlemen?" Dan demanded.

Reiter shrugged. "One meets people and always hopes to advance."

"Addresses? Phone numbers? Radio signal I.D.'s? And a special code book for communications. I think you're in league with them—or at least hoped to be—for a much more intriguing reason."

"What?" Reiter asked boldly.

"That's what I want you to tell me. It's what you *will* tell me before I'm finished with you, you piece of Nazi shit!" Dan suddenly exploded.

Fear leaped onto Reiter's face and he took a step backward. Brooks was silent a moment to allow his unexpected fury to dissipate. He forced himself to be cool, yet he had seen the look of fright on the *Obersturmbannführer's* face and knew that anger and threats were weapons he might ultimately use effectively against him.

He showed Reiter the papers with the long numbers and the Zurich addresses. "What do these mean?" he asked calmly.

"They are not mine."

"They were in Schmidt's wallet."

"I do not know what they mean. It is Siegfried's private business, I imagine."

Reiter stared at the papers nervously and his tightly closed lips twisted against each other. He *did* know something, Brooks realized. It was something that worried and excited the *Obersturmbannführer.*

"I'll make a simple suggestion then," Dan said.

"What is that, *Hauptmann?*"

"I will copy one of these and give you the original. Tell your rocket scientist I inadvertently left it here when I was questioning you. I'll arrange for you to spend time alone with him again after we reach England. Find out what it means."

Reiter stared at him speculatively. He was no longer in a frame of mind to make great sacrifices for the Third Reich. What was the point of it anymore? He might devise some sort of deal with the captain. The sums involved, he imagined, were enormous. Even if he only ended up with a small portion, it would be worth losing a larger amount to gain his freedom. He would have to convince the American that only he could gradually wheedle from Siegfried Schmidt the information to unlock that immense fortune.

"What's in it for me?" he demanded.

"Depends how cooperative you are and what you find out."

"Very well, *Herr Hauptmann.* I will try."

Twenty-seven

✠   *Obersturmbannführer* Dietrich Reiter awoke on the second morning of his captivity and for a few moments didn't know where he was. He felt a sense of dread and was bathed in sweat.

Had he just come out of a nightmare? he wondered, or had the memories of scenes and voices that rose in his mind been real?

He touched himself... arms, legs, face... to verify his existence. He felt, then saw, the familiar cloth of his own pajamas, rumpled, dirty, needing to be washed. The hard, plain bed was strange, the walls and spartan room furnishings unfamiliar, the bars on the window. Then he remembered.

In the darkness in the middle of the night, as he and *Herr* Schmidt had been led to the building that now housed them, it looked like a two-story stone cottage. In the distance, across vast grounds, he had seen dimly the silhouette of a huge fortress-like structure.

"What is this place?" he had asked the American captain.

"Your jail, Reiter," Brooks had replied. "Not as notorious as the Tower of London, but the British have been trying and executing their enemies here for hundreds of years. They've loaned it to us for the duration."

"Execution!" Reiter had almost screamed. "For what! I am a prisoner of war."

Without reply, they had been taken up a stairway, Schmidt to one room, he to another. His aching arms, which had been bound tightly at the wrists all during the flight from Innsbruck, had been untied at last. After mention of *jail*, Reiter had expected a dismal cell and had been surprised to see a plain but not unpleasant room, though there were the bars on the window.

Brooks had stayed behind a few minutes after his men left. There was a bathroom in the hall, he had said. If Reiter needed to use it, he was to call for the guard and would be escorted. There would be at least two

American sergeants on duty in the hall outside the prisoners' rooms around the clock, he had said, and others on reserve downstairs.

"I ask you again, *Herr Hauptmann,* why do you speak of trial and execution?" Reiter had implored, futilely trying to make it sound like a demand. "I have done nothing to warrant such treatment."

"For the crimes of the SS, *Herr Obersturmbannführer,*" the captain had replied coldly. "Each day new and unspeakable things are uncovered by our armies. Not just simple brutality, but death camps... murder factories for hundreds of thousands, maybe millions of innocent civilians and prisoners of war. Hitler might be dead, but the rest of you will pay."

Reiter had known of these things—and now, as he had feared, so did the rest of the world. "I will try to help you," he had said hurriedly then to his captor. "As you requested before we left Austria."

"About what?" the captain had asked, as if he had no memory of it.

"The papers you showed me. The Zurich addresses. The numbers."

The American had stared at him with contempt. "Whatever they are, they are insignificant compared to what I've learned the last few days about the atrocities committed by you Nazi bastards."

"No, they are not insignificant," Reiter had said softly.

The captain had stared at him appraisingly. "How do you know, if you don't know what they mean?"

"A feeling I have... that is all," he had answered, his voice all flustered. "And my belief that nothing *Herr* Schmidt is involved in is insignificant."

"Okay. I'll arrange for you to spend a little time alone with your friend Siegfried tomorrow," the American had agreed. "Next time I see you I'll expect answers." He had given him only one of the papers.

"Must I continue to wear this?" Reiter had asked, touching the hood on his head.

"You may take it off now," the captain had said. "In the presence of anyone else you must wear it. The guards will always knock before entering. You must put it on before they see you. They've been instructed."

Lying there fearfully on his cot in the morning, the *Obersturmbann-führer* was suddenly yanked into a moment of hope by the sounds of strong German voices outside. Had he dreamed all he had just reviewed in his mind?

He leapt from his cot and rushed to the barred window. He saw platoons of men, robust German faces and physiques, spread out over the grounds between his jail and the fortress in the middle distance. The men wore athletic shorts and shirts. They were doing exercises and running, responding with German drill chants to the loud commands of German *Feldwebels.*

Was he going mad? Reiter wondered. Were *they* prisoners too? They didn't look it. Their shirts and shorts were blazoned with emblems of the U.S. Army.

"What is the name of this place?" he had asked the American captain last night.

"Milton Hall," had been the answer.

Reiter had heard of the notorious Tower of London as a place of execution, but he had never heard of Milton Hall.

Captain Brooks did not visit him all day. Meals were brought on trays—unappetizing prison food—carried by silent guards who refused to engage in conversation. As the captain had ordered, they announced themselves at the door and waited for him to cover his head before entering. Reiter did not understand this hood business. He felt suffocated when he had to put it on, like a man hooded in his last moments before hanging, the noose already around his neck, the trapdoor about to drop from under him.

No knives were included among the utensils brought in with the food, nor was there anything in the room that could be fashioned into a weapon for attack or suicide. He was permitted to use the toilet whenever necessary and to shower and even to shave with a safety razor prepared in advance, but always with one of the sergeants escorting him and watching him closely throughout the most intimate functions.

As the captain had promised, Reiter was taken to *Herr* Schmidt's room to talk to him alone for an hour in the afternoon, but he mostly had to listen to him complain. Concerned about secret microphones, their macabre, hooded heads almost touched as they spoke in the barest of whispers in prudent, cryptic phrases.

Schmidt told him the American medic had examined his wounds and changed his bandages again. The healing was going well, he reported grumpily. That distressed Reiter very much. He thought the captain had agreed that, in exchange for his cooperation, only he would administer to his companion. What if the healing process went too well, too fast? What if Schmidt's features were restored and the Americans recognized him at last? Reiter was no longer as much concerned about the fate of his charge as he was about his own. The situation would grow much worse for the aide to such a man!

He showed Schmidt the paper with the numbers and Zurich addresses, and whispered, "The American captain stupidly left this behind in my room. He wants to know what it means."

Schmidt grabbed the paper. "What did you tell him?" he demanded, stuffing it into his pocket.

"Nothing, Siegfried. It is your business."

"Do not call me Siegfried when we are alone together, Reiter. That is disrespect. I will not tolerate it."

Reiter drew back before he could launch one of his irrational outbursts.

Herr Schmidt had just abrogated his own request to call him by his first name. He was behaving with the authoritarian personality Reiter remembered. Fortunately, he could do him no harm in their present circumstances—except for the fact of his existence here.

Reiter spoke no more about the confiscated paper. Actually it had not even been necessary to approach him about it, except to appear to be following the captain's instructions. The paper was the same list of numbers and words Reiter had received by radio at the Hotel Edelweiss, had memorized and given to Schmidt three days earlier.

Captain Brooks's superiors were waiting for him in the oak-paneled meeting room at OSS headquarters in London when he arrived from Milton Hall late that afternoon. Only Colonel Robert Hoose, commander of all the agency's United Kingdom and European activities, and Larry Dillard, civilian Chief of Special Operations, appeared this time. They greeted him with exuberance, standing immediately when he entered the room and flashing great, warm smiles.

The colonel returned Dan's salute, then added a firm handshake and a spirited, "Welcome home, Captain!"

Dillard tipped his brow with his fingers in a comradely semblance of a salute. "How are you, Dan?" he said, grasping his hand and looking at him with admiration and concern, as if he might not have expected to see him there again.

"Fine, sir," Brooks answered.

He'd only had a few hours sleep after getting the company and captives squared away, but he felt sharp in his Class A's, still invigorated by the action of the past few days and mentally ready for the debriefing.

"Any news of a surrender yet?" he asked.

"No. But it could come in the next hours. Certainly not more than a few days," Colonel Hoose declared. He motioned Brooks to a chair close to him at the big table. "More important for now . . . Who have you caught, Brooks?"

Dan delayed the answer by asking, "Is anyone else coming, sir?" He remembered very well his November briefing in this room and how cagey they all had been. Today *he* held the upper hand and he intended to keep it. "Major Blakely and Lieutenant Colonel Pearson?"

"Alan Blakely's been sent home," Hoose divulged crisply. "That was a bad bit of business with the girl and the Russian. No excuse for it."

"He's dead," Brooks said. "Major Mikhail Schepilov and sixteen men he had with him."

Dan told them about the *Spetsnaz* ambush at night in the mountain forest and the Russians' attempt to take his captives away from him.

"I sent a detail back the next day to strip their uniforms and phony I.D.'s and bury them in the mountains," he related. "This must go no further than this room. Even now we can't be sure that the Russian connection has been broken. They're tenacious sons of bitches when they want something."

"Of course, Dan," Hoose said in a tone of humility. "I agree with you completely."

"What about Lieutenant Colonel Pearson?"

The head of OSS's Paris branch had been important to the beginning of Knight's Cross before Brooks had been brought into it. He had been at Dan's first briefing here. Though no longer made privy to the most secret aspects of the mission, he had seen Dan and his pilot team off from the Dijon airfield that night in early March when they had parachuted into the Inn Valley.

"Transferred to China with a lot of our European personnel," Hoose told him.

Brooks was glad of that, that Blakely had been sent home and Pearson to China. It meant fewer people sniffing around, asking questions, maybe stumbling on answers.

"Then no one else will be made aware of what I tell you about Knight's Cross?" Dan pressed.

"No. We're limiting the need to know to Mr. Dillard and myself," replied the colonel. "Commander Cassidy wanted to be here. He knows you're back—we'll get to that later—but he was refused. Now, please tell us who you captured."

"I don't know," Brooks said simply.

The two OSS executives stared at him in disbelief.

"What do you mean you don't know!" Dillard demanded. "Do you realize the priority operation I mounted when you sent 'The fox is bagged' signal?"

"Not 'The fox... 'A fox', sir. I certainly..."

"I understand that, Dan," Dillard interrupted in exasperation. "I knew it couldn't be Hitler."

"I certainly do appreciate the priority operation you mounted, Larry," Dan said, trying to mollify his boss. "By acting as quickly as you did you averted potential disaster for all of us. The entire Knight's Cross operation might have been blown, including our prisoners. Sending us directly to Milton Hall was an excellent move. We can maintain security there without the British or any of our own military interfering."

"Who do you *think* you've captured, Brooks?" Hoose persisted.

"I've got two prisoners, Colonel. I know the identity of one of them." He told them about *Obersturmbannführer* Reiter. "He'll be helpful, I'm sure, if I can work on him long enough without interference. But it's the other one who's the important one."

"How the hell do you know that, Brooks, if you don't know who he is?" the colonel demanded.

"Let me tell you first what I do know," Dan insisted. "You can confirm my conclusions or suggest your own."

He described the circumstances leading to the kidnapping of his two captives: the SS unit dug in at the Hotel Edelweiss; his reasoning that they were there to protect Nazi leaders fleeing from Germany; the covert arrival of the bandaged man from Berlin with his *Sicherheitsdienst* escort; the kidnapping and battle.

"He's badly wounded... disfigured," Dan revealed. "There's no telling who he is just yet. I know because I've taken the bandages off. I haven't let anyone else see him except my medic, who compared what he saw to the pictures of Nazi leaders you gave me. He couldn't identify him either. However, the man carried papers under the name of Siegfried Schmidt and both he and his escort claim he's a rocket scientist who was burned in an air raid."

"Even one of those boys would be useful to us," Colonel Hoose stated. "Looking to the future, that is. But I don't think he was worth mounting the operation you did, the loss of dead and wounded to kidnap him and the massive extraction Larry ordered to bring you out fast."

"I don't either," Dan agreed. "But our captive is as much Siegfried Schmidt, rocket scientist, as you are, Colonel."

"Then who the hell is he? And how do we find out?"

"I have a hunch he's somebody *very* important," Brooks said. "Maybe someone as high up as Heinrich Himmler or Martin Bormann. However, I won't really know until his wounds heal, or if I'm able to squeeze it out of him or Reiter before then."

"Himmler or Bormann! By God, Brooks, that would be a feather in our caps!" exclaimed the colonel. "What evidence do you have?"

Dan unzipped a canvas bag he had carried into the room and upended its contents onto the table. "This is some of it," he said with satisfaction. "More than a hundred thousand dollars in the currencies and gold coins of various countries. Schmidt and Reiter were on the ratline out of the Reich. Reiter has already admitted it. They were at the Edelweiss waiting for further instructions. Only somebody very high up in the government or party would have access to funds like this."

Dillard lifted a pile of the gold coins, clinked them in his hands and poured them into Hoose's palms; then he riffled through a few packs of the banded currencies and passed them to Hoose for closer inspection. Dan could sense Dillard's banker's mind at work.

"I suggest we deposit this into one of the agency's covert accounts," said the SO chief. "Eventually, there will be a full accounting made to the agency, of course, and the money would be returned to the U.S. Treasury as leftover operating funds."

"How would you like a few million more like that?" Dan asked, startling them.

222

"Very much, Captain," replied the colonel. "It would validate the operations of this agency, which the regulars have bitched about since we were established."

"I have a strong hunch there's a lot more where this came from," Dan told them. "This is only walking around money."

"What makes you say that?" asked Dillard.

"This does," Brooks said. He withdrew a folded sheet of paper from his inside jacket pocket. "It's a copy I made of a note found in Herr Schmidt's wallet. The original is in my quarters at Milton Hall."

Colonel Hoose read the note. "Is it some sort of code?" he asked, and handed it to Dillard.

Dan smiled. He had copied and brought with him only one of the long numbers and Zurich addresses. There had been six in Schmidt's wallet. "Yes, sir, in a manner of speaking it's a code," he answered. "I've looked up the Zurich address." He took a notepad from his pocket and read from it. "It's a bank. The International Bank of the Four Cantons. I believe the number is a secret Nazi account to finance their escape and a lush life in a foreign country."

Colonel Hoose immediately saw the prospects in that, yet he asked, "Didn't Hitler issue a directive a year or so ago that all Germans with foreign accounts were to return their money to the Reich or be considered traitors?"

"Yes, and face imprisonment or death," Brooks acknowledged. "But I'll bet there were thousands who didn't pay any attention, particularly the higher-ups running the show."

"You're onto something, Dan," Dillard said excitedly. "At the bank I was associated with before the war, we had trouble with the Swiss over secret numbered accounts."

"How do we get hold of the money?" Brooks asked. "Is the number enough? Does someone just walk in, show the number and ask for what he wants? How about withdrawals and transfers at long distance?"

Dillard frowned in thought. "Maybe the number is enough, but perhaps there's a code word or I.D. also needed."

"Our own experience with OSS's covert accounts in Switzerland might help," Colonel Hoose said. "I would think that Allen Dulles in Bern or someone among his staff would be able to help."

"There are conditions that must be met before you go ahead," Brooks spoke up.

"What?" asked Hoose huffily.

"The source of the number and address must not be revealed to Dulles or anyone else," Dan insisted. "Until I uncover the identity of Siegfried Schmidt, the origin of the information must remain secret between the three of us."

"That's reasonable," Dillard granted.

"If Dulles can effect the transfer of funds, he must do it with maximum secrecy," Brooks continued. "If the transaction takes place it should be reported only directly to you."

"I think you're getting a bit out of your depth and responsibilities, Captain," the colonel said brusquely. "These details are for us to decide. Not you."

Dan remained unrelenting, rank be damned. "It would violate our security, sir, for anyone else to know there are people like Reiter and Schmidt being held by OSS who are a conduit to such funds," he argued. "The intelligence services and governments of any one of our allies and any branch of our own military services or government might insist upon priority or try to interfere. And that goes for the Germans, too."

"The Germans are in no position to interfere with anyone," Hoose retorted with satisfaction.

"Then the Russians!" Brooks contended. "Look at the trouble they've already caused Knight's Cross."

"I think you're overly concerned about something which is no longer your business, Captain," the colonel retorted.

"You will recall, sir, at my original briefing, that you gave me orders not to reveal information to anyone until I was ready," Dan insisted.

"He's right, Colonel," Dillard spoke up.

"Schmidt's true identity is still unknown and I believe I am in the best position to find out what it is," Brooks declared.

"You are not unexpendable, Captain," Hoose snapped.

Brooks was brought up sharply by that. He remembered, *No agent was ever recruited to work for the agency without thought being given to the possibility of having to dispose of him, if necessary, after his usefulness had ended.*

Entwined with that thought he heard the colonel continue, "We can take the prisoners away from you and find out what we want ourselves."

"I'd advise not doing that, sir," Dan said calmly, aware he was teetering on the edge of insubordination.

"Why not?"

"There has already been one major security leak in this building, Colonel," Dan reminded him, "but not one single breach in my company, even while we were surrounded by the German army, with every opportunity for my men to defect back to them, or for any of us to do something stupid that would have blown our cover. There's something much bigger at stake here than authority and chain of command."

"What might that be, Brooks?" demanded the colonel sarcastically.

"The likelihood of millions of dollars salted away in secret Nazi accounts like this one," Dan said. "OSS can be the agency that recovers it. Having captured these two men and established a difficult rapport with them, I'm in the best position to see this aspect of Knight's Cross through successfully."

224

The two OSS executives stared at him appraisingly. "I think he's right," Dillard said, shifting his gaze to the colonel.

With reluctance, Hoose finally came around. "Very well, Brooks. They're yours for now. Until it's decided what follows."

"Thank you, sir."

"However, there's another disturbing matter that has to be resolved right away," Colonel Hoose hurried on. "Commander Cassidy is very angry about your treatment of his agent, Karl Bergen."

"I've preferred charges against Bergen."

"I know. That's part of the problem."

"Bergen's lucky I didn't shoot him on the spot," Dan retorted. "I don't know the man's game, but he interfered with Knight's Cross and could have caused fatal damage."

"Bergen disputes your charges, Captain. He says it was you who turned him in to the Gestapo."

"He thinks it was the Gestapo... and it's important that he continue to think that way," Brooks explained. "In fact it was a Kripo inspector working for us who took him and his radioman out of circulation at my request. The radioman is clean. He contacted us when he realized what Bergen was up to."

"That's one of the reasons we recommend against pressing your charges," Dillard said. "Would you want Bergen to hear such testimony and have it on the record?"

Brooks mulled that over. His intense dislike of Bergen and his anger about what the man had done to try to thwart Knight's Cross had clouded his judgment. He realized that his own testimony would not be sufficient to convict Bergen. Inspector Klung and Willy Hupnagel would have to give evidence at a court-martial. He didn't want that. Aspects of the mission would go on public record.

"You're right, sir," Dan agreed. "I withdraw the charges, but urge you to get him out of the ETO as quickly as possible. Send him back to the States and discharge him. He's not to be trusted."

"I'll suggest that to Commander Cassidy, but I don't think he'll go for it," Colonel Hoose said. "He has other plans for Bergen."

"The war's almost over in Germany. What in hell does he need him for?"

Colonel Hoose said, "Cassidy still wants to use him. Counterintelligence in the Reich. There will still be a lot of Nazis to round up and Cassidy thinks Karl's the man to help do it."

"I don't want him crossing my path again, Colonel," Dan said angrily.

Dillard and Hoose exchanged furtive glances. "I think we'd best let you in on some of the rest of it," the colonel spoke. "However, nothing we say here now is ever to be revealed to anybody. That's *never*. That doesn't mean not until after the war is over, it means forever and beyond."

Dan couldn't imagine what the colonel was driving at. He was an executive in a posh office not an operative immersed in blood, shit and fear, surrounded by enemies. What in hell did he know about keeping silent under the most dangerous circumstances. "I don't think you need have any concerns about my maintaining security about anything, sir," he said crisply.

"Give him the gist of it, Larry," Hoose said. "As a civilian it might be best coming from you. I'm still held to a stricter set of rules."

Dillard began hesitantly, but soon spoke with excitement as he related to Brooks what the captain realized was an astonishing briefing.

"This is something new for us, Dan," said the SO chief, "and you can be in on the beginning of it. Except in the Far East against the Japs, there's no more need for SO or Cassidy's SI as we knew it. Oh, there will still be Criminal Investigation Division and Counter Intelligence Corps operations, but that's regular army, not OSS. Many of us in the agency, however, have resolved that we need an independent intelligence and covert action organization such as the United States has never had before. The British and French have had it for hundreds of years, the Germans have had it for almost as long. The Russians have got more of it now than anybody and have had since the communist revolution."

"That's the direction we've got to go now," Colonel Hoose said enthusiastically. "Against the Reds, as well as cleaning up after the Nazis."

Brooks absorbed their meaning only too well. "What's our mandate for it? Where are our orders?" he asked.

"We improvise as we go along," Dillard stated. "Until there's a new official agency in place, we will do whatever we think is necessary for the good of our country."

"Lieutenant Commander Cassidy does have new orders," Colonel Hoose revealed. "That much is official. He is to find and use Nazis who can help us against the Russians. Intelligence people who have secret files and established networks on the other side. We don't have that capability yet."

"Does it make any difference if they're SS, party leaders, murderers and war criminals?" Brooks asked with mock insouciance.

His bosses missed the sarcasm. "Anything we can get away with, if it serves our purpose," Dillard replied.

"We excluded Commander Cassidy from this meeting until we could assess what you were going to reveal to us, Captain," Colonel Hoose told Brooks now. "However, because of his new responsibilities, he is very interested in who you've captured."

"I don't want him or Bergen snooping around anywhere near my prisoners," Dan said adamantly. "If he ever got wind of what we're onto now, he would be as dangerous as Bergen was in the Inn Valley."

Dillard and Hoose considered that a few moments, shifting in their chairs, looking away from him almost in embarrassment at having to agree with him. Yet they could not possibly be so unaware and unimaginative as to not understand the truth of what he'd said, Brooks thought.

"Very well. I think we can ease out of it tactfully," the colonel commented coolly.

Then a new, smug smile spread across Larry Dillard's face. "Something just occurred to me," he said with satisfaction. "Do you realize, Colonel, that the money Captain Brooks has brought us today and the funds we might manage to get out of the account in Zurich can serve us well in this new direction we're going? They are funds we don't have to account for. They can finance our work until a new agency and funding is set up."

The next morning, after OSS security officers brought Karl Bergen to his office, took off his handcuffs and left, the first question out of Lieutenant Commander Cassidy's mouth was, "Who did Brooks get, Karl?"

"I don't know, sir."

"That's the same answer he gave the brass at a meeting here yesterday." Cassidy wasn't supposed to know anything about what had been said in that meeting, but he'd managed to ferret that much out of Colonel Hoose. "I don't believe Brooks," the SI chief said. Or maybe Hoose and Dillard were holding out on him.

"I wouldn't believe anything that bastard said!" Bergen spat out in fury.

Cassidy knew he should reprimand him for speaking that way about another officer, but it wouldn't have served his purpose. He smiled sympathetically.

"I want you to know how much I admire the job you did in Austria, Karl, and how much I regret that you were prevented from accomplishing more."

"*Danke, mein Herr,*" Bergen replied, then remembered he was back in England, speaking to an American. "Thank you, sir."

"I'll help you get out of this court-martial nonsense," Cassidy continued. "But I must have your word that what we speak about here today and in the future will never be revealed to anyone. Ever. Can you live up to that?"

"Of course, sir. Didn't I just spend six months living among the fucking Nazis, feeding you military intelligence?" Bergen challenged. He sounded both hurt and angry.

Cassidy appraised the man sitting across the desk from him. He knew him, but he still didn't *really* know him. He didn't really know what had driven him to want to be an agent and be willing to live as precariously as he had in enemy territory all that time. He was thinner, but looked just as mean and dangerous.

"You're right, Karl. Forgive me for even bringing up the matter. I should probably ask you first if you want to continue working for me. You certainly have done your share already. If you turned me down I'd understand."

"What would my assignment be, Commander?"

Cassidy leaned closer, as if speaking in confidence. "We haven't even finished this war yet, but we've got to start preparing for the next. You're an American now. You can help, Karl."

"Yes, sir, I'm proud of my citizenship," Bergen answered, "but I'd like to spend some time in Germany when the war's over."

Cassidy hadn't thought it would be this easy. "That's exactly what I have in mind, and I can probably get you a promotion," he said cheerfully. "You might have to operate a lot in civvies, but more rank would make a difference in your authority and paycheck."

"What can you do about those lying charges Brooks brought against me?"

Cassidy leaned back in his swivel chair and tapped the tips of his fingers together in a pensive gesture. "There are no grounds for a court-martial," he said. "I've convinced the brass that we should handle the matter administratively and quietly. I've also told them that I still need you, Karl, for a very important mission." Cassidy recognized that he was the *brass* himself, but saw the advantage of using the word to ally himself as *us* against *them*.

Bergen leaned forward in his chair. "What would the mission be, Commander?"

There was no point in dilly-dallying, Cassidy thought. "To go into the former Third Reich as soon as the surrender comes and find high-ranking Nazis who are willing to work with us against the Russians."

Bergen forced his voice into a calmer tone than the excitement he felt. "I'd like that," he acknowledged. "Finding the worst Nazi bastards and seeing that they get what they deserve."

"You misunderstand," Cassidy corrected. "I'm not speaking of retribution. We want people we can work with."

Bergen stared at him in astonishment. He realized now that he'd missed the full implication of what the lieutenant commander had said. He had never considered the possibility of such a thing. What he'd always had in mind was exacting retribution for crimes against himself and his circle of Brownshirt friends who had been betrayed and butchered a decade ago; and afterward to plunder for his own enrichment whatever property and treasure were left for the taking.

"Of course in some circumstances punishment might have to be meted out," Cassidy continued as if he were giving a philosophical lecture. "Because of public demand...widespread awareness of specific crimes. But even there we might be able to make some accommodation, provided

228

we were quick enough and clever enough about it. Secret arrangements while we held punishment over their heads. You understand what I mean, don't you, Karl?"

Bergen did, and yet it was all too sophisticated for him. He had his own agenda and that was the one he intended to stick to. "Yes, sir," he replied politely.

"In particular," the SI chief elaborated, "I want you to find high-ranking officers and government officials who have amassed intelligence about Communist organizations in any country in Europe, and about Soviet military plans and capabilities."

"I understand, Commander Cassidy," Bergen said. "Would Willy Hupnagel go with me again?"

"No, you won't need a radioman for this assignment. We'll arrange other ways to communicate."

"You will clear my record with OSS?"

"Of course."

"There is a lot of back pay due me."

"I'll take care of it today."

"Will there be a further briefing...leads to follow up?"

"Yes."

"I am free to go now? No more handcuffs and guards?"

"Absolutely."

"My promotion?"

"Will take a little time. Don't let it hold you up."

"Is Brooks around? Am I liable to run into him?"

"He's at Milton Hall, but he'll be coming in from time to time like he did yesterday."

"What do I do if I run into him?"

"Avoid him, Karl," Cassidy instructed. "Except for one important matter."

"What's that?"

Cassidy knew he was treading on very dangerous ground, but felt compelled to go on. "Everybody has been refused permission to see or question the captives he brought in," he said in a quiet, measured voice. "We've got to do something about that, Karl, and I think you're the man to do it."

"Where are they being held?"

"Milton Hall. But that would be impossible even for you. The place is locked up tight. You couldn't get near them."

"What am I to do?"

"They'll likely be moved. I don't know when or where, but I'll get word to you. Be ready for it." Cassidy stared at Bergen and wished, for this moment, he could transform himself into someone who looked as rough and intimidating as that. "I warn you," he said in a low, harsh voice, "if you ever drop even a hint of what we talk about to anybody...the consequences will be terminal."

Bergen's gorge rose at the threat, but he gave one of his terrible little smiles in response. "I understand, sir," he said softly.

"Since Brooks won't let us talk to his prisoners, we've got to force him to," Cassidy went on. He felt like Iago now, planting an idea, suggesting mischief. "Go around him. Get close to anybody who's close to them. Or get rid of them."

"The prisoners?"

"Brooks."

Twenty-eight

✠   It would be two or three days, Brooks knew, before news could reach him about the success or failure of the transaction in Switzerland. They would at least have to wait until the banks opened for business again on Monday.

In the morning, he strode across the grounds of Milton Hall from his quarters in the Elizabethan main building to the gatekeeper's cottage, exchanging salutes with *Feldwebels* supervising squads of men engaged in the exercise, sports and drill program laid on to keep them busy.

Lieutenant Becker was running the company now with the help of *Oberfeldwebel* Helmut Jung and the other German noncoms. Jung had gladly given up his temporary rank of *Oberleutnant,* happy to be a master sergeant again. All the American sergeants were guarding the captives, except for Paulsen who had set up a dispensary for the company in the main building and was on call when Brooks wanted him to tend to Siegfried Schmidt.

To satisfy curiosity and eliminate speculation about the identity of their prisoners, Brooks had given a briefing to the Germans in the mess hall, and separately to his OSS cadre in the cottage. Implying that he was able to take them into his confidence at last, he had told them, without revealing names, what was still the surface truth and could cause no harm: that one of the captives was an important rocket scientist and the other his SS watchdog. Then he had bound his men to secrecy again by commending them for the loyalty they had shown to each other and to him all these months and ordering them once more never to reveal what he was telling them to anyone else.

Dan had never expected to be quartered at Milton Hall again, but it had been the ideal choice to temporarily lodge the Knight's Cross company and its captives. There were sixty rooms in the main building alone, more than enough to house the men in great comfort. They were quite impressed too, as he had been when he had trained here two years earlier, by the baronial halls with beamed ceilings and the corridors lined with medieval armor. He had been pleased also to find Lieutenant Chadwick and the same excellent OSS support group on hand that had handled the mess and housekeeping duties for them at St. Germain. They were accustomed to having the Germans around, knew how to mind their own business regarding matters other than preparing fine meals and keeping the rooms and grounds in tip-top shape, and they were less likely to blabber elsewhere.

He hadn't told the men yet, but Brooks hoped to be able to deactivate the company soon. Colonel Hoose and Larry Dillard had concurred with him that as soon as the fighting ended they should try to arrange a speedy transfer to Germany and demobilization for the former POW's. That would fulfill one of the promises made when he had recruited them. Those who had been civilians in France before enlisting for the mission would be returned there if that was their wish.

Dan glanced quickly into the downstairs sitting room of the cottage where cots had been set up for his off-duty cadre. Sergeant Mangold, on alert with an M-3 submachine gun now instead of the German Schmeisser he had carried for months, greeted him softly. Maurer and Brunner were sacked out.

Brooks climbed the stairs to the second floor. Before he reached the top, Sergeants Schafer and Blumberg had their submachine guns aimed at him. It was their watch in the corridor outside the prisoners' rooms.

"Any problems or complaints?" Dan asked.

"All quiet, sir," Schafer reported.

"I'll be talking to them now. One at a time," Brooks said.

Obersturmbannführer Reiter heard the knock on his door and quickly put on the hated hood, adjusting the cutout holes to his eyes, nose and mouth. The American captain entered and Reiter stood to attention, unexpectedly glad to see him.

Brooks noted the gesture of respect. "How are you today, Colonel?" he asked cordially. He decided to be solicitous, maybe even butter the man up a bit and try to make him feel relaxed rather than frightening him again.

"As well as can be expected under the circumstances, *Herr Hauptmann*," replied the SS officer.

He wore the dark gray suit and black shoes he had been given in the Austrian farmhouse, and had been issued clean underwear, socks and shirt, though no tie and belt. Reiter surmised it was a precaution to keep him from hanging himself, which he had not even considered doing.

"Did you learn anything from Schmidt yesterday about the numbers and the Zurich address?" Brooks continued in a pleasant voice.

"Yes, *Herr* Hauptmann. I think you will be pleased," Reiter asserted with satisfaction. Alone in the night, his fears mounting, he had decided to be less hostile, more cooperative, perhaps even obsequious if it would buy him freedom. "May I remove the hood?"

"Yes. You may also sit down."

Reiter lifted off the black cloth and sat on the edge of his bed. Brooks took the one chair in the room. "What did you learn?" he asked.

"The address is a bank. The numbers are the entry code to a secret account."

Brooks feigned a look of surprise. "How much is in the account?"

Reiter spoke prudently. "He didn't say. But he mentioned that *Herr* Speer, who had arranged it, would take good care of him. I would guess at least a million Swiss francs."

Dan kept his expression immobile. Reiter appeared to be telling as much of the truth as his knowledge allowed him to, though perhaps he was just being judicious in the amount suggested.

"Sounds plausible," Brooks said affably. "I'll convey the information to my superiors and see if it checks out. If it does, we'll consider your status again."

"*Danke sehr, mein Herr,*" the *Obersturmbannführer* said in a humble voice.

"Would I be right in assuming that the other numbers I found in *Herr* Schmidt's wallet are for additional accounts at various banks?" Brooks prodded.

"Yes," Reiter agreed readily. He had made up his mind during his restless night that if he were to cooperate fully with the American captain it would still be possible to get his hands on some of the money himself. "Siegfried told me that once out of the Reich we wouldn't have to worry about funds. I will help you, *Herr Hauptmann,* but I must have something in return."

"What do you want?"

"To be treated as an officer in the Wehrmacht. A temporary prisoner of war to be released at the earliest opportunity, rather than as a member of the SS who would be made to face the charges you have spoken about. Also to share in some of the funds you will be able to acquire with my assistance. And to be released in a neutral country. Switzerland, Spain or South America."

Brooks went right along with him as if it were already a *fait accompli.* "Switzerland, of course, would give us closer access to the money."

"That would be good, *mein Herr.* From there I would make my own arrangements. I promise you that I will disappear—most likely to South America—and never make trouble for you, never speak of this matter to anyone. If I were able to start a new life with substantial capital, there would be no reason to. It would be foolish of me."

Along with every other Nazi who has something to hide, Brooks thought to himself. He didn't believe he really needed the man to get information from Schmidt about the numbered accounts, unless there were caches not indicated by the notes he already had. But he still needed Reiter to reveal Schmidt's true identity, which he was sure the SS officer knew.

"And what shall we do about *Herr* Schmidt, to whom you seem so devoted? Brooks asked.

"I would want to take him with me, to continue the journey you interrupted at the Hotel Edelweiss."

Brooks took from his pocket another one of the notes that had been in Schmidt's wallet and handed it to the *Obersturmbannführer.* "I want you to question your rocket scientist about this one today, Reiter. And this time see if you can find out exactly how much money is in the account."

He didn't want to overwhelm them with demands for information on every one of the accounts at one time. He wanted to give them a chance to be a little bit more cooperative each time in exchange for going easier on them. He intended to manipulate them gradually and work his way slowly but surely into their confidence.

In Zurich, on the 7th of May, Sascha Gorchavek made his rounds of several message drops belonging to his Soviet intelligence network. He traveled this particular circuit often as part of his assigned duties, rarely knowing in advance if he would find anything. He didn't mind that his task was frequently unprofitable. It was not very demanding work and his excursions from Bern, where he was based, were made through beautiful Swiss mountains and valleys that had not been ravaged by war as his homeland had been. He liked too the quality of life in the civilized, sophisticated Swiss cities, though he could never speak of that to his comrades.

There was no official, legal representation of the Union of Soviet Socialist Republics in Switzerland, this most capitalist of capitalist nations. Yet ever since Vladimir Ilyich Lenin and his small band of associates had plotted their Revolution in a whorehouse in Zurich, there always had been Russian agents operating in Switzerland, though from time to time the Swiss police swooped up entire networks.

Capitalist matters interested the intelligence organ of the army, the GRU, very much. One of its functions was to become aware of new weapons and military technology and try to steal them. The GRU also knew that there was military intelligence to be learned from industrial and commercial espionage.

This day, under some brush close to a familiar tall pine tree in Bauer Park, Captain Gorchavek retrieved a small, capped container which he placed in the pocket of the finely tailored Swiss suit he wore with pride. His suit and well-crafted black businessmen's shoes were part of his cover in order to look as much like the local populace as possible. While in his stooped position, Gorchavek pretended to retie his shoelaces. Then he stood up, gazed all around him to be certain he was unobserved and made his way to the railroad station, from where he took the mid-afternoon train back to his safe house in Bern.

Gorchavek was on his first posting outside the Soviet Union as a GRU operative. A stocky, round-faced peasant with a quick, sly mind, he had risen to the rank of captain in the Red Army due to his forcefulness and obedience to orders during years of combat against the Hitler armies that had invaded the motherland. His bravery had brought him to the attention of the regimental commissar, who had considered him trustworthy enough to serve in intelligence. A nine-month course at the Language Academy had made him sufficiently proficient in German, which permitted him to operate well in the *Schweizerdeutsch* areas of Switzerland, though not in the French and Italian speaking cantons.

In his apartment on Seefeldstrasse, Gorchavek read the note while sipping a glass of beer, which he felt he had earned after his day's labors. He had developed a taste for beer and wine since coming to Switzerland, rather than the vodka he previously had been accustomed to; but he was prudent in their use, not wanting to risk the ire of his superior, Major Cherensky, who kept a close watch on his budget and even begrudged him this pleasant little apartment, though it had been considered safer for him to live alone rather than share quarters with other operatives.

The message he pondered now was from one of the deep moles for whom he was the contact. The mole was a Swiss national who was the third ranking executive of the International Bank of the Four Cantons. He had access to who owned what secret numbered accounts and what transactions were made. For substantial payments, he had been recruited to report unusual activity in accounts that belonged to leading German, French, British and American industrialists and their corporations; also high-ranking government and political figures of those countries, and accounts suspected of belonging to their intelligence services. Though he was breaking Swiss banking laws by disclosing privileged information, the mole didn't know he was working for the Russians. He had been led to believe he was giving insider tips to a financial analyst whose arcane habit it was to examine curiously diverse factors before advising his clients on investments.

The note from the mole asked for a meeting. To Gorchavek this meant the man was in possession of high grade intelligence which he couldn't commit to writing. He regretted now that caution had kept him from opening the container and reading the message while still in Zurich. He would have to return there immediately, to the same message drop, after putting rendezvous instructions in the container.

It required, therefore, two more round trips and another day before the furtive meeting was effected and Gorchavek received the intelligence orally and made the usual payment to the mole. During his return journey home on the 8th, he became aware of unusual excitement around the newspaper kiosks in the train station at Zurich and heard strangers calling to each other happily that the war was over. He bought a newspaper before boarding the train and read it with elation. The official unconditional surrender by the German government, such as it was, had been signed that day.

When Gorchavek finally reached his apartment in Bern that night and wrote down what he had learned from the mole, he felt he had his teeth in something juicy but still couldn't figure out exactly what. It was time to call in his superior.

Major Sergei Cherensky, a blond, slender man of forty-two, looking even more tailored and prosperous than his subordinate, arrived at Gorchavek's apartment in the evening. He preferred not to have his agents come to his own apartment or office unless absolutely necessary. Fluent in German and French, he posed successfully as an investment adviser with a limited clientele. He insisted that no Russian be spoken when he met with his men.

"You have heard the news, Gorchavek?" the major said excitedly in German after the door was closed behind him.

"It is wonderful," Gorchavek responded, shaking his superior's extended hand. "What joy there must be at home tonight."

"Complete victory at last. Yet for us, Sascha, the war goes on."

"The mole," said Gorchavek, "reports that two million Swiss francs have been transferred from one numbered account belonging to a German company to another numbered account belonging to Blackstone Trading Company, an American firm. The transaction was made by telephone and the correct numbers were given."

Major Cherensky's interest picked up immediately. "Blackstone is a covert account of the American Office of Strategic Services," he said. "We can assume that a German company isn't making payment to OSS for services rendered or any other commercial reasons."

"Then what?"

"Suggest something, Sascha," coaxed the major.

"More likely it is plunder secreted in Switzerland by the Nazi hierarchy," Gorchavek declared with confidence.

"Now you're thinking," Cherensky complimented. "But you have forgotten your manners. Do you have a little wine, Sascha? Something to celebrate victory and help lubricate our brain cells."

"Of course. Forgive me, sir." Gorchavek rushed to pour them each a glass of a dry white wine he had in his ice box, and brought with it cheese and crackers. "To our victory, Major," he said, sipping delicately from his stem glass. At home he would have tossed off a hefty shot of vodka and immediately poured another. He hoped his superior noticed how he had adapted to prudence and refinement.

"If your supposition is correct, Captain," Cherensky continued, "why would any of these Nazis reveal the existence of their plunder, much less turn it over to OSS?"

Gorchavek put his glass on a table between them and bit daintily into a piece of cheese on a cracker after his superior had preceded him to the plate. He chewed as he thought. When he had swallowed, he said, "To make a deal."

"It could be a banker or industrialist, a politician or solder," Cherensky speculated. "Who do we know about, Gorchavek, who would fit that profile? A man in a position to bargain for his freedom in exchange for Swiss francs."

"We can discount Hitler."

"Only if we believe the report of the German high command."

"Our own leaders have confirmed his suicide."

Cherensky opened his mouth to say something disdainful, then altered it as he spoke. "Our commanders in Berlin have not exhibited the corpse. But perhaps Moscow does not want them to."

"Goebbels suicide has been confirmed," Gorchavek ruminated, "but we have heard nothing about the capture of Göring, Himmler or Bormann. Or Speer, their Minister of Arms and Munitions. Or their financial wizard, Schacht."

"Good candidates, Sascha."

"Then we must ask Moscow to demand of the Americans a complete list of their high-ranking prisoners, Comrade Major."

"Unlikely they would comply. If there is a deal cooking, would the OSS even report the capture of someone suspected of having a hoard to tap? I don't think so," said the major patronizingly.

"What action can we take?"

Cherensky smiled. "Were you ever posted to a *Spetsnaz* unit, Sascha?"

"No, sir. GRU considered it, but then it was decided I would be more useful in this assignment."

Cherensky stared at him appraisingly, then nodded as if they had entered into a pact. "Many weeks ago, Sascha, I received an unusual message from GRU headquarters in Moscow. I was told to be on the lookout for a *Spetsnaz* team who might be making their way over the mountains into Switzerland from Austria. It was not certain they would come this way, but it was a possibility."

"What was their mission?"

"I was not told. However, one perceives things about certain operations even when one isn't supposed to," he said softly. "You associate one matter with another but keep your mouth shut about what you think you know—since GRU apparently doesn't want you to know it—until, eventually, something about what you're not supposed to know can be useful to you."

Gorchavek had been waiting for the point of it all, not wishing to intrude upon his superior's mental concentration. But as the major drank his wine, with apparent appreciation, his talk seemed to wander about philosophically. He emptied his glass and held it up to indicate a refill would be appreciated. As he poured from the bottle, Gorchavek finally prompted, "To what did you link the *Spetsnaz* team, sir?"

"In my mind, Sascha, I associated it with an inquiry that had been sent to me earlier," Cherensky told him. "Moscow wanted to know if we had run across anything about an OSS mission to capture high-ranking Nazis escaping to the Inn Valley. They thought that Dulles, the OSS station chief here in Bern, might be involved or at least know of it. It was suggested that there might be somewhere we could obtain the information."

Gorchavek drained his wine glass and decided he would not refill it. "Did you learn about it, sir?"

- "Regrettably, no, Sascha. But now I believe it would be to our advantage to pursue it."

"How do you want me to proceed, Major?"

"Go to the Inn Valley and snoop around. We have the names and addresses of Austrian Communists who were with the Resistance. They have been helpful to us in the past and stand ready to help again."

Twenty-nine

✠   The guns in Europe fell silent five days after Knight's Cross returned to England. That same day Larry Dillard telephoned Brooks at Milton Hall to tell him Allen Dulles in Bern had completed the transfer of two million Swiss francs—almost one million American dollars—to one of the agency's own covert accounts.

That was twice as much as Reiter had estimated, but Dan was disappointed. He had speculated that the secret accounts might give OSS access to Nazi plunder worth tens or hundreds of millions in American dollars.

"Will there be more account numbers?" Dillard prompted.

"I'm confident there will be," Dan told him. "Let me continue to handle this my way and maybe we'll be able to pay off the national war debt."

"I doubt there will be that much money, Captain, but stay with it. We're backing you all the way," the SO chief said.

Dan could have given him another account number right then, but he didn't want to make it appear too easy. He intended to dole them out to his superiors only as his own agenda progressed.

The previous day he had brought Reiter into Schmidt's room to treat his wounds again. He had stayed there himself, listening for any chance remark between them that might prove useful, observing the medical procedure closely and scrutinizing the patient's features for recognizable changes. There were none, except for a fuzz of brown and gray hair beginning to grow on his face and skull; and Schmidt had been grumpy and suspicious and hardly any words had passed between the captives.

It was Brooks, however, who had given Schmidt the shot of morphine afterward, drawing a sigh of appreciation and a *"Danke"* from him. It was always Dan who gave him the longed-for shot now, even when Paulsen treated the burns. He was establishing his own bond with the man, casting himself as the means of delivery from pain and depression.

Later in the day, he had sent Reiter back alone to fawn on Schmidt and try to worm more information out of him. What Brooks wanted in particular was to know the amount in each account, but the *Obersturmbannführer* had reported that Schmidt angrily refused to divulge anything. For two days he had not even confirmed another account number. Reiter claimed Siegfried was being extremely perverse and had confiscated the note, as he had the first one after presumably divulging what it meant. But Dan now suspected that Reiter's supposed questioning of Schmidt might itself be a ploy. He had a feeling the SS officer already knew the answers and had been holding them back for reasons of his own.

After news of the surrender had been broadcast, Brooks returned to the gatekeeper's cottage to interrogate his captives again. Walking across the grounds of Milton Hall, *Oberfeldwebel* Jung caught up to him before he entered the cottage. "Sir, may I speak to you a moment?"

"Of course, Sergeant. What is it?"

Jung looked unsure of himself. "I have a favor to ask."

"Go ahead."

"I do not want to go home with the others yet," he said. "I would prefer to stay under your command, if you can use me to help guard your prisoners, or whatever your next duty is, *Herr Hauptmann.*"

Brooks had never considered keeping any of the Germans on for the next stage, but now he replied, "It's a possibility, Jung. You know how highly I regard you. I'll give it some thought."

"*Danke, Herr Hauptmann,*" Jung said gratefully. He saluted, turned smartly and strode across the grounds toward a platoon that was waiting for him.

Brooks watched him pensively. He would have thought the man would want to get back to Hamburg as fast as he could to try to locate his father and mother, if they had survived. The idea of keeping him on, however, did have some appeal.

Dan entered the cottage, looked in on the off-duty section of the security detail to make them aware of his presence, then climbed the stairs to the second floor, spoke briefly to Sergeants Maurer and Brunner on guard in the hallway, and headed for Siegfried Schmidt's room with a medical kit.

The prisoner greeted him courteously. It still gave Brooks a macabre feeling to hear the muffled voice through the mouth opening in the bandages and hood, to catch an occasional glimpse of eyes through the slits and to try to read a facial expression he couldn't see.

"Germany has surrendered," Dan told him.

"What terms?" Schmidt demanded.

"Unconditional."

"Disgraceful."

"Necessary."

"It would not have happened if *der Führer* had lived," declared Schmidt angrily. "The word surrender was not in his vocabulary."

"Then he should not have committed suicide and left the others to take the blame for him."

"He was betrayed by the General Staff. Deserted by the German people."

"But not by you."

"By me? No. Not in my heart, *Hauptmann*. But I am only a scientist, not a politician or soldier."

"Yes. So you said."

Brooks did not intend to tell him anything about the expropriation of his account in Switzerland. "I will look after your medical treatments myself from now on," he said. "Take off the hood."

"If you are as capable as your medic or Reiter," Schmidt commented.

"I am."

"I am certainly in no position to object. I have no desire to go to a hospital and I do not particularly care for doctors."

"Then you are in good hands, *Herr* Schmidt," Dan said. As he uncovered the prisoner's burns, cleaned them and applied ointment, he scrutinized the disfigured face and tried to imagine what it had been like before. There was something almost familiar about it, but he attributed that to his own imagination and wishful thinking. "You are improving slightly," he said. "It will probably take many weeks, but one day you will look like yourself again, perhaps with some scars."

"That is all right. I shall wear them proudly. I am not vain."

Brooks fell easily and slyly into the role of innocent questioner. "Did you have a full head of hair before or were you bald?"

"Full hair."

"A beard?"

"No."

"A mustache?"

There was a moment's hesitation. "No. I always preferred to be clean shaven."

"Bristles are beginning to push through where the scabs have come off," Dan told him.

Schmidt appeared to ponder that news approvingly. "Then I will grow a new head of hair and a full beard and mustache," he said with unexpected enthusiasm. "It would interfere with the healing process if I attempted to shave."

"Yes, I agree," Dan said. "You're mostly scabs and fuzz now, but you'll be covered with bandages for many weeks anyway."

When the fresh bandages were fully wrapped, holes cut and hood replaced, Schmidt stepped away a few feet and stared at his captor appraisingly. "You did that as well as any eminent professor or society doctor in Berlin, *Hauptmann*. Perhaps you have missed your calling," he said waggishly. "May I speak to you man to man now?"

"Of course. There is no need for formality between us, *Herr* Schmidt. Only courtesy and cooperation."

"Then why do you keep sending Reiter to try to worm information from me?" Schmidt demanded, his voice suddenly rising with anger and his manner becoming imperious. "I am not stupid. I know what you and he are up to. Neither of you will ever get anything out of me."

The prisoner suddenly put his hand to his forehead and tottered back a few steps, then put his other hand to his belly and doubled over as if gripped by acute pain. He staggered backward until his legs touched the cot and he sat down on it heavily. "I am ill, *Hauptmann*," he gasped out. "I am sweating underneath all these *verdammten* bandages and I have an ache in my stomach. Please, I must have my injection now."

"In a few minutes," Dan said calmly. "I'm glad you finally told your aide the meaning of the address in Zurich and the numbers."

"He tried to get this information from me," Schmidt wheezed, "but it is private business. *My* private business. I told *Obersturmbannführer* Reiter nothing."

Brooks believed he was telling the truth. It seemed to confirm his suspicion that Reiter had relayed only information he already knew. "He gave me certain details," he said.

"About Zurich?"

"Yes."

"Have you used this information yet, *Hauptmann*?" Schmidt asked in a low, halting voice. One of his legs kicked involuntarily and he pressed a hand against it.

"No. I haven't had the opportunity," Brooks lied.

"Perhaps I can prevail upon you not to," the captive said with difficulty. "You would not go unrewarded, I assure you."

He began to sneeze and Brooks recognized it as yet another symptom of morphine dependency that Paulsen had briefed him about, along with the twitching leg, sweats and cramps. But Schmidt's anguish didn't move him.

"There are only two or three things I want from you, *Herr* Schmidt," he said calculatingly, "and then maybe we can reconsider your status as a prisoner of war. For the present, I'm the only one responsible for you."

Schmidt stopped sneezing and stared at him. Brooks fixed on the dilated pupils within the holes of the hood and bandage. The man appeared surprised and confused.

"What is it you want, *Hauptmann*?" came the hesitant question.

"Your name and position in the Third Reich. You're no more a rocket scientist or any other kind of scientist than I am."

"You know my name and the position I held," Schmidt retorted stubbornly—and sneezed again. Brooks saw the man's right hand shaking as he tried to make a little gesture of dismissal. "You have the documents in your possession. You took them from me."

"They're fraudulent. With the war over, we'll soon be able to investigate you further in Germany itself. You're going to have to stay in custody until then." Dan looked around the room as if he were rating its degree of comfort. "This place is a palace compared to some of the others we're using to hold prisoners. You'll probably be moved to the worst of them. And you won't have me around to cater to your new little habit. If you cooperate now, things will go much easier for you."

"What else do you want from me?" Schmidt rasped. He pressed his belly and bent over as another cramp gnawed at him.

"The procedure to gain access to your accounts in Switzerland and the amount of money in each of them," Brooks demanded. "I suspect that, whoever you really are, you and your cronies have got tens of millions and more salted away for your retirement."

"Millions!" Schmidt screamed in pain and anger, rocking up and down as he pressed at his gut. "Maybe you are right. Even I do not know. The thieves took everything away from Germany against *der Führer's* orders. Maybe billions, you insignificant fool!" He suddenly realized what he had spewed out in his outburst. "No, forgive me. I do not mean to insult you, *Herr Hauptmann*. It is the pain speaking, not me. Give me morphine now, *bitte!*"

Dan watched him squirm, but didn't enjoy it. Maybe there actually were billions, he contemplated with a nervous feeling of awe. "I know the account numbers and bank addresses already, Schmidt," he said calmly. "They were in your wallet, so it is foolish of you not to confirm that they exist and tell me the additional details. I'll find them out anyway without your cooperation. Help me now and your status as a prisoner will be reconsidered."

Schmidt tried to sit rigidly in control, but a leg kicked out again and his arms trembled. He started to speak, but was interrupted by a fit of sneezing. "Very well, they exist," he finally muttered hoarsely, straightening himself up. "An injection, *bitte*. Then we will talk. I promise you."

Brooks held out his hand. "I want the two memos you confiscated from Reiter."

Schmidt went silent a moment, wrestling with his torments. "He too has betrayed me," he murmured. He shoved a hand into his jacket pocket, brought forth the two memos and handed them over.

Dan didn't really need them. He had copies. But he was making the point with his captive that whatever power he might have had in the past, he no longer had it; and also that even the smallest cooperation would bring its reward.

He gave Schmidt the shot of morphine he craved.

Relaxed and calm again a few minutes later, the hooded man tilted his head in a sly, appraising movement and said, "You are interested in money, eh?"

Brooks decided to keep it simple. "Yes," he responded.

"I am not the depositor, *Hauptmann*. I am merely the caretaker, the administrator of the funds you are interested in." Schmidt shook his head like a worried bookkeeper. "It is a grave responsibility. Perhaps you and I might make some mutually satisfactory arrangement."

The hint of negotiation came as a surprise to Dan, though he had put the monkey on Schmidt's back, made him dependent on his morphine fix for this very reason. "What do you want in exchange?" he asked.

"I will help you gain access to one of the numbered accounts. I do not know how much is in it, but ten percent will be yours," Schmidt said, as if granting munificent largess. "The rest of it I will deposit in a new account, the number of which will be known only to me. You will then release me in a neutral country. Switzerland, Spain or South America."

The proposal was familiar, similar to what Reiter had presented, except that Schmidt was greedier.

"And you plan to remain in possession of all the other accounts?" Brooks asked with seeming ingenuousness.

"Yes. That is my offer. As I told you, the money is not mine. I am merely the caretaker. I have responsibilities regarding it."

"It sounds like a bribe to me."

"If you wish to turn your share of the account over to your government, that is your business entirely, *Hauptmann*."

"And what shall we do about *Obersturmbannführer* Reiter, who seems so devoted to you?"

"I do not give a damn what happens to Reiter. He is getting on my nerves. It would be better if he were not here."

The notion startled Brooks, as if Schmidt had read his mind. He had given some thought to the idea himself. The SS officer's usefulness to him had been nil so far. He was perhaps more of a potential liability: a man who knew just enough to know too much; a man who might reveal what he knew to others or take action on it himself if freed. Unless Reiter was concealing additional information about secret bank accounts and treasure hoards, Dan didn't want him around anymore either. Except that he also believed the *Obersturmbannführer* knew the real identity of Siegfried Schmidt and he was determined to get it out of him.

For a long, silent minute, Brooks made it appear that he was seriously considering what his captive had just proposed. Then he said bluntly, "Your offer is unacceptable, Schmidt."

The prisoner reared back, as if such an answer were incomprehensible to him. "I ask you to consider it again, *Hauptmann* Brooks," he said in a tightly controlled voice. "It is possible that I might be able to increase the portion set aside for you. Or your government, as you prefer."

With exaggerated politeness, Dan said, "If you will allow me a day or two to think about it, I'll return to you with a counter offer."

Schmidt replied stoically, *"Danke, Hauptmann."* And he turned away as if it were he who was dismissing Brooks from an audience.

Dan didn't bother with Reiter again that afternoon. From the baronial study he used as his office in the main building, he telephoned Larry Dillard at OSS headquarters in London and gave him a second long number and the address of a branch of the Federated Bank of Switzerland in Zurich. He told the Special Operations chief he had been able to ferret the information out of one of his prisoners in just the last hours, and that he had a strong hunch there would be even more soon.

"Good work, Dan," Dillard responded enthusiastically. "I'll pass the information on to Bern for immediate action."

Brooks actually felt resentment at having to bring someone else in on the payoff, though he knew there was no other way to proceed. "What about repatriation of my men?" he asked. "The sooner the better now."

"Travel orders are being cut for them," Dillard reported. "We have to pay them off, but their documentation is completed. I think we'll be able to arrange a squadron of transports in two or three days. They'll fly out of Peterborough to our base at Dijon, where we still have control. Your POW's will have their original German uniforms waiting for them to change into on the plane and will be flown directly to Frankfurt from Dijon. The men who were in the French Resistance have permission to return to France and will change into their own civvies on their plane. Captain LeGrange is handling these aspects of the transfer. Send Lieutenant Becker to Frankfurt with the POW's."

"That will be fine, Larry," Brooks said. "But I do want to keep one of the POW's, *Oberfeldwebel* Helmut Jung, with me for a while longer."

"No problem if he agrees."

"He's volunteered."

Dan slept restlessly that night. He woke early in the morning with a feeling of incompleteness, of something not being quite right in his world. It wasn't just the realization that Knight's Cross, which had built to such a combat triumph for him, was winding down, leaving him without a driving purpose; it was also his awareness that the mission had not achieved its intended goal. Yet, within this sense of incompleteness, he apprehended also the glimmer of an as yet unknown beginning. His sixth sense told him there was something profound, as yet unperceived, that still lay ahead of him.

When he got up, he put on shorts and a sweatshirt. He attributed his uneasiness to not getting enough physical activity during the past few days. He went out and ran swiftly and did vigorous calisthenics with the men before breakfast, and felt better for it. He had changed back into his Class A's when Larry Dillard called.

"It didn't work this time," said the SO chief. "Dulles was unable to effect a transfer from the account you gave us. There's a code word needed in addition to the number. His contact doesn't know it. The word is written down and locked in a safe and only the number one man at the bank has access to it. It's necessary for you to come up with that word before we can try again."

Obersturmbannführer Dietrich Reiter saw the expression of anger on the American captain's face as he came into the room and he knew that it boded him no good. Had he made an error in the account number in Switzerland? Had something else gone wrong? Had he been mistaken regarding the amount of money in the account? It had been only an educated guess on his part. Perhaps there had been no money at all . . . no account.

"Take off the hood, Reiter," Brooks snapped.

It was not a kindly suggestion, as it had been the last few times. Reiter removed the cloth quickly and waited nervously for the enumeration of his unknown offenses.

"I've treated you with undeserved consideration," the captain said coldly. "You've behaved like what you are: an *Obersturmbannführer* in the *Sicherheitsdienst*. Your type can never change. That's the way you'll be treated from now on, Reiter. You'll be charged with war crimes and brought to trial, which is more than you goddamned Nazis have done for others. And then you'll be strung up by your neck, as you deserve."

"What is the matter?" Reiter pleaded, aghast. "I have cooperated with you. I told you about the bank and the number."

It was true that the first one had worked, but Dan didn't intend to divulge that to him. Nor did he know why that account—which had come up first only by chance—hadn't also required a code word. He thought maybe it was bait, risking a relatively inconsequential amount to warn the Nazis that someone was tapping into their scheme and that the speculatively greater plunder in the other accounts was vulnerable. Or maybe they figured anyone raiding the account would be satisfied with what was in it and not try for the others. There were other maybes. But he didn't know the answer.

"You tricked me," he accused Reiter. He felt rage and the tone of his voice sounded as if he were on the edge of doing something violent to the SS officer. "You withheld vital information from me when you pretended to cooperate. There is a code word needed to get into the Zurich accounts. What is it?"

"A code word! About this I know nothing. I swear to you, *Herr Hauptmann!*"

"Then find out from your phony rocket scientist. Do you understand me, Colonel? Find out from Schmidt today—or you're both *kaputt.* I might not even wait for a trial. You're a prisoner of OSS. Not the army. You're familiar with OSS?"

"Of course, *Herr Hauptmann!*"

"Dealing with swine like you, Reiter, we've had to unlearn every decency taught by God and country. We have ways of tending to matters like this that would make your fucking Gestapo look like a girl scout troop. *Verstehen Sie?*"

The *Obersturmbannführer* felt new fear clutch at him. He had thought surely the American captain would behave honorably in exchange for the information he had given him. Reiter had even imagined ahead to what a fair share of the money would be and what kind of life he would be able to live and where. But he truly had known nothing about code words.

Yet Siegfried Schmidt must have known. Even now he must have the words locked in that feverish brain of his. During all those weeks they were preparing their escape he must have secretly specified the passwords despite not yet knowing the numbers and locations of every one of the accounts that would be set up for him.

Reiter saw now that he was going to have to do a lot better than he already had in order to bargain for his freedom and win it. Facing him, he feared, were the certainties of the fate threatened by the OSS captain. He felt that it was no longer very important that he be rewarded with a portion of the Nazi plunder that lay waiting in the Swiss bank accounts. He simply wanted to survive and be set free in a place where he could breathe again and make a new life for himself. Even a life of poverty and toil was better than what he now faced; though he had enough confidence in his own abilities to believe he would find a position of substance and do well in a distant, safe country.

But to be made to pay for the sins of *Herr* Siegfried Schmidt and his accomplices was unjust. If the Americans held him prisoner long enough, that was exactly what would happen. He had to distance himself from Siegfried Schmidt as quickly as possible.

"Don't you *know* who he really is?" the *Obersturmbannführer* gasped out.

Brooks felt a quickening of his heartbeat. "Who?" he asked calmly.

"*Herr* Schmidt," the SS officer whispered.

"Siegfried Schmidt. A rocket scientist, as you've both told me again and again. I have the documents found on him to prove it," Dan said with scorn.

"No," Reiter moaned, shaking his head, unable to meet Brooks's gaze.

"If I tell you the truth about him, you must not associate me with him. I am not one of his inner circle. I am not guilty of his crimes. I have been with him only a few weeks."

"Who is he?"

Dietrich Reiter took a deep breath, looked up into Dan's eyes, and murmured, "Adolf Hitler, *der Führer* of the Third Reich."

Brooks felt such exultation that he could hardly control his voice. Yet he continued to speak softly and rationally. "Hitler is dead. He killed himself in Berlin. You Germans announced it. The Russians have confirmed it."

"Did they show proof? A body?"

"There is supposed to be a burned corpse wearing the remains of Hitler's clothes. Parts of the skull and dental work are said to have survived the fire and are believed to match Hitler's, but that's still to be verified by forensic experts. Hitler's surviving aides and high officials in the bunker have apparently reported to the Russians the details of what happened."

"They don't *know* the details!" Reiter exclaimed. "They only think they know, as Hitler intended. Only I know."

"Sit down, Reiter," Dan ordered.

The SS officer stepped backward until his legs hit his cot and he dropped heavily into a sitting position. Brooks picked up the one wood chair in the room, brought it close to the prisoner and straddled it in a reverse position. Reiter looked very apprehensive, as if he expected a blow and would duck instantly out of the space of a few inches that separated him from his captor.

"Don't you believe me?" he pleaded.

"Who else knows?" Dan asked gently.

"Nobody."

"Not the pilot who brought you into the auxiliary field at Innsbruck?"

"He knew nothing."

"Not the SS officer who met you and the personnel at the Hotel Edelweiss?"

"Totally fooled," Reiter insisted with a small note of pride.

"Nobody else back in Berlin was in on it?"

"In on it, yes. The planning and arranging. But it was all done by a tight, secret cabal of contacts and cutouts in the inner circle of the SS who had absolutely no idea who it was for. Each was ordered to perform a certain function. That was it. He did his duty, kept his mouth shut and knew nothing more. None of the higher-ups who saw him every day in the bunker even suspected. Hitler did not trust any of them. Not even Eva Braun, whom he married on the last day, knew how he was going to use her. Poor woman."

"He killed her?"

"She took cyanide. It was her wish to die with him," the SS officer said, shaking his head with a somber expression. "*Der Führer* had told everybody he was going to stay in Berlin to the end and commit suicide before he would allow himself to be captured. That was what he feared most. Not to die, but to be put on display by the Russians. Even his faithful dog, whom he loved dearly, had to sacrifice herself for him."

"Blondi?"

"Yes. You know this?" Reiter asked in surprise.

"I know a lot. What happened to the dog?"

"Hitler needed a demonstration that the poison would work. A vial was forced down the poor creature's mouth. She died instantly."

"Tell me how you got him out."

Intimidated by Brooks's threatening presence and his fear of what he might do to him, Reiter also wanted to demonstrate he was as clever as his captor and could be useful to him. With a quiet sense of pride, neither boastful nor humble, he related the details in a matter-of-fact tone.

A dying soldier with a severe head wound, who was the same size as Hitler and bore somewhat of a facial resemblance to him, had been carried into the bunker on a stretcher, completely bandaged like a mummy, supposedly to be awarded a medal in his last moments by *der Führer* himself.

"There were many dead and dying soldiers in the streets around the *Reichskanzlei* in those last hours," Reiter recalled. "The stretcher bearers were instructed to wait in the reception foyer after placing their burden, under my supervision, in an empty room next to *der Führer's* bedroom. They were given food and drink from the wedding table. Hitler's substitute died within minutes. Not even time enough to get his medal, poor bastard. I think at that moment Hitler would have given him the Knight's Cross with diamonds. On Hitler's orders, nobody was permitted to enter that area of the bunker afterward."

Reiter described how he had stripped the body of bandages and uniform and dressed it in a complete outfit from Hitler's wardrobe. At the appointed hour, Adolf and Eva had made their farewells to those left in the conference room and retired to the privacy of his bedroom. Eva had swallowed the cyanide and died as her new husband watched. Then Hitler darted into the next room where Reiter had been waiting and together they carried the substitute *Führer* into the bedroom. Hitler changed quickly into traveling clothes that had been prepared in advance. Reiter bandaged him like a mummy and Hitler went to the adjacent room and lay down under a blanket on the stretcher where the dead soldier had been minutes before.

"I myself had to blow the dead man's brains out with one of Hitler's Walthers and drop the pistol there," Reiter related grimly. "There was plenty of disfigurement and blood from my shot and the earlier wounds.

Nobody would have recognized him and, in any event, Hitler had ordered that no one was to look upon his face after he shot himself. I had only a minute to take care of the rest. I knew that the sound of the shot would bring others. I left for just a few moments to see that Hitler was ready to be carried out of the adjacent room on the stretcher, then rushed back to the bedroom just as others from the conference room reached the doorway.

"I pushed my way in front of them, covered the body and head completely with a blanket and reminded them what *der Führer* had ordered, that he was to be taken outside and burned immediately. As far as I know, nobody looked under the blanket."

While the others carried the bodies of Eva Braun and the dead surrogate out of the bunker for cremation, Reiter had summoned the two litter bearers from the reception foyer and together with them brought the blanket-covered, disguised *Führer* to an underground garage where a prepared car waited, packed with their luggage and money for the escape. Reiter had propped the covered, supposedly dead soldier in the front seat, then dismissed the stretcher men.

"I could not bring myself to shoot them, which had been considered," he admitted. "I thanked them and told them to save themselves as best they could. They left quickly. Then I drove out of the garage into the most horrendous bombardment, heading toward an emergency landing strip in the Tiergarten where we were to rendezvous with the aircraft. We were not even one hundred meters from the *Reichskanzlei* when we were almost killed."

As the *Obersturmbannführer* recounted the rest of it—the automobile blown onto its side, Hitler's bandage-disguise ignited by phosphorous that blazed through to burn away his hair and flesh, the hurried medical treatment, the commandeering of a second vehicle—Brooks could not help but feel a sense of the strange, retributive justice that had been meted out to *Herr* Siegfried Schmidt during his frantic escape from the cataclysm he had created.

"It is a miracle that we made it, that the Storch came for us, that we were able to fly out," Reiter said in wonder. "The miracle ended, of course, when you kidnapped us from the Hotel Edelweiss. If that had not happened, we would probably be well on our way to safety by now."

"Why did he want to leave?" Brooks demanded. "Why didn't he just kill himself and have done with it, or join the millions of poor bastards he sent to their deaths? If your *Herr* Schmidt is really who you say he is, he should have died in battle alongside his soldiers like the great leader he always claimed to be."

"For an answer to that, you will have to ask Hitler himself," Reiter replied, shrugging. "What he told me was that he intended to inspire National Socialism to rise from the ashes, to regenerate it in more fertile ground elsewhere in the world. In my opinion, it is the futile fantasy of a madman."

"I think you're trying to cover your own ass, Reiter," Dan said quietly. All the same, he believed him because he wanted to believe him. To accept the incredible story meant Knight's Cross had accomplished its mission beyond anyone's imagining. Yet Brooks retained a shred of doubt. The tale had been spun by a die-hard Nazi like the ones who had related the story of Hitler's suicide.

"Will he admit it?" Dan asked. "I must have further proof."

"No, he will not admit it. Not without an exceptional reason. You do not believe me?" Reiter challenged, offended. "Take me now to *Herr* Schmidt's room. I will leave the door slightly open and you will hear everything to satisfy you."

"Put on your hood," Dan ordered.

His heart was beating faster. If what Reiter told him was true, what would he do about it?

He escorted the hooded SS officer into the hallway. "Schafer. Blumberg," he said to the two sergeants on guard. "Give me the key to Schmidt's room and go downstairs with the others until I yell for you."

They left with a surprised "Yes, sir," but no further comment.

Brooks unlocked the door and stood to one side. *Obersturmbannführer* Reiter opened it just enough to squeeze through. With his hands behind him and his back to the door to hide the opening, he eased it toward the closed position and left it a fraction of an inch ajar.

Herr Siefgried Schmidt wanted respect, thought Reiter bitterly. He would give it to him. He raised his arm in a stiff Nazi salute. "*Heil,* Hitler!"

Brooks placed his eye at the tiny slit of open door. He could see the two macabre, hooded men inside and hear the words spoken. Schmidt did the same little wrist flip of a salute that Brooks had seen Adolf Hitler do in dozens of newsreels. Then he tilted his head to the side in a questioning pose. "Why do you suddenly address me in this way, *Obersturmbannführer?*" he asked in almost a jocular tone.

"Because you reprimanded me, *mein Führer,* when I called you Siegfried, as you had asked me to."

"No, Reiter, because you and the American captain still think you can try to trick me out of what is rightfully mine," Schmidt said angrily.

"I do not know what you mean, *mein Führer,*" the SS officer protested.

"But *der Führer,* Adolf Hitler, is dead, is he not, Reiter?" Schmidt contended in a voice that was now a chortle. "All the world heard this on the radio, announced with such tears by that oaf Doenitz. Why do you bother to *Heil* a man who is dead?"

"Because *you* are still Adolf Hitler, beloved *Führer* of all the German people."

Siegfried Schmidt's voice grew louder as a fit of anger struck him. "A *Führer* who was betrayed by his General Staff and long before the end was himself deserted and betrayed by the German people he loved and died for!"

"Shhhhh, *mein Führer.* Someone will hear you."

"Let them hear," Schmidt shouted. "Who will believe that a dead man is alive?"

Dan Brooks believed, with a wave of exultation sweeping over him.

He slipped quietly away from the door, to let Reiter lean against it and close it. In a few minutes, he would call Schafer and Blumberg to bang on the door and take Reiter back to his room.

Thirty

✠   At 1000 hours, Thursday, May 10, Captain Brooks was admitted to OSS's red brick mansion on Grosvenor Street. He felt unaccustomedly nervous. As soon as he passed the entry guards, he heard one of them pick up a phone and announce his arrival to someone upstairs.

Larry Dillard and Colonel Hoose were expecting him in the conference room, but the alert had apparently not been to them. On the second floor landing. Lieutenant Commander Francis Cassidy burst out of his office and confronted him angrily.

"Who in goddamn hell do you think you are, Brooks!" the Secret Intelligence chief shouted. "I want access to your two prisoners."

"I'd like to take tea with the king and queen, Francis," Dan snapped back, "but they haven't invited me."

"You wise ass son of a bitch. I'm going to break you if it's the last thing I do."

Dan resisted the urge to slug the naval officer. He felt he ought to thank him instead for getting his adrenaline up, relieving his anxiety and helping him bury deeper the extraordinary secret he carried.

"May I make a suggestion, Commander?" Brooks asked in a reasonable voice.

"Try me!" Cassidy replied belligerently, still blocking the way to the conference room.

"When I'm through with the prisoners and Knight's Cross is closed out, I'll try to get you permission to question them."

"How long is that going to be?"

"My guess, if all goes well, is that it will take us at least another month. Maybe two."

"Fat lot of good that's going to do me."

"It's been a long war, Francis," Dan said. "I hope it's going to be a much longer peace."

"Damn it, Captain," Cassidy said, "that's exactly what my function is now, to make sure there *is* going to be a long peace. Doesn't that mean anything to you?"

"It means a lot, Frank, but my orders are to keep my mouth shut and my prisoners sequestered until our job is done," Dan said, trying to move around him.

Cassidy looked bewildered, not sure if Dan was trying to be pleasant. Then he attacked again. "What you did to Bergen and Hupnagel in Innsbruck is unforgivable."

"They're lucky to be alive, Francis. And that was *my* doing. Bergen is untrustworthy. The man is a menace. I hope to hell you sent him home."

"I did send him home," replied Cassidy, smiling. "To Germany. He's working for me there."

Brooks stepped around him and strode down the corridor, shaking his head. "Just keep him away from me," he warned.

Larry Dillard and Colonel Hoose greeted Captain Brooks in the conference room with less exuberance than they had the week before. Dan had asked for the meeting without telling them why.

"Have you brought the password, Captain?" the colonel asked.

"No, sir. But I believe I have a way of getting it."

Hoose looked at him gravely. "I'm not criticizing you personally, Brooks, but perhaps you are too close to the matter. Maybe it's time we relieved you and let someone else take a crack at your prisoners."

"That would be the worst possible thing to do," Dan replied. He turned to Dillard for support. "Nobody but we—and maybe a hint of it now in Bern and Zurich—are aware of the possibilities in what we're doing."

Hoose complained, "Dulles was upset that one of his important banker agents had to place himself at risk without any results."

Dillard pressed, "Who's the mystery man, Dan?"

"He's still Siegfried Schmidt," Brooks replied. He wondered if anything in his voice would give him away. "If I can keep after him he will eventually break. Even if it turns out that *Schmidt* is who he *really* is, he's our only access to the account password. I've got about all I think I'll ever get out of the SS officer who escorted him. I don't think he knows any more."

"What do you want to do?" asked Colonel Hoose.

Dan hesitated. He asked himself, *Why didn't he just tell them that Siegfried Schmidt was Adolf Hitler? Let them announce it to the world, put him on trial, find him guilty, then hang the son of a bitch?*

Could the head of state of an enemy nation, as monstrous as this one was, be executed under international law? In ancient times that had happened with regularity, but they had made no attempt at international law then. A hundred and thirty years ago, when they were perhaps trying to be more civilized in Europe, a deal had been made with Napoleon Bonaparte after he had screwed up the world in *his* time and been captured. He had escaped and they had to do it all over again and send him once more into exile, where he finally died from high living. And what had the fine and eminent powers-that-be done to the major offender after the First World War? They had merely banished the German Kaiser to live and die in luxury.

Dan wondered, too, if maybe the real reason he continued to withhold his astounding bombshell was that if he told them now that he'd had *der Führer* in his custody for ten days without knowing it, it would make Captain Brooks look like a damned fool.

But that was *not* the reason, he felt certain. It was because he didn't trust *them! His superiors!*

They were making deals with useful Nazis to help them perpetuate their confraternity and abet their plans against the Russian bugaboo. That was what Bergen was doing for Cassidy now. Why wouldn't they make a deal with Hitler, too? Brooks knew that he himself was capable of duplicity, of letting *Herr* Schmidt believe he would release him after squeezing him for every bit of Nazi plunder he had. But he would never let Adolf Hitler go scot-free. He could personally kill him without any qualms and with a sense of justice.

"I want to take Siegfried Schmidt to Switzerland with a security team and work on him there," Dan told them. "Despite this temporary setback over the password, there is no one who can uncover it quicker than I can. I'm sure Schmidt knows the password."

"Why do you have to do it in Switzerland, Captain?" the colonel challenged. "Why not right where you've got him at Milton Hall, or bring him down here and we'll get an interrogation team on him around the clock until he breaks."

"I know I can make a deal with him on the password once we're in Switzerland."

"What kind of deal?" Dillard demanded.

"All the secret bank numbers and passwords he might know about, and I'm confident there will be more," Dan assured them. "Complete and unfettered entry into the accounts in exchange for letting *Herr* Schmidt vanish there in Switzerland, which he has suggested, or in some other neutral country."

He couldn't tell them that Adolf Hitler, self-assured about the secrecy of his true identity, had already made him an offer he had refused; that Hitler and he would both have to up their antes as the game progressed, and that he would be lying to *der Führer* himself about buying his freedom with the money in the banks.

The Special Operations chief stared at him dismayed and spoke more sharply than he usually did. "We don't even know who the hell the man is. How could we possibly let him go?"

"You've already told me you're playing ball with other Nazis who are willing to give you what you want. Why not this one?"

"Not if he's Himmler or Bormann," Colonel Hoose insisted. "That kind will have to stand trial for their crimes."

"What about the other prisoner, the SS officer?" Dillard asked.

Brooks stared at him and said nothing and it made his boss nervous. Colonel Hoose also sensed what the silence meant and it made him uneasy too.

Dan broke the silence. "He knows too much. He's a danger. If you treat him like the war criminal he probably is, if you try him and sentence him, he can talk to others, reveal things in court, things we don't want him to talk about. If we turn him loose, which is what I hinted to him if he cooperated—which he has done to a certain extent—he can also talk, or try to empty the account himself if he knows how to do it."

"You don't seem to have a choice, Brooks," said the colonel with a grim expression on his face.

Dan waited for him or Dillard to say more. He wanted them to *order* him to do what they were all thinking.

"What you do, and the details of it, will be strictly up to you," the SO chief said, unable to meet Brooks's eyes.

Colonel Hoose changed the topic. "Get your mystery man to reveal the password. If it works, and if you also find out there are more accounts, we'll arrange your trip to Switzerland."

"Bleed the son of bitch, whoever he is!" Dillard added with uncharacteristic vehemence. "It makes no difference who he is if he produces."

"Will any of it be shared with our allies? Dan asked.

"No. I don't believe there's any reason to do so," the colonel stated. "Certainly not with the Russians, who owe us a fortune in Lend-Lease matériel anyway. This is our private business, Captain. Even you have expressed that you want no one else to know about it."

Private business was the phrase that Siegfried Schmidt had used too. "I agree, sir," Brooks said.

He felt a sense of great personal power. He had always followed orders, admittedly with some variations when expedient. Now he would carry out an operation because *he* wanted to do it.

There was a great emptiness on the grounds of Milton Hall. The *Jäger Einheit* had been dispersed to France and Germany. Except for a few maintenance staff, Lieutenant Chadwick's support unit also had left. *Oberfeldwebel* Helmut Jung was happy that Captain Brooks had granted his request and kept him on, though he was uncertain what his duties would be. He was not yet included in the rotation of guards at the cottage

where the mysterious prisoners were kept. The American sergeants—
Schafer, Blumberg, Maurer, Brunner, Mangold and Paulsen—were
assigned that duty.

Helmut often thought of Kurt von Hassell, buried in a cemetary in the
Inn Valley with the other *Jägers* killed in action. He also thought about
the notion Kurt had introduced to him months earlier about who they
were being trained to capture. Hitler and Goebbels had cheated them.
Göring had been taken prisoner in Bavaria. Nothing had been heard yet
about the fate of Himmler or Bormann.

Each day, Helmut tried to keep in shape by running and doing
calisthenics. Occasionally Captain Brooks or one or more of the American
sergeants joined him for the exercise, but there was very little talk
between them. The captain also took each of the hooded prisoners out
separately for a half-hour walk each day, followed a short distance behind
by two of the armed sergeants. Jung found himself wondering often about
the captives, particularly the one who had been bandaged like a mummy
when they captured him. Were they really the persons the captain said
they were?

After a few days, Captain Brooks summoned Jung to his study in the
great manor and asked him to sit in a comfortable wing chair while they
talked. It was the captain who stood and stared down at him.

"You have killed men, Jung?" he asked tersely.

The question made Helmut uneasy, but he recognized it was not idle
talk for a *Bierstube* in Hamburg. "Of course," he answered. "I have just
been through a military operation with you and you have seen it with
your own eyes."

"And before that?"

Helmut felt even more uncomfortable, unaware what Brooks was
driving at. "In the war, yes," he replied. "I regret there were Americans
among them, but it was combat. They were shooting, we were shooting.
Who knows who killed whom?"

He thought then of *Unteroffizier* Otto Würster, whom he had killed in
the grenade "accident," and wondered if he was expected to talk about
that now. He didn't want to. He still felt some guilt about it, though he
had known it had to be done. The captain knew about it in any event.

"What I tell you now is private and must never be spoken about with
anyone else," Brooks continued tensely. "I ask you this as a point of honor
between soldiers. I'll have no control over you, of course, once you are
discharged."

"I agree, sir, whatever it is."

"There is a man who must be eliminated. If I ask you to help me, will
you?"

Dan had given much thought to the matter. If he could avoid it he
preferred to keep his American cadre out of the Reiter affair, though they

were the kind of men who would follow his orders and just do it. Maybe they would forget about it afterward or maybe they would be haunted by the manner of it later. He thought the former, though they wouldn't take it lightly, as he didn't. Jung, though, had told him often how much he hated the Nazis and SS who had taken over his homeland and destroyed it. Perhaps he would be more than willing to help eliminate the *Obersturmbannführer*. In any event, he felt he could trust the man completely.

Helmut looked away from the captain toward a leaded window that opened onto a view of the gardens. "An assassination?" he asked apprehensively.

Brooks stared at him with a grim little smile. "In my branch of service the euphemism is *termination*," Brooks said, beginning to pace the room. "But yes, you are right, an assassination."

"Who?"

"The SS officer in the gatekeeper's cottage. He was with the *Sicherheitsdienst*. The worst of them."

"Not the other prisoner too?"

"No. I think he will still be of use to us. I have other plans for him, in which you will be included. But the SS officer must be terminated to protect our security."

Jung looked at him questioningly. "The war is over, is it not, *Herr Hauptmann*?"

"In Europe, yes."

"How can a prisoner under guard affect our security?"

"Because of the knowledge he has."

"Not the deeds he has done?"

"I am sure he is guilty of crimes too."

"Why do you not put him on trial? Prove his guilt. Let the judge sentence him to death if that is the penalty for his crimes."

"Because he will talk about what we don't want him to talk about. And he still has the power to hurt us."

Helmut stared at the captain, who had stopped pacing in front of him and met his eyes. "And for this you want me to help you kill him?"

"Yes."

Jung looked at him sadly and shook his head. "That's what I did for Hitler."

"It's not an order, Sergeant. You are free to refuse."

In great distress, Helmut said, "Please forgive me, *mein Herr*, but I must decline. In combat I would have no problem, as you already know. But I never did have the stomach for something cold-blooded like this."

Dan nodded. "I respect your answer, Sergeant, and I don't think less of you for it," he said. In a curious way, he thought even more of the man, for having refused to commit a deed that went against his conscience. Maybe

Jung had learned something more from his years of war than he had himself. Pensive a moment, Brooks said, "This is all you will ever hear of it. I ask only that you forget that we ever had this conversation."

A moment later, Dan was startled to hear Jung say, "Even if it was Adolf Hitler himself, I think now that I would want him first to be brought to trial for his crimes. To do otherwise would be to behave like a Nazi."

Obersturmbannführer Dietrich Reiter heard them coming in the night and knew it boded him no good. All his business with the Americans since being brought here had been in the daytime. Except for the threats by the captain, he and his guards were not brutal men, they had treated him well, though Brooks had not let him see *der Führer* since that day he had revealed to him the true identity of Siegfried Schmidt. The captain had warned him that he was never to divulge what he knew to anyone else and Reiter had dutifully complied. His captor had continued to interrogate him, but there had been less urgency in the questions, as if the answers no longer made any difference. Even the somewhat comforting sound of many German voices outside on the grounds also had disappeared.

Reiter knew well the implications of sudden, unannounced visits in the night. He lived with memories of pounding feet on stairways, the crashing of doors and the hopeless cries of victims dragged from their homes, for he had been with the instigators and attackers.

His own oppressors came to him silently and perhaps that was worse. They were on him almost before he knew it. He had finally fallen into his usual restless sleep when the sound of the door being opened woke him. He was momentarily blinded by flashlights and then the overhead light snapped on. The American captain and three of his men, including the medic, stood over him before he could rise up.

Brooks clamped a hand over the SS officer's mouth as his eyes went wild and he started to shout. Moving in quickly were Maurer and Schafer. They easily overwhelmed Reiter as he struggled. Paulsen pulled off the prisoner's pajama shirt and jabbed into his arm a hypodermic with a stiff shot of thiopental sodium.

They held Reiter until his struggles stopped and he passed out. The medic left quickly. He would be out of it now, with no knowledge of what was to happen next and orders to never reveal to anyone what he had been asked to do this night. If another shot was needed along the way, he had supplied a filled hypodermic and Brooks would give the injection to Reiter himself. The other three men in the security team had been told nothing. They had been given the night off, told to go into town and have a good time, get laid, and take Helmut Jung with them. They were not to return to Milton Hall until 0800.

A stretcher was brought in from the hall. The unconscious SS officer was strapped onto it, carried outside and placed in an ambulance borrowed from Special Operations Wing. Schafer, who had requisitioned it, drove. Brooks and Maurer sat in back with Reiter. If stopped for any reason and questioned, they were taking a heart case to the airport for transfer to a hospital in London.

Dan's mood was icy and melancholy. He felt none of the heady challenge and anticipation he experienced when he was about to go into combat. They reached the Peterborough airport and loaded their cargo on the Special Operations Wing C-46 waiting for them. The pilot and co-pilot were already in the cockpit, the only crew aboard. They had not been told the purpose of the flight, but were used to the shadowy doings of spooks. They had been ordered not to leave the flight deck and enter the cabin and not to see and hear anything that did not concern their jobs operating the aircraft.

The plane took off, heading southwest for the Atlantic coast. They flew over England and Wales and then out over the black ocean south of Ireland. Brooks waited two hours until they were well out over the sea, then gave another knockout injection to the prisoner. Weights and ropes were tied to Reiter's body and the stretcher straps released. Dan went forward and checked the aircraft's position with the pilot. It was well away from land.

He returned to the cargo hold. "You know how to open the door, Schafer?" he asked.

"Yes, sir."

"Do it."

The sergeant slid the door open and they were hit by a blast of cold air from the night. Brooks and Maurer lifted the limp body of Adolf Hitler's last aide and flung it out. *Obersturmbannführer* Dietrich Reiter's arms and legs flailed as his body tumbled around the weights and disappeared toward the Atlantic Ocean 5,000 feet below.

"Poor jump posture if you ask me," muttered Schafer.

The joke didn't assuage the guilt that he, Maurer and their CO felt. Dan went forward and told the pilot to return to Peterborough.

He was Siegfried Schmidt's sole contact now.

Brooks waited until the middle of the next afternoon before going to the cottage to attend to his burns and interrogate him. He did not intend to reveal that he knew his true identity. As *der Führer* exposed, he might not be willing to cooperate. He might as likely let the money go unclaimed as a last form of *Götterdämmerung*. Nevertheless, Brooks had to keep up the game of making *Herr* Schmidt believe he was still trying to find out who he was.

As he changed the bandages—and as Schmidt agonized through all the familiar symptoms of his morphine dependency, knowing he would get his shot only in exchange for some scrap of information—the captive nervously tried to make small talk.

"How are things in my Reich today?" he asked.

Dan examined the man's disfigured features, his scabbed, blistered, scarred, discolored and fuzz-covered face and skull with new sight. He began to discern the identity he now knew to be there.

"All is quiet. There is no more Reich, *Herr* Schmidt," he replied as he cut holes in the head wrappings. Then he remembered there *was* something, based on news he had learned that morning. He decided to use it to try a new approach to his prisoner. "No, that's not quite true," he said blithely. "At least I am sure now that you are not Heinrich Himmler."

"Aachhh! Why do you torment me with Himmler? Of course I am not Himmler, as I've told you again and again!" Schmidt declared angrily. Then, twisting his head so that he could see Brooks better through the eye holes, he added warily, "But why are you so sure now, *Hauptmann?*"

"Himmler is dead. A suicide like *der Führer*," Dan related.

A cackle of satisfaction escaped from Schmidt's lips, but then his mood changed to one of foreboding as he listened further.

"He was captured by the British a day or two ago," Dan continued. "He carried false identity papers and had a black patch over one eye. Under interrogation, he admitted his identity, then bit down on a cyanide pill hidden in his mouth. They tried to pump him out, but were too late. He died within minutes."

"His disguise did not save him," Schmidt murmured, almost as if in sympathy.

"That still leaves Bormann," Brooks goaded. "Are you Martin Bormann?"

"*Gott im Himmel!* How many times are you going to ask me that stupid question, *Hauptmann?* Martin has not been captured too?"

"Not yet, as far as I know."

Schmidt got up from the chair where he had been sitting while Brooks tended to his dressings. He paced the small room nervously, glanced out the window, aware of the silence outside, the absence of the men who had appeared to be German *Soldaten*, perhaps prisoners like him.

"Ahh, Martin, Martin," he murmured. "Most loyal and faithful to the end. He would not leave until *der Führer* ordered him to." He sat down on his cot, trembling and sneezing, then grabbed at his belly and began to rub it. "It is time. You must give me morphine."

"Where is Bormann? Where did he go?" Brooks demanded.

"If I knew, you would never get it from me, *Hauptmann*," the prisoner gasped out in pain. "Such information would not be negotiable. Poor Martin. The shelling and bombing from the Russians were terrible when he left. Most likely he was killed."

"You weren't."

"I am Siegfried. I am Germany," Schmidt proclaimed. "I do not die easily. A charmed life."

"Not so charming at the moment, *mein Herr*," Brooks muttered. He took one of the morphine syrettes from the medical kit. "Do you want your shot? Or do you want to start breaking the habit? I'm sure your pain is not as bad as it was a couple of weeks ago."

"Pain. What do you know of pain, *Hauptmann*? Your medicine gives me peace for a few hours."

"You're going to give me something in exchange this time, *Herr* Schmidt," Dan said bluntly, holding up the morphine syrette.

The captive's eyes focused on him through the bandage slits. They alternately blazed with rage and softened imploringly. "What do you want?" he moaned, bending to the floor, then suddenly rearing back with a succession of sneezes.

"I know your bank account numbers, as you are aware, so there's no need to play games about them anymore," Dan told him. "In fact we've already expropriated two million Swiss francs from one account. I didn't even need you for that one."

Schmidt stared at him aghast, then groaned and rocked from side to side as he gripped his belly. "How could you do such a thing? The money was not yours."

"Nor, if I may hazard a guess, did it ever belong to you or the depositors for whom you claim you're merely the caretaker. It's Nazi plunder, Schmidt. We'll get it one way or another. The only way you'll ever see a penny of it is to cooperate with me now."

The captive's eyes beseeched Brooks. "I am in great pain now, *Hauptmann*. What do you want from me? My injection, *bitte!*"

"First tell me why we didn't need a password for the account we were able to enter."

"It was a small one. Of no consequence," Schmidt whimpered. "If someone tampered with it, we would find out and take action. I thought maybe Reiter would try."

"*We?* Who are *we?*"

"I do not know, *Hauptmann*. *I* am *we*. Others are *we*. Accounts were set up for such emergencies. I am just a German citizen doing his duty, as instructed. I did not know everything." He dropped back onto the bed, curling his knees up into his stomach, moaning in pain.

Brooks wanted to kick him and roust him out, but instead he took a note from his pocket and read it out loud. It was the name of the Federated Bank of Switzerland and the numbered account Dulles's contact had not been able to get into. "What is the code word for that account, Schmidt?" he demanded.

The captive rolled over and thrust his feet down hard onto the floor, tensing his body to resist the gnawing craving in his guts.

"Morphine and I will help you," he promised. "Did I not make you an offer before? I will make you a better one."

"The password, Schmidt," Dan said calmly. "We need proof that you control these funds. And the sums must be substantial. One or two million dollars is not substantial. It's hardly worth the effort."

"Take me to Switzerland and there will be more, much more," Schmidt beseeched, reaching out one bandaged hand to grasp Dan's arm.

Brooks felt the trembling and tension in the man's body running through him. He left the hand there though it gave him the same crawly feeling he'd had at the man's touch before he'd known he was Adolf Hitler.

"The password first. Otherwise it's *kaputt* for you, Siegfried," Brooks said in a pleasant, cajoling voice. "No morphine, no Switzerland. And most likely Moscow in a day or two. We're giving some of our better class prisoners to the Russians. I'm sure they would enjoy having you as their guest, no matter who you are, since you control all this money."

It was this last, as Dan had expected, added to his captive's panicky craving for morphine, that made him scream out, *"Wotan!"*

"Is that the password for the account at Federated Bank in Zurich?"

"Yes. It will remove all doubts of the magnitude of the sums I control," Schmidt shouted hysterically.

He struggled out of his jacket, rolled up his shirt sleeve and bared his arm for the needle. Brooks gave him the shot and he relaxed onto his bed with a sigh. In a few minutes he began to speak again—softly, slowly, out of his fantasy world, but seemingly in control of himself.

"Where is Reiter?" Schmidt asked. "I have not seen him for days."

"I sent him to a prisoner of war camp," Dan replied. I noticed he was getting on your nerves."

"He was no use to me anymore," Schmidt said. "His job was to protect me...." He hesitated a moment to formulate a good reason. "...for the good of German rocket science, for the future of the Reich. Look how the fool allowed you to capture me. I assure you, *Hauptmann* Brooks, that despite our temporary setback, one day German rocket men will rule the world. There are even those among my colleagues who talk of German pilots flying to the moon. But I do not really believe that will be possible. Fairy tales."

"I am sure that you, as a scientist, *Herr* Schmidt, know much more about that sort of thing than I do," Dan conceded.

He wanted to establish now in Adolf Hitler's mind the illusion that he had accepted him finally as Siegfried Schmidt the rocket scientist and innocent keeper of someone else's secret bank accounts. Then he opened

the door and called down for Brunner and Mangold to return to their
guard posts in the corridor.

From his quarters in the great house, Dan telephoned Larry Dillard
and said to him one word:

"*Wotan.*"

Thirty-one

✠   Sascha Gorchavek returned to Bern from his mission to the Inn Valley on the afternoon of May 20, bursting with remarkable intelligence but stunned by the strange happenings he had uncovered.

The crossing both ways at Bregenz—in a Mercedes provided by Major Cherensky, which he had enjoyed driving enormously—had been made without problems. With the war over, border controls were less stringent; though, in any event, his Swiss car license and various personal identification papers were more than adequate. In the Inn Valley, now under control of American occupation forces, he had behaved like a tourist, which was the part of his job he enjoyed most. He had been passed through military checkpoints with courtesy. They were looking for Nazi war criminals, he had been told, and he had wished them, *"Viel Glück!"*

When he reached home and had poured himself a refreshing bottle of beer brought back from Innsbruck, Captain Gorchavek telephoned his superior and Major Cherensky arrived within the hour. Gorchavek had a choice of chilled wine or beer ready for him.

"I'll try one of those Austrian beers you imported, Sascha," said the major. "Then I am eager to hear your report."

"It is hard to know where to begin," the captain told him. Then he began to relate the information he had gathered during two weeks in Austria.

He had started his investigations by contacting Austrian Communists on the list the major had provided. These connections had led to others, once credentials had been verified on both sides. He had continued his spying by drinking and eating in more *Bierlokale* and *Gasthaüser* between Innsbruck, Solbad Hall, Wattens, Schwaz and Schlitters than Major Cherensky might have approved, except that his extravagance had brought results. He had talked to many men flushed with victory and drink who claimed to have been in the anti-Nazi Underground and had spoken about astounding events.

Gorchevek had learned that a company-size OSS unit had indeed operated in the Inn Valley for almost two months in the disguise of a German mountain infantry company. Also that *Spetsnaz* agents and ultimately an operational team had shadowed them constantly.

Major Cherensky leaned toward him with a look of great satisfaction on his face and said fervently, "You see, Sascha, *there* are the reasons for the inquiries from Moscow that I told you about."

Cherensky was taking credit to himself for having had the shrewdness to send his subordinate across the frontier on his own authority. But Gorchavek didn't mind. He had enjoyed the journey and the actions he had taken would look good on his record.

"Did you learn anything about the capture of high-ranking Nazis?" the major asked.

"There is evidence they might have succeeded in one circumstance."

"*Spetsnaz?*"

"No. The Americans," Gorchavek told him unhappily. "Two passengers, believed to have flown from Berlin, were observed arriving in a small plane at an emergency landing field near Kematen at dawn May 1," he related, referring to notes made during his journey. "The same men stayed for two nights at a secluded hotel guarded by an SS detachment in the mountains east of Innsbruck. Late on the second night, this place was attacked by the American *Jäger Einheit*. The two men and all their possessions disappeared. They were next observed—at least it is believed they were the same men—on the night of May 3 at the same flying field where they had arrived. They were in the custody of the Americans, who were then wearing U.S. Army uniforms. They left Austria with them in a squadron of transports."

"Their identities, Sascha?" urged the major.

"Outwardly they appeared to be no one of the level of importance that both OSS and *Spetsnaz* were apparently expecting to find there," Gorchavek said, referring to his notes again. "One was a civilian whose name was given to me as Siegfried Schmidt, a rocket scientist. The other was identified as an SS *Obersturmbannführer* named Dietrich Reiter, a handsome, brown-haired man in this mid-thirties."

"What was the age of Schmidt and a description?"

"No one knew. His face was completely swathed in bandages. Also his hands. Like an Egyptian mummy. He needed assistance to get out of the plane and enter the car that took him to the hotel. He either had been badly wounded or it was a good disguise."

"Perhaps both, Sascha," Cherensky speculated.

"Both men were wearing civilian clothes when last seen," Gorchavek continued. "This was reported to me by Party members and Resistance people who helped move the company to the airfield in buses and trucks.

266

The captives' hands were bound and each was wearing a hood over his head, as if he had been prepared for execution."

"To hide their identities, Sascha," Major Cherensky suggested. "The Americans do not execute prisoners without trial. They are too fastidious in these matters. However, what you have told me indicates that Schmidt and Reiter are more important then their tentative identifications would make them appear. Otherwise, why would the Americans have mounted such a dangerous, clandestine operation to capture them and then immediately fly them secretly out of Austria? They could have held them there like thousands of others. Even Skorzeny, the Nazi commando leader, is in their custody there, but the Americans won't let our people question him. I tell you, Sascha, I suspect they are using fellows like that. Making deals with them. How else do you think they were able to transfer money from the Nazi account two weeks ago?"

"That is my conclusion also, Comrade Major," stated Gorchavek.

"And what about *Spetsnaz*?" Cherensky asked. "The war has been over in the Tyrol for three weeks. Have they been heard from? What became of them?"

It was the question Gorchavek had dreaded. "Terrible news, Comrade Major," he responded gloomily. "One pair of agents who operated in the western sector of the Inn Valley is believed to have been killed early in April. Though a second pair operating in the eastern sector around Schlitters is thought to have escaped to the Soviet occupied zone in the last days of the war."

Cherensky shrugged philosophically. "And the operational team you spoke about?"

"Vanished into thin air, sir," Gorchavek said softly, still reluctant to report it. "According to a partisan who was on the reception committee, there were seventeen in the group. They were disguised as American soldiers."

An expression of new understanding spread across Cherensky's face. "So that was their game," he murmured. "Dangerous, but it might have worked. The local population, except for our Communist friends, would have been more receptive to Americans than Soviets. What did this *Spetsnaz* group do, Sascha?"

Gorchavek looked at him uncomfortably. "I heard a rumor that I hesitate to repeat, Comrade Major. It is too devastating and it was suggested by only one person, an Underground member in the eastern part of the Inn Valley. He was not a Communist, though some who served with him in the Resistance were. In fact, he spoke against the Soviet Union, which kept me from revealing myself to him and made me very cautious in what I could discuss in his presence. A man like that would be willing to say such things."

"What things, Gorchavek?" demanded Major Cherensky.

"That the *Spetsnaz* squad followed the Americans to the same target and were all killed in a battle with them or the Germans and were buried in the mountains without a trace."

Major Cherensky was pensive again. "There has been no further inquiry about them from Moscow," he finally said.

Gorchavek nodded in acknowledgment. They both knew about silences that screamed with unspoken meanings.

Cherensky snapped himself out of the gloom. "Sascha, you have done splendidly," he said. "For the time being we must keep what we know secret. Is that understood?"

"Of course, Comrade Major."

"Tomorrow, I would like you to begin making your rounds again between here and Zurich, checking the message drops. Be sharply alert for contacts. I have a feeling there will be more banking activity soon."

Two days later, Captain Gorchavek found another message container in Bauer Park from his mole in the International Bank of the Four Cantons. He slipped it into his pocket and went to a restaurant, where he ordered coffee and cake. Afterward he went to the men's room and secluded himself in one of the booths. He admired the civilized toilet facilities in Switzerland and was optimistic that one day such handsome conveniences would be surpassed in the Union of Soviet Socialist Republics.

Reading the note, he was glad he had not returned to Bern before opening it. The message was dated the previous day and the mole had requested another personal contact "regarding a matter of extreme importance, similar to the last one."

Gorchavek wrote a rendezvous place and time for the next day on another slip of paper, put it in the container and hurried back to leave it at the message drop. Not wanting to wait another day, however, he didn't depart this time, but kept the site under observation from a short distance away. He surmised the banker would look for a reply on the way home from his office.

His expectation was rewarded when he spotted the elegantly dressed man retrieve the container shortly after six o'clock. Gorchavek followed behind him as the mole hurried out of the wooded area to his car. Shortening the distance between them, he called out the man's name and was acknowledged. They talked in the car as the mole drove him to the train station.

"I don't know what it all might mean to your financial friend," the mole concluded after his information had been conveyed and payment received, "but that is an extraordinary sum about to be put in play for *something* and I was sure he'd want to know about it right away."

268

"*Danke schön!*" responded the Russian, enormously gratified as he left the car quickly and raced for the next train to Bern.

He could hardly wait to tell Major Cherensky that this time a sum in Swiss francs equivalent to $2,000,000,000 American had been transferred to OSS's covert account. It was almost beyond his reckoning.

Two billion dollars!

At OSS headquarters in London, Larry Dillard and Colonel Hoose listened to Dan Brooks outline his plans.

They were elated about the news that had come from Bern a few days earlier, and seemingly agreeable to almost anything he suggested now. They knew that his handling of the end game was going to make them look mighty good once the funds were transferred to the U.S. Treasury. In the interim, no one but the inner cabal would know how much of the money was being used for their new unofficial intelligence and espionage operations being carried out all over Europe.

However, they weren't going to let Brooks get completely away without answering some troubling questions.

"What does *Herr* Schmidt expect in return for revealing the additional accounts you think he knows?" the Special Operations chief asked.

"Not *think*. I'm positive he knows them," Dan replied. "It's just a matter of getting them out of him."

He could never tell them now why he was so positive, that he had found six account numbers in Schmidt's wallet the night he kidnapped him from the Hotel Edelweiss. All he lacked were the additional code words like *Wotan*.

"Very well, Dan. You've done so extraordinarily well so far. But what does he expect in return?" Colonel Hoose pressed.

"Freedom... as I told you at our last meeting. A safe haven in a neutral country, with proper documentation. Switzerland would do for starters. And part of the money for himself."

"Without ever learning his true identity?" Hoose asked.

"I've accepted that he's Siegfried Schmidt," Brooks told them. "We could check it out further, of course, in the German records of their rocket people, but I understand the Russians have made off with a lot of those records and the scientists and engineers."

"It's not likely they'll share it with us," Dillard acknowledged.

Colonel Hoose, about to speak again, was suddenly edgy and he looked away. "I assume the SS officer is no longer in your custody," he said quietly.

"That's been taken care of—as discussed," Brooks confirmed.

The colonel turned his gaze on him fully. "Have you considered the same possibility for Schmidt—after we've gotten all we can from him?"

Dan wasn't about to let them off easy. "That would depend on your orders, gentlemen," he said quietly, throwing the responsibility back to them.

"The decision will be yours, Captain," Hoose pronounced carefully. "Only you will know when your mission is over and what to do about it then. Except for the amount of money expropriated, there is to be no after action report written on this or any other aspect of Knight's Cross."

"Agreed, sir," Brooks acknowledged crisply.

It was exactly what he wanted: not to be accountable to anyone but himself for the way things went from here on.

During the next six weeks, while Brooks kept his security team and captive isolated at Milton Hall and staved off further interference and pressure from outside, he waited for Schmidt's healing to progress and his beard, mustache and hair to grow out.

In the early stage, whenever he was unbandaged, Schmidt looked like some injured, newly hatched bird with only partially formed, damp, matted feathers. Though he craved morphine twice a day and his mood alternated between euphoria and tantrums, he seemed more heartened from the moment Dan divulged to him that he was devising a plan to smuggle him into Switzerland.

"Then you had success with the *Wotan* account?" he said in a voice that combined hope with accusation.

"Yes. You've earned the reward for your cooperation," Dan responded.

"But you and your accomplices, your government perhaps, have taken the money. So what is the point of cooperating?" Schmidt said with a sigh of resignation.

"You'll begin your journey toward freedom. In Switzerland you will live in better circumstances and you will be even more cooperative."

"What do you expect of me, *Hauptmann*, when we get there?" the captive pressed.

"The passwords to enter each of the remaining accounts," Brooks responded.

Schmidt's euphoria diminished. "All of them?"

"Yes."

"Then there is no reason to go. What will be left for me? For those who trusted me? I offered you ten percent once. I will increase that to fifteen."

"Unacceptable, Siegfried," Dan said firmly. "It is *we* who offer *you* the terms now. And consider yourself lucky to be allowed any at all."

"It is *I* who hold the secrets."

"Then take them to the gallows with you. The alternative is a public trial for war crimes, in which the Soviets will participate."

"I committed no crimes. I served my country as a scientist."

270

Brooks watched for subtle changes in the prisoner's eyes and unbandaged face as he posed the next question: "Do you know the amount of money that was in the *Wotan* account, *Herr* Schmidt?"

"No. But I assume it was quite a lot."

"Two billion dollars."

The prisoner's eyes opened wide and his mouth gaped in amazement. He repeated the figure in a low murmur. Dan assessed his reaction as genuine.

Almost meekly, Schmidt ventured, "You have expropriated so much already. Is it not reasonable of me to expect you not to take everything?"

"When we reach Switzerland, we will negotiate further," Dan suggested. "If that is acceptable to you."

The captive nodded and murmured, *"Danke."*

As Dan turned to leave he saw how Schmidt's hand trembled, how he fought not to give himself away. In Berlin, he was sure the man would have thrown a hissy fit and ordered him shot, as he had so many others.

Brooks needed these weeks to get cover stories, passports and documents prepared. Larry Dillard had OSS agents study border crossings and airport passenger controls. Brooks thought it advisable also to wait to see if there were going to be any repercussions from Swiss bank officials or their government about the transfer of the huge amount of money. Or any move by the Nazi depositors to indicate they knew what was going on. Or Allied governments, particularly the Russians.

When nothing turned up to alert OSS in Switzerland or London that anyone was onto them, Dan went to London for another meeting in Grosvenor Street and told Dillard and Hoose he was ready to make his next move.

Civilian travel to the continent was permitted again, and on Friday June 15, 1945, a party of three prosperous looking gentlemen boarded a Swiss airline DC-3 flying to Zurich from London.

Dan Brooks, dressed in an American-made blue serge suit, looked around at the unaccustomed comforts of the interior cabin of an aircraft he had jumped out of many times in its C-46 military version. There were two plush armchairs on each side of the aisle and two pretty young women to guide them to their seats and see to their comfort. It brought a smile to his face. He carried a passport in the name of Lawrence Travis, a businessman eager to reopen trade channels between his import-export firm in New York and the newly liberated nations of Europe. But first a stop in Switzerland to arrange for international banking and credits.

The bearded man who sat beside him wore dark-tinted bifocals and carried a Luxembourg passport in the name of Felix Reinhardt. His cover story and papers identified him as a financier and factor who had been trapped in England when the Nazis overran his country and was returning to Luxembourg via Switzerland where he would begin to reestablish business connections with people who might have thought him long dead.

Reinhardt knew only a few phrases in English, hastily learned, and therefore felt quite comfortable flying via an airline whose personnel spoke a form of German. He wore a navy blue suit originally manufactured in Luxembourg City. He spoke very little to anyone during the flight, responding to the stewardesses with one or two mumbled words in a hoarse voice. He remained engrossed in a Zurich newspaper, though from time to time one hand strayed to his well-sculpted reddish-brown beard and full mustache—as if surprised to find them there. His hair had grown out about two inches, had been tinted the same color as his beard and mustache and was combed back away from his forehead on both sides. There were also burn scars at the hairline, and a few spots on his head had been filled in with bits of a toupee.

Dan scrutinized his companion occasionally, quite pleased with the barbering, coloring and patch-up job he had done on *Herr* Schmidt in the privacy of his room at Milton Hall. The day before leaving, the rest of the security team had been surprised to be introduced to the quiet, bearded man finally revealed out of the chrysalis of bandages and black hood. Following orders, they questioned nothing and accepted as reality the information that Brooks had given them about Felix Reinhardt of Luxembourg. They were to continue to guard him as closely, however, as when he had been Siegfried Schmidt.

Schafer, Blumberg, Maurer, Brunner, Mangold and Jung—also using aliases on American passports and cover stories prepared for them by the OSS documents section—had been sent ahead during the previous two days to test Swiss entry and customs procedures at the Zurich airport and then take up residence at a safe house arranged for them on Lake Zurich by Allen Dulles. Brooks had been concerned that Jung might have a problem going through Swiss entry controls because he carried an American passport but spoke only a few phrases in English. However, a message received that morning confirmed he was waiting in the safe house with the others.

Peter Paulsen, the medic, sat immediately behind passengers Travis and Reinhardt on the airliner. His passport and credentials, also in a phony name, identified him as an American physician on his way to Switzerland for additional study. In his doctor's bag he carried a plentiful supply of morphine syrettes.

Karl Bergen received the private, coded dispatch from Cassidy by courier while he was interrogating Nazi prisoners held at the Dachau concentration camp near Munich. He read the message, smiled with anticipation and tucked it into his pocket.

Bergen loved the power that his assignments and impressive credentials bestowed on him. But Dachau didn't mean to him what it meant to others. His inclinations were no different now than they had been when he was a Nazi party member himself. He had never given a damn about the Jews, political prisoners and *Untermenschen* who had been slaughtered here. But he thought it was funny that Nazi bigwigs and war criminals were imprisoned in their own concentration camp now, awaiting investigation and trial.

Before receiving the latest dispatch from Cassidy—one he had been anticipating for weeks—Bergen had spent many hours at Dachau interrogating Colonel Otto Skorzeny, the big, scar-faced Austrian who had planned and led some of the Nazis' most notorious unconventional warfare operations. Karl knew his reputation well enough to feel a certain amount of awe. Locked alone with him in his cell, he had tried to intimidate him.

"Where's Hitler?" he had demanded.

"Dead in Berlin," Skorzeny had replied calmly. "If you want the body, you should go ask the Russians."

"You helped him escape, didn't you?" Bergen had accused. It was part of the line of grilling that Cassidy had told him to pursue.

Skorzeny had laughed. "You are the hundredth investigator who has charged me with that. It is not true. The last time I saw *der Führer* was in March in Berlin. As far as I know, he never left the city."

The man had given a rational answer to every question. Bergen wanted to shoot the arrogant bastard on the spot, as a symbol of all the others he wished to get back at and kill. Skorzeny, after many hours, had told him nothing and could not be intimidated. They were too much alike, Bergen thought.

Now, after receiving the new orders from Cassidy, he got into his car and headed toward the Swiss border at Meersburg on the shore of Lake Constance, a drive of five or more hours west through the night. There was a guide who would take him secretly across the lake into Switzerland. Karl had a new I.D., cover story, money and changes of clothing prepared in advance.

Cassidy had alerted him that the Knight's Cross commander, that son of a bitch Brooks, had taken one of his prisoners to Zurich. The chief of OSS's Secret Intelligence branch in London still wanted to know who the mystery man was. He had told Bergen he didn't care what he had to do to find out.

Thirty-two

✙   Dan Brooks watched the lakeshore road from Adolf Hitler's bedroom in the safe house at Meilen. Across the way was the chalet's pier and speedboat on Lake Zurich.

Brooks's eyes scanned the water, looking for a boat that might linger too long within surveillance distance. He didn't know who might come after them now in Switzerland, but he didn't trust anyone, even the man who was due at the house in twenty minutes. On the telephone, Allen Dulles had said he would arrive from Bern about eleven in the morning.

Dan turned angrily toward the captive sitting on his bed, sweating, sneezing and trembling with morphine dependency symptoms. Felix Reinhardt had been stubborn and peevish all morning, refusing to cooperate. Brooks had withheld his shot.

"I must have another password before my superior gets here," he demanded. "I can only protect you if you help me. Otherwise you'll be thrown in with every other war criminal."

"You are no better, *Hauptmann* Brooks!" the prisoner shouted at him. He pressed his belly and doubled over with a spasm of pain.

Since their arrival two days earlier, Brooks had been trying to let the man feel less like a prisoner. He had assigned him the best room and instructed the security team to behave more like bodyguards than jailers. Yesterday he had taken Reinhardt for a pleasure drive into Zurich, like a rich tourist in the back seat of a fancy Mercedes, with Schafer at the wheel and Blumberg sitting shotgun up front. Dan had directed Schafer past two banks on Paradeplatz where the secret accounts were held. He had closed the glass partition between the front and rear of the vehicle to keep private any spontaneous revelations by the captive. But the man had merely smiled enigmatically.

Catering to him further, Brooks had promised to take him for a spin in the speedboat and to Jelmoli's department store if he wanted to acquire a new wardrobe for his imminent freedom. The captive had responded to all such suggestions enthusiastically.

"Do I feel the bindings loosening?" he had asked.

"If that's what you sense, it must be so," Dan had responded.

He had brought all Reinhardt's meals to his room personally. Vegetables, fruits and grains only, as was his preference. He had carried up trays of food for both of them and had tried to engage in conversation that didn't sound like interrogation. He had to be careful so that he did not reveal he knew whom he was talking to. In any event, *der Führer's* table talk had not been effusive. He had asked questions about life in America, but seemed to be only vaguely interested in Brooks's responses. He would not talk about the life and work of *Herr* Siegfried Schmidt.

Dan had continued to administer the morphine twice a day and to tend to what was left of his burns. Yet none of his good treatment of the man was having the desired effect. Hitler apparently was accepting it merely as his due. Dan wondered if while he thought he was taking control of Adolf Hitler, the master manipulator was really taking control of him. Underneath the beard, full mustache, new hair style, tinted glasses and Luxembourg suit, he had to keep reminding himself, there still existed the deranged, murderous tyrant who had been the scourge of the world.

Brooks turned away from his captive and looked out to the road and lake again. He had expected to be able to give another bank password to Allen Dulles in person this morning. In his anger and frustration, he had to resist the temptation to lash out physically at the whining, tortured wretch on the bed.

From behind him he heard the captive beseech, "You cannot leave me with nothing. I have already given you too much, *Herr Hauptmann!*"

Dan whirled on him. "Don't call me that. Here in Switzerland I'm Lawrence Travis, a businessman like you, *Herr* Reinhardt. If you ever blow my cover when we're out in public, you're finished. Do you understand?"

"Yes, yes, of course. I am sorry. You must give me morphine now, *Herr* Travis. *Bitte!*"

Brooks fixed his gaze on the man and tried a different course. "Do you know the name Allen Dulles, *Herr* Reinhardt?" he asked.

Reinhardt stopped trembling and cocked his head. "I have heard of him," he said. Then he sat rigid, his arms wrapped around himself, his eyes going angry. "The American spymaster here in Switzerland," he grumbled. "It was he who did business with those traitors Canaris and Himmler. It was he who corrupted many German officials into betraying their country, who talked the traitor General Wolff into surrendering my..." He caught himself in time and looked away. "Dulles, who talked General Wolff into surrendering the German armies in Italy."

"How do you know these things, Felix?" Dan taunted. "A man who works as a rocket scientist wouldn't know things like that. Surely they didn't appear in your Nazi newspapers."

Reinhardt couldn't meet his eyes. He rocked from side to side. "I had friends in high places, as you already know," he answered. "Yes, it is even true that I met *der Führer* on a number of occasions."

"This morning you will have an opportunity to meet Allen Dulles," Dan told him, smiling.

The captive looked startled. *"Ich verstehe nicht . . .* I don't understand."

"Quite simple. He's the superior I'm expecting. He doesn't know anything about you yet. But if he knew that a man of your exalted position was here, he . . ."

"Nein. Ich will ihn nicht begegnen."

"What do you mean you don't want to meet him? He would be insulted, *Herr* Reinhardt. Besides, you have no choice in the matter."

Hitler's eyes darted to the window, then the door, as if looking for escape. Brooks wondered if Allen Dulles would be amused at how his name and persona were being used. He was threatening the prisoner with the bogeyman of his own imagination, like a bad boy being threatened with a visit by Adolf Hitler.

"Das lasse ich mir nicht gefallen!" Reinhardt shouted, shaking his head.

"You won't put up with it?" Dan echoed. "Neither will I, Felix. I've been too damned easy with you. Dulles will have it out of you in five minutes. If you think you're feeling withdrawal pain now, you don't know what pain is. He'll laugh at your pain. Not only will he get the password out of you, he'll just as quickly break through your cover story. He'll know you're not Felix Reinhardt and will do a better job of finding out who Siegfried Schmidt is. He's clever at that sort of thing, as you know."

Hitler's eyes darted wildly around the room like a trapped animal, uncertain whether to cower or rage. "Morphine, *bitte!*" he squeezed out. "I must have my injection. I cannot think straight when I am like this."

"You have only one or two words to think of, *Herr* Reinhardt. That should not be too difficult for you. What is the password into the account number I showed you?"

"You will leave me nothing!"

"There is much more," Brooks reminded him. "You know it. I know it. But no one else knows it yet. Six account numbers were found in your wallet, Felix, and we are only working on the third."

"What you are doing is criminal."

Dan tried to place himself in the mind of Adolf Hitler. What did the man want most besides an immediate shot of morphine? The late *Obersturmbannführer* Dietrich Reiter had given Brooks the clue many weeks ago. *Der Führer* wanted to plant National Socialism somewhere else in the world, nurture it with as much money as he could retain from this hoard of secret plunder and make it grow. Victory out of defeat. Ultimate triumph. That was the conceit Brooks had to play to.

"Cooperate now and we will negotiate how some of the additional money might be left for you to enjoy in your freedom," he cajoled. "Continue to be stubborn and you will deal with Allen Dulles and lose everything."

"It shall remain private between us?"

"Yes."

"*Valkyrie*," Hitler whispered.

"That is the password?"

"Yes."

"Take off your jacket and roll up your sleeve," Dan ordered with satisfaction.

He jabbed the morphine syrette into Hitler's arm muscle, emptied it and withdrew it. Felix Reinhardt murmured, "*Danke*," and eased himself into a reclining position on his bed with a sigh. He would rest for a while now, perhaps nap.

Brooks heard a car outside, looked out the window and saw the nondescript vehicle turn into the short, steep driveway of the safe house. The driver got out, scanned the chalet and grounds quickly, swiveled his head to the road, the cars moving on it, and the dock and lakefront across the way. When he was satisfied, the driver opened the rear door of the car and a slender, well-dressed man, smoking a pipe and carrying an attaché case, stepped out. He too scanned the building, grounds, road and lakefront before walking toward the front door of the chalet.

"You are to stay in your room and away from the window until my visitor leaves, *Herr* Reinhardt," Dan ordered.

He went to the bedroom door and called down for Mangold and Jung. They came bounding up the stairs on the double. Mangold was directed to stay in the room with the prisoner. There was to be no talk between them, Dan reminded, as he always did when one of the men was assigned close to Reinhardt. Jung was posted in the hallway. The rest of the security team were already at windows and entries around the chalet and hidden among trees on the grounds.

Bruno, the houseman, was supposed to be in the kitchen preparing lunch. When Brooks descended to the lower floor, however, he was not surprised to find him already greeting Dulles, ostensibly fulfilling his role as major domo. He was a taciturn, wiry man in his forties, who spoke *Schweizerdeutsch* and some English and French. Brooks didn't trust him. He seemed too acutely alert to everything that was said and done in the chalet, whether it had anything to do with housekeeping, shopping and meal preparation or not. Dan suspected he was as much a personal operative for Dulles as he was a den mother. He kept him away from Felix Reinhardt and had ordered him not to speak to any of the other men or eavesdrop on their conversations or try to take note of their comings and goings.

Dan had never met OSS's Bern station chief before, but recognized him from pictures. He was patrician in bearing, wore a gray homburg, which he was just handing to Bruno as they spoke softly, and a charcoal gray, pinstriped suit. He did not give Bruno the attaché case. As he looked toward Brooks coming down the staircase, Dulles's eyes were clear and direct behind rimless glasses. His small gray mustache was as elegantly groomed as the rest of him. He greeted Dan in a cultured, modulated voice. His manner was urbane. He certainly didn't look or sound like a spymaster or bogeyman, and that, of course, was to his advantage.

"Mr. Travis?" he said with a knowing smile.

"Yes, sir," Brooks acknowledged. "A great pleasure to meet you. You'll stay for lunch, won't you?"

"Let's see how it goes. We've got things to talk about," Dulles responded. He gestured toward the small study off the entry hall. He obviously had been in the chalet before. They walked into the room and he closed the door.

Dan moved a chair close for his guest, then sat in the swivel chair behind the desk. Dulles, who had been heading toward it, looked slightly displeased that he had not been deferred to. He settled into the side chair and laid his attaché case on the desk.

"Are the arrangements we set up for you satisfactory?" he asked blandly.

"Perfect," Dan responded brightly. "Thank you for coming. I would have called at your headquarters in Bern if you had preferred."

"I didn't," Dulles replied brusquely and then launched right into a complaint. "I have no idea why you and your people were sent here. I know, of course, from Larry Dillard, that you're the man who has been uncovering Nazi accounts—but it seemed to me you were doing quite well in England. I certainly do not want you to make an appearance at my apartment or the embassy and risk compromising my position with the Swiss government."

"I understand, sir."

"I don't really think you do. The war has been over almost two months. We're winding down here, moving into Germany, and I see no reason for London to have sent additional operatives who are not under my control. Do you care to enlighten me?"

"I wish I could, sir, but you, of all people, must understand that I'm not permitted to."

Dulles shook his head. "Even I, in my own territory, am to be kept in the dark?"

"Not completely in the dark, sir. After all, you're included for the touchdown play, so to speak. You've done extraordinarily well transferring the money to the OSS account."

278

"Are you patronizing me, Travis? Or whatever the hell your name is?"

He was losing his urbanity, Dan thought. "Of course not, Mr. Dulles. I'd like to know how you do it."

Dulles smiled. "Seems we're playing to a draw. You know I won't reveal that, Travis. Suffice to say that it is done. In the same vein, I'd like to know how you've come upon these account numbers and passwords."

"Can't reveal that, sir," Brooks said crisply. "Not even Mr. Dillard or Colonel Hoose have been told."

"You mean it's your intelligence exclusively, Travis?"

"Yes, sir."

"What if you die?"

Dan wondered why Dulles had put it just that way. "I take it with me," he replied coldly.

But he remembered: *No agent was ever recruited to work for the agency without thought being given to the possibility of having to dispose of him, if necessary, after his usefulness had ended.*

"I'd have thought Lieutenant Commander Cassidy would be in charge of something like this at the London end by now," Dulles commented. "Seems more an SI function than SO. In fact, Cassidy telephoned me a few days ago, inquiring about what I presume was this operation, though I can't be sure."

Brooks felt his fury rise. "Cassidy has nothing whatsoever to do with my mission," he declared angrily.

"Sounded as if he was just tossing a line out to see if he could hook something. Wanted to know if someone named Brooks and his Knight's Cross people had settled in all right. Is that you?"

"No."

"I told him I didn't know those names."

"I hope you told him nothing about me and my team."

"Of course not, Travis," Dulles declared indignantly. "But he seemed to know that some new operatives had been slipped into Switzerland."

"Not a word of our presence here is ever to be breathed to him," Dan said forcefully. "If he or any of his agents come sniffing around, tell them nothing. And I want to know about them immediately."

Dulles stared at him as if he had been struck. "You've got a rather high-handed opinion of yourself," he said.

Brooks forced himself to a humbler tone. "Sorry. Didn't mean it to sound that way. It's the security of the mission that concerns me. Not internal politics or chain of command."

He didn't mind being deferential, because he knew that he still held extraordinary power. Though Dulles outranked him, that status was nothing when weighed against the secret knowledge Dan possessed.

"Actually, I don't know who you really are, Travis," Dulles said with a tired smile. "You probably know more about me, to my regret. However, we have business to conduct. Let's get to it."

He unlocked his attaché case, withdrew thick bundles of Swiss currency and handed them across the desk. "I've been directed to supply these funds and anything else you need. Looks like you might be here for a while."

"No way to tell yet, sir," Brooks replied. "As long as it takes to conclude the operation successfully."

"Couldn't I have handled it?"

"No, sir. And I don't mean that as a slight of you or your office in any way."

"The money is for the personal expenses of you and your men," Dulles told him. "We'll take care of household expenses through Bruno."

"What's his real status?" Dan asked. "Agent or servant?"

"A highly trusted servant," replied Dulles, clearing his throat and smiling.

To Brooks that meant an informant to keep tabs on him. But was it Dulles's idea or did it come from Larry Dillard and Colonel Hoose in London? Either way, he thought it best to change the arrangement immediately.

"Who are the men you've brought in with you?" Dulles inquired casually. "London saw fit to give me only your cover name."

"They're OSS operatives, that's all."

"All seven? That's more than I had to work with all during the war. No, there are eight, aren't there? I'm particularly intrigued by the older, bearded fellow who's apparently quite shy and uncommunicative. I'd at least like to meet *him*."

Bruno obviously had been reporting to him. "When you leave, sir, I want you to take the houseman with you and see that he doesn't return," Brooks said.

"That's rather high-handed of you."

"Cautionary," Dan rebutted. "I recommend him as a major domo, but we'll not be needing his services anymore. You've provided adequate funds to take care of our needs for a while. If more is needed, I'll be in touch with you. We can handle our own housekeeping. Bruno presents a danger to our security."

"If he does, then so do I."

"Precisely."

"*That* is the most insolent remark out of you yet, Travis." Dulles declared angrily. "Mr. Dillard and Colonel Hoose will hear about this."

"You'll be wasting your time, Mr. Dulles," Brooks replied calmly. "I have carte blanche to proceed any way I see fit. I'm not to be interfered with at any level. The continuation of the mission is strictly in my hands."

Dulles snapped the attaché case closed and locked it. "I'll be going now," he said testily. "I'll forego the pleasure of lunch with you and I'll take Bruno with me. Though I do think you're making a great mistake. He'd be a valuable man to have around in case of trouble."

280

"I'm sure he would be, Mr. Dulles," Dan granted, smiling. "But I've already got excellent men with me for that purpose."

"You're a very cautious man, Travis. I suppose I really ought to approve, seeing the business we're in."

"Thank you, sir. I do have something highly classified for you, though, if you have another moment," Brooks dropped in casually.

"What might that be?" Dulles asked, standing up.

"The number of another Nazi account," Dan said insouciantly. He took a sheet of paper from his pocket and read off the digits. "This one is at the main branch of the Swiss National Trust Corporation on Paradeplatz. The password is *Valkyrie*."

Allen Dulles dropped down into his chair again, staring in wonder at the man he knew only as Lawrence Travis. "*Valkyrie*," he repeated in a whisper. Then he quickly rummaged for a notepad and pen in his jacket. "You do have a way about you, don't you?" he said with grudging respect. "Does London know about this one?"

"No, sir. I'm to deal directly with you now. You're to report the results to them and to me."

"With the greatest of pleasure. May I have that number again, please?"

Sascha Gorchavek stood close to the fence and stared down at the great brown creatures ambling around the deep pit below. Some lolled in apathy, others stood on their hind legs, stretching up along the wall to the men, women and children beyond their reach. Captain Gorchavek always wondered if they were seeking freedom or handouts of food. Or maybe something more ominous and primal. It filled him with sorrow and rage whenever his duties brought him to the Bear Pits in this wooded park in Bern. To him the great bears signified Mother Russia. Never mind that the Bernese had their own native claim to the animal and had named their city after it. He likened their captivity to what the capitalist world had been doing to the USSR since the revolution—holding it down.

Standing beside him, *Herr* Sturm, his mole from the Zurich branch of the International Bank of the Four Cantons, seemed oblivious to the fate of the bears. He was facing away from them, scanning the Sunday crowd, hoping no one he knew would see him there.

Gorchavek too glanced around at the people, looking for Major Cherensky, who was to rendezvous with them. A few days earlier, when Gorchavek had told his superior about the third transfer of Nazi money to the covert OSS account—again in excess of two billion American dollars—the major had decided to break precedent and have Gorchavek bring Erich Sturm, their mole in the Cantons bank, for a personal meeting.

"We need to force the Americans out into the open, Sascha," Cherensky had said. "So that we can follow them and locate the source of their information."

"How do we do that?"

"If the bank refused to make the transaction, if a highly placed executive requested the physical presence of the account holder of record before authorizing transfer of the money..."

"How do we arrange to have something like that happen?"

"A substantial payment to your mole. Or perhaps the threat of exposure of your mole. We want him to enlist in his aid the comparable executives of the other banks from which these transactions are originating. Have them all agree privately to set up a new rule that an owner or representative of these particular accounts must appear in person. We can have someone outside the bank waiting to pick up the trail."

Herr Sturm had objected strenuously when Gorchavek presented the idea. However, he finally agreed—for an additional payment—to join him in Bern to meet the man he was only dimly aware of as the financial analyst who had been bribing him for years to provide certain insider information about special accounts.

Gorchavek saw his elegantly dressed superior strolling in their direction along the wall of the bear pit. He stopped every few meters to look down again, as if trying to find the most advantageous viewing position. He finally paused again, just on the other side of *Herr* Sturm.

"My employer is here,"Gorchavek whispered to the banker.

Sturm turned to see the slender blond man who had sidled up close to him. "How am I to address you?" he asked.

"Franz will do," said Cherensky.

"You understand caution then, Franz, as well as I do," Sturm said. He glanced back at Gorchavek, whom he also had known only by a cover name. "As well as your friend Theo here."

"Of course."

"It is regrettable that my name is known to you but I suppose that was necessary before you ever approached me."

"Of course."

"I have explained to Theo and I will try to convince you that you are asking for the impossible. It is not a procedure required by the banking laws of Switzerland. To suddenly ask the holder of a numbered or password account to present himself in person before making a transaction will create suspicion regarding me."

"Not if you and your counterparts at the other banks use the ruse only in these limited instances. These particular account holders are not people who will make trouble for you. They will comply because it will be the most prudent thing for them to do."

"What am I to say to my counterparts at the competing banks? They, after all, might not want to cooperate."

"Tell them it is a discreet procedure you had to institute temporarily in order to protect not only your bank but the reputation of all of Swiss banking. Tell them the truth, that there has been sudden unexpected activity in these accounts and you wish to make certain that nothing criminal is taking place."

Sturm looked at him grimly. "Merely giving you information is criminal."

"But personally lucrative, *Herr* Sturm. And it harms no one, I assure you. Will you comply with my request?"

Sturm looked around to see if anyone was observing them, then looked down into the bear pit and spoke softly. "It will require a payment to me of five thousand francs. In cash, as previously."

"Two thousand, *Herr* Sturm, and my promise that we will not disclose to the banking authorities the assistance you have given me in the past. Surely that is a fair business proposition."

Sturm took a handkerchief from his breast pocket and dabbed at his damp forehead. "What if the others ask for payment?"

"There is no reason for them to do so. They will merely be helping a colleague for the good of all. If any of them asks for payment, I would be shocked."

Sturm met the eyes of the man who called himself Franz. He had the feeling that he was more dangerous than the beasts in the pit below. "Very well," he said. "I agree."

"Admirable," said Cherensky, smiling. He took a pen and notepad from his pocket, wrote a phone number and handed it to Sturm. "As soon as you know where and when an ostensible holder of one of these accounts plans to show up to arrange a transfer, please telephone this number."

"Am I to delay or prevent the transaction?"

"No. Conduct your business in your usual efficient way. However, as a gesture of courtesy, you and your counterparts at the other banks will escort whoever appears to the exit when their business is concluded. You will then go outside with them for a few moments. You will carry a folder of papers and clumsily drop the folder while waving goodby to the client. That is all that is required."

"All?" Sturm protested. "How am I to explain such a complicated procedure to the executives at the other banks?"

"Call upon their good will as colleagues and compatriots. Tell them what I suggested earlier, that a discreet investigation is being conducted, that it is necessary to verify the integrity of these clients and maintain the security of the entire Swiss banking establishment."

Sturm looked dubiously at the supposed financial analyst. This procedure sounded more like espionage than money management. "I will try," he said, "and hope for the best. I shall expect payment as agreed, whether you succeed with your investigation or not. May I go now?"

"Of course. A pleasure to meet you," said Major Cherensky effusively.

He extended his hand so that Sturm could not avoid shaking it. Captain Gorchavek did not bother.

They watched Sturm walk hurriedly from the park and Gorchavek commented, "There is no chance that he will report us to the authorities, is there, Comrade Major?"

"No, Sascha. He is already in too deep. He has too much to lose."

Gorchavek turned back to look into the bear pit and dared to ask another question that had occurred to him during the weeks since this banking business had come up. "Perhaps it is none of my business, Comrade Major," he began hesitantly, "but have you informed GRU Moscow about what we are doing?"

Cherensky also pressed close to the fence, stared down at the imprisoned beasts for a few moments, then glanced sharply at his subordinate. "No, Captain, I have not. Nor are you ever to breathe a word of it to anyone. If I tell headquarters about it now, all it will mean is that I am reporting failure. GRU is not interested in failure. Not until we get our hands on the man who controls these accounts—or, better still, the money itself—will I report it to headquarters."

Thirty-three

✠   As he drove along the shore road in the panel truck belonging to the Meilen *Schwimbad*, Karl Bergen slowed near the chalet where he had finally uncovered his targets three days earlier. He looked quickly left to the driveway, house and grounds but saw no one. Glancing right into Lake Zurich, he spotted the wet, brawny figure of Sergeant Blumberg climbing up the ladder from the water to the private dock.

"Jew bastard," he muttered to himself.

Bergen had never forgotten or forgiven the angry words that had passed between them at OSS headquarters in London eight months earlier. There'd be a bullet for him too, if all went well.

It had taken Karl more than three weeks to follow up all the leads to Brooks's possible safe house that Lieutenant Commander Cassidy had sent him. The process of elimination had led finally to this chalet in Meilen and a repeat of the furtive surveillances he had gone through elsewhere. Through binoculars, from the nearby *Schwimbad*, he had spotted Brooks at last, coming out of the chalet with Blumberg and two other men, getting into a big Mercedes at the top of the driveway. One of the men was older and bearded and Bergen felt confident he was the prisoner, one of the two who had been flown out of Austria with their heads covered by hoods.

Karl had applied immediately for a flunky's job at the bathing pavilion. They had been satisfied with his identification as a displaced person and glad to hire him at this busy time of year. He took care of towels and lockers and drove the panel truck on runs for supplies. He wore a slate blue porter's uniform with the visored cap pulled low over his forehead. The job included a room to live in, looking out toward the lake, the road and the nearby safe house. It gave him opportunities for surveillance of the exterior layout of the chalet grounds and its waterfront facilities and the comings and goings of the occupants.

Bergen was about to glance once more toward the chalet on the other side of the road when he spotted another man within his view on the lake side. A tall, husky fellow wearing slacks and sports shirt stood in the shadows cast by one wall of the boathouse and a couple of trees. He had a military bearing about him and looked to be about forty years old. He seemed on guard there, his head and eyes moving, alert to the swimmer climbing onto the dock, to the boats on the water, the traffic on the road, the grounds of the chalet. In the few seconds he had to size him up as he drove past, Bergen thought there was something familiar about the man.

Then he remembered! The *Goethe Stube* of the *Goldener Adler* in Innsbruck, that Sunday late in March when he had been summoned for a bawling out by Brooks disguised in a *Jäger* corporal's uniform and by *Kriminalinspektor* Klung. At another table there had been a tall, husky *Oberleutnant* and slender, blond *Schütze*, each looking like a Nazi recruitment poster. The man in the shadows of the boathouse was the lieutenant. Bergen remembered seeing him again wearing an American uniform without insignia during the airlift out of Austria.

With this one, whom he hadn't spotted before, Karl had counted eight men in the chalet besides the prisoner. He knew that they took turns at the separate guard positions; that they swam one or two at a time at various hours of the day, including Brooks but not the bearded man; that they went out, two or three at a time, for joyrides in the speedboat; that if the prisoner was taken out in the boat, Brooks was always with him with one or two other guards; and that when the prisoner was taken some- where in the car, Brooks was always with him with two other men.

Bergen realized it would be extremely difficult to get at the captive through the tight ring of watchdogs. He had not yet determined the interior layout of the chalet or which room the bearded man was staying in, but he doubted he could penetrate the place. The only possible moves seemed to be to get to the captive outside after eliminating whoever was with him; or to eliminate the security team one by one until there was no one left to interfere. Brooks was the key to it. Eliminate the leader and the others might become confused and vulnerable.

It seemed to Karl that he already had been given permission by Cassidy to kill Brooks if that was the only way to get at the prisoner. He wanted to, whether it was necessary or not.

Late on the afternoon of July 10th, Dan Brooks took Felix Reinhardt out for what had become a daily excursion in the speedboat. It was always the highlight of the prisoner's day. It gave him a feeling of exhilaration, of freedom, particularly when he was allowed to take the wheel and control the throttle and turn the bow in any direction he pleased. This day they left the dock a little later than usual and Brooks took none of the security team with them, as he always had before.

"Don't expect us back until after dark," he said to Schafer and Blumberg as they untied the bow and stern lines from the dock bollards and tossed them into the boat. The men looked concerned. "Don't worry," he assured them. "We'll be all right."

Brooks wanted to be alone with Adolf Hitler, to talk about things that concerned only them. He felt secure in the boat on Lake Zurich. He wore his pistol in a shoulder holster under his open-necked sports shirt and there was a silencer and extra magazines in the pocket of the jacket he had brought along.

Dan took a heading northwest toward Thalwil. The sun was beginning to dip behind the mountains in the middle distance. The shoreline and low hillsides were filled with chalets, hotels and business areas. He needed to work out his final moves.

He had to continue the charade for Felix Reinhardt—and perhaps for himself—that he eventually was going to drop off the prisoner in secret somewhere along the opposite shore to make his escape to freedom. But he also had to devise in detail how he was going to kill Adolf Hitler in secret and make him vanish without a trace, if it finally came to that, which he believed it must.

Brooks was convinced it was much too late in the game to even think of revealing that Adolf Hitler was alive and then to turn him over to superiors he distrusted; or to President Truman himself in Washington; or to the international tribunal being planned to try war criminals. It was too late, not only in this end game he had chosen to play his own way for good and substantial reasons, but, more important, too late in the precarious international game. To reveal to anyone that Adolf Hitler was alive, that he had been in his custody for almost three months, that billions of dollars in Nazi plunder were being coerced out of him, and that OSS and maybe the United States government did not want to share any of it with its allies, would open up a Pandora's box worse then the container of troubles the wily gods had given as a gift to the ancient Greeks.

More immediately, Allen Dulles had been able to transfer more than four billion dollars from three of the accounts, but Brooks still didn't know how much might be in the remaining three, and he allowed for the possibility of additional caches. He already had the password for the fourth account, but combat for it between him and Hitler had been fierce. The prisoner had held out so long that Dan had thought he was going to kick his morphine addiction cold turkey. But he had caved in at last when he could no longer withstand the torture of his craving and his fear of being turned over to the Russians.

The new password—"*Nibelungen*"—had confirmed for Brooks the significance of all the code words. They were names from Wagner's operas of the Ring Cycle. Hitler was known to be a great admirer of Wagner and an apostle of the Teutonic myths on which Wagner had based his work. Regrettably, though, Dulles had come up against a new obstacle this time.

Offshore from Oberrieden, Brooks turned the boat around, put her on a heading southeast and gave the wheel to Reinhardt. "Keep her in the middle of the lake on the same course," he said, tapping the compass. "No more then twenty knots. We need to talk."

"Okay, Mr. Travis," the captive replied. He was quite pleased by the few American phrases he had picked up and used them at every opportunity.

Dan continued to speak to him in German, his voice raised just above the steady, modulated thrum of the engine. "Are you enjoying yourself?" he asked as an idle opener, watching him weave his way with surprising deftness between passing sailboats, throttling down and up as necessary.

The prisoner glanced at him and attempted a smile. "As much as I can," he replied, then looked forward to steer. "Of course it would be much better if I were out here as my own master."

"Perhaps your wish will be answered soon," Brooks said in an offhand way.

It amazed him that so complex and perverted a mind could be absorbed, with almost childlike delight, in running a boat. He couldn't recall ever seeing a picture of Hitler at the wheel of a car. There always had been a driver. Maybe he had never learned to drive and this was a new thrill for him.

"However," Dan continued, "we have a problem at the bank."

"What is wrong?" Reinhardt asked, worried.

"The bank will not transfer money without a personal appearance by one of the account holders of record."

Reinhardt let out a shriek of delight. "Hah! This you cannot hold me responsible for. I have cooperated with you completely and I shall expect you to fulfill your promises to me, *Herr* Travis," he contended with surprising composure.

"I've fulfilled them so far, haven't I?" Brooks insisted.

He understood the reason for Reinhardt's chortling satisfaction. If OSS couldn't transfer the money, there would be that much more left for *der Führer*. Dulles had thrown the matter to Brooks to resolve. The Bern station chief dared not risk a personal appearance by himself or a member of his staff at any of the banks.

"Yes. But always to your advantage," Reinhardt retorted.

"Do you have a contact who can go to the bank for us?" Dan probed.

Reinhardt throttled all the way back and let the boat drift as they passed offshore Wädenswil in the dusk. He spoke with surprising confidence. "That is no problem, Mr. Travis. I am a signatory to the account."

Brooks looked at him dubiously and asked, "Under what name?"

"My own name, of course. Siegfried Schmidt."

"Is it the only signature?"

"What makes the difference to you?" Reinhardt challenged. "I will go with you and help myself at the same time I help you. I do not enjoy being a pawn."

"Once again, Felix," Dan demanded in exasperation, "is Siegfried Schmidt's signature the only one on that account?"

The captive stared at him haughtily, enjoying his moment of ambiguous control. Then he prudently backed off. He seemed to have genuine difficulty remembering. "The *Nibelungen* account?" he asked hesitantly.

"Yes. At the International Bank of the Four Cantons where the first account was also located. The one that didn't need a password."

"Reiter signed the card too. In his own name. I believe there were at least three others who were to sign with *noms de guerre*."

"Who were they?"

"I don't know. That was the reason for the *noms de guerre*. All would have equal access to the money, but would have to defend their withdrawals to the others, if asked."

"You actually went to the bank to endorse the signature card?"

"No. It was prepared in advance in Germany and delivered to the bank by someone residing in Switzerland."

"Who?"

"Why is it necessary for you to know these things, Travis?" Reinhardt whined in irritation.

"Because I ask them," Dan snapped back at him. "You have a penchant for quickly forgetting the precarious position you're in, Felix. Stop fighting every step of the way. You've been warned about the consequences of that. And you've seen the rewards for cooperation. You are living in a fine chalet in Switzerland, being looked after well and receiving your medication. Right?"

"Yes, of course," Reinhardt acknowledged. "According to Reiter, the account was opened by a man named Meyer Bernstein, who is also a signatory."

"A real person or a *nom de guerre*?"

"A real person, regrettably. A Jew, formerly resident in Germany, who moved to Switzerland before the war. The Swiss were apparently more willing to open such a numbered account for a rich Jew than an honest German. He was warned, however, that he must never attempt to steal any of the money. If he did, he and his family would be hunted down and killed."

Brooks could visualize Nazi agents in Switzerland having forced a refugee to perform a service like that against his will. Perhaps, at the time, they had held members of his family hostage.

"Was his name on any of the other accounts, too?" he asked.

"I believe so, though I didn't approve."

"But you are only the caretaker of this money, *Herr* Reinhardt," Brooks said. "Why should it even concern you."

The captive looked away, eased the throttle open and the boat powered forward again. "Merely a personal preference. Of no importance, of course."

"You have no qualms about going to the bank with me?" Dan prompted.

"Of course not," replied Reinhardt with confidence. "Why should I? My name is registered there, though I might have to prove I am Siegfried Schmidt. You took my papers from me."

"They're at the chalet."

"Good. Then it is settled. We will go."

He was too eager, Brooks thought. What if the whole deal was blown? What if someone found out that Felix Reinhardt and Siegfried Schmidt was really Adolf Hitler?

"Why are you so enthusiastic to go to the bank?" Brooks demanded. "What mischief do you think you're going to commit there?"

Reinhardt glanced at him a moment. In the dusk, Dan could not read his expression. "I am bored by this game. I want to move on."

"What do you have in mind?"

"I will attempt to straighten out the problem you are having with the *Nibelungen* account. Since I am a signatory, they cannot refuse to authorize whatever transaction you request."

"It will be *you* requesting the transaction as *Herr* Schmidt. I'll give you the name and number of the account to which the money is to be transferred."

"How much?"

"However much is in it. Ask for their records of deposit," Dan told him. "The money will merely be moved in the bank's ledgers from one account to another. Even if the amount is in the billions, it will be no loss to them and shouldn't distress them."

Reinhardt maneuvered the boat past sailboats and power craft now showing running lights and eased off the throttle so that they moved at trolling speed toward the dam at Rapperswil. He turned on the speedboat's running lights, then faced toward Brooks. "I have additional requirements this time," he declared.

"Go ahead," Brooks said warily.

"Assuming there is enough there to make your superiors content, I would like to make a proposal, *Herr* Travis."

"I'm listening."

"I don't want you to get the wrong impression," Reinhardt continued. "In no way do I wish to tarnish your integrity. You are obviously a brave and honorable soldier. You remind me of *der Führer's* most trustworthy and courageous officer, Otto Skorzeny. You are both specialists in secret warfare."

"What are you driving at, Felix?"

"I intend to repay you for your decent and humane treatment."

"How do you propose to do this?" Brooks asked.

"First I must know when, how and where you intend to free me?"

"*When* depends on how soon we conclude our business transactions. The easiest *how* and *where* is for us to go out in the boat together as we did this evening. I'll let you off anywhere convenient on the opposite shore or take you to a dock in Zurich if you prefer. After that, you're on your own.

"Is this to be your decision or will your headquarters dictate it?"

"I have quite a bit of latitude in this regard."

"I surmised as much," Reinhardt commented, favoring Brooks with a self-satisfied smile barely perceptible in the darkness. "How will you account for my absence when you return?"

"Let that be my secret," Dan told him. "What are *your* plans?"

"I intend to disappear."

"As Reinhardt, Schmidt or someone else, maybe even Meyer Bernstein?"

"Let that be *my* secret," the prisoner said curtly. "I certainly will never disclose to anyone what happened between us."

"What's your proposition?"

"Does your agency know all six numbers you took from my wallet?"

It would have been so easy to lie but, on a hunch, Dan decided to tell the truth. He didn't see how it could harm him. "No."

"I thought not. Is there a reason?"

Brooks felt a curious sense of guilt and perceived that their roles were suddenly reversed. Adolf Hitler was the prosecutor and he the defendant.

"I deemed it prudent to move cautiously. The success of the operation is my responsibility, not theirs," Dan said. "If you were a military man, Felix, which you obviously are not, you would know how often the high brass and their political masters screw up the men in the field who know what they're doing."

Reinhardt went on, "I think you didn't want them to try to expropriate all the accounts immediately because it would have aroused suspicions."

"Very perceptive of you, Felix," Dan agreed. "Perhaps that's what's happened now."

"Very well, Travis," Reinhardt declared in a tone of authority. "I will help you transfer the money in the *Nibelungen* account to your agency. But this will be the last of it."

"No it won't, Felix. There are two more accounts that we both know about."

"My proposal concerns those accounts," Reinhardt rushed on with enthusiasm. "We must assume that the presence of a signatory will be required for them too."

"Perhaps. Perhaps not. But plausible to assume."

"Again, I do not know how large the deposits are, so it is a risk for me. But from each of them I will open an account for you in the amount of five million dollars. They can be numbered or in whatever name you wish."

It amused Brooks to see the game go forward, though he wondered too if he actually *could* be corrupted. "What if there isn't five million in the accounts?" he asked.

"I will transfer to you all that is there," Reinhardt said emphatically. "We each take a risk. But we must do it right away. First the *Nibelungen* account tomorrow to satisfy your headquarters' demands. Then we will go immediately to the other banks and complete our private transactions."

Dan almost laughed at the gall of the man. "You seem to have forgotten something, Felix."

"What is that?"

"The rest of the money in the last two accounts."

"That will remain my personal business, *Herr* Travis," Reinhardt insisted. "No matter how large or small an amount is left after my gifts to you, I will transfer the funds to a number known only to me and the appropriate bank executives."

"And the other signatories to the accounts?"

"They, too, of course. I do not intend to steal their money. I will merely tell the bank to use the same signature card. I will see that the new number reaches them."

"Including Meyer Bernstein?"

Reinhardt was thoughtful a moment. "It would be practical, would it not? In case he is needed as an agent again."

"I would advise it," Brooks concurred, feigning approval as if he were already part of the plot. "However, what if there is nothing left after your five million dollar gifts to me?"

Reinhardt brooded a few moments. "It is a circumstance I cannot imagine," he said. "Do you agree to my proposal?"

"*Jawohl, mein Herr,*" Brooks said. "We will go to the banks tomorrow and you will be Siegfried Schmidt again. I'll take the wheel now."

He picked out the navigational blinkers and steered for the dock at Meilen, four kilometers northwest. The shoreline and hills wore a bracelet of lights and most of the boats had returned to land. He could swim it easily if he had to.

From his position in the right front seat of the Mercedes parked at the curb, Helmut Jung watched the façade of the stately gray stone building which Mr. Travis and *Herr* Reinhardt had entered a few minutes earlier. He did not know exactly who or what he was looking for, but his orders were, as always, to keep an eye out for anyone or anything that looked suspicious or seemed out of the ordinary. Besides scrutinizing people entering and leaving the bank, Jung moved his head and eyes frequently to observe pedestrians on the sidewalk and vehicles in the road. Next to him behind the steering wheel, Freddy Blumberg went through the same maneuvers of constant alertness. They were each dressed in conservative suits and wore pistols concealed in shoulder holsters.

Helmut took note again of a black, pre-war American Lincoln sedan that had been parked twenty meters beyond the bank's entrance when they arrived. He could make out the figures of two men in the front seat. The driver wore a chauffeur's uniform and cap. The man on the passenger's side wore a light summer suit. He was twisted around, watching the bank's entrance, as if expecting someone to come out at any moment. Other cars pulled up to the curb between the Mercedes and Lincoln from time to time, a few driven by chauffeurs, and let passengers out to do business in the bank.

Jung hardly thought of himself anymore as an *Oberfeldwebel* in the Wehrmacht. Though he still felt some guilt about not rushing home to Hamburg to look for his parents, he also felt a strange, compelling need to stay with the Americans and help them complete their mission. He believed he was doing it not only for himself, but also for Kurt von Hassell and the other men of their company who had been killed and wounded in Austria. He was obsessed by the feeling that there was still some unknown, unfinished business that he must be present for and that he was there representing all of them. He thought it had something to do with his confused emotions toward their prisoner, identified first as a German rocket scientist, then a Luxembourg businessman, and treated now more like a guest than a prisoner.

There was something distressing to Helmut about the appearance of the man. None of the Americans seemed to react that way, although he never really had talked to any of them about Reinhardt. It was against orders, as it had been against orders to discuss Schmidt before him. He would have talked to Kurt about it eventually, if von Hassell hadn't been killed in action. He had never forgotten, though, what Kurt had suggested to him during their training in St. Germain and later during their campaign in the Inn Valley, that it seemed to him as if they were being trained to capture the highest ranking Nazis, perhaps even *der Führer*.

Yet this Reinhardt, this Schmidt, did not look like Adolf Hitler, nor like any of the others in the Nazi hierarchy whom Jung could conjure up.

Or did he?

There had been *something* familiar and disturbing about him from the first moment he had snatched him from his bed in the Austrian mountains. Though Helmut had never seen the features beneath the mummy-like bandages until the captive had been unveiled as the bearded Felix Reinhardt just before they left Milton Hall, he still remembered the voice at the Hotel Edelweiss crying out, "*Reiter! Reiter! Helfen Sie mir! Wir sind unter Angriff!*"

He rarely had heard the man speak since then, and it always had been in a soft, strained, unfamiliar voice. But that night at the Hotel Edelweiss the voice had sent a chill through him.

Since coming to Switzerland and observing how Lawrence Travis catered to the prisoner, brought him his food, took him on excursions in the car and pleasure rides in the boat, and now on a visit to a big bank in Zurich, Jung was even more willing to believe that he had helped Captain Brooks capture someone much more important than he would ever be willing to admit. He believed that was why *Obersturmbann- führer* Dietrich Reiter had been secretly assassinated.

What was the point of it all? They seemed always to be waiting for something to happen. How long would it go on? The war in Europe had been over more than two months. Even as he tried to do his job as an integral member of the security team, Helmut never ceased to wonder about these things.

He forced himself to stop thinking about matters not pertinent to his immediate task. He saw that the black Lincoln was still parked at the curb twenty meters beyond the bank's entrance.

Inside the International Bank of the Four Cantons, the transaction was going smoother than Brooks had expected. He had briefed Siegfried Schmidt in advance not to complain about being summoned in person, not to grouse that it was counter to previous bank policy.

"Just let it ride," Dan had warned as they walked up the stairs to the wide entrance where the glass door was opened by a guard. "Be courteous. Behave as if you do this sort of thing all the time. Be a gentleman and they will treat you the same way."

"*Natürlich*, Herr Travis," Schmidt had responded amiably as they went up a few more steps where another guard had opened a second door. "I am not a child on his first visit to the bank."

In the large regular banking area with tellers behind rows of counters, Brooks had leaned close and added, "Don't take any shit from them either. I don't know what their problem is, but just order them to transfer the *Nibelungen* account to the Blackstone Trading Company number I've given you."

Schmidt had looked at him sharply, not wanting any more gratuitous instructions. Then he spoke to another guard in the hushed chamber, telling him he had an appointment with *Herr* Erich Sturm, an executive in charge of numbered accounts. Sturm was the man to whom his call had been transferred that morning when he telephoned the bank and said he wanted to schedule a personal meeting to conduct his business, as requested.

The guard had led them up a wide marble stairway to an office on the second floor, where a dark-haired, stocky man, elegantly dressed, had identified himself as Eric Sturm.

"Please forgive us for asking you to make this transaction in person, *Herr* Schmidt," Sturm had said solicitously after Schmidt had identified himself and given the account number and password.

Schmidt had made an imperial gesture of dismissal with his hand to indicate the matter was of little concern to him. But *Herr* Sturm had found it necessary to explain further. "It's simply that there has been no activity in this account since Mr. Bernstein opened it for you and the other gentlemen and himself. The sum involved is so large that we thought it best to take this precaution for your protection."

"*Danke sehr*," Schmidt had replied graciously. As an afterthought he gestured toward Dan and said, "Mr. Travis, my associate," which required Brooks to shake the banker's hand.

Then Schmidt had taken over the meeting with authority. He had asked first to see the records of deposit, which he checked against some meaningless numbers he had scribbled on notepaper earlier at Dan's request and affected holding so that neither the banker nor Brooks could see them. He copied the sum from the bank's statement onto the same piece of paper, murmured his approval and went through the paperwork for the transaction swiftly.

None of the worst possibilities that Dan had worried about earlier took place. No challenging bank officials, no police, no piercing of the identity of Siegfried Schmidt, no skepticism about him being one of the account holders of record. The arrangements went quickly, accompanied only by a few seemingly normal remarks from the bank executive.

"You are acting for the other depositors of record?" Sturm inquired nonchalantly.

Schmidt looked at him coldly. "You have noted, have you not, *Herr* Sturm, that my associates and I have equal rights in this account," he declared in a voice that could not be doubted. "One acts for the other."

"Of course. The records are clear on that. I surmise that Blackstone has big postwar development plans."

"Yes," Schmidt replied sedately. "An American company, you know. An excellent investment. But I am not at liberty to say more."

Brooks was eager to know the amount of money that had been transferred to the OSS account, but he contained himself. Business completed, they rose to go. *Herr* Sturm, engaging in chatter about economic opportunities in the postwar world, made a point of escorting them downstairs and outside the front door, all the time clutching a folder of papers in his hand, which he managed to drop as he waved goodbye from the front stairs.

"Turn left off Paradeplatz onto Bahnhof Strasse, Freddy," Dan directed as soon as he and Schmidt settled into the back of the Mercedes. "I'll give you the next stop in a couple of minutes."

He closed the glass partition to the driver's compartment as Blumberg turned out into the traffic lane. He also couldn't help noting that Helmut Jung had his head twisted around and was looking back with intense alertness toward the bank and at cars parked along the curb.

"The amount, Siegfried," Brooks prompted, tapping the jacket pocket where he had seen him place the sheet of paper he had used in the bank.

Schmidt pouted, but handed it to him. "I do not know whether to be pleased or displeased," he said.

Dan read the number his captive had jotted down in the bank and felt ecstatic. The amount of Swiss francs that Adolf Hitler had just been forced to turn over to OSS would convert to about one and a quarter billion American dollars. The total so far was close to five and a half billions. Surely, headquarters in London would be more than satisfied with that.

There was suddenly an insistent banging on the glass partition to the front and Brooks looked up to see Jung demanding his attention. Dan slid open the divider.

"I think there is a car following us, Mr. Travis," Helmut told him. "I don't wish to point, in case they can see me, but it is the big black American car two vehicles back. They were parked close to the bank before we arrived. As soon as we passed them, they pulled out after us."

Blumberg found the car in the rear view and side view mirrors and said, "It's a Lincoln, sir."

Brooks sensed Felix Reinhardt starting to twist his body to see and he reached out and grabbed his shoulder to hold him straight. "Don't look around, Felix. Don't let them see you take notice of them," he ordered. "Make the left on Bahnhof Strasse, Freddy, and we'll see if they follow."

"There was something else, sir," Jung said. "The man who came out of the bank with you dropped some papers. I had the feeling he did it deliberately as a signal."

Thirty-four

✠   Sascha Gorchavek, driving an old Peugeot sedan, made a U-turn in Paradeplatz and managed to slip into the traffic flow only three cars behind Major Cherensky's black Lincoln.

They had staked out the bank immediately after *Herr* Sturm's call that morning, having each moved from Bern into temporary quarters in Zurich since making the new arrangement with the bank mole. Cherensky had been parked near the façade of the building. Gorchavek had been parked on Talacker Strasse, more than a block from the bank, facing the opposite way, unable to see who had been fingered by the mole. But he had seen Cherensky's Lincoln leave the curb, driven by an agent in chauffeur's livery; and he had understood his superior's mouthed words and hand signals as he swept past.

The additional backup agent sitting beside Gorchavek had confirmed his interpretation of the major's gestures: their quarry was in the Mercedes two cars ahead of Cherensky's vehicle. Gorchavek had launched eagerly into his part of the prearranged tracking procedure and was determined not to lose the car in which the Americans rode. They would follow them until they learned where they were staying, then would set up round-the-clock surveillance and plan the next step.

Up ahead, he saw the Mercedes turn left on Bahnhof Strasse. Cherensky's Lincoln turned right, as planned, in case the target vehicle had spotted them. Gorchavek turned left, staying on the track, following the Mercedes, now four cars ahead. His superior would go one block further toward the lake, then order his driver to double back to pick up the hound and fox again.

"They turned the other way," Blumberg said, darting quick glances into the rear view and side view mirrors.

Felix Reinhardt started to twist his head around for a better look and Brooks physically restrained him. "Make a few casual left and right turns

297

off Bahnhof, Freddy, at normal speed. Don't make it look like evasive action. We'll see if they try to pick us up again."

"I am sorry, sir," Jung spoke up. "I felt certain they were following us."

"Perhaps they were," Dan allowed.

After a few turns, as they were driving south on Löwen Strasse, Blumberg said, "Now there's a dark blue Peugeot shadowing us."

"Just draw him on, Freddy," Brooks directed. "Go to the Federated Bank of Switzerland on Bahnhof near Pelikan. Mr. Reinhardt and I have business there. We'll see if the tail follows."

When Blumberg parked the car, the Peugeot drove past them and out of sight. "Maybe I was wrong," he said.

As they entered the grand lobby of the Federated Bank, again under the watch and guidance of deferential guards, Brooks played a little mental game, trying to guess what the code word to the account was. There had been no reason to attempt to force it out of the prisoner this time, the man would have to reveal it at the bank. Dan ran over names he could recall from a performance of the Ring Cycle he had seen in Bayreuth before the war. Since *der Führer* had selected Siegfried for himself, that one seemed unlikely. Brooks opted for the heroine, Brünnhilde.

In the office of the bank executive, after pleasantries that included identification of "Herr Travis, my associate," Schmidt handed the banker the written account number and told him he wished to make some withdrawals and transfers.

The executive waved them into comfortable chairs beside his desk and reached for his ledger. Finding the number, he looked up and prompted, "*Das Kennwort, bitte?*...The password, please?"

"*Brünnhilde,*" said Schmidt.

Dan smiled inwardly and felt confident he himself could come up with the password for the last of the six accounts.

"I see there has not been any activity in this account since it was opened," the official commented.

"Yes," Schmidt acknowledged. He darted a quick glance at Brooks, then went on confidently. "Today I wish to withdraw a slight amount in cash. But, more importantly, I want to open two new numbered accounts. One will be for my associate here and the number will be given by you directly to him."

"In other words, even you are not to be privy to it?" asked the banker, raising his eyebrows.

"That is correct," Schmidt affirmed calmly.

"And the other account you want to open?"

"That number—and a new password I will provide you—are to remain the private knowledge of the bank and me, but not *Herr* Travis."

Brooks kept thinking of the name *Fafnir*, the dragon of the Ring Cycle. He silently urged the word toward Schmidt's mind, hoping that by some mysterious process of telepathy he might infuse it and make it the new password.

"Will the other signatories to the *Brünnhilde* account also have access to your new one?" the bank official inquired tactfully.

"Of course," Schmidt declared with unquestioned firmness.

Dan was sure the man hoped that none of the others ever came near the remaining money.

"This is merely a matter of additional privacy and security for us," Schmidt continued. "Use the original signature card when the others come. As you are aware, we each have equal rights of withdrawal. I act for them as well as myself and they will be informed of the new number and code word."

"How much do you wish to withdraw in cash today?"

"For the moment, twenty thousand Swiss francs."

"How much to Mr. Travis' account?"

"The equivalent of five million American dollars."

Brooks felt a strange new fear clutch at his gut, a kind of anxiety and apprehension that he had never felt in combat. Adolf Hitler and this oblivious banker were making him an instant millionaire five times over. It wasn't a sense of guilt that he felt, for he knew that what he was doing was a ploy. He marveled, however, at the casualness of it all, the blasé references to sums of money that most people had to work years and lifetimes to aspire to and never earn, the moving around of fortunes that few people ever saw.

"And the balance, *Herr* Schmidt? Quite a huge sum, as you are aware. Is it all to go into your new account?"

"Let me see your total," Schmidt requested.

The banker looked it up, jotted the figure on a piece of paper, folded it and handed it to Schmidt. Again Dan wanted to know what it was but forced himself to look discreetly away.

Schmidt read the numbers but gave no sign of being pleased or displeased. He said, "*Danke*. That concurs with our own records," then went on to give further instructions as if he were used to this sort of high-level financial wheeling and dealing all the time. As he might well have been, Brooks realized.

"Immediately after the transfer," Schmidt directed, "I want you to invest two-thirds of the new account's total into top grade Swiss bonds and keep reinvesting the interest until further notice."

Dan had his own request, an inspiration of the moment. "In addition to the private number," he said, "I want a name put on my account. Not a password. Just a name."

"What is it?" asked the official politely.

Staring at Adolf Hitler with a smile of satisfaction, Brooks quickly made up a name: "Anti-Nazi Relief Fund."

"Who will be the signatories?" asked the banker, looking at him with unexpected warmth.

"I will, of course. At least temporarily," Dan told him while he watched Siegfried Schmidt squirm in his seat. "But not *Herr* Schmidt. There will also be Mr. Meyer Bernstein, who is a signatory to the *Brünnhilde* account, as you know. None of the others. Just *Herr* Bernstein or me for the time being."

The official wrote down the instructions and had Dan authorize them with his signature. "That is good, Mr. Travis," he said happily. "You too, *Herr* Schmidt. For the longest time I thought this money belonged to Nazis. It is gratifying to learn that it will be used against them and to help their victims."

To Brooks it was worth the five million bucks just to see Adolf Hitler's eyes burning with fury and frustration.

Half an hour after entering the bank, they left it. Siegfried Schmidt had a fat wad of Swiss francs in an envelope in his jacket, plus the record of money deposited into the new secret account, plus his receipt for the purchase of Swiss bonds. Brooks had the deposit slip for $5,000,000 in the new account. The bank official escorted them courteously to the front door, waved goodbye as they climbed into the Mercedes and dropped the folder he was carrying.

"You're right, Jung," Dan said as they pulled away from the curb. "Don't anybody turn around."

"The Lincoln's behind us," Blumberg called out, watching it in the rear view mirror.

"I'll bet the Peugeot is somewhere close by," Brooks said. "They're switching off, playing leap frog with each other. Drive back to Meilen, Freddy. Keep a sharp lookout for hostile moves, but don't try to shake them. It's better to know who we've got tailing us."

He had intended to make one more stop in Zurich to deal with the remaining account at the Swiss National Trust Corporation, but thought it best now to put it off until he knew who the shadows were and what they wanted. The banks—or at least the executives they had dealt with— were obviously in on it. Yet they had seemingly cooperated fully with the transactions, which was puzzling. Dan closed the glass partition so his men couldn't listen in on the complaints he expected to hear now from Felix Reinhardt.

"Who is the bearded man, Sascha?" asked Major Cherensky.

"I have the feeling he is one of the hooded captives the Americans flew out of Innsbruck," replied Captain Gorchavek cautiously in a muffled voice.

They were dining alone early that evening on beef fondue in a lakefront restaurant in Meilen. Cherensky waited patiently for his chunk of skewered beef to sizzle to his satisfaction in the pot of hot cooking oil.

"I agree, Comrade Captain," he said, speaking softly so that the other diners couldn't overhear them. He paused to sip from a glass of red wine, then turned the crystal to admire the play of light through it. "As you know, Sascha, I have always believed that there is a relationship between the OSS and *Spetsnaz* operations in the Inn Valley, the inquiries from GRU in Moscow and the business taking place here now. But I pose to you again the question: *Who* is the bearded man?"

Gorchavek intended to remain cautious. "I don't think we can know the answer to that, sir, until we have him in our hands," he answered. "He looks like no one I have ever seen before. Yet it would seem from these extraordinary bank transactions with OSS that he must be one of the big ones."

"Bormann is apparently the only one from Hitler's inner circle still not accounted for," Cherensky said. "The rest are either dead or held captive."

"Whoever it is, Comrade Major, he can't get away from us now," Gorchavek declared with confidence.

They had followed the Americans to their safe house where the prisoner was being held, and apparently had done so without being spotted. At least the quarry had never tried to take evasive action while their Mercedes was being trailed from Zurich to Meilen. The Russians had then rented rooms in a hotel about half a kilometer from the chalet. One of the team's operatives had the place under surveillance at that very moment from a rented boat on the lake; another operative, dressed in hurriedly purchased Swiss hiking gear, had been assigned to amble along the shore road and up into the hills around the property, to try to determine the exact layout of the house and grounds and get an accurate count of how many people were there.

Gorchavek removed his long cooking fork from the bubbling oil. The meat on it was done just right and he remembered not to put the hot fork in his mouth this time, having earlier burned his lips in his eagerness. He placed the meat on his plate, to be cut into smaller pieces and dipped in the array of sauces he relished.

He looked around the restaurant and assured himself again that, if he spoke softly, he could not be overheard. "We've already been close enough to kill him, if that's what you wanted, Comrade Major. If we can't kidnap him, it can still be done. That would at least stop the Americans from taking money from the enemy which rightfully should be ours."

Cherensky stared through the window into the gathering dusk on Lake Zurich. "No, Sascha. The people guarding him, yes. It may be necessary. But not their golden goose, whoever he is. That, too, would be failure."

Dan Brooks didn't change the routine at the safe house during the next few days. He wasn't ready for any more banking transactions in Zurich, but he wanted to provide a chance for whoever had them under surveillance to make their move. He had placed the security team on an even more intense alert to thwart any physical attack on them or the possibility of an attempted kidnapping.

Both the Lincoln and Peugeot had followed them from Zurich and had gone past the chalet within a minute of each other after Blumberg turned the Mercedes into the driveway. None of the occupants of the cars had been observed clearly enough to make an identification. Only the Peugeot had come by again; it had drifted slowly past that first night.

Brooks had telephoned Allen Dulles in Bern immediately and, feeling quite smug, had told him he'd succeeded in transferring almost one and a quarter billion dollars from the *Nibelungen* account in the International Bank of the Four Cantons to the Blackstone Trading Company account in the same institution. But he had deliberately not told him they had been followed. For all he knew, it might have been Dulles's operatives. Nor had he even hinted at the transactions he'd been involved in that same day at the Federated Bank of Switzerland. If the shadows were Dulles's men, which he doubted, Dulles would likely know about it already—though, in theory, no one in OSS except Dan knew that the *Brünnhilde* account existed at that bank.

Neither the Lincoln nor Peugeot had been seen again since that day. However, Brooks and his men, and even a newly worried Felix Reinhardt, had become aware that other cars were being used in clumsy attempts to shadow them whenever they went out. The local car rental business, Brooks surmised, was apparently doing quite well.

They continued to keep a sharp eye for any vehicle that passed the chalet often. The one most noticed was the panel truck belonging to the Meilen *Schwimbad*. No one ever got a good look at the driver, though. He wore what appeared to be a porter's uniform, with a visored cap pulled so low that his shadowed face could not be distinguished. Dan figured that truck belonged there, in any event, since the bathing pavilion was a short distance away.

Despite their awareness of being stalked, Brooks, his security team and their captive still led what appeared on the surface to be the leisurely life of a group of semi-vacationing businessmen enjoying the summer weeks in Switzerland. They took turns swimming in the lake, except for the captive, and went out for joyrides in the speedboat. Brooks took Reinhardt for his cruises in the late afternoon and evening. He even fulfilled his promise and drove with Reinhardt and two of the security team into Zurich to let him buy clothes at Jelmoli's department store and Fein-Kaller's haberdashery.

Reinhardt/Schmidt/Hitler had used his own money, since for the moment he had a lot of it. Dan had never asked him, though, how much he had transferred from the *Brünnhilde* account into his new one. That would have appeared as if he were trying to break their agreement; the prisoner might have balked at doing further business with him. There was still the last account to get into. Brooks guessed, however, based on the previous accounts, that there probably had been between a billion and two billion dollars in *Brünnhilde*.

On none of their trips had anyone made an overt threat toward them, though there continued to be reasons to believe they were being followed, sometimes by a vehicle, other times by men on foot who seemed to take particular interest in their mundane routines.

The day before, when they had gone for an excursion in the Mercedes, they also had stopped at food stores to stock their larder. Brooks, Reinhardt, the driver and security man always moved from one place to another together, like a Roman cohort in tight formation, ever watchful, protecting each other and especially their prisoner. In Sprünglis' *Konditorei* in Zurich, Dan had been sure a man was eyeing them who also had been observing them in a produce store earlier. He was a slender, blond man, perhaps in his forties, well dressed, who looked as if he'd just dropped in from a nearby financial institution to lunch on the bakery's extraordinary pastries and coffee. But why had he been in the greengrocer's earlier?

Each of the security team, including Brooks, had been taking turns in the kitchen since he had discharged the houseman. They were self-sufficient men and each could prepare one or two specialties. Helmut Jung made a particularly good sauerbraten the others enjoyed, though it wasn't served to the prisoner. Reinhardt was the easiest to cook for. He required only vegetables, spaghetti, grains and cereals.

Jung had taken particular note of this ever since Milton Hall. He had wanted to talk to *Herr* Travis about it, but had not had the audacity to do so. He remembered, though, with uneasiness, that the man who had brought Germany to ruin also had been a vegetarian.

Sunday evening, July 15th, Dan baked chickens for the men and prepared mashed potatoes, vegetables and a salad. Brunner and Maurer took turns serving the food to their comrades in the dining room as the men relieved each other at their posts in the house and outside. Brooks carried his food upstairs to Reinhardt's room and brought him spaghetti with a light, meatless tomato sauce, the salad and a glass of milk. They sat at a small table near the open window, looking out at the lights on the opposite shore.

"It might be pleasant to eat with your men for a change," said the prisoner.

"You can eat with whoever you want to in a few days. Preferably in

303

another country a long way from here," Dan told him. "I've decided to wrap up our business on Tuesday. There's no doubt we're under surveillance, but I have no idea who they are. They might even be *your* friends. However, there have apparently been no adverse reactions from our last bank transactions. I'm willing to go ahead with the final one if you are."

"It is my dearest wish, *Herr* Travis."

"We will deal with the final solution a day or two after that," Brooks said, intending the double entendre. He still wasn't sure what he would do, what he was capable of doing, except that Felix Reinhardt and Siegfried Schmidt would have to disappear and never be heard from again.

Reinhardt stopped chewing his food. "Final solution?" he repeated in a worried tone.

"Sounds familiar, doesn't it, Felix?"

"I have never heard the phrase before."

"I'm surprised. It was quite popular in Germany during the last few years. But, then again, your mind was involved with science and high finance, wasn't it?"

"Rocket science, *Herr* Travis, as I've told you many times."

"Of course."

It was one of their more animated table talks. Usually they ate in strained silence, for Brooks couldn't ask him all the questions he was eager to. He usually listened only to the sounds of cutlery against the plate, chewing noises, the gurgling of *der Führer's* stomach, an occasional fart. He had noticed how much the room smelled like an outhouse in the morning or after the man had been in it alone for any length of time.

But tonight, maybe because Dan knew it was so near the end, there were important matters, questions he was bursting to ask his prisoner, but they were on subjects he could talk to him about only if he told him he knew that he was Adolf Hitler. Military and political questions. Why, why, why? Personal questions. Did he really marry Eva Braun and then kill her or let her kill herself? Did he ever fuck her or anybody else or was she just someone to have hanging around for show?

He could ask him anything he wanted to, speak for the three billion people of the world and the millions who had been butchered in his name. He could probe the mind, history and psyche of this man and find out what really made him execute the heinous crimes he had committed upon the people of the world, including his own *Volk*.

Dan even wanted to ask him something so simple as, Was there really supposed to have been a Last Redoubt in the Tyrol or was it a clever ploy to mislead the Allied command? He thought the latter. But what did Adolf Hitler *know*?

304

Yet Brooks understood that he couldn't talk to Siegfried Schmidt or Felix Reinhardt about any of these matters because the moment he did Adolf Hitler would no longer play the game and be useful to him to the end.

He carried their empty dinner plates downstairs to the kitchen and brought up two of the rich pastries from Sprünglis and steaming cups of coffee topped with whipped cream.

Ahh, wunderbar. Wiener Kaffee mit Blätterteig," murmured Adolf Hitler. "It reminds me of better days."

Karl Bergen picked Monday night to make his move. He didn't enjoy working as a flunky handling other people's wet towels, cleaning up the locker rooms and running errands for the management of the Meilen *Schwimbad*. In the late afternoon, he observed the chalet's dock through his binoculars from the grounds of the swimming pavilion.

Since he had located Brooks and his group, he had observed the daily and nightly activities of the occupants of the safe house. He had noted the rotating guard duties, the excursions into Zurich, the alternating swim periods and the boat rides. Brooks and the bearded man always took their jaunts on the lake in the afternoon and during the past week had been leaving at a later hour and returning after dark.

Karl saw them now walking down the driveway and crossing the road with two other men. It was the Jew sergeant and the Nazi lieutenant. They disappeared for a few seconds through a grove of trees and around the other side of the boathouse, then came out onto the dock where the speedboat was tied up. He watched Brooks and the bearded man step into the boat, then saw the other men pass jerrycans of extra fuel to Brooks. He saw no signs of weapons, but that didn't mean they weren't wearing them in concealed holsters. He knew the drill.

Bergen watched the men on the dock untie the lines fore and aft and toss them into the boat. He saw Brooks take the wheel, as he usually did, turn over the engine, put it in gear and ease the boat away from shore. Brooks's two men watched the boat for a few moments, waved to its occupants, then walked back across the road and up the driveway to the chalet.

Brooks and his companion would be out about two hours, Karl knew, during that period when most of the other boats on the water were heading home; and by the time they returned to the pier in the darkness there would be light traffic on the road and few pedestrians around. Bergen intended to park the Meilen *Schwimbad* truck nearby and slip down to a hidden vantage point as close to the dock as he could get to wait for them. The element of surprise would be in his favor. He would shoot Brooks and shoot whoever came down to the dock to meet the boat, as one or two of the men usually did. He would snatch the prisoner, shove him in the truck, knock him out if he had to, and head for Lake Constance to cross the border again and hole up in his safe house at Meersburg. Once there he would squeeze out the identity of the bearded man and contact Lieutenant Commander Cassidy.

Sascha Gorchavek wondered if there were really any fish in the lake and if the way he had baited the hook and was handling the pole, reel and line was correct. It was not a subject they had covered at the GRU Academy in Moscow. Major Cherensky had given him only a few brief instructions when they rented the fishing gear earlier. Gorchavek had hardly ever been in a boat before in his life. He had even wondered if it was possible to get seasick while posing as a fisherman here on Lake Zurich.

The major had rented the half-cabin fishing boat at a pier across the lake in Wädenswil. He had piloted it to this location about a kilometer out from the Americans' safe house. The engine was stopped now and they had a sea anchor out to hold their position, but there was a swell and chop to the water from the wind and passing boats. Captain Gorchavek could feel the rising and falling of the hull in his stomach. He believed he was dressed properly, at any rate, in slacks, sports shirt, deck shoes, light windbreaker and a long-billed fisherman's hat. Major Cherensky, who knew about these things, had helped select his costume for this phase of the operation. The major was similarly dressed, as was the third operative in the boat. Each was armed with a pistol in a shoulder holster under his jacket.

"They are coming out now," said Cherensky. "Work your reel. Take no direct notice of them."

The speedboat passed on the starboard side, heading northwest as it usually did. Gorchavek observed it with practiced sidelong glances. The same two men were in it who went out every day at this time: the tanned, wiry man at the wheel, in his thirties, wearing an open-necked sports shirt, whom they assumed was the American commander, and the older, bearded man with his head thrust up into the wind as if grateful for the fresh air he was breathing. That was the man they wanted.

For days and nights the Russians had conducted a surveillance of the residence and activities of the Americans and their captive. Individually and in pairs, they had observed them from a distance, strolled by the property and hiked up in the hills behind it. They had driven past the chalet to spy on it, followed their quarry's car on excursions and tailed them on foot into and out of stores. After discussing all the options, Major Cherensky had decided that a successful abduction during one of their quarry's trips would be extremely difficult and a surreptitious attempt to enter the chalet would be equally dangerous. There were men on guard constantly, even when one or two of them were swimming or off duty elsewhere.

306

The one weak link they had perceived was the daily boat ride when only one guard, the one they assumed was the commander, was with the prisoner. That man had been with the bearded one on every trip out, had been with him in the banks and was with him now. Major Cherensky had concluded that the most feasible method to accomplish his goal was to intercept the speedboat after nightfall when there were few other boats on the water and when the quarry were moving at what he observed in past days to be a leisurely speed back to their dock in Meilen.

He expected, optimistically, that the surprise of their planned hijacking, with guns aimed and ready to be fired, would startle their quarry into immediate compliance without anyone getting hurt. He didn't want the American, only the prisoner, who obviously had control of what Cherensky believed was an enormous hoard of Nazi plunder; a man he was almost sure had himself been one of the German hierarchy. He intended to kidnap him and head for the dock on the other side of the lake at Horgen where their fourth operative was waiting with another rented car.

Captain Gorchevek agreed that the plan was their best option. However, he was a man who, before being invited to join GRU, had experienced more fierce hand-to-hand combat in the war then his superior had ever faced as an undercover agent. He did not feel quite as hopeful about the likelihood of non-violent, stupefied reactions from their targets. One way or another he was determined to complete the operation successfully.

Thirty-five

✠ Two kilometers out from their dock, Brooks switched seats with Felix Reinhardt and gave him the wheel. The captive opened the throttle a little more and pointed the bow toward Thalwil.

"I wish my freedom would be tonight," he shouted above the throb of the engine.

Herr Reinhardt seemed in unusually good humor. He had not had a morphine fix since morning and wasn't to get his second shot of the day until just before bedtime, but he appeared to be at the top of his manic wave. These last few afternoons he had been speeding the boat to the opposite shore, then slowing down and cruising along closer to the villages and docks, looking for potential landing sites. Always the same question, which he asked again now, "Have you decided where you will leave me?"

"No, I haven't. But I will consider your preferences, Felix."

"I'm inclined toward the municipal docks at Zurich."

They had cruised the twelve kilometers to the north end of the lake a number of times and, to Dan, it presented no logistical problems. "That's okay," he said.

"I believe there will be less reason for anyone to take notice of us there. Easier to become lost among the larger population," Reinhardt continued. "It will also place me closer to the railroad station and the airport."

"Have you considered what will happen to you without morphine?" Brooks asked.

"Freedom itself will be a sufficient narcotic for me," Reinhardt replied as he slowed the vessel off Rüschlikon and nosed along the docks.

"I doubt that," Dan challenged.

"You will give me a temporary supply then, *Herr* Travis. To use only if absolutely necessary. But I assure you that I have the strength of character to break this habit as I have others. Cold turkey, as you say."

308

Brooks looked at him dubiously. "I'll give you whatever we have on hand just before you leave."

"Perhaps tomorrow night?" the prisoner said eagerly.

"No. The bank tomorrow for our last business," Dan told him. "Then we wait a day or two to see what our shadows are up to. They're not *your* friends, are they, Felix?"

"Germans? Highly unlikely, *mein Herr*. Nobody knows I'm here."

For the next hour, as Reinhardt steered the boat where he wished, Brooks wanted finally to tell him he knew who he really was, that he had not got clean away with his scheme, that his captor was not as naive as *der Führer* believed. But he could do that only when he had no more need for him and if he was about to kill him.

Twilight turned to dusk to night. Running lights went on. Boat traffic on the water dwindled. Shore lights sparkled. "Take her in, Felix," Dan finally said, his quandary unresolved. "Playtime is over."

The prisoner knew the way back to their dock and he took it, cruising along leisurely, checking the navigational blinkers from time to time, concentrating on his steering. He eased off on the throttle and gave leeway to a brightly lit passenger ferry coming down the middle of the lake from Zurich to Pfäffikon. When the ferry passed, he increased speed slightly and steered toward their dock at Meilen.

Out of the darkness, little more than a kilometer from shore, a half-cabin fishing boat suddenly loomed on the port side where Reinhardt was absorbed in conning the helm. He didn't see it, but Brooks did. It was a boat he had seen earlier, drifting on a sea anchor at about the same position while three men were fishing. They were not fishing now. Their running lights were on and there was dim illumination in their cabin and a soft glow from their instrument panel. He could faintly make out the man at the interior wheel. He was maneuvering to come alongside.

Instantly apprehensive, Dan undid another button on his sports shirt to give him easy access to his shoulder holster. "Hard to starboard!" he shouted to Reinhardt, who at that moment became aware of the closing vessel and followed the order.

Brooks saw the man at the wheel of the other boat twist it to follow their turn. A stocky man in the stern of the cockpit stood ready with a line to loop over one of the speedboat's cleats and he held a pistol pointed in their direction. The third man leaned over the gunwale, his arm thrust forward, a pistol in his hand. Then the hulls touched. Reinhardt was between Dan and the intruders.

The man at the gunwale called out, "If the gentleman with the beard will step into our boat there will be no trouble."

The words were German but the accent was Slavic.

Spetsnaz! thought Brooks. He instinctively grasped Hitler around the ribs, pressed him against himself as a shield and whipped out his Luger.

He had two seconds to aim while their attackers busied themselves in securing the boats, which continued to move in tandem, turning in a tight circle. He fired twice at the man who had called out and saw him pitch backward and slump into the cockpit. The stocky man at the stern roared an oath in Russian and returned fire. Dan swung his weapon on him, squeezed off two rounds and saw him falter, drop his gun, clutch his chest and fall to the deck. Without pause, Dan sighted on the helmsman just coming out of the cabin discharging a pistol blindly in his direction, and he shot him twice. There were no more answering shots.

Brooks released Hitler to take the helm. The boats had bumped against each other a few times and then moved apart. "Let's get the hell out of here!" he shouted.

Hitler fell off his seat into the leg space under the instrument panel. Dan reached over him to cut the throttle and shove the gear shift into neutral, but had to struggle to keep his balance in the circling boat. He reached down and pulled Hitler up to push him aside and take the wheel. He felt clammy wetness on his bare left arm. He touched the wetness and raised his fingers close to his eyes. Even in the feeble glow of the boat lights he knew it was blood. But not his own! His arm was not injured. He had felt no impact there.

He grasped his captive's shoulder, pulled him up and shouted, "Felix!"

There was no reply. Not even a moan. Adolf Hitler's eyes were wide open and fixed. Blood oozed from a hole in his temple and ran down his face to soak his beard. Brooks shook him and called out, "Siegfried!" There was no reply. He propped him against the seat cushion and saw the gaping, bloody chest wound that had stained his own arm.

In anger and frustration, Dan roared the name, "Adolf! You son of a bitch, Hitler!"

The head slumped and the corpse collapsed into the corner of the seat. The Russians had killed him and never realized who he was.

Gentleman with the beard... step into our boat... no trouble... that's what one of the intruders had shouted. They had wanted to kidnap a man whose identity they still didn't know.

They had never given up the scent. They had been onto Knight's Cross since Schepilov in London. Brooks felt rage at the loss of his prisoner before he was done with him. But a moment later he perceived the dilemma they had resolved for him. He glanced at their drifting boat. If one of them was able, he would have taken the wheel by now. Dan felt he either had killed the three of them or wounded them so severely they couldn't function. He scanned the nearby waters quickly to assure himself nobody had seen the action or heard the shots. He saw boat lights far away, but no one close enough to observe or interfere with his plan.

Hitler first. Brooks took a heavy wrench from the tool kit and, with fury and revulsion, beat the corpse's face to a pulp. "*Auf Wiedersehen, Herr Schmidt...Herr Reinhardt...Herr Hitler!*" he roared.

Then he guided his boat to the side of the other craft, grabbed the gunwale and, with his pistol leading the way, peered cautiously into the cockpit. The three men were sprawled where they had fallen. Dan quickly tied a line to hold the boats together and climbed onto the other deck, carrying one of the jerrycans of extra gasoline. He confirmed that the three attackers were dead. He searched their pockets and found Swiss residency permits and driver's licenses made out in Germanic names. There was nothing to tie them to the USSR. He stuffed the I.D.'s back in their pockets and went to the controls. The engine was still idling, the shift in neutral, the boat slowly drifting. He left it that way.

When he emptied the jerrycan of fuel into the cabin and cockpit, he leaped back into the speedboat, untied the line and moved his boat about a hundred meters south. While the engine idled and the boat bobbed, he poured the second can of gasoline onto the flooring, seats and deck and fully drenched the corpse of Adolf Hitler. He moved swiftly through his paces as if he had rehearsed his actions and knew exactly what to do. In a way he had. This was close enough to how he had planned to make his prisoner vanish.

Let that be my secret, he had told Hitler.

An accident, he had planned to tell the others when he swam back to the dock at Meilen alone. *The boat caught fire and blew up. Poor Reinhardt drowned.*

None of the security team would question him further. They knew the nature of their work, as did the men in Grosvenor Street.

He stripped to his shorts, then had a moment's uncertainty about what he would take with him and how he would get it back. His eyes lit on a ring buoy and line hanging in the cockpit and he swooped it up. Removing a box of matches, he bundled all his clothes and gear into his jacket, tied it to the top of the life preserver and floated it off the stern with a push toward Meilen.

Once more he looked around to assure himself there were no other boats nearby to worry about. The nauseating stink of gasoline filled his nostrils as he went forward, put the transmission in gear and the speedboat began to move. He aimed it toward the drifting craft one hundred meters away, tied the wheel with rope to hold its course and slowly increased his speed. At fifteen knots, he glanced for the last time at the corpse of Adolf Hitler. Then he looked toward the target hull, looming ever larger.

"Thanks, *tovarishchi!*" he yelled into the wind.

He advanced speed to twenty knots and moved as quickly as he could back to the stern, tottering on the slippery surface and balancing against the pounding, rocking hull. The distance between the boats diminished quickly as he crouched above the transom, turned his back to the wind and struck three matches as one. They flared, he thrust them into the box to ignite the others, then flung the incendiary into the cockpit and dived into the water, pointing himself downward, plunging deeper and deeper, stroking and kicking to stay down as long as his breath would hold.

Karl Bergen parked the *Schwimmbad* panel truck just off the road on the lake side, about thirty meters from the boathouse and dock. He turned off the headlights and let his eyes grow accustomed to the darkness. He was satisfied with his place of concealment, a site that was darkened further by the branches and thick foliage of a grove of trees. Intermittently, the blackness was cut by the lights of a passing vehicle. Through his binoculars, Karl focused on the dock and saw no one. He glanced toward the driveway and chalet on the uphill side. Outside lights were on, interior draperies drawn. None of the security team was within his view, but he knew they were there.

He scanned the lake for the returning speedboat, but did not see it. He had watched it come in on other nights and thought he would recognize it by the pattern of its running lights while it was still far out. He had noted that Brooks also put on the spotlight to sweep the dock and surrounding area before approaching, then turned the light off before reaching the landing. By then, one or two of his men were usually down there to help him tie up. Karl felt no qualms about his ability to take care of them, too.

He put the binoculars down on the seat beside him, withdrew his Luger from his shoulder holster and screwed on the silencer. He had checked the pistol and ammunition before leaving his room earlier with all his clothing and personal gear. There was a round in the chamber, a full cartridge clip in the grip and four extra magazines in his pockets. He laid the weapon down on the seat and retrieved the binoculars.

As he searched the lake again, Bergen was startled to see a sudden flare of light and hear the boom of an explosion. He focused on what appeared to be a small boat, about a kilometer offshore, enveloped in flames.

Anxiety seized him. He remembered the extra cans of gasoline loaded aboard Brooks's boat. Had some quirk of fate cheated him of his prey? *Goddamn it, no!* he almost shouted. He wanted to rush down to the end of the dock to get a better view. But he had to wait where he was and move only when he saw Brooks and the bearded man return. He had to keep watching the lake and the dock, to see if the security team took any action.

Brooks felt the shock of the explosion underwater. He stopped going for depth and swam instead for distance. He didn't want to come up into a lake of fire. He didn't want to be where would-be rescuers could spot him. He hoped the remains of the burning boats and bodies would sink without a trace.

The water was cool but not so cold as to be uncomfortable. He stayed under the surface as long as he could, then came up for air, took a few deep breaths and looked around to fix his position. The bright flames of the fire were reflected and magnified by the lake. He was as far away from the burning wreckage as he'd been when he'd started the speed-boat's final run. The light reached him, and the crackling of flames. The fire was doing its work well, consuming the evidence.

He saw the lights of a few boats very far away. No one seemed to be heading toward the site of the collision yet, but he was sure people had noticed by now and somebody would be doing something—if only to call the authorities. He craned his head as he rose on a swell and the flickering light helped him spot the white ring buoy with his jacket on it. He swam to it, tied the loose end of the long line around his waist and started stroking and kicking toward the chalet's dock. He figured he was about a kilometer out and could make it in fifteen or twenty minutes.

He wasn't really late returning. It had all happened so fast. But he was concerned his men might become anxious about what they may have seen. If they came looking for him, it would only screw things up. As he plowed along with his rhythmic crawl stroke, he thought of those matters he would still have to deal with.

He was little concerned about being embroiled in an investigation here. If he wasn't intercepted in the water or run over by a stray boat, he and his men would be gone before any inquiry could begin. He would have his men out of the chalet within an hour after hitting the dock, be in Bern before midnight and out of the country in the morning. Dulles would help, though Brooks would give him no explanations. The executives in London might be a different matter.

What have you done with Schmidt/Reinhardt?

I decided it was best to kill him.

Why?

We had gotten all we could out of him. I thought it best not to risk having him talk about it later or try to blackmail us.

There was no reason for them not to believe him. They knew he had terminated *Obersturmbannführer* Reiter at their mutual pleasure and knew all the other disagreeable things he had done on their orders.

Would they ask *where* and *how?*

No, they didn't really want to know that sort of thing.

Did you ever learn Siegfried Schmidt's true identity?

Another identity? No, I never did, except for Felix Reinhardt. I came to accept that he was Siegfried Schmidt.

Martin Bormann is still missing. Perhaps he was Bormann.

He wasn't.

Do you think there were any more bank accounts?
Perhaps.

A five and a quarter billion dollar return on their investment seemed more than adequate to Brooks. He wasn't sure he approved of what the powers that be were doing and would do with the expropriated Nazi plunder anyway. It didn't bother him to hold back a while on the rest of it, to see what developed, to think about how it might best be used. A mere captain employed on the point, as he was, rarely had the chance to control results and influence policy. He was seizing his chance.

Dan stopped swimming to check his position. The flames behind him were less bright, as if the boats had already burned to the water line. Nor was he able to glimpse any other craft going toward the wreckage yet. Ahead of him he could pick out familiar lights and landmarks on the shore. He was making good time. Perhaps another eight to ten minutes and he would be at the dock. He started swimming again. He wasn't tired. As he cut the water with strong strokes and kicks, he continued to ponder what lay ahead.

His conscience didn't bother him about the five million transferred to the account opened in the name of the Anti-Nazi Relief Fund, nor about the unknown amount Schmidt had transferred, nor the cache that hadn't even been tapped. Those sums could also be transferred to OSS and the U.S. Treasury in time, once he was able to figure out a way to make it happen but stay out of the transaction himself. He felt no urgency about it. The money wasn't going anywhere. But he didn't think he would be able to live with himself if he used any of it for his own benefit.

It troubled him, too, to know that the original owners of the wealth were not being considered in the agency's thinking so far. Millions of men, women and children had been robbed and murdered. International relief organizations were already at work and desperate for funds to help additional millions who had barely escaped to resettle and build new lives.

Among them, he had reason to believe, might be the man who had been forced to establish the Nazi accounts and was a signatory to them. He had the notion of going in search of Meyer Bernstein. Between them they might figure out how to get into the accounts that hadn't been tapped yet—and the best use for the wealth they recovered.

Helmut Jung and Fred Blumberg ran down the driveway from the chalet, crossed the road and halted at the end of the dock. They searched the dark waters in front of them and raised their eyes to the diminishing flames a kilometer offshore.

Ten minutes earlier, scanning the lake through binoculars from an upstairs room—as he usually did when the captain and their prisoner were due back—Jung had caught sight of the sudden flareup on the water and had heard the dull boom of the distant explosion. He had watched the conflagration with apprehension for a few minutes, trying to figure out what it was, for he had not witnessed the events preceding it. Then he had summoned the sergeant.

Blumberg had taken the night glasses from him and focused on the offshore scene. "It looks too big to be ours," he had said anxiously, "But maybe somebody rammed them. Let's get down to the dock. If they don't turn up very soon, we'll get another boat and go out looking for them."

When they rushed from the chalet they had alerted the others. Before crossing to the boathouse and dock, Blumberg had glanced up and down both sides of the road as he usually did, checking for suspicious vehicles and pedestrians. A car had passed in front of them going north and its headlights had momentarily illuminated a panel truck parked under some trees on the lake side about thirty meters away. It had registered in Blumberg's mind as a truck he had seen often in the area, belonging to the nearby *Schwimmbad*. But it struck him now, in a delayed reaction as he stood at the end of the dock, that he only remembered seeing it moving on the road, never parked. He would check it out on the way back. He was more worried about Captain Brooks now.

Jung had the binoculars again and was studying the lake, sector by sector. It was a clear summer night, the sky over the mountains sparkling with stars reflected in the water. "The flames are dying down," he reported.

Blumberg could see that without the glasses. "How about other boats?" he asked, staring through the dark space to the many lights on the opposite shore. "Anybody heading in that direction? Maybe the captain stopped to give assistance," he added optimistically. "Yeah... that's what he'd do if it happened to somebody else."

"I see other lights approaching the site," Jung said. "I think the boat that was on fire is sinking."

"Jeezus, give me the glasses, will you, Helmut," Blumberg said in agitation. He could remember times in France and Italy when he had stayed up all night like a mother hen waiting for Brooks to come back from some goddamned escapade. But this time they weren't in enemy territory and he didn't have orders to stay put. He would get somebody else's boat and go out looking for him if he didn't turn up in a few minutes.

He took the binoculars and slowly swept the long, wide expanse of waters between their dock and the vanishing site of the calamity. He spotted a small white life preserver gliding on the surface as if being towed, and he moved the glasses down a fraction and saw the swimmer. The head was low in the water, hardly coming up for air, and he couldn't make it out, but he had the feeling it was the captain.

"There's somebody in the water swimming toward us," Blumberg said softly.

Jung watched with mounting relief as the swimmer came closer. Three minutes later he gripped *Hauptmann* Brooks's wet hand, helped him off the top of the ladder and drew in the ring buoy with the bundle tied to the top.

Brooks was breathing heavily from his exertions and began to shiver now that he was out of the water.

"Where's Reinhardt?" asked Blumberg.

"*Kaputt,*" Dan answered. He kneeled over the life preserver and untied the bundle on top of it. His jacket was soaked. "We're leaving here tonight. Let's go."

They waited for him to elaborate, then realized that was all he intended to say. They turned toward the road and started to walk off the dock when a man appeared out of the close grove of trees, moving stealthily, face indiscernible. They thought at first he was one of their own.

Karl Bergen stopped and raised his pistol in a two-handed grip. He tried to aim, but they were still moving, his nemesis partly blocked by the others. Fury rose in this throat. "Brooks, you son of a bitch! Where's your prisoner?" he shouted.

Dan couldn't see him, but recognized the voice and the venom. He saw the stance and knew there had to be a pistol stuck out in front of it. Anger rose in him at the stupidity of being caught like this and he braced himself for a bullet.

Jung saw the gun but ran toward the attacker, reaching into his holster for his own weapon. He never heard a sound, just felt a tremendous impact against his chest that stopped him, then a second blow in his belly that crumpled him onto the planks.

Blumberg had time to aim. He squeezed off his shots carefully. The first one bored a hole through Karl Bergen's head and carried him backward. As he started to topple, Blumberg shot him in the torso. He moved closer to his fallen target, stepping over Jung and firing again. Standing over the body, he saw that there was no need for another shot. He recognized the bloody face of Karl Bergen.

From behind him, he heard Brooks shout, "Freddy! Get Paulsen!" He turned and saw the captain kneel at Jung's side, and Blumberg ran toward the chalet for the medic.

Schafer, Maurer and Mangold, having heard the shots, were running down the driveway, pistols in their hands. "You won't need those," Blumberg said. Then he realized he was still holding his own weapon and he shoved it into his shoulder holster and rushed up to the house, shouting for Paulsen.

Brooks felt helpless, kneeling there on the dock in his shorts, dripping water, unable to do anything for Helmut Jung. He tried to stanch the flow of blood with part of Jung's shirt, but it quickly soaked through. He looked toward where Karl Bergen was sprawled out dead about fifteen feet away from him and he felt rage again. *If only I'd killed him in Austria like I should have*, he thought with remorse. He turned back to Jung. He was conscious, looking at him, trying to say something.

"Tell me, *Herr Hauptmann*," he murmured. "Who was the man with you in the boat?"

"Our prisoner," Dan answered softly.

He heard the pounding of feet behind him, looked up and saw his three men rushing up to give assistance. They each paused to glance at Bergen's body and recognized the rogue agent they'd brought back from Innsbruck.

"I need Paulsen and the medical kit," Brooks demanded.

"He's on the way, Captain," Schafer said.

Dan made an angry gesture toward Bergen's body and ordered, "Get that piece of shit wrapped into a tarp in the boathouse. We'll get rid of it later."

They lifted the body and moved it away fast, each dismayed by what he felt he had let happen.

Brooks heard Jung still whispering and he leaned closer to hear him.

"Was it the monster himself? Please. You must tell me. Was it the swine Hitler?" Jung murmured.

"It was Schmidt," Brooks answered guiltily. "The same Schmidt who has been with us all these weeks. The same Schmidt we captured in Austria."

Dan heard running feet again and looked up to see Paulsen with the medical kit. Paulsen dropped down beside him, opened Jung's shirt and began to examine the wounds.

"Oh, shit!" he muttered. Then, "Just hang on, Helmut. You're gonna be okay." He tried to sop up the blood with compresses and more poured out. Jung winced and closed his eyes. Paulsen gave him a shot of morphine, looked at Brooks in despair and shook his head. He poured sulfa powder on each of the wounds, pressed down new bandages and moved Jung's hands to rest on top of them.

Dan stood up, touched the medic's shoulder and beckoned him away. "If we got him to a hospital?" he asked, not knowing how he would explain it to the Swiss if he called for help.

"He's a goner, sir. No matter what you do," Paulsen said softly. "I've done all I know how."

Brooks heard Jung calling weakly, "*Hauptmann.*"

He wanted to be alone with the man now. "Go up to the house and make a litter with some sheets and blankets," he ordered the medic. "Take the men in the boathouse with you. Bring the litter and we'll carry him up there."

Paulsen left and Dan kneeled close to Jung again. "I'm here," he said.

"I must know, *Herr Hauptmann*," Helmut murmured. "Why should somebody named Schmidt...just an ordinary Schmidt...be of such importance to you? It was *Hitler*...I *know* it was Hitler." He coughed and spit up blood.

Brooks looked around. They were alone. He said what he had vowed he would never say to anybody. "It is a secret, Helmut," he whispered. "You must promise that you will never tell anyone else."

Jung spoke very weakly, in a voice suitable to great secretiveness..."*Natürlich, Herr Hauptmann.*"

"Yes, it was Hitler," Dan said softly. "You and your comrades helped to capture him. He thought he had tricked us, but he didn't. It was we who tricked him...made use of him."

"He is dead now? Truly dead?"

"Yes. Somebody was trying to take him from us on the lake, but they killed him by mistake. They're dead too. Nobody knows except you and me, Helmut."

"Nazis?"

"Russians, I think. But I couldn't swear to it."

Jung relaxed for a moment with a deep sigh, as if he'd passed out—or died. But then his eyes flickered open again and he said, "I owe you a great debt that I will never be able to repay."

"It's I who owe you," Brooks told him. "You saved my life. If not for you, Bergen would have shot me."

Helmut coughed and struggled to breath. He focused all his remaining strength just on being able to speak, to get out the idea he had to impart. "Life is so strange, *Hauptmann*," he murmured. "For so many years I wanted to kill Hitler. Look what I had to go through in order to be part of the event. A miracle...truly a miracle."

He faded into unconsciousness. Dan called his name, but he didn't answer. He leaned closer and realized Jung was no longer breathing. He felt for a pulse in Helmut's wrist but knew that there was none.

As he waited for his men to bring the litter, Brooks tried to make sense of what had happened in this last hour.

The war was over. But the war went on. Men were still killing each other in the name of something good or bad.

They had to pay someone, of course—someone to stay sharp, move fast, kill if necessary.

Someone like him.

KNIGHT'S CROSS

Area of Operations in the Austrian Tyrol

GERMANY

Inn River

Innsbruck

Kematen

Oberperfuss

Sill River

Lüsener Ferner
drop zone

A U

FRANCE

GERMANY

CZECHOSLOVAKIA

Munich

Vienna ★

AUSTRIA

Zurich

Bern ★

SWITZERLAND

HUNGARY

Area of
detail

ITALY

YUGOSLAVIA